May 1'

W9-CHF-356

The Sinful Suitors

Sabrina Jeffries's delightful Regency series featuring the St. George's Club, where watchful guardians conspire to keep their unattached sisters and wards out of the clutches of sinful suitors.

THE STUDY OF SEDUCTION

THE ART OF SINNING

SABRINA JEFFRIES

To Pleasure a Prince

POCKET BOOKS

New York   London   Toronto   Sydney   New Delhi

Pocket Books
An Imprint of Simon & Schuster, Inc.
1230 Avenue of the Americas
New York, NY 10020

This book is a work of fiction. Any references to historical events, real people, or real places are used fictitiously. Other names, characters, places, and events are products of the author's imagination, and any resemblance to actual events or places or persons, living or dead, is entirely coincidental.

This Pocket Books paperback edition September 2016

POCKET and colophon are registered trademarks of Simon & Schuster, Inc.

For information about special discounts for bulk purchases, please contact Simon & Schuster Special Sales at 1-866-506-1949 or business@simonandschuster.com.

The Simon & Schuster Speakers Bureau can bring authors to your live event. For more information or to book an event, contact the Simon & Schuster Speakers Bureau at 1-866-248-3049 or visit our website at www.simonspeakers.com.

Manufactured in the United States of America

10 9 8 7 6 5 4 3 2

ISBN 978-1-4165-2386-4

To my curmudgeonly husband of twenty years,
this one's for you. I love you exactly as you are.

And to Deb Dixon—
thanks for all the advice on this book!

Prologue
London, April 1814

A young lady's sponsor at court must be above reproach. If her family is not, they should have the good sense to absent themselves from the proceedings.
—Miss Cicely Tremaine, *The Ideal Chaperone, a Guide for Governesses, Companions, and Tutors of Young Ladies*

He couldn't see a damned thing from here.

Marcus North, the sixth Viscount Draker, rose from the marble bench and crossed the terrace to survey the ballroom through the glass doors. Much better. Too bad he couldn't stand here. But someone might see him. It wouldn't do for him to be caught skulking about like a French spy.

"What in God's name are you doing?" asked a voice behind him.

Marcus turned to find his half brother scowling at him as he came up the steps from the garden of his new town house. So much for not being caught.

Alexander Black, the Earl of Iversley, strode onto the terrace. "I thought you went home to Castlemaine hours ago."

"I did." Strolling back to the marble bench, Marcus picked up the glass of Madeira he'd left there. "But halfway to Hertfordshire, I decided to come back."

"Why?"

He sipped the wine. "To watch and make sure everything goes all right."

"And if it doesn't? What will you do, leap inside and take care of it?"

"Very amusing." Marcus stared through the glass doors into Iversley's ballroom. The guests were entering, and at their center was Marcus's half sister.

He caught his breath. All he could see of his precious Louisa was her head, but with her hair up in a fashionable coiffure adorned by a large ostrich feather, she looked beautiful. And too damned grown-up. Sloe-eyed and black-haired, she was the very picture of their late mother, and that could not be good.

Marcus drank deeply. What did Iversley and his wife Katherine really know about presenting a young woman to society? Especially one whose pariah of a brother was only mentioned in vicious whispers.

He tore his gaze from the doors. "How was Louisa's presentation at court?"

"It went very well. She didn't trip over that ridiculously long train they make the girls wear, and according to Katherine that's every girl's greatest fear."

When the crowds parted enough to reveal Louisa's low-cut bodice, Marcus cursed the day he'd agreed to let her come to town. Confound it all, she looked more like a married woman of twenty-five than a maid of nineteen. "I hate that gown. It shows too much."

"Ah, but they like the girls to wear gowns cut down to their navels," said a familiar voice from behind Iversley. "Louisa's is actually modest by comparison."

"Why the hell are *you* here?" Marcus asked as his other half brother, Gavin Byrne, walked up holding a glass of champagne. "She's my sister, not yours."

Byrne shrugged. "Louisa's debut was part of our bargain when we began the Royal Brotherhood of Bastards. The least I could do was attend her ball." He shot Marcus a faintly contemptuous glance. "Since her own brother won't."

"You know damned well I can't—it would ruin everything."

"Then for God's sake, don't sneak about out here. If you won't come inside, you overprotective ass, go home and leave things to Iversley and me."

Marcus snorted. "Iversley, I can trust, but *you*—"

"Come now, gentlemen," Iversley broke in, "we're all on edge this evening. But the worst part is over, so there's nothing more to worry about."

Fat lot *he* knew. There was always more to worry about with a sister.

Marcus glanced through the glass, then scowled when he saw Louisa smile shyly at some handsome devil being introduced to her. "Who's *that* rascal?"

"Relax," Iversley said. "He's perfectly respectable and quite a catch, I'm told. Simon Tremaine, the Duke of Foxsomething."

"Foxmoor?" Marcus growled. "Katherine invited the duke to this?"

"Why not? He's young, he's rich, he's unmarried—"

"He's Prinny's close friend, that's who he is," Byrne put in. He walked up to stand beside Marcus. "How very interesting."

Iversley blinked. "I'm sorry, we didn't know. Neither of us pays much attention to society gossip."

Byrne shot Marcus a knowing glance. "They're too busy doing . . . other things."

"There hasn't been much of *that* lately," Iversley grumbled. "Katherine had a baby two months ago, remember?"

"Ah, the life of the married man," Byrne said smugly. "Give me a bachelor's life any day, eh, Draker?"

"Damned right." But Marcus actually envied Iversley his adoring wife and infant daughter. He'd trade all his riches to have either.

But he never would. He had to accept that. Marcus narrowed his gaze as he saw Foxmoor take Louisa to the floor. "Was Prinny at court today?"

Iversley made a sound of disgust. "I heard he was. I didn't see our blasted father myself, however."

"You've never met him, have you?" Byrne asked Iversley.

"No. Not that it would matter if I did. He doesn't even realize I'm his by-blow. What about you?"

"Saw him once at the theater when I was a boy. Mother pointed him out to me from backstage." Byrne scowled. "She never stopped trying to make him acknowledge me, if only privately. Of course, Prinny would die before he'd admit to fathering a child by a common Irish actress. What would his bloody friends think?" He shot Marcus a glance. "He only admits to the ones like Marcus, born to 'respectable' wives of gentlemen."

"Trust me," Marcus muttered, "the last thing you want is Prinny in your life. Why do you think I've kept Louisa away from him all these years?"

Iversley blinked. "Louisa is Prinny's, too? You said it was just you, but if we have a half sister—"

He scowled. "It *is* just me. Louisa was born the year Prinny got married, while he and my mother were on the outs. But although the girl is definitely the viscount's daughter, Prinny has shown a sudden interest in her. The devil sent a messenger a month ago requesting a meeting 'to discuss Louisa's future.' I sent the man packing."

Byrne lifted an eyebrow. "Perhaps Prinny knows something we don't—he never claims any by-blows he doesn't have to."

"She's *not* his," Marcus growled. "The year of her birth was the only time he avoided our estate. Besides, if he'd believed her to be his, he would have challenged me for guardianship long ago, like he did with that girl Minney a few years back. The viscount believed Louisa to be his own daughter, society accepts her as the viscount's, and I'd better not hear you implying otherwise."

"But she must know that *you're* Prinny's son—"

"If she does, she never speaks of it. And I won't have you rousing painful questions in her mind about her own blood when there's no reason for it. So keep your damned mouth shut, do you hear?"

"Fine," Byrne muttered. "I don't know why you're so testy about it. It's not as if being Prinny's by-blow would hurt her. The ones he's privately acknowledged have done quite well as a result of the association. Hell, you could have done well yourself if you hadn't publicly tossed him and your mother out of Castlemaine."

That one act had tarnished him in society, but his mother's revenge, the lies she told her friends about him afterward, had blackened him forever. Nine years later, he was still paying for it. And all because of that damned lecherous prince.

"He deserved what I did." The old anger boiled up inside Draker. "So did my mother. They were lying in each other's arms a mere week after Father died."

"So what?" Byrne drained his glass. "The viscount never protested it. Why should you? He was dead, for God's sake, and he wasn't even your father."

"He acted like one. And he deserved some respect from them for treating me like a son all those years."

Byrne snorted. "He let his wife cuckold him—"

"You're certainly one to talk," Marcus ground out. "If not for obliging husbands, you'd have no bed companions."

Byrne's blue eyes hardened to chips of ice. "Now see here, you pompous—"

"That's enough, both of you." Iversley stared through the window. "It's Louisa we should worry about. Should Foxmoor be kept away from her?"

Marcus gulped some wine. "Most certainly. It can't be coincidence that Prinny's most ambitious friend is sniffing around Louisa."

"Fine. After tonight, he won't be invited to our functions."

"You can't stop him—or Prinny, for that matter—from approaching her at other affairs." Marcus stared sullenly into the jeweled depths of his empty glass.

"Oh, yes, I can," Iversley said. "I won't let anyone near who might harm her. In the months Louisa has been coming here to prepare for her debut, Katherine and I have grown fond of the girl. We wouldn't want her caught in Prinny's machinations."

"You're both probably worrying for nothing." Byrne sipped his wine. "Just because Foxmoor is dancing with her doesn't mean Prinny put him up to it. She's a beautiful girl, after all."

"True. But it makes me damned nervous." For the first time in years, Marcus wished he could go into society without stirring up nasty comments and drawing hateful looks. He wished he could shave off the beard that hid his ugly scar without fearing it would draw even more vicious rumors. He didn't care what they thought or said about *him,* but Louisa . . .

He couldn't mar her come-out by accompanying her.

Nor could he demand that she remain exiled with him at Castlemaine, much as he wanted to. Louisa deserved better. And the only way she would get it was if he trusted Iversley—and Katherine—to look after her in the next few weeks while she lived in their home, flitting from party to ball to soiree.

Without him.

He stared back through the glass. "I hope you and Katherine know how much I appreciate what you're doing for her."

"It's the least we can do after all you did for *us,*" Iversley said in a voice deep with emotion.

"It was nothing," Marcus mumbled, unused to being thanked. Unused to having friends—brothers—who could thank him.

An awkward silence ensued before Iversley cleared his throat. "I'd best return to my guests. Do you two plan to stand out here all night?"

"So Draker can grumble whenever Louisa dances with someone he doesn't like?" Byrne retorted. "Not on your life. We're going to the Blue Swan."

Marcus shot Byrne a dark scowl. "I'm not sitting around your dingy gaming establishment while a lot of sots speculate on my beard and my past and my—"

"Clearly you've never been to Byrne's club if you think it's dingy," Iversley remarked. "And I'm sure he has private rooms."

"Not to mention the best French brandy a smuggler can provide," Byrne said. "Come on, you big grouse. This bloody ball will go on for hours, and you know you don't want to lurk about out here cooling your heels until it's over."

He hated to admit it, but Byrne was right. "I suppose I could go home." But he wasn't in the mood to return to Castlemaine and the emptiness that Louisa would have left in her wake. "Do you indeed have private rooms?"

"Of course." A devilish smile broke over Byrne's face. "And if you like, I can have female company fetched for us. I'll even pay for it myself."

Marcus was sorely tempted. Although he'd never kept a mistress and he seldom used whores, tonight wasn't a night for scruples. And Castlemaine might seem less lonely if he returned by light of day.

"Go on, Draker, go with him," Iversley prodded. "We brothers have to stick together when we can."

Brothers. The pain in Marcus's chest eased. "All right, I'll go."

"Excellent." Byrne picked up the bottle of Madeira and refilled Marcus's glass; then handed the bottle to Iversley and raised his own glass in a toast. "To the Royal Brotherhood of Bastards."

They echoed the toast, with Iversley swigging straight from the bottle.

Then Marcus lifted his glass again. "And to our royal sire. May he rot in hell."

Chapter One
Hertfordshire, May 1814

*Discourage your charge from gossiping, but be
aware of all the latest on-dit yourself, so you can
separate the sheep from the wolves.*
—Miss Cicely Tremaine, *The Ideal Chaperone*

*T*he carriage crested a hill and Lady Regina Tremaine
gasped at her first glimpse of Castlemaine, nestled in one
of the Chiltern hills' verdant valleys. The place lived up to
its name gloriously. Despite its lack of a moat, it was the
very picture of a Tudor castle with its battlements, para-
pets, and pointed gothic windows. How odd to find it
plunked down here in Hertfordshire among the oxen and
the barley, only twenty miles from London. It was like
stumbling upon Camelot in the midst of Whitechapel.

"Interesting, isn't it?" said Cicely Tremaine, her spinster
older cousin and chaperone.

"Fascinating." Though she'd expected something of the
sort, after hearing Louisa wax rhapsodic over her home.
"If it's not too gloomy on the inside. You know how dank
and dark these old piles can be."

Shortly after, as a footman ushered them inside, she
discovered that the place wasn't gloomy in the least. Yes,
someone had gone a bit wild with the theme. Rumor had
it that the previous viscount had spent a fortune over-

hauling the castle some twenty-five years ago; inspired by Walpole's Strawberry Hill, he'd turned the crumbling old building into a gothic masterpiece.

It had been finely done, however. The burnished dark woods and the ironwork gave an impression of strength. Despite the faded hues of the ancient tapestry hanging on one wall, the overall impression was of lush colors—the rich gold-shot silk of the drapes and the vibrant reds and blues of the stained-glass window at the top of the magnificent mahogany staircase.

Cicely edged closer to her. "On the inside it's not quite what one expects."

"No." Regina knew Lord Draker was rich, but given his notorious reclusiveness, she'd expected sooty ceilings and cobwebs lurking beneath every chair—not this immaculately clean foyer with its sparkling crystal chandelier and a Tintoretto painting that proclaimed the owner's wealth and taste.

But only to those who knew art. Either Lord Draker was more sophisticated than she'd realized, or he merely liked interesting pictures.

She hoped it was the latter. She had her best successes with shallow or simpleminded men; clever ones were a bother, although even they could be gotten round easily enough if she put her mind to it.

The butler approached, looking flustered. "Good morning, ladies. There must have been some mistake. Miss North is in London at present and—"

"I'm not here to see Louisa," Regina said with a smile. "Would you kindly tell his lordship that Lady Regina Tremaine would like a word with him?"

The butler's face turned an interesting shade of purple. "H-His lordship?"

She raised one eyebrow. "This is Castlemaine, isn't it?"

"Certainly, my lady, but . . . well . . . you do mean that you wish to see the viscount, don't you? Lord Draker?"

"Of course."

"Marcus North, the sixth Viscount Draker."

"Yes, yes, that is the one," she said impatiently. "Have we come to the wrong house?"

"Perhaps this is a bad time," Cicely whispered, her pallor deepening.

"Nonsense." Regina offered the butler a cool smile. "Would you inform his lordship that I am here to see him?" She added archly, "If it's no trouble."

The butler colored again. "Of course not, my lady. Forgive me, but ladies rarely . . . that is, his lordship does not . . ." He trailed off weakly. "I will inform him of your arrival at once."

"Sweet heaven, what a servant!" Regina told Cicely, as he hurried up the main staircase. "You'd think his master was a troll from the way that fellow acts."

"They do call him the Dragon Viscount," Cicely said.

Regina glanced up at the Tintoretto portraying St. George slaying the dragon, the Draker coat of arms with its black dragon rampant, and the mahogany newel post with a coiled dragon atop it. "I can't imagine why," she said dryly.

Cicely followed her gaze. "Not just because of that. Why, I heard that only last year he reduced a bookseller in the Strand to tears over some moldy old book the man had promised to him, then sold to Lord Gibbons. And he actually struck one of His Highness's messengers last month."

"I also heard that Lord Maxwell keeps a goat in his bedchamber, but you don't see me sending someone to milk it. One mustn't let idle gossip govern one's actions."

"There's more than just rumor surrounding his lordship." Cicely breathed heavily, having her usual trouble with her weak lungs. "What about his treatment of his mother? Don't you remember the horrible claims Lady Draker made when she used to visit your parents?"

"I remember that Lady Draker had a knack for dramatic exaggeration. Besides, his lordship can hardly be as awful as she claimed and raise a sister as lovely as Louisa. Who, incidentally, says that her mother lied about her son's supposed mistreatment."

Cicely looked mutinous. "Miss North is probably too terrified of her brother to say anything else."

"She doesn't act terrified, I assure you. She seems to think he walks on water." Indeed, the incongruity between Louisa's and society's respective images of Lord Draker intrigued her. Even if she hadn't needed to pay this visit, she might have come just to determine his character. "That's why Louisa won't accept my brother's attentions without his lordship's permission. Because she respects Lord Draker's opinion."

"Yes, but—"

"Shh," Regina interrupted. "Listen."

The butler's plaintive voice wafted down the stairs. "B-But milord, what shall I tell them?"

"Tell them I'm indisposed," answered a deep male voice. "Tell them I'm in India. I don't care what the hell you tell them as long as you send them away."

"Yes, milord," came the butler's meek reply.

Regina scowled. So Lord Draker refused to let her have her say? Not if she could help it. Spotting the servant stairs down the hall, she started for them.

Cicely grabbed her by the arm. "What are you doing? You can't just—"

"Stay here and keep the butler occupied." Regina shook

off her cousin's weak grip. "I mean to speak with Lord Draker one way or the other."

"But, my dear—"

Regina didn't stay for further reproaches. If his lordship thought she would drive twenty miles from London only to be put off like some importunate creditor, he was in for a surprise.

Upstairs in the lengthy hall, it took her only minutes to find—after peeking inside the rooms behind every other massive oak door—the one that must lead to his lordship's study. She hesitated just long enough to examine herself in a nearby mahogany-framed mirror. Cheeks pleasingly flushed from their drive, check. New Bourbon hat firmly in place, check. Matching lilac mantle that gaped open to reveal just a hint of bosom, check. Lord Draker did not stand a chance.

Before she could lose her nerve, she opened the door and swept inside, right into the dragon's cave. Except that it wasn't lined with blackened stones smelling of sulfur . . . but with gilded leather smelling of ink. Books. Thousands of books marched around the walls in varying shades of brown and dark blue, further proclaiming their owner's education and wealth.

The room was enormous, probably spanning the entire length of the house. How could a person own this many books, let alone read them?

Sweet heaven. She was in deep trouble now. Not only was the viscount probably a clever man, but a clever man with lots of knowledge at his fingertips. She brushed off that unsettling thought. He was a man, after all, and a bookish man at that, with little knowledge of society, current affairs . . . feminine wiles. Surely her usual charm and a flirtatious smile would suffice.

If she could find the dratted fellow. The library appeared to be empty. She closed the door behind her more loudly than she'd meant to, and a rich baritone voice wafted down to her from the heavens.

"I take it you got rid of Foxmoor's sister."

She jerked, then glanced up to see a ledge directly over her head. Moving farther into the room, she turned around and found the Dragon himself. He was up on a little gallery that ran along the near side of the high-ceilinged room and contained even more bookshelves. His impressively broad back was to her as he took down a volume and opened it with almost paternal care.

It was the only careful thing about him. Everything else was haphazard—the raggedly trimmed hair that fell unfashionably below his collar, the dust-smeared fustian suit, and the scuffed boots.

And he was huge. No wonder everyone believed the rumor that he was actually Prinny's son. He certainly had Prinny's height and large frame, but without the corpulence that plagued His Highness.

The shaggy-haired giant returned his book to the shelf, then squatted to remove one lower down, giving her a view of his well-shaped behind and the impressive thigh muscles straining against the fabric of his ill-fitting trousers. Her mouth went dry. Even she could appreciate a fine male figure when she saw one.

"Well?" he asked. "Did Foxmoor's sister give you any trouble? I hear she's the troublesome sort."

The words jerked her back to the matter at hand. "No more troublesome than the average lady put off by a rude gentleman."

He stiffened, then rose to face her, and she sucked in a breath.

He was nothing like his rumored sire after all. For one thing, he wore an exceedingly unfashionable beard. His Highness would eat nails before he'd grow his whiskers that long. But the prince would certainly not mind having this man's body. A pugilist's meaty shoulders and burly chest tapered down to a surprisingly trim waist. Even his calves appeared to be well-turned, though his stockings . . .

She blinked and looked again. His stockings didn't match.

"Are you finished yet?" he snapped.

She jumped. "Finished what?"

"Looking me over."

Drat it, she hadn't meant to stare. She jerked her gaze up to his bushy beard. "You can't blame me for being curious. Few people ever get to see Castlemaine, much less its owner."

"There's a reason for that." He turned his back on her to restore his book to the shelf. "Now if you'll excuse me—"

"I certainly will not. I wish to talk to you."

He removed another volume. "Like brother, like sister, I see. Can't take 'no' for an answer."

"Not when the 'no' comes without an explanation."

"I'm busy. That should be explanation enough."

"You're not busy; you're a coward."

He whirled to face her, his scowl raining dragonly fury down on her. "What did you call me?"

Excellent, Regina—why not just slap his face with your glove?

But drat the man, he'd really roused her temper. "A coward. You're perfectly ready to slander my family to your sister, but heaven forbid you should state your objections to our faces."

A laugh echoed in the library. "You think you and your brother scare me?"

Her annoyance increased. "Simon said you refused to speak with him."

"He knows perfectly well why I prefer to communicate through the Iversleys. And if he insists on continuing to corrupt my sister—"

"Corrupt!" she protested. "My brother would never corrupt anyone!"

"—I'll be happy to meet with him in person." Lord Draker fixed her with his hard gaze. "So tell Foxmoor that sending his sister here won't soften me one whit."

"He doesn't even know I've come. I'm not here on his behalf. I'm here to argue for your sister."

She didn't miss the subtle gentling in his features. "Louisa sent you?"

"She said you would never listen to her, since she's so inexperienced in society. But she hoped you might listen to someone who knows it well enough to point out the advantages of an alliance between her and my brother." Especially since the Iversleys upheld Lord Draker's refusal to let Simon near the poor girl.

His face closed up. "Louisa was wrong. My mind is set."

"What possible objection could you have to Simon? He's one of the most eligible gentlemen in London."

"I'm sure he is," he said, with an impatient wave of his hand. "Now if you'll excuse me, I have work to do."

Regina was *not* used to being dismissed or ignored. And to have this . . . this beastly devil do so was beyond the pale. "I'm not leaving until I hear some reason for your objection. Because I certainly can't see a good one."

"You wouldn't." He swept his gaze from the tip of her lilac hat to the points of her expensive kid shoes, and she would have sworn she saw admiration flicker in his gaze. Until he added with a sneer, "Your sort never does."

She bristled. Tired of craning her neck up at this obnoxious creature, she approached the stair that led up to the gallery. "And what sort is that?"

"A wealthy lady of rank moving in the highest circles of society."

She began to mount the little stairs. If he wouldn't listen, she'd trap him on the gallery and *make* him listen. "Your sister is a wealthy lady of rank moving in the highest circles of society."

He scowled at her. "She's only there until she finds a decent husband. I want a better life for her than that of a society chit." He swept her with a contemptuous gaze. "The sort who spends her days dithering over what color ball gown to wear."

His blatant assumption stoked Regina's temper even higher. She stepped onto the gallery and walked toward him. "I suppose you'd rather she marry a bushy-faced hermit like you. Then she can spend her days listening to him rebuff all her visitors."

His lordship shot her a scalding look. Sweet heaven, he had the most beautiful eyes she'd ever seen—a rich brandy brown, with long dusky lashes a shade darker than his hair.

A pity those eyes presently burned a hole through her skull. "Better that than spend it catering to Prinny and his ilk," he said.

The light dawned. "Oh, I see. You object to Simon because of his friendship with His Highness. You don't like your sister being around your father after you went to such great pains to throw the man out of here all those years ago."

"You're damned right I don't. And what's more—" He

broke off suddenly. His frown disappeared, only to be replaced by a suspicious crinkling at the corners of his gorgeous eyes. "You do realize you just called me a bastard."

"I did not!"

"In the eyes of the law, my father was the fifth Viscount Draker. And since you were clearly not referring to *him* . . ."

He had her there, drat him. Clever gentlemen were such a bother.

He went on smugly, "One would think a duke's daughter would know better than to throw salacious rumors about a man's parentage right in his face." He settled his hand on the gallery rail. "But then, we both know how thin is the facade of manners that your sort put so much stock in."

"Now see here, you overgrown oaf, I've had enough of your half-baked ideas about me and my 'sort.'" Pivoting on her heel, she headed back toward the little stair. "If you want to force Simon and Louisa to sneak around behind your back, then fine by me. Who cares if they're caught in some compromising position and tarred by scandal? I shall simply tell my brother to go right ahead setting up their secret meetings—"

"Stop!" he roared.

She halted near the stairs, a smile playing over her face.

He came up behind her. "What the devil are you babbling about?"

"Oh, no, I shan't trouble you with it—you're far too busy." She continued toward the stairs slowly—very slowly. "Clearly I've taken up too much of your precious time already. So I'll be on my way."

She'd already reached the stairs when he grabbed her arm and swung her around to face him. "Not until you tell me what's going on, damn you."

Fighting a smile, she removed his hand from her arm. "Are you sure you can spare the time?" she said sweetly. "I don't know if I should impose."

He marched forward, forcing her to back down the stairs. "Your hints about 'secret meetings' had better be more than the figment of your imagination. Because if you think some paltry trick will gain you my attention—"

"Trick? Surely you don't think a woman who spends her time dithering over which gown to wear could trick a clever gentleman like you."

He swore under his breath.

Take that, you big lout. She was so busy congratulating herself that she didn't pay attention and missed a step. She stumbled and was about to tumble backwards to the floor when his lordship snagged her about the waist.

For a moment they stood frozen, with only his broad arm beneath her back preventing her from falling. Thank God he was strong.

And surprisingly clean, for all his mismatched stockings and rough looks. A heady scent of bay rum and soap wafted through her senses, making her wonder if he were not quite the oaf he seemed.

Then his eyes dropped to where her pelisse had fallen open to reveal her low-cut bodice, and his gaze lodged there as if stuck.

Men often stared at her breasts—on occasion she'd even used that to her advantage. But for some reason, *his* staring unsettled her. He looked as if he wanted to devour them . . . and make her enjoy the devouring.

As her breasts pinkened beneath his gaze, she opened her mouth to rebuke him, then noticed the edge of the scar that crawled above his beard and onto his cheek. She'd heard he had a scar, but no one seemed to know how he'd received it or how bad it was. His heavy beard covered most of it, but the part that showed looked rather nasty.

He lifted his eyes to her face. Catching where her gaze was fixed, he scowled. "Watch your step, madam. You wouldn't want to go tumbling."

His thinly veiled threat sent a shiver along her spine. And what had he done to gain such an awful scar anyway? She shuddered to think.

Shifting her in his arms, he lifted her as if she weighed less than nothing and set her firmly on the floor two steps below, then descended to loom over her.

"Now, Lady Regina, you're going to explain exactly what you mean by my sister and secret meetings. Because you're not going anywhere until you do."

His low rumble of a voice sparked a peculiar quivering in her belly. Apparently, she'd awakened the sleeping dragon.

Now she must figure out what to do with him.

Chapter Two

*Never trust a young man, whether he be a poor
mister or a titled and wealthy gentleman, alone
with your charge.*
—Miss Cicely Tremaine, *The Ideal Chaperone*

As Foxmoor's sister strolled to the center of the library,
Marcus followed, trying hard to keep his eyes in his head.

It was impossible. The woman moved as sweetly as a
sonata, and it had been too damned long since he'd heard
one. He couldn't take his eyes off her fine bottom, swathed
in what was undoubtedly the latest fashion. He'd give half
his fortune to have that fashionable ass settled on his lap.
To have *her* settled on his lap, where he could touch and
squeeze and plunder every honey-perfumed, muslin-
draped inch.

He scowled. As if a haughty female like her would let
him within ten feet. Even after he'd rescued her from a
near fall, she'd regarded him as if he meant to ravish her
right there.

He'd wanted to. Who wouldn't, when a woman's lovely
breasts were served up like that, begging him to dive in
and enjoy?

And dash his brains out on the rocks. It could be no
coincidence that Foxmoor's pretty sister had come to

argue for him, no matter what she claimed. That's who was always sent to appease a dragon—a beautiful young virgin.

But this virgin was braver than most. Not many society misses would storm right into his study without an introduction, especially given the gossip about him. And the woman was sophisticated enough that society had dubbed her "La Belle Dame Sans Merci"—the woman without mercy—after that poem by Chaucer about a heartless beauty.

That's why her brother had sent her. Marcus had best remember that. She was what poets meant when they spoke of dying for love.

She was trouble.

"Well?" he snapped, desperate to get the damned woman out of his study before she put a siren's spell on him. "What's all this about secret meetings?"

Boldly she faced him. God help him, why must she be a blonde, too, his particular weakness? The gilt curls peeking out from beneath her feather-adorned hat practically begged to be stroked and fondled and—

A pox on her and her fancy kind. He didn't need this right now.

She regarded him with cool composure. "Your sister and my brother are determined to see each other. If you don't consent to their courtship, they'll sneak around behind the watchful eyes of her guardians. Then they're sure to be caught in a compromising situation that would harm Louisa more than my brother."

"Which is why she would never behave so recklessly."

"No?" Lady Regina stared him down. "I'm here precisely because she doesn't want to go behind your back until she's sure you can't be moved."

Alarm seized him. "You talked to Louisa about this?"

"I talked her *out* of it. She was ready to go along with my brother's plans, but I convinced her that even a duke is not above reproach in such matters and that if they were caught, the ensuing scandal—"

"Damn the scandal! I just don't want her anywhere near your brother and his confounded circle of friends!"

Her gray eyes hardened to steel. "Clearly Louisa doesn't share your aversion to His Highness."

That was the trouble. Louisa didn't even understand it. She'd been ten when their mother left. All she remembered of Prinny was an indulgent "Uncle George" who occasionally brought her treats; Marcus had worked hard to keep her from hearing rumors about the true nature of their mother's "friendship" with the man.

He'd only heard them himself when he'd gone to Harrow at eleven. Some ass had called him Prinny's bastard the very first day. That's when he'd discovered he was the sort of abomination people joked about—an affront to the very values of respectable society. So when Louisa was born shortly after that, he'd vowed to do whatever he must to keep her from suffering the same stigma. Especially since her blood wasn't tainted like his.

He'd held to that vow ever since. And now this seductive harpy and her brother threatened to expose Louisa to everything he'd tried to protect her from. He would not have it! "Surely you realize that Louisa isn't wise enough to the ways of society to be a good choice of wife for your brother."

"She'll learn. She makes him happy—that's all that matters."

He laughed bitterly. "Strange sentiments coming from you, madam."

She cocked her head, setting her ostrich feather aquiver. "What do you mean? You don't even know me."

"I know of you. Who hasn't heard of Lady Regina Tremaine, who despite refusing scores of gentlemen manages to acquire more marriage proposals with each passing year? Can't find one to make you happy, madam? Or just can't find one lofty enough to suit your family's fine lineage and high expectations?"

Two spots of color stained her pretty cheeks. "I see you've been listening to idle gossip."

"It doesn't seem so idle now that I've met you."

"I could say the same for the gossip about you."

"Oh? What do they say about me these days?" He waited for her to hem and haw—no one in society ever gossiped about a man to his face.

She skewered him with a sugared dagger of a smile. "They say you're a hard man with a foul temper. That you have secrets too dark to speak aloud, and that you will do anything to keep them."

He snorted. "They say that *you* enjoy putting upstarts in their places. That your sharp tongue has made you the darling of our corrupt society during the seven years since your come-out."

"Six," she corrected tightly. "And they say that *you* browbeat tradesmen and toss hapless messengers out on their ears for no reason."

He stalked toward her. "They say that some idiot poet is writing a poem to your heartlessness."

Her features grew stony. "They say that William Blake, that daft artist, got the inspiration for one of his horrible dragon paintings from *you*."

He happened to own one of those "horrible dragon paintings." Blake himself, one of Katherine's acquaintances, had given it to him. But he'd thought it was Blake's idea of a joke. Until now.

Scowling, he bent his head until he was nose to nose with the impudent chit. "They say that you're a haughty bitch of a beauty who thinks the sun rises and sets for her because she's daughter to a duke."

When her glittering gaze met his, he thought he saw hurt in it. But that was absurd. Women like her did not hurt.

"They say you eat small children for breakfast," she countered. "With jam."

The deliberate absurdity of that last one startled him. And he didn't like being startled. He glared down at her. "They call you 'La Belle Dame Sans Merci.' "

She thrust her face so close to his that her ostrich feather brushed his forehead. "They call *you* 'the Dragon Viscount.' But that's because society entertains itself by attaching titillating names to those they fear, envy, or admire. It says nothing about either of our characters, as you, of all people, should know."

That astute assessment of society gossip gave him pause. Drawing back from her, he said sullenly, "You left out the worst of the gossip about me. That I bullied my mother and forced her to rely on the kindness of friends— your parents, for example. That I refused to honor the terms of my father's will. That I even used to beat her. Or had you not heard that, too?"

"I heard."

"Then why didn't you mention it? Unless— You believe it, don't you?"

She thrust out her chin. "Should I? Is it true?"

That took him aback. No one had ever bothered to ask him. "You'll think what you want to, so it hardly matters what I say."

"It matters to me."

She said the words so sincerely he almost believed her. And that infuriated him. "Think what you wish then," he growled. "It makes no difference."

"Very well, I'll do that."

When she said nothing more, he cursed her for not indicating what she'd chosen to believe. Not that he cared what she thought. He didn't care in the least. Even if she *was* the most attractive female ever to enter his library.

Then she had the audacity to cast him a sultry smile that sent his pulse pounding. "But I don't know how we got so far off the subject," she said. "This isn't about you or me. It's about Louisa."

Louisa, right. Damn her, Lady Regina was driving him mad, with her crazy assertions about her brother's happiness. She was such a little hypocrite. A dangerously seductive, thoroughly enticing hypocrite with a body made for—

He gritted his teeth. This reaction was exactly what Foxmoor had probably hoped for when the man had sent her here, damn it. "Yes," he said tightly. "We were discussing how you and your brother have corrupted my sister. Otherwise, she wouldn't even think of going against my wishes. She can be headstrong, but she isn't a fool."

She arched one delicate brow. "Clearly you've never been in love, or you would understand that two people in love aren't liable to behave rationally."

"In love, hah. After a couple of dances at her comeout?" A sudden chill seized him. Circling around her, he headed for the fireplace. "They can't have seen each other beyond that."

"Girls do wander onto balconies at parties, you know." She watched as he reached for the poker. "And gentlemen enamored of them do follow them into gardens. Attraction can blossom into love after only a few encounters."

He stabbed the poker into the fire. "My sister might fancy herself in love, but that brother of yours has no such noble motives."

"If you think my brother would attempt to steal your sister's virtue—"

"No, that would certainly not be to his advantage." Not if this courtship had anything to do with Prinny, as Marcus suspected.

She blinked. "You can't possibly think he wants her fortune. He has one of his own."

"Good." Thrusting the poker aside, he faced her. "Because if she does marry him, I'll cut her off. He won't get a penny from me."

When Lady Regina eyed him as if he were a slug, he considered taking back the blatant lie. He'd only said it so she would think twice about helping the couple.

"Such a threat is unlikely to keep my brother from courting your sister," she said quietly. "It will merely encourage them to sneak around behind your back. And make me more than happy to help them."

"What? And risk a scandal?" He sneered at her. "You would never do that."

She assessed him coldly. "If they're willing to risk scandal to be happy, then I'm certainly willing to help."

He bit back an oath. Perhaps it was time Lady Regina learned Foxmoor's true character. Because if she actually believed all that rot about love, she might not approve of his machinations.

And if she already knew Foxmoor's true plans? Then it was better to lay their cards on the table. "Haven't you asked yourself why your brother, who could marry any woman he pleases, would pursue a girl whose family and friends are so opposed to him?"

She lifted her chin. "He's in love."

He snorted. "He's in love, all right. With the idea of being prime minister." He chose his words carefully, not wanting her to know Prinny's claims about Louisa's parentage. "You see, Prinny—your brother's friend—grew fond of my sister in the years he was playing 'Uncle George.' He's annoyed that I refuse to let him near her now—"

"You won't let His Highness see Louisa? And he allows that?"

"Why shouldn't he? He knows he can't press it—he has no connection to her. She's merely the daughter of his former mistress. But that doesn't stop him from trying to stick his nose in where it doesn't belong. Look at what he and Mrs. Fitzherbert did with that poor girl Minney after the death of her mother, his mistress. Everyone knew the girl wasn't his, yet he fought her family for custody and won, solely by abusing his power."

He glared at her. "Fortunately, I know enough of the prince's secrets that he would never dare such a thing with me. Which is why he's trying to get at Louisa through your brother, a man who will do anything to further his political career—including scheme to bring Louisa into Prinny's sphere against my wishes."

Blanching, she reeled away from him. "You think that my brother . . . that the prince is using my brother—"

"I think your brother is using my sister. At Prinny's behest. Your brother is more than eager to give Prinny what he wants, in exchange for his support once Prinny becomes king in truth."

When she faced him again, her eyes were glittering. "Why has Louisa never mentioned your suspicions?"

"Because she doesn't know about them. I've never told her about Prinny's interest in her future. Or your brother's aims. I do not want to hurt her."

"Neither do I. And I certainly wouldn't be here arguing his case if I thought my brother intended such a thing. I assure you that if he wanted to marry her for a political purpose, he would state that outright."

"I'm not sure that marriage is his true intention. A courtship would be enough excuse for bringing my sister around the prince—"

"How dare you! Simon would never use a woman in such an underhanded manner, preying on her feelings merely for some political advantage." She brightened. "Besides, if that's all he wanted, he would have told her of the prince's aims the first time they danced. Yet she has never mentioned that. Clearly, you are wrong about his intentions."

"I'm not wrong. I don't know why your brother hasn't told her, but I assure you it's not out of any great 'love' for her. And all this talk about sneaking around is to bring her to Prinny, so the man can flatter her and undermine my authority."

"Don't you think she should know of the prince's interest in her future?"

"Absolutely not. She's just young enough to be dazzled by the idea of traveling in court circles, without being wise enough to understand how dangerous Prinny can be." Stepping nearer, he lowered his voice. "And so help me, if you dare tell her any of this—"

"I am not a tattler, sir," she retorted with a mutinous set to her chin. "Besides, I am not about to tell her some unfounded nonsense about a plot between His Highness and my brother."

Her loyalty to her brother was commendable but misplaced. "If you don't believe me, ask Foxmoor why he's courting her. See what he says."

A hint of uncertainty showed in her eyes before she stepped away with a sniff. "I don't have to. I know my brother. He is not the calculating devil you make him out to be." She arched one elegant eyebrow. "Nor are you giving your sister enough credit. She's a lovely girl. Any man would be happy to marry her."

"The sister to the Dragon Viscount, whose mother was as notorious in her day as Delilah was in hers?" He leaned against a nearby bookshelf. "When I sent Louisa out into society, I hoped she might find some handsome young baron or kindly merchant who might overlook her country manners and her connection to me, who could marry her for her own sweet self. Then lo and behold, she snags the interest of a wealthy duke with a brilliant future ahead of him. Can you blame me for being suspicious?"

"I assure you, my brother is only one of her admirers."

The observation rubbed him raw. He hated that this confounded society chit knew more about his sister's prospects than he did. "Then let one of *them* court her. Because I'll never approve a courtship between your manipulative brother and my sister. I know that the prince is mixed up in this somehow, and I won't have it."

"If you ever met my brother, I know you would reverse your bad opinion—"

He laughed harshly. "Not damned likely. Unlike those idiots in Parliament, I'm not swayed by 'gifted oratory' from an insolent, lying pup."

She bristled, her cheeks awash with scarlet and her bosom quivering. God help him, but Lady Regina with her dander up was an awe-inspiring sight. What he wouldn't give to have her beneath him unleashing all that fire and passion—

"You will drive them to elope with your bullheaded refusal," she snapped.

He tamped down his wayward thoughts. "I doubt he means to elope. But now that I know what he's up to, I'll bring her back here out of his reach."

"You would ruin her chances to make any match, simply to keep her away from my brother?"

He shrugged. "She can always have another season next year. By then, she'll see the situation more rationally."

"By then, she'll resent you even more for your stubbornness, which will give her justification for deceiving you at every turn." She shot him a withering glance. "Unless you intend to lock her in the dungeon you supposedly have downstairs?"

"Don't be absurd. Once she's at home, I'll make her see I'm right—"

"Or your draconian measures will drive her into running away. And I tell you now, if she ever seeks refuge in *my* home, she will have it."

"Confound it all! If you help her, I will . . . I will—"

"What? Slander me in society? Do you think anyone would listen to you over me and my brother?"

He clenched his fists. The duke had friends in high places. Marcus had only his money and his gruff temper.

And his half brothers. "All right, I'll let her remain in society. But you and your brother will both be banned from seeing her."

"Then Simon will find some other woman to help him sneak her off, some woman you don't know. And Louisa will gladly go along."

"A pox on you," he roared. "What do you want from

me? You give me no recourse. I don't want them sneaking about, but I refuse to let your brother court her if he only does it to get her into Prinny's clutches!"

"Then you should determine for yourself his motives."

That brought him up short. "What do you mean?"

"Let them court . . . but oversee the courtship yourself. Why not go into society and see how matters really stand with your sister and my brother? Once you see them together, you can't possibly continue in your ridiculous suspicions. And if by some small chance you are still convinced of his duplicity, you'll have better control over the situation if you're out in society yourself."

Among the rumormongers and the scornful *ton*? Marcus shuddered. "You don't know what you're asking. I loathe society. And it loathes me, I assure you."

"Over some old gossip? I doubt that. There will be grumblings at first, but that will die soon enough when they witness your concern for your sister."

Lady Lofty was insane if she thought it would be that simple. Still, he *could* watch out for Louisa so much better than heretofore. "There would be no sneaking around behind my back? No secret meetings?"

"You have my word on it. *If* you give them a month to court properly, so my brother can prove that his intentions are honorable."

Honorable, hah! Foxmoor didn't know the meaning of the word. If Marcus could show that the man's motives for courting Louisa were suspect, wouldn't Lady Regina leap to condemn Foxmoor's behavior?

Not if she was part of his plot. But if she *was*, she ought to realize that Marcus's interference would be detrimental to her brother's plans. Out in society, he might even keep Foxmoor from doing what he planned.

He glowered at her. "You hope I'll refuse your little proposition, don't you? Then you and your brother can tell Louisa how unreasonable I am and give her an excuse for disobeying me."

She rolled her eyes. "Don't be absurd."

"Come to think of it, it's a clever plan. Did you dream it up yourself, or did your brother help you concoct it?"

Her silver-grey eyes impaled him. "Is that what you do out here in the country all day—imagine intrigues and plots against you? I hate to disappoint you, sir, but I want only the happiness of my brother and Louisa."

He didn't believe that for a minute, and he would prove she was lying if it killed him. "Very well, I accept your challenge. I'll go into society and observe my sister and your brother together. I'll endure the gossip and the speculation if that's what it takes to make her see sense."

"That's all I want," she said primly. "For you to give them a chance."

"Then you won't mind agreeing to one small condition."

She grew wary. "Oh?"

The more he thought about it, the more he liked this idea. He smiled down at her. "It seems to me that I'm taking all the risks in this arrangement. You want me to go into society, where I'll endure old gossip and social affairs I detest, and all I might get for it is the removal of your brother from my sister's affections. Fine. I'll brave the gossipmongers, but only if you brave them with me. I'll let Foxmoor court Louisa . . . if you let me court *you*."

She stared at him, mouth agape.

I've got you now, Lady Lofty, he thought smugly.

La Belle Dame Sans Merci let herself be seen welcoming the attentions of the disgusting Dragon Viscount? Never.

She wouldn't risk the damage that would do to her reputation as the darling of society. And then he could show Louisa once and for all how shallow her new friends were.

As a smile tugged at his lips, her eyes hardened. "Now *you* think *I'll* refuse."

"Of course not," he said mockingly. "You have only my sister's best interests at heart. So you'll happily endure my company just to unite two lovers."

"I might. If I knew *why* you want to court someone of my 'sort.' "

He shrugged. "If I must go out into society, why not do it with a beautiful woman on my arm?" He let his gaze trail insolently over her, waiting until the color rose in her cheeks before adding, "In the right place, even the company of a woman like you can be enjoyable."

Her eyes narrowed on him. "Are you sure you're not wanting to court me just to annoy my brother?"

"I'll admit that adds to the attraction, but no." He threw out the first reason that came to him, knowing she would refuse his terms anyway. "It's time I acquired a wife. Why not start my search at the top of the social ladder?"

"How very flattering," she remarked coldly.

"I'm not asking you to marry me. I merely want you to give me your company exclusively, the way I'm letting your brother have my sister's. If a woman of your station champions me, it will ease my way in society."

She regarded him intently for a long moment, then tipped up her chin. "Very well, I accept your proposal, sir."

His smile faltered. She couldn't be serious. "Perhaps I didn't make myself clear. I don't mean a private courtship where I take you riding in the country or accompany you to a play in a darkened theater. You must dance with me publicly and ride in my carriage on Rotten Row. To truly soften the blow of my return to society, you must attend at least two or three public events on my arm."

Her eyes twinkled. "Is that all? I say we make it an even month of events. You're allowing Simon and Louisa a month to court, so we should have the same."

"You think I'm joking—"

"No, indeed. You don't strike me as the sort to joke."

"Damned right, I'm not." But could he really mean to go through with this?

Oh yes. When it came to Louisa, he would brave anything. While it might hurt his sister's standing to have him appear in public, her being found in a compromising position with the duke would destroy it. And having Prinny wheedle his way into her affections would be disastrous. Marcus knew firsthand how easily his manipulative father could ruin a life. Well, the man wouldn't ruin Louisa's.

And if Foxmoor could use Marcus's sister, then Marcus could certainly use Foxmoor's. He'd make sure Lady Regina's outings in society with him gave her a good taste of what being related to him would be like. Then Lady Lofty would beg her brother to stop courting Louisa. "So we're agreed," he said. "Simon courts Louisa; I court you."

She didn't even flinch. "Fine by me."

"Very well. The Iversleys are having a soiree tomorrow evening to exhibit Louisa's musical talents. I'll be at your town house at seven to fetch you."

He thought she might balk, but she merely set her shoulders. "And Simon, too. I was invited, but he was not, since the Iversleys apparently share your disapproval of his interest in Louisa. But I'm not going anywhere unless he—"

"I'll take care of that right now." He strode over to a writing table to scribble a note. "Since you're so fond of paying calls, you can call on Lady Iversley this afternoon to give her this." He handed the note to her. "Go ahead and read it if you don't trust me to word it properly."

A strange panic filled her features before she masked it. "I'm sure it's fine."

"Then I'll see you tomorrow."

He headed back toward the gallery stairs, hoping she would understand she was being dismissed. She'd found her own way in, so she could damned well find her own way out.

"One more thing before I go, Lord Draker," she said. "You should shave off your beard before tomorrow. Beards aren't considered fashionable these days."

He turned a cold gaze to her. "Neither are impertinent women, but that doesn't seem to stop you. Good day, madam."

"I just thought you'd wish to know—"

"Good day, madam," he repeated firmly.

She looked as if she might retort, then sniffed and turned toward the door.

As she swept from the room in a swirl of white muslin, he snorted. Shave off his beard indeed. Was that why she'd agreed to his proposal? Because she thought she could turn him into a suitable gentleman?

If so, she was in for a surprise. He wasn't one of her fawning suitors to be wound about her little finger for her own amusement. No sharp-tongued duchess's daughter would tell *him* how to groom himself.

Let her flash her winsome smile and flaunt those glorious breasts that begged to be kissed and fondled and—

A sweat broke over his brow, making him curse. He

could handle this damned attraction. He *could*. He just had to keep his mind focused on his goal. Besides, even if he wanted to turn his life upside down for the haughty chit—and he didn't—it wouldn't suit his purpose. The more he offended Lady Lofty's sensibilities, the sooner she would beg her brother to end his association with Louisa.

That couldn't be too soon for Marcus.

Chapter Three

Your duty is to your employer,
not to your charge, for if she falls,
they will blame you, not her.
—Miss Cicely Tremaine, *The Ideal Chaperone*

"Are you all right?" Cicely asked Regina as they settled back into the carriage. "You look flushed."

"I'm fine," Regina lied. Who wouldn't look flushed after half an hour of the Dragon Viscount's scorching insinuations and fiery glances? It was no wonder the brazen scoundrel had no friends.

Cicely looked unconvinced. "He didn't shout at you? Or . . . or touch you?"

Regina stared out the window, trying not to remember his powerful arm around her waist, holding her suspended in space. "We had a perfectly reasonable conversation. He *is* a gentleman, you know." With a hard head, a million thorny prejudices . . .

And a clever mind, drat him. She should never have agreed to his bargain. Let the Dragon Viscount—a man as unpredictable as a typhoon—court her? She must be daft.

But what else could she do after all the nasty and ridiculous claims he'd made about Simon? He'd cast a slur on the family honor. If she'd refused his bargain, the arrogant lout would have considered that proof of her family's lack of character. He would have used her refusal against her brother.

And the blackguard had the audacity to call *Simon* calculating! At least her brother knew how to act like a gentleman. Simon didn't growl at a lady or give her his back. Simon didn't make outrageous proposals that any lady with an ounce of sense would reject.

If I must go out into society, why not do it with a beautiful woman on my arm?

Her breath quickened involuntarily. More men than she could count had called her beautiful. But few had dared to couple it with a hot, avaricious stare that played over her so insolently . . . so boldly—

"Are you sure you're all right?" Cicely asked. "You look rather pink-cheeked."

"It's this heat, that's all." Regina opened her reticule to find her fan. It was *not* the viscount's burning stares. Decidedly not.

When she drew out her fan, a note fell into her lap. Drat it, she'd forgotten about that. With a glance at Cicely, who was now pulling down the shade to block the afternoon sun's unrelenting rays, Regina unfolded the paper. She stared hard at it, praying that this time she'd magically be able to make sense of the letters that other people claimed formed words.

But as usual, the magic eluded her, and no words that she could understand would form. A d, then a p, then an l . . . or perhaps an e. What sort of word was that? She turned the note sideways—or at least she thought it was sideways. But she couldn't even make printed letters form words properly—how in God's name was she supposed to make sense of this scrawl?

When her head began to throb, she tossed the note aside with a curse. Lifting her gaze, she found Cicely watching her with concern.

"What's that?" her cousin asked.

Regina shrugged. "A note I'm supposed to take to Lady Iversley. His lordship didn't even seal it—he showed it to me for my approval."

Cicely's eyes went wide. "Oh, dear, what did you do?"

"I pretended to read it, and that seemed to satisfy him."

Cicely donned her spectacles. "Shall I read it to you then?"

Gritting her teeth, Regina handed it over. "If you don't mind."

"Of course I don't mind, dear."

As Cicely scanned the note, Regina suddenly felt six again, watching her cousin and childhood tutor read easily what she couldn't read even with a struggle. "I did try, you know," she said.

"Uh-huh," Cicely murmured, absorbed in the note. Then Regina's words sank in, and she lifted her gaze. "You don't have to try. I'm always happy to read for you."

"I know, but I fear I don't try hard enough. If I really worked at it—"

"Oh, but you mustn't!" Cicely's face showed clear alarm. "Didn't it give you the headache?"

"Well, yes, but—"

"What if it hurts your brain permanently? Who knows what could happen? Remember what the doctor said—it's not worth trying to read if you tax your brain so much that you injure it. Do you really want to risk losing your facility for speech or thought, too?"

Regina gazed out the window. "Of course not."

Despite the claims of the private doctor Cicely had secretly consulted when Regina was young, neither of them had any idea what might happen if she braved the headaches. No one else seemed to suffer pain merely from staring at a few words. No one else looked at letters and saw them backwards or upside down.

Why was her brain so different? She generally understood spoken words, and whenever someone read to her—and she'd grown very clever at convincing them to do so—she understood what they read. She enjoyed hearing a good story, and she absolutely delighted in attending the theater.

So why did her brain fail her when she opened a book or even tried to read music? Why must the letters and notes always look wrong?

Cicely believed it was because of the terrible fever that had struck Regina when she was two. Regina had been told that her nanny had nearly despaired of her living through it. And she had taken longer than most children to learn to speak.

"Well, what does it say?" she asked, as Cicely continued staring at the paper.

"His lordship doesn't have the finest hand I've ever seen, but if I read this correctly"—she flashed Regina a smile—"then you succeeded in changing his mind about Miss North and your brother. He asks that Lady Iversley invite Simon to a soiree at her home tomorrow evening." Cicely gazed at it more closely, a puzzled frown creasing her brow. "And he says that he'll be attending as well. With you? Surely I can't be reading that correctly."

Regina drew herself up. "Yes, I agreed to let him . . . er . . . accompany me." She didn't dare tell Cicely the true nature of her arrangement with Lord Draker; Cicely would faint dead away.

As it was, Cicely's head shot up so fast it nearly fell off. "My word, are you sure you should do that?"

"No," Regina said wryly. "But I had little choice. It was the only way Lord Draker would agree to let Simon court his sister."

Cicely sat back and fanned herself furiously with her reticule. "Oh dear, oh dear . . . the Dragon Viscount . . . and you . . ." She stopped fanning to remove her spectacles and hand the note back to Regina. "Are you sure Simon will allow it?"

Regina tucked the note back inside her reticule. "He will if he wants to see his sweetheart." She smiled smugly. "Besides, he won't find out until Lord Draker shows up at our town house, and by then it will be too late. Simon doesn't even know I went out to Castlemaine to talk to the man." When Cicely blanched, Regina's eyes narrowed. "You didn't tell him, did you?"

"No! I-I mean . . . well . . . I did leave a note for him. But I doubt he'll get home before we do, and as soon as we're back I'll retrieve it from his desk." When Regina began to scowl, Cicely added hastily, "I merely wanted to make sure someone knew where we were in case something happened to us out there."

Regina rolled her eyes. "What did you think Lord Draker would do—lock us in his famous dungeon?"

Cicely leaned close, her eyes feverishly bright. "You jest, but I've heard that he chains women down there and does unspeakable things to them."

She bit back a smile. "What sort of unspeakable things?"

"Regina!" Cicely said, clearly horrified.

"I'm only teasing, dear." Or half-teasing anyway. Because the thought of Lord Draker "doing unspeakable things" to a woman chained in his dungeon provoked an odd fluttering in her chest.

She could picture the scene—a woman bound and helpless before him . . . subjected to his unsettling gaze greedily raking her scantily clad body. Then his hands would follow where his gaze had traveled, touching and stroking until the woman sighed with pleasure—

She snorted. Pleasure, hah! How could she even think that such a thing would be pleasurable? And from that arrogant scoundrel, too—how absurd. She was as bad as Cicely with her fertile imagination.

"You've really got to stop reading those gossip rags," she grumbled to her cousin. "They give you the wildest ideas." *And me, too, unfortunately.*

Cicely flinched. "I only read them so I can keep you informed about what's happening in society."

Regina was instantly contrite. "I know, dear, I know. And I do appreciate the sacrifices you make for me. What would I do without you?"

That seemed to mollify Cicely, who drew out her netting with a hesitant smile.

Regina meant every word. If not for Cicely, all the world would know about the duke's daughter whose brain was so damaged that she couldn't read. People would pity her—and her brother. They would dredge up every inconsequential tale about her family and search for deficiencies in Simon and Cicely and—

No, it couldn't be borne. No one must ever learn her secret.

Thank heaven for Cicely's quick-wittedness. The minute she'd discovered Regina's weakness, she'd scrambled to hide it, even from Regina's parents. Cicely had known even then what Regina had taken years to learn—

that the duchess demanded perfection from her children. The family honor must be upheld, after all.

Fortunately, Mama's expectations for Regina had focused on womanly accomplishments over scholarly ones. Since Regina had learned to play the harp by ear and could sing well, Mama had been content right up until her death shortly before Regina's come-out.

Regina didn't miss not being able to read. She could go to plays, and Cicely read the papers to her. And if sometimes she burned to know what people were talking about when they discussed some poem—Cicely hated poems, so they never read any—she soon got over it. It wasn't as if she could do anything to change the situation.

But it *was* an inconvenience, and it became more so every day. Not to mention the burden it put on her cousin. Cicely was twice Regina's age, and her eyes were failing. She'd never been in the best of health, but now she was downright sickly. Soon, being Regina's companion would be too much for her.

"What was the viscount like?" Cicely asked from across the carriage. "Was he as frightening in person as everyone says?"

"Not at all." No reason to alarm Cicely any further.

"I heard that he was handsome before his riding accident."

Regina's curiosity was roused. "Is that how he got the scar on his face?"

"That's what his mother told yours."

"What kind of riding accident was it?"

Cicely's nimble fingers continued netting at an even pace. "Lady Draker was vague on the details, but it happened around the time his father died, right after he reached his majority. The viscount was probably too grief-stricken to heed where he rode, so he took a fall. No one really knows for sure."

The thought of Lord Draker grief-stricken and wounded muddied the image Regina had formed of him. She had assumed he'd received his scar from some fellow who didn't appreciate his acting like his usual obnoxious self.

The carriage rumbled along for a few moments. "A pity about the scar," Cicely finally said. "I suppose it makes him hideous now."

"No, indeed," Regina said quickly.

Curiosity shone in Cicely's face. "Then he's still handsome?"

"Not exactly." He was arresting. Powerful. A most intriguing man.

But not handsome, not with that fur all over his face. Then again, if he were clean-shaven and dressed like a gentleman instead of a dusty hermit—

"It hardly matters what he looks like, does it?" she said peevishly. "I only have to endure the courtship while Simon courts Louisa."

"*Courtship?*" Cicely squeaked. "He's *courting* you?"

Drat it all, she hadn't meant to say that. "Well, sort of—"

A shout sounded from the road ahead, and the carriage jerked suddenly to a halt, throwing her forward into Cicely.

"What the dickens—" Regina muttered as she scrambled off her cousin.

"Your Grace!" came the alarmed voice of the coachman from up on the perch. "Did you require—"

"I require my sister!" boomed a voice that made Regina groan. Then the carriage door swung open to reveal the one person she didn't presently want to see.

Her brother.

Simon glared at her through the open door, his golden hair disheveled and his blue eyes glittering. "This time you've gone too far." He flung himself into the carriage beside Cicely, then ordered the coachman to drive on.

As the carriage lurched forward, Regina glanced out to see Simon's tiger wheel his phaeton around. Sweet heaven, Simon had come after her in his fastest phaeton, which he reserved only for dire emergencies or rides with His Highness.

That could only mean trouble, so Regina didn't give him the chance to launch into a tirade. "How kind of you to come all this way to accompany us, Simon. But you needn't have bothered."

He scowled. "Don't you try to turn me up sweet—you know very well you had no business going out to Castlemaine."

"What's wrong with paying a visit to my friend's brother?"

"You risked your reputation by going to a bachelor's home—"

"Cicely was with me. Besides, no one saw me out there. And since when do you care about my reputation? You wanted me to risk it by helping you sneak a young woman away from her guardians to meet you privately."

Simon eyed her with suspicion. "You didn't tell Draker that, did you?"

"What I did was convince him to let you court Louisa for a month."

He blinked. "You must be joking."

"No, indeed," Cicely put in. "Regina's got a note from him to take to Lady Iversley, asking her to invite you to the soiree at her house tomorrow night."

Looking flummoxed, Simon fell back against the squabs. "How the devil did you manage that?"

When Cicely started to answer, Regina cast the older woman a warning glance before flashing a smile at her brother. "He's a perfectly nice man once you make him listen to reason."

"I doubt that seriously." Simon gazed out the window with a speculative expression. "So what are the terms of this courtship? Can I call on Louisa at the Iversleys'? And accompany her to balls?"

"Of course."

"I assume I can take her riding in the phaeton."

Regina swallowed. "His lordship would probably expect to . . . er . . . go along, and short of making him ride behind you, I don't think—"

His gaze swung to her. "Why would Draker expect to go along?"

"Because that's his condition for allowing this—that you let him oversee the courtship."

"I don't want him overseeing it! What sort of courtship is that?"

"The proper sort, that's what."

"But I can't have him hanging about while I'm with Louisa. It will ruin everything."

Her eyes narrowed. "How so?"

The veiled look that came over his features gave Regina pause. *I think your brother is using my sister.* Could that cursed man be right about Simon's motives, after all?

Her brother caught her staring and stiffened. "Draker will spend his time sniping at me, and I'll be forced to defend myself, which will surely make Louisa angry. How can I court a woman when her brother is insulting me at every turn?"

She searched Simon's face, but his words made sense. "Tell me something, why do you want to court Louisa? You met her only a few weeks ago, and you barely know her."

"I know enough. She's a fine girl—well-read, interesting, accomplished—"

"So you want to marry her for herself," she prodded, ignoring the fact that "well-read" was at the top of his list. Thank God Simon didn't know of her own weakness.

He looked her right in the eye. "Of course. Did Draker say otherwise?"

No point in rousing Simon's temper by telling him of the viscount's suspicions. Especially when they were clearly unfounded.

"No, I merely wanted to be sure." *Aha, Lord Draker—I told you that you were wrong about him.* "So you truly don't care that there's scandal associated with her family. And that she's not all that sophisticated."

"Do *you* care?" he countered.

"No. But I'm not considering marrying her."

Regina was, however, going to be living with any wife Simon chose, since she never intended to marry herself. That's why she fully intended to have a say in his choice, whether he knew it or not.

She needed Simon to find someone who could help Cicely with her duties, so their poor cousin would not be so overtaxed. And both she and Cicely liked sweet Louisa. Louisa wouldn't try to change their way of living or put on airs like the saucy females Simon always seemed to fancy. Louisa would be a friend who could be trusted with her secret, and Regina had none of those.

Oh, she had female friends, but they all believed in her carefully cultivated image of sophistication. Take that away, and they would devour her whole. Mama was not the only person in society to demand perfection.

But Louisa wouldn't. And once the dear girl married Simon, her loyalties would be with the family, thank God.

Which was why Regina had to bring the girl's wretched brother around. "Since you mean to marry Louisa," she told Simon matter-of-factly, "you'll need her guardian's consent, or you'll have to elope. And now that I've arranged a way to obtain it, why not take advantage? How can it hurt to show him that your intentions are honorable?"

A muscle tightened in Simon's jaw as he settled back against the squabs. "I suppose you're right. It isn't as if we have to spend much time with the blasted fellow. A party here or there. I can still see Louisa in private as we discussed."

Regina stiffened. "Absolutely not. For one thing, Louisa won't do it now that her brother has approved a formal courtship. And part of my agreement with his lordship was that the courtship would be entirely public and proper."

Simon's eyes narrowed. "For how long?"

"A month."

"Regina!" Cicely exclaimed. "You agreed to let that devil court you for a *month?*"

"Devil?" Simon demanded. "Court who? What are you talking about?"

Oh, dear, sometimes Cicely was entirely too overprotective. Regina shot her cousin an exasperated glance before turning to Simon. "His lordship and I made a bargain. In exchange for his agreeing to let you and Louisa court, I agreed to let him court me."

"Are you out of your mind?" he roared. "You agreed to

let the Dragon Viscount court you? A man who'd ravish you as soon as look at you?"

"Don't be absurd. He may be gruff, but he's a gentleman." Assuming that one's definition of "gentleman" was rather broad.

"The man can't get a woman even to look at him, yet you promise to endure his attentions for a month? Why, Regina?"

"Because he practically dared me to do it, that's why. He's so sure that you—that we—are wicked creatures who will corrupt Louisa. I couldn't refuse his challenge and confirm his opinion."

"Even if it means you're banned from parties because you have the notorious Dragon Viscount in tow?"

"Stuff and nonsense. I should hope my own standing is secure enough to allow me the occasional eccentric suitor. I might even reverse his outcast status, and think what a coup that would be. All of society would be talking about it."

"Is that what this is about? You're bored with your volunteer work at Chelsea Hospital and need a new project? You think to tidy him up and teach him some social graces?"

"Not exactly, but I do believe that with a little subtle persuasion—"

Simon snorted. "Not likely. Draker isn't like those poor saps who worship at your feet. You won't train *him* to behave with just your icy reproofs." He eyed her consideringly. "But it could be entertaining to watch you try. Very well, see if you can civilize his lordship. If anybody can force him to his knees, you can."

"I wish you wouldn't put it like that." Bad enough that the viscount and everyone else thought her a "haughty bitch." Must her brother do so, too?

"In fact, let's make the endeavor more interesting. I'll wager that even a month of your 'subtle persuasions' cannot turn his lordship into a gentleman suitable for society. And if I win the wager, you agree not to interfere anymore in my courtship with Louisa."

She'd been going to refuse his detestable wager, until his last words. Why wouldn't he want her to help him in his courtship? He ought to be grateful.

I'm not sure that marriage is his true intention.

She stiffened. "If *I* win, then you agree to ask Lord Draker formally for Louisa's hand. And to abide by his answer."

With indrawn breath, she waited for his response. If Simon accepted her terms, then he did mean to marry Louisa, and Lord Draker was wrong.

Simon cocked one eyebrow. "Done. But you will not win. The man may take the chance to court you, but he will never become another of your toadying puppies to command."

She glowered at him. "Why do you assume that's what I want from him? I might be interested in the man for himself, you know."

Simon laughed. "You've never shown interest in any man who wasn't a blindingly handsome nitwit you could make dance to your tune."

True. But that was because clever men were liable to unveil her secret shame. At least the nitwits never guessed that she couldn't read.

But then they didn't care either, which is probably why she never did more than let them squire her to parties. She couldn't bring herself to marry a nitwit.

Or anybody else. Even if her husband accepted her defect, she dared not risk having children. What if she passed it on to them? What if her children's brains were even more damaged than hers? She couldn't take that chance.

"By all accounts," Simon went on, "Draker is ugly—"

"He's *not* ugly."

Simon arched one eyebrow. "If you say so. But he's a clever man of letters steeped in scandalous rumor. Definitely not your sort."

"Perhaps my tastes have changed."

"You mean you've decided to cut your teeth on something meatier? Be careful, dear girl. Setting your sights higher is an admirable goal, but starting with the likes of Draker is insanity."

"I told her that," Cicely put in. "She just won't listen."

Because she couldn't bear to let the man continue his arrogant assumptions when she had the power to prove him wrong. "Think what you wish, but I will take your wager, and I will win." If only to make sure Simon did this courtship properly.

He laughed. "Very well, have your fun. And when you fail, and the devil continues opposing our match, Louisa will wash her hands of him at last, leaving us to do as we please."

Regina gritted her teeth. "I shall not fail. No brother of mine shall sneak about town with his ladylove like some reckless rogue. I'll make sure of that."

Chapter Four

*The best weapon against unwanted suitors is a
dire look. Use a mirror to practice your
disapproving glances.*
—Miss Cicely Tremaine, *The Ideal Chaperone*

Marcus frowned as he paced the foyer of Foxmoor's spacious and extravagantly furnished mansion in town. The butler had told him that Lady Regina would be down momentarily, but she'd already kept him waiting a full fifteen minutes. That was probably part of her attempt to bring him to heel.

Very well, let her play her little games; they would not affect him. She might be a siren, but he was as immovable as Ulysses tied to the mast. Like Ulysses, he would allow himself to hear her dangerous song without succumbing to its allure.

"You must be Draker," said a voice from behind him.

He turned to find a man approaching—young, blond, and dressed in a fine suit of dark blue silk. If Marcus hadn't recognized the duke from Louisa's coming-out ball, he still would have known him by the marked resemblance he bore to Lady Regina. The man was too handsome by half, certainly too handsome to make a sweet girl like Louisa happy.

Marcus hated him instantly. "Hello, Foxmoor."

The man stopped short. "Have we met before?"

"Not exactly, but I know who you are."

"Excellent." The duke held out his hand, but Marcus ignored it. After a moment, Foxmoor dropped his hand. "So you're here to court Regina?"

Marcus eyed him warily. "She told you about our . . . er . . ."

"Bargain? Yes. Very peculiar, that." His mouth hardened. "I'm not sure I approve, but Regina has a tendency to do as she pleases no matter what I say. One of the trials of having sisters, I suppose."

"I haven't had that sort of trouble myself." Marcus gave a thin smile. "My sister knows better than to act without my permission."

Foxmoor's eyes narrowed. "I wouldn't count on that. Miss North has a mind of her own, which you'll learn soon enough if you force her to choose between us."

"Louisa will never choose you if I have anything to say about it."

Foxmoor's smile stopped short of his eyes. "You won't."

Marcus scowled. "Now see here, you calculating weasel—"

"That's enough, both of you."

They whirled toward the stairs at the same time. But while Simon began to frown at the sight of his sister in her evening gown, Marcus was struck dumb.

Had he thought her beautiful before? He'd been deranged. That had been the plain Lady Regina, the one who paid calls to reclusive country gentlemen. *This* was Lady Regina in full society regalia, La Belle Dame Sans Merci in all her glory. A vision of loveliness in pink crepe and pearls.

And he'd thought she couldn't bring him to heel. If he

didn't watch it, she'd soon have him leaping into the water to drown himself at her siren feet.

He watched as she descended the stairs, her overskirt floating around the white satin gown skimming her shapely curves. Another hat adorned her gilded hair, this one pink satin with two dangling white tassels that barely trembled as she glided toward them. He hadn't known a woman could move as smoothly, or as sensuously, as that. Even her stern expression couldn't quell the quickening of Marcus's pulse at the sight of her.

"Behave yourself," she said, and for half a second, Marcus thought she was talking about the heat rising in his loins. But no, she was speaking to Foxmoor. "I refuse to spend the evening listening to you bait his lordship," she told her brother in a silky voice that made Marcus's blood run even hotter.

"Me!" Foxmoor protested.

"He was kind enough to indulge my request that he give you a chance, and I won't have you go at him with daggers drawn. Either behave civilly, or we will leave you here, and you'll have to take your own carriage."

"A capital idea," Marcus muttered.

That only drew her withering stare to him. "As for you, my lord, I suppose I shall have to overlook your deplorably unfashionable evening clothes." While a footman scurried to help her don a pelisse, she eyed Marcus askance. "I suppose you lacked the time to purchase new evening attire for your entry into society—"

"The time *and* the inclination to spend money so frivolously," he retorted. "Especially when I possess a perfectly good coat already."

"And here I thought you were wealthy. Apparently I was mistaken." Before he could respond to that insult, she continued in that sugary voice of hers, "But razors aren't costly. So what reason could you possibly have for ignoring my advice about shaving off your beard?"

Did she mean to lecture him with impunity? Not damned likely. "What lies beneath my beard is no sight for a lady. You of all people should understand that, given how important you deem physical appearance."

If she realized he was insulting her, she didn't show it. "That means you should let *me* judge whether what lies beneath your beard is a sight for ladies."

"Ah, but then if you shrank back in horror, it would take me weeks to grow the beard back properly, during which time I'd be deprived of your company."

She smiled. "Would that be such a loss for you?"

"We made a bargain, and I mean to hold you to it." He held out his arm, ignoring the way her smile faltered. "Shall we go?"

As she took it, a snigger from his left made him glance over to find Foxmoor fighting back a laugh.

She glared at her brother. "Something wrong, Simon?"

"No, nothing," he answered, eyes alight with amusement. "I'll just fetch Cicely. She's in the drawing room."

When he walked off, his shoulders shaking with laughter, Marcus glanced down at Lady Regina. "Was it something I said?"

"My brother thinks you're incapable of behaving like a gentleman. And you prove him right with every word out of your mouth."

He suppressed his irritation. "As I recall, our bargain didn't include any assurances that I'd behave like a gentleman."

"True. But I didn't realize you meant to spend our time together trying to embarrass me."

He stared her down. "I'm planning to be myself. If that embarrasses you—"

"No need to get all dragonlike and huffy about it. I assure you I'm very hard to embarrass."

"No, your forte is probably embarrassing other people."

She flinched, then glanced away. "Of course. That's what my sort excel at. How clever of you to have found us out."

Damn. Had he actually hurt her feelings?

No, that was impossible. Her "sort" prided themselves on being able to shame someone with a word. She was only angry that he'd beaten her to the insult.

Moments later, her brother returned with a woman in tow. As Foxmoor performed the introductions, Marcus examined Miss Cicely Tremaine, who was clearly her ladyship's duenna. Even the great Lady Regina couldn't venture into public without a chaperone.

But the fiftyish Miss Tremaine, though wan and thin, looked alert enough to keep even the most determined suitor at bay. She obviously meant to do her duty, which was fine by him. Marcus didn't need to insult Lady Regina with physical overtures. Just showing up at the soiree with her would be enough to make her reconsider any association between their families.

Indeed, her lesson had already begun, for clearly her duenna found him repugnant. When they entered his carriage, and he and Foxmoor situated themselves across from the two ladies, Miss Tremaine couldn't look at him without frowning. And when Marcus tried to make himself more comfortable in the cramped carriage and his leg brushed hers, her look of horror was almost comical.

Almost.

Gritting his teeth, he reminded himself that he *wanted*

this reaction. He wanted Lady Regina to witness how people outside Castlemaine always regarded him—with fear, revulsion, suspicion, or contempt.

Except for the lady herself, that is. But she was probably well schooled in disguising her reactions.

As the carriage set off, his gaze shot to where she sat across from him. She truly was a master at hiding her feelings. She was the only person whose opinion of him he couldn't read.

All the more reason not to trust her.

When she caught him watching her, she smiled. "I hear that Louisa is to play both the pianoforte and the harp this evening. I had no idea she was a harpist."

"She isn't. She plays it very ill. But whenever I point that out, she insists that I don't appreciate harp music sufficiently to judge."

"Miss North plays the harp like an angel," Foxmoor bit out.

Marcus eyed him askance. "Yes, she looks perfectly angelic when she plays it. Too bad the music she produces is about as angelic as an owl's screech."

Lady Regina laughed. "Simon wouldn't know—he's practically tone-deaf. An owl's screech or a nightingale's warble are all the same to him."

"And you?" Marcus asked Lady Regina. "Do you have an ear for good music properly played?"

"I've been told that I do. And though your sister may not play the harp very well—I'll have to reserve my judgment since I haven't yet heard her—she has a lovely singing voice and is more than adequate on the pianoforte."

He snorted. "She ought to be, considering how much I paid her music teachers."

"I thought you didn't spend money frivolously," she quipped.

"It isn't frivolous to protect one's ears."

A reluctant smile touched her pretty lips. "Is that why Louisa paints such nice watercolors? Because you took measures to protect your eyes?"

"The best art teachers money could buy."

"Sweet heaven, all that protection must have cost you dearly." Her eyes twinkled at him from across the carriage. "What with the dancing masters to protect your feet and the riding masters to protect your Thoroughbreds—"

"Not to mention the tutors to protect my reason from daily assault." He shot her a deprecating glance. "Ah, but then you probably don't consider it important to educate a woman's mind. God forbid she should know Shakespeare or read Aristotle to improve her reasoning. As long as she's pretty and accomplished in the feminine arts, it doesn't matter if she's stupid, does it?"

Her smile vanished. "Of course not." She glanced out the carriage window. "We've reached our destination— what a pity for you. Now you'll have to wait until we get through the door to continue enumerating my faults."

His jaw tightened. He wasn't sure how he'd done it, but this time he knew he'd wounded her.

Fine. That would teach her not to play with dragons, wouldn't it?

After they left the carriage, and Lady Regina swept ahead of him, arm in arm with Miss Tremaine, Foxmoor fell back to join Marcus. "Good show, old man—excellent courting technique, the whole insult thing. She'll be yours in no time."

As Foxmoor then hurried ahead with a smug smile,

Marcus nearly called out that he didn't *want* her to be his. But that would tip his hand to the enemy, and he wasn't about to do that.

Nonetheless, even the sight of Louisa waiting impatiently in the doorway for their arrival could not banish his disquiet.

"Marcus!" Louisa cried as he approached. "You really did come! Lady Iversley said that you were going to, but I didn't dare believe her."

A lump lodged in his throat as he looked her over, marveling again at how grown-up she seemed these days. "How could I miss my sister's grand performance?" he said gruffly as he bent his head to kiss her cheek.

She swatted his arm with her fan. "Fiddlesticks—you missed my court presentation and you missed my coming-out ball. I hardly think you came here for *me*." With eyes sparkling, she glanced inside to where Lady Regina and Foxmoor were being greeted by the Iversleys. "But I don't mind."

The lump in his throat slid down to settle like a rock in his belly. Damn, he hadn't even considered how Louisa would react to his showing up here with Lady Regina. Louisa thought this was a real courtship, which couldn't be good.

"Don't get your hopes up, angel," he murmured. "Dipping one's toe in the water isn't the same as going for a swim."

"It could be," she said brightly. "If one discovers that the water is fine."

He wasn't expecting the water to be fine. But he could hardly tell her that.

He didn't have to. As he led her inside the bustling foyer, the sounds of chatter died. Except for the conversation continuing between their hosts and Lady Regina, complete silence reigned as every eye turned to him.

For a second, he was transported to his first ball all those years ago. A bumbling seventeen-year-old, he'd tried to be the gentleman his mother wanted, but he'd been too big and awkward to do more than embarrass her.

Back then, however, the looks leveled on him had merely been pitying or contemptuous. Now they were downright hostile.

He reacted as he always did. Badly. "I've come to devour the virgins," he growled. "Anyone care to tell me where they sit?"

That broke the silence, largely because people fled the foyer in a noisy rush. Here and there he heard their whispers: "the audacity of the man" and "how dared they invite him?" and the words "Dragon Viscount."

"I see nothing has changed in society in nine years," Marcus told Louisa. "Sorry, angel, I didn't mean to ruin your party."

She sniffed. "You haven't ruined it, but if you keep on being such a surly—"

"Ass?" he said helpfully.

"There, that's what I mean. You say these crude things even though you know better. If you'd give people a chance, and at least *try* to be courteous—"

"Lord Draker!" Katherine hurried over. "How good of you to come!"

"No need to shout," he said. "I've already run everyone off."

Katherine paled. "I'm sorry, Marcus—I meant to catch you at the door, but I thought you and Louisa were still outside. I should have paid better attention—"

"It's all right." He hadn't meant to upset Katherine,

whom he respected enormously. "I'm used to people's reactions. Rolls right off my scaly back."

At least it was only for one night; Lady Regina wouldn't
last beyond that. After this soiree, she'd think twice about
linking her brother to his sister. He'd make sure of it.

His resolve hardened when Foxmoor said, "Shall we?"
and held out his arm to Louisa, who left Marcus's side to
join the devil.

Marcus glared at the man's back, then turned to Lady
Regina. "Shall we brave the crowd, too, madam?" He offered her his arm, waiting to hear an excuse.

She merely took it and smiled. *Smiled,* for God's sake! If
he hadn't known what she and her brother were up to, that
smile would have knocked him back on his heels. But he
wasn't about to let it. Bad enough that the mere touch of
his hand on her arm was stirring very ungentlemanly . . .
thoughts.

As they headed down the hall, she murmured, "I suppose that comment about the virgins was your idea of a
joke?"

"I merely said what everybody was thinking." He cast
her a sly glance. "Why? Have you decided you're capable of
being embarrassed after all?"

"No, but Louisa is."

He groaned. Damn, the woman knew just how to get at
him. But Louisa was the reason he was enduring this torture, though she might not appreciate it at the moment.
"I'll do my best not to shame her."

He'd do his best, all right . . . to separate his sister from
that devil Foxmoor. And if that meant subjecting Louisa to
a little public embarrassment and crushing his unwanted
physical attraction to Lady Lofty, then so be it. In the end,
Louisa would thank him.

Chapter Five

*A lady can enjoy any party where the company is
well-mannered, sprightly, and amiable.*
—Miss Cicely Tremaine, *The Ideal Chaperone*

After fifteen minutes at the soiree, Regina wanted to lecture nearly every person present. After thirty, she wanted to strangle them. And these people were the nicer members of society—they should at least tolerate Lord Draker to be polite. Yet they either gave him a wide berth, as if he had the pox, or insulted him within his hearing, as if he were invisible.

Nor was he any help whatsoever. The cooler they were, the more snide he became. If the scoundrel weren't so huge, she'd rap his knuckles with her fan. He probably wouldn't even feel it, the big lout.

As if matters weren't bad enough, he now stood with that notorious Mr. Byrne, his supposed half brother. His lordship wasn't satisfied with shoving his scruffy appearance in people's faces—oh no, he had to remind them that only the previous viscount's indulgence had saved him from being a bastard in the truest sense. God forbid Lord Draker should let sleeping dogs lie—that would be too easy.

Only half-paying attention to the Marchioness of Hungate beside her, who nattered on about some outrage, Regina stole a glance at them. When Lord Draker cast her a smug smile, she narrowed her eyes. He was actually enjoying the results of his churlish appearance and behavior. Why didn't he understand that he only made things worse for himself?

He murmured something to his half brother, then headed toward her, and she jerked her gaze away. Wonderful. Now he was coming over *here* to wreak havoc. Just what she needed to improve her mood—the sour Lady Hungate *and* the surly Lord Draker sniping at each other.

"What is wrong with young people today?" Lady Hungate complained. "They pay no attention to the proprieties. In *my* day, girls couldn't go riding with young gentlemen until their come-out. Yet I heard that Miss Spruce was actually seen in the park with Mr. Jackson last week. She's not out yet, is she?"

"No," Regina said absently, only too aware of the viscount's approach.

Lady Hungate glanced behind Regina, then lifted her lorgnette to study Lord Draker with a moue of disgust. "And in my day, good grooming was a requirement for anyone going into society."

Before Regina could retort, Lord Draker said, "In *your* day, gossips were horsewhipped in the square. You should be glad we're *not* in your day, madam."

Lady Hungate sniffed. "Well, I never—"

"No, you never were, more's the pity."

That finished her off. With a glance at Regina that said, "How dare you inflict this person on us?" the marchioness swept off to find better company.

Regina couldn't decide whether to be impressed at how

effectively he'd silenced the irritating Lady Hungate or annoyed by the rude methods he'd used to do it. "I think you enjoy being a bear."

"Every bear-baiting needs one. I'm only giving them what they want—somebody for them to sharpen their claws on." He eyed her closely. "Don't tell me you *like* listening to the old battle-ax complain."

"Even if I don't," she said primly, "I am not so rude as to—"

"Remind her that it's equally rude to gossip? No, apparently I'm the only one you lecture. I don't see you pointing out their rude behavior to *them*."

"They're only being rude because you are."

"No, they're being rude because they're ignorant and shallow and don't have a thought in their heads beyond the latest rumors and fancy fashions."

No doubt he included *her* in that assessment, drat him. "Perhaps. But the proper way to deal with ignorant people is to brush off their gossip with witty retorts—not vicious insults. If you'd turn the rumors to your advantage by making jests of them, people would stop baiting you."

He raised an eyebrow. "Are you trying to manage me, madam?"

She snorted. "You must be joking. You're the most unmanageable man I've ever met. I'm only trying to help."

His eyes blazed at her. "I don't need your help, damn it."

Lady Iversley's announcement that the concert was beginning prevented her from retorting. Not that he would have listened. Lord Draker was the most pigheaded man she'd ever met. And how was she to improve his standing in society when he fought her every attempt? He'd said he wanted her to smooth the way, and now he rejected all her suggestions. She did not understand him.

Regina took her seat. To her surprise, he took the one next to her. When he dropped heavily into it, however, she could barely keep from pointing out that he didn't have to throw himself into chairs like a lumbering dragon who couldn't keep his tail straight. Not that he would listen to that, either. He took direction badly. Sometimes she even admired him for it. A pity that no one else would.

At least he would cause no trouble while Louisa was singing. Clearly, he thought the world of his sister. So why didn't he try harder to behave at her party?

As soon as the music began, Regina relaxed. Music was her favorite enjoyment. She turned to her harp whenever she needed to be soothed, though she could only play it by ear since she couldn't read notes. Thankfully, she had a talent for picking out melodies. And she loved hearing any sort of song, especially when the performer sang as beautifully as Louisa.

After the second piece, Regina glanced over to see Lord Draker smiling proudly at his sister. Something clutched at her heart. Just now, he didn't look the least bit forbidding. He looked surprisingly young.

She did some figuring in her head. Why, he couldn't be more than thirty-one, only seven years older than she. Did he really mean to molder out at Castlemaine for the rest of his life? What a waste.

He caught her watching him, and something flickered in his eyes—something scorchingly wild, and so raw it sparked an unfamiliar and oddly delicious tingle along her spine. Whoever had said that music soothed the savage breast had never met Lord Draker.

Because the way he looked at her now was decidedly savage. No man had ever dared to rake her with his gaze like that, yet she did not find it offensive. If anything, it made her wonder . . .

With a blush, she jerked her gaze from his. But her powerful awareness of his presence beside her only heightened as the hour wore on. Every approving murmur in response to his sister's playing resonated deep in Regina's belly. Every time he shifted in the flimsy chair, she was reminded of how incredibly massive he was—broad back, impressive shoulders . . . exceedingly muscular thighs.

Nor did it help that he kept time to the music by tapping his fingers on those very thighs. Or that said thighs strained most impressively against the worn fabric of his outdated evening attire, making her wonder how it might feel to brush up against those thighs when one was dancing. Or perhaps when one was . . . being embraced. Or . . . kissed passionately . . . on the mouth and the throat and—

A hot flush flooded her cheeks. This was absurd—what sort of woman was she to have such flights of fancy about a man she hardly knew? She should be paying better attention to Louisa's lovely singing.

When they came to the part where Louisa was supposed to play the harp, Louisa stood before the crowd and smiled. "I hope you'll forgive me if I deviate from the program, but tonight is too special to resist. You see, a very dear member of my family also possesses a fine singing voice. I hope you'll help me persuade my brother to join me in a duet."

As Louisa began to clap, a smattering of lackluster applause echoed around them. Lord Draker muttered, "Damn the foolish girl."

Regina cast him a sidelong glance. "Don't you dare disappoint her."

He glared at her. "Damn you both." But he rose and strode to the front.

Regina settled back in her chair, curious to see if Lord Draker's "talent" was genuine or the result of a doting sister's fond imagination. As the song began and a rich baritone sounded in the room, Regina smiled to herself. Well, well, did wonders never cease? The dragon could actually sing.

It was very clever of Louisa to use that on his behalf. How better to soften the guests toward him than to illustrate Lord Draker's talents?

The young woman had picked a fine song for him, too—"The Last Rose of Summer." The rumble that made his speaking voice a menacing growl lent his singing voice the proper depth for the plaintive tune, and his somber countenance seemed perfectly appropriate for the sad lyrics about death and old age.

Clearly the audience appreciated the performance; they were rapt with attention. Even Regina, who considered herself something of a connoisseur of fine singing, was moved, especially when his voice swooped low, vibrating through her blood, reminding her of how he gazed at her sometimes.

As he was gazing at her now. Her breath caught in her throat. When he sang of reflecting "back her blushes," she felt a fresh blush rise in her cheeks. And when he finished with the mournful line, "Oh! who would inhabit this bleak world alone!" she wanted to leap up to assuage his loneliness.

Sweet heaven, what a performance! Nor was she the only one affected. As the last notes died, the audience held their breath one aching moment before breaking into enthusiastic applause.

To her delight, Lord Draker actually looked flummoxed by their response. Murmuring a gruff thank-you, he started to return to his seat.

But his beaming sister stayed him. "Don't go yet. You must sing another."

He shook his head. "No one wants to hear me again, angel, but perhaps one of the other ladies will oblige you." His gaze swung to Regina. "Lady Regina might be willing to grace us with a song."

As a burst of applause sounded around Regina, she could only stare at Lord Draker with her heart fluttering. Did he truly want to hear her sing, or was he just choosing this way out of another performance?

"Yes," Louisa prodded. "Lady Regina must sing."

The growing applause made it impossible for her to refuse, as did the burning look his lordship leveled on her.

As she rose to walk toward the front, Louisa added, "But the two of you must sing a duet. Oh, do sing 'Tho' You Think By This to Vex Me.' Lady Regina has just the right voice for it, and it's my favorite."

Regina faltered. She knew most of the standard pieces by heart, but the song Louisa wanted had over twenty-five lines that Regina hadn't memorized. And Lord knew she couldn't read them.

She continued toward the front more slowly. "No, not that one, Louisa, if you please. What about 'Chastity, Thou Cherub Bright'?"

Louisa looked at her oddly. "But that's not a duet."

"Right. Then perhaps . . . er . . . how about . . ." Why couldn't she think of a single duet she knew by heart?

"Is it my sister's song choice you object to?" Lord Draker asked coldly as she frantically searched her blank mind. "Or her choice of partner for you?"

A stillness fell over the audience, fraught with tension. Regina's panic increased. "It's not . . . I mean . . . I merely don't—"

"So it's both." He added in a sneering aside to the crowd, "La Belle Dame would never sing a duet, because that would require sharing the center of attention. And God forbid she should share it with a man, especially one who—"

"Lord Draker, an urgent message has come for you," called a voice from the back. Everyone turned to see Lady Iversley wearing a forbidding scowl.

He narrowed his eyes. "From whom?"

"Your estate. It requires your immediate attention." She leveled a quelling glance on the now-murmuring crowd. "But that's no reason for the rest of you not to enjoy the performances. Please, Louisa, do play something for Lady Regina to sing. I'm sure everyone would love to hear her."

When the viscount looked as if he might speak again, their hostess added tersely, "If you would just come with me, sir, I'll take you to the messenger."

Lord Draker glowered at Lady Iversley, but with an icy, "Excuse me," marched out of the drawing room, leaving Regina shaking from head to toe in mortification.

It was swiftly followed by anger. What on earth was wrong with the man? Had he *no* sense whatsoever of proper public behavior? Granted, she had handled the situation badly. If she hadn't acted so alarmed, he wouldn't have pounced on her slip. But why must he always say such appalling things?

Look at the crowd—they were shocked. He'd just destroyed any gains Louisa had made for him. Even Lady Iversley's quick thinking could not fix this.

Still, she refused to let the woman's efforts be ruined.

She moved to the pianoforte, where she murmured to Louisa, "Can you play 'Chastity, Thou Cherub Bright'?"

Louisa nodded, then said in a decidedly cool undertone, "Forgive me, but I didn't realize you would object to singing with Marcus."

"I don't. I simply don't know the other song well enough to perform it."

Though Louisa looked skeptical, she said nothing as she played the introduction. Regina began to sing, but even her favorite tune couldn't raise her spirits. If Louisa didn't believe Regina's protest, her brother surely wouldn't. Nor would anyone else. They would assume that she'd deliberately insulted him.

But honestly, it wasn't *all* her fault. He hadn't even given her a chance to think of something else.

Frustration wound a knot in her belly. Since she refused to give up on Simon and Louisa, she must persist with his thorny lordship. Somewhere in that thick head of his, he *must* know how to be a gentleman. She simply had to appeal to his better nature. She knew he had one; no man could sing that soulfully without having a soul.

Chapter Six

*Let your charge have her head from
time to time. It will teach her to value
your judgment all the more.*
—Miss Cicely Tremaine, *The Ideal Chaperone*

Marcus fought to restrain his temper as he strode down the hall after Katherine. The strains of Lady Regina's sweet soprano followed him, a siren's voice to match her siren's cold heart.

Damn her. "So where's this messenger?" he bit out.

Katherine stopped short to face him. "You know perfectly well there's no messenger. I had to remove you before you embarrassed dear Louisa any further."

"Me?" He snorted. "Louisa's harpy of a female friend is the one embarrassing her."

"Because she didn't want to sing with you? Can you blame her? You've been a perfect monster all evening. Lady Regina has done nothing but—"

"Scheme with her brother to ruin Louisa."

Katherine blinked. "What?"

"You don't know the situation, so stay out of it." He turned back toward the drawing room. "Now, if you'll excuse me, I must return—"

"Oh, no, you don't." Katherine moved to block his path. "You are not going back in there."

It was like a mouse facing down a bear. He ought to laugh. But having his brother's wife angry at him was unsettling. "Are you trying to send me off to bed without my supper, Mother Katherine?" he tried to joke.

She colored. "Don't be silly. I merely want you to stay out of the drawing room until the concert is over. Then you can come insult people at dinner if you please. At least there you'll be limited to the people sitting on either side of you."

"Fine." He couldn't believe sweet little Katherine was taking Lady Regina's side. "I'll sit in Iversley's study until dinner. Assuming he has something decent to drink in there." He headed off that way.

She followed him. "Getting foxed will only make everything worse, you know. Lady Regina already thinks you're a rude lout—do you want to make her think you're a drunk as well?"

He shot her a cold glance. "I don't give a farthing what Lady Lofty thinks. I will damned well get as foxed as I damned well please. So trot on back to your guests before I change my mind and decide to embarrass those harpies after all."

She looked as if she might retort. Then, pursing her lips into a line, she pivoted and marched back to the drawing room.

He strode into Iversley's study and headed straight for the whisky decanter. After pouring himself a generous splash, he drank it, savoring the hot burn.

Lady Regina's voice wafted to him from the drawing room, as pure and high as his sister's was throaty and low. A pox on that confounded female. The night wasn't half-over, and she was already balking at their agreement.

He ought to be ecstatic. His plan was working beautifully; Lady Regina wanted nothing to do with him already.
She'd actually snubbed him in front of Louisa, which
would surely anger his sister. It was exactly what he
wanted. So why was he annoyed?

Because he'd seen the look on her face when Louisa
had suggested she sing a duet with him. A love song, of all
things—what delusion had possessed his sister? Lady
Regina's horror had been unmistakable. She'd quickly
tried to hide it, but it had been too late. He could only
imagine what she was thinking: Sing a love song with the
oafish Dragon Viscount? What will people say? It might
lead people to think they were courting, and she would
never allow that.

Why did he even care? This wasn't a real courtship. It
was a bargain, pure and simple. And the more his presence
mortified her, the better it was for his plan.

Behind him the door to the library opened, and he
scowled. No doubt his sister-in-law had returned to make
sure he didn't drink too much.

"You already said your piece when you banished me
from the drawing room, Katherine." Defiantly, he poured
himself more whisky. "You're wasting your time continuing the lecture."

"Yes, you don't take lectures from anyone, do you?" answered a soft female voice from the doorway.

A knot twisted in his gut. Damn, damn, damn.

He faced Lady Regina with a scowl. "I certainly won't
take them from you. So if you thought to teach me a lesson
with your little display in the drawing room—"

Her chin quivered. "I wasn't trying to teach you anything." With a glance down the hall, she entered and closed
the door.

"Are you sure it's wise to be alone with me with the door closed, madam?" He tried not to notice how prettily her cheeks flushed and her eyes sparkled when she was upset. "What would people think?"

"I don't care. And anyway, no one saw me come in here."

He gave a harsh laugh. "Of course not. You're no fool when it comes to preserving your image as society's reigning queen." But she wouldn't be so cavalier about it if she knew that just the sight of her looking like a goddess in that gossamer silk gown made him want to grab her by the throat and shake her.

Or kiss her senseless.

When she neared him, he tensed. "If giving me the cut indirect did you no good," he said, "what makes you think—"

"I was not giving you any sort of cut whatsoever," she said stoutly.

"Right." He took a deep swallow of whisky.

"I simply didn't want to make a fool of myself by bumbling through a song I didn't know."

Damn her for thinking he cared. And damn him for caring. "Whatever you say, madam. I understand how these things work."

"Drat it, I am trying to explain!"

"There's nothing to explain. I've already forgotten it."

"I haven't," she said in those dulcet tones that cast a spell on every man who heard them. "I didn't intend to hurt your feelings."

A red haze formed behind his eyes. "Don't flatter yourself. I'm not one of your slobbering sycophants who might moan and threaten to do himself in when you give him one of your set-downs. I don't give a damn what you think of me. Go on back to your friends. I've no interest in listening to you chastise me for exposing your true nature to the crowd."

"*My* nature?" Her eyes narrowed. "Now see here, you thickheaded dolt, the only nature you exposed in that drawing room was yours. You merely proved that you have absolutely no sense of proper behavior or gentlemanly discretion. What you said about me wasn't true in the least, and everyone knew it."

"Really? So you acquired your nickname by accident, La Belle Dame Sans Merci?"

Her flinch told him he'd wounded her. It should have pleased him. It didn't.

"Say what you wish about me," she retorted, "but you ought to at least care how your reputation for churlishness affects Louisa. It's the only thing marring her standing in society."

"If this is society, she's well out of it."

"Oh? She's better off stagnating in the country with no one but you for company? *You,* who'd rather bury himself in a book than have a civil conversation with an actual person?"

"And what's wrong with that?" With his whisky glass, he gestured to Iversley's many books. "I'm not the only person who takes refuge in books. Just because *you* don't like them—"

"I never said that." She sounded surprisingly defensive. "I merely think there's more to life. A person cannot find everything in a book."

"Ah, but you're wrong. I can find whatever I want in my library."

"Music?" She strolled up to him. "You can't find music."

He set down his glass and turned to Iversley's bookshelves. Searching until he found the right volume, he opened it and read aloud, "'Golden slumbers kiss your eyes/ Smiles awake you when you rise.' It's a poem by Thomas Dekker, now used as a common lullaby. You probably heard the tune in your head as I read it."

"That's not the same as hearing it sung. Reading the words of my favorite opera, for example, certainly wouldn't satisfy me."

"But one can't always attend the opera. One can always open a book."

She uttered a frustrated sound. "What about physical things, like dancing? There's no dancing in books."

"No?" He drew down another book. "Here's one that explains how to perform dances." He flipped through it and showed her the diagrams. "You see? You *can* find dance in books."

She shook her head. "Reading about dancing isn't the same thing as performing a dance."

"Actually, it's better. If I read about it, I don't have to deal with too-hot ballrooms or having my toes stepped on." He cast her a cold glance. "Or superior females who think themselves too fine to dance with me." *And sing with me.*

She flushed, yet she wouldn't let go of her argument. "You also don't know the joy of touching another human being." She approached him, and he sucked in a heavy breath. "Or the thrill of passion. Don't you dare tell me you can get *that* from a book, because I know better."

"Oh? I would have thought a well-bred lady like yourself hadn't experienced 'the thrill of passion.'"

A faint flush turned her cheeks rosier than before. "You know perfectly well that's not what I meant."

"Ah, yes." He scoured her with a contemptuous look.

"From what I've heard, you won't even allow your sniveling admirers to kiss your hand."

"At least I dance with them. The only females *you* allow near your estate are servants, for heaven's sake. Unless there really *are* women in your dungeon."

"What are you talking about?"

Her blush deepened. "The gossips say that . . . that you chain women up in your dungeon to . . . have your way with them."

Oh, for God's sake— "And you believe that?"

She thrust her chin out at him. "I might. Especially given how much trouble you seem to have with pleasing women who *aren't* chained up."

He stalked up to loom over her, but that proved a mistake, for now he could smell the seductive scent of honey-water wafting off her and could see the golden tendrils feathering her neck. Her aristocratic arch of a neck that he wanted to—

He dragged his gaze to her face. "I know how to please a woman well enough when I set my mind to it."

"Do you?" She arched an eyebrow. "I've seen little evidence of that."

"That doesn't mean I can't."

"No? Then prove it. Prove that you can please a woman."

Somewhere in the dim recesses of his fevered brain, he realized she meant a different sort of pleasing than he did—compliments and courtesies and gentlemanly behavior. But at the moment he didn't care. He'd had enough of her lies and her condescending taunts. He'd show her once and for all what happened to any woman foolish enough to bait him.

"Fine. Since you insist . . ." And without giving her a

chance to protest, he bent his head and kissed her right on the lush red mouth that had tortured his dreams last night.

She jerked back, her eyes wide. "What are you doing?"

"You told me to prove I can please a woman."

"I didn't mean *that* kind of pleasing."

"But I did." She hadn't yet slapped him, which emboldened him enough to add, "Apparently I wasn't convincing, however, so I'll have to try again." Reaching up, he caught her chin in one hand.

Alarm flickered in her eyes. "This is not acceptable. We are not in your dungeon here, I'll have you know."

"What a pity." He snaked his free arm about her waist. "You could use some chaining up."

She fisted her hands against his chest. "You'd never dare. And I'd never allow it."

"Oh? What would you do to stop me? I hate to tell you, but your little 'cuts direct' won't work in the dungeon."

"I did not give you the cut di—"

He blotted out the words with a fiercer, bolder kiss. He didn't want to hear her lies. He didn't want to think about those bastards in the drawing room. He only wanted to kiss her again.

She made a token resistance, pushing feebly against his chest. But she didn't pull her lips from his, and soon her hands flattened against him. That left him free to really kiss her, to linger over her mouth, driven by the impulse to prove her wrong about him, to make her acknowledge him as something more than a loutish beast.

But that wasn't all he wanted. He wanted to eat her up, get inside of her, figure out why she drove him insane with just a look.

God help him. He'd expected kissing her to be like kissing a marble Venus, the lips cold and unyielding, her body stiff against his. Instead, her lips were warm and trembling, her body fluid in his arms and growing more so by the moment.

When she actually clutched at his coat lapels, triumph surged through him. He drew back to stare at her smugly. "Now, tell me again that I don't know how to please a woman."

Her closed eyelids drifted open to reveal dove gray eyes dazed with need. "You know how to be impertinent," she said in a throaty voice. "I'll give you that."

"You haven't begun to see me impertinent." Cupping the back of her neck in his hand, he drew her close for another kiss. This time he dared to deepen it, thrusting his tongue against her parted lips until he gained entry to the heady warmth of her mouth.

Great God, what a seductress's mouth she had, as sweet and bewitching as any siren's. He wasn't idiot enough to question why Lady Lofty was letting him kiss her so outrageously. He merely took advantage of the fact that she was, relishing the heartfelt moan she made in response to his bold forays.

She lifted her dainty arms to encircle his neck, and that emboldened him further, until he was plundering her soft lips over and over, drinking in every richly perfumed breath. How many chances did a man have to taste the elusive Belle Dame? To bury himself in the hot silk of her mouth and stroke the eloquent contours of her waist and hips with his greedy hands?

Not until he had her boneless and limp in his arms did he tear his mouth from hers. "Now *that's* impertinent."

Her breath came in staccato bursts. "It certainly is," she said, but without rancor.

"So is this." He brushed a kiss to her blushing cheek.

"And this." He explored other parts of her with his mouth—her fragile eyelids, the throbbing pulse at her temple, the delicate curve of her ear.

But when he traced it with his tongue, she gasped. "Lord Draker—"

"Marcus," he corrected. "If we're courting, you should call me Marcus."

She hesitated, then breathed, "Marcus," in that seductive whisper that drove him insane. There was nothing for it but to kiss her again.

Pressing her back against the bookshelves, he ravished her mouth the way he wanted to ravish her body, until the taste of her so filled his senses that he actually contemplated lifting her skirts and—

She pushed hard against his chest. Only then did he stop kissing her.

"We should not be doing this, Marcus. Someone might find us here."

Frustration made him growl, "And that would not do for my lady, would it?"

"If my brother found us, it would not do for *you,* either."

He smiled grimly. "It might. Foxmoor would demand satisfaction on the dueling field, and I could—"

"Don't even think such a thing!" she cried, covering his lips with her fingers.

They stood frozen a moment. Then she traced his mouth with a gentleness he wasn't used to from anyone. He dragged in a ragged breath, but didn't stop her.

Until she ran one finger along his scar.

"Don't," he murmured.

Curiosity glinted in her eyes but she changed the direction of her exploration, slipping her fingers down to caress his jaw. "Your beard is soft. I expected it to be prickly."

Her tenderness unsettled him. "It's no different from other hair," he said gruffly. "It's only prickly after it's shaved off. But I'm surprised an elegant female like you would even touch a man's beard."

A coy look crossed her face. "Believe it or not, sometimes elegant females try things they're not supposed to."

"Right." That was why she'd let him kiss her. Apparently even La Belle Dame craved excitement occasionally and couldn't get it from her idiot suitors. He bent his head to nibble her earlobe. "Try anything you want with me," he whispered. "I won't tell a soul."

She jerked back, her face aflame. "I didn't mean—" She broke off at the sound of the doorknob turning, then wriggled out of his arms just as the door swung open.

Iversley stepped inside, then froze. His gaze swung from Marcus to Regina. "Sorry to interrupt," he said tersely.

When Regina turned to face Iversley the reserved expression she generally wore was already in place, banishing the tenderness of a few minutes before. Marcus wanted to howl his frustration.

"It's no problem." Her voice was as unruffled as if she'd just been taking tea. "His lordship and I were merely talking."

Marcus knew she was perfectly in her rights to preserve her reputation. But with his blood still in wild riot, he reacted to her calmness as if it were an assault.

"Yes." He couldn't keep the sarcasm from his voice. "Lady Regina was explaining to me why she prefers private duets to public ones."

The gaze she swung to him was so hurt that he realized her reserve had been only a facade. Anger flared in her eyes, and she slapped him. Hard. "Go to the devil," she choked out. Then she fled.

As soon as she was gone, Iversley shut the door. "You deserved that."

"I suppose." Marcus rubbed his jaw. For an elegant female, her ladyship had quite a swing. And quite a little temper. "But I was merely stating the obvious."

Iversley shook his head. "Any other woman you set your sights on might put up with your grousing and your insults, but not Lady Regina, society's reigning—"

"I don't have my sights set on her." Marcus strode over to the table with the whisky decanter and picked up the glass he'd left there.

"Liar. I've seen how you look at her."

"No differently than I look at any other attractive female." His hand shook as he poured himself more whisky. "I'm sure I look at your wife exactly the same."

"If you did, we'd be dueling at dawn," Iversley said dryly. "Because you look at Lady Regina as if you want to bed her."

God help him, he did. "Any man who looked at her would want to bed her." He downed the whisky. "What of it?"

"Be careful, is all I'm saying. She's not . . . er . . ."

"My kind? We were doing just fine until you interrupted us."

And until I insulted her.

No, he wouldn't chastise himself for that . . . or for her look of betrayal. She'd experimented with kissing the Dragon Viscount, then turned around and expected him to pretend it hadn't happened because *she* was ashamed. A pox on her. "Why are you here, anyway?" he asked his brother.

"Katherine said you were getting drunk. I didn't think that was wise. Of course, if I'd realized you were engaging in another vice—"

"Didn't you hear Lady Regina? Nothing happened. So go back to your guests and send someone for me when dinner is served."

"All right." Iversley opened the door. "But take my advice—next time you engage in 'nothing' with Lady Regina, you might want to lock the door."

As his brother left laughing, Marcus gritted his teeth. Damned interfering relations. Louisa with her matchmaking duets, Katherine with her lectures, and Iversley with his annoying observations. They were blind to the truth—that Foxmoor and his sister represented everything wrong with polite society that Marcus had spent his life avoiding. Foxmoor was a schemer, and Regina . . .

Well, he hadn't figured her out yet. No one had forced her to come in here to "explain," so why bother? Was she genuinely sorry she'd balked at singing with him, or did she have some other motive?

It hardly mattered. After her slap, she couldn't possibly mean to continue their bargain. She would make that clear later, and he could demand that Foxmoor stay away from Louisa, too. So he would win.

And there would be no more kisses. No more tender caresses, no more—

With an oath, he slammed his whisky glass down on the table. There wouldn't have been any more kisses, anyway. Lady Regina's little adventure had surely taught her what he already knew—they were not suited for each other in any way.

Too bad he already ached to kiss her again.

Chapter Seven

*If your dire looks and somber reproofs do not
work, you can never go wrong by bringing the
young lady's male relations into the picture.*
—Miss Cicely Tremaine, *The Ideal Chaperone*

Cad! Impudent oaf! Blackhearted devil! Him and his
"private duets"—she would make him regret his insults,
just see if she didn't.

If he insisted on believing she had cut him publicly, if
he refused to listen when she tried to explain, then she
washed her hands of him. Let him spend the night growl-
ing at everyone who crossed his path. She would not stay
to endure it.

A lock of Regina's hair drooped onto her neck, and she
groaned. No doubt that devil had dislodged her Platoff
hat with all his rough handling of her. He'd probably done
it on purpose, too, so everyone would see that she'd been
doing something scandalous.

Ducking into an alcove that contained a mirror, she
examined her attire. Thankfully, her hat was secure, except for the lock of hair that had come free of its pins in
the back. Quickly she repinned it. If not for her cheeks
flushing as pink as her overskirt, no one would guess

she'd just been engaging in the most outrageous behavior
with that . . . that boor of a man.

And he thought he knew how to please a woman—hah!
He didn't know the first thing about it.

She caught sight of her unnaturally red lips and winced.
All right, so perhaps he did know a thing or two. He kissed
well. Quite well. Beyond well. He could make a woman
forget her name and her reputation and everything in between when he gathered her close to press his hot mouth
to hers—

Drat the man, why must he affect her like this? She
should have slapped him much sooner, the second he'd
given her that first rude buss on the lips.

Or perhaps when he'd dragged her into his bold embrace. And certainly after he'd dared to thrust his tongue
into her mouth, so deliciously that she'd wanted to find
out how it would be if she let him kiss her a little . . . bit . . .
longer . . .

Her knees buckled, and she jerked herself upright.
What was wrong with her? He'd had her acting like some
shameless wanton, coaxing her into letting him do wicked,
heavenly things to her, and she hadn't even protested!

But that was because he'd kissed her so daringly that it
had knocked all her will to resist right out of her.

Until he'd turned nasty again. She scowled. That was
the trouble with the Viscount Draker. One minute he was
kissing her tenderly and asking her to call him Marcus; the
next he was biting out insults.

And she had no idea how to handle it. Men did not generally behave this way to her. So why did he? And why was
she letting him get away with it?

Afraid to face the answer to that question, she gave her
gown and her hat one last check, then sallied forth into the

fray. The concert had apparently ended, and now people were milling about Louisa in the drawing room. Her brother, of course, was one of them.

He approached her with a smile. "I see you've rejoined us. Where were you—administering one of your famous lectures to Draker? I suppose you expected him to react more appropriately after you snubbed him."

"I did not snub him!" she practically shouted. Then realizing that people were watching, she lowered her voice. "And no, I was not lecturing him. But I tell you one thing, when you and Louisa are married, you'd better treat me well, considering all I am putting up with to bring you together."

"Of course. You'll have my undying gratitude, dear girl."

"And stop calling me 'girl,'" she grumbled. "I've been a full-grown woman for years. You know I hate your calling me that." Which is precisely why he did it, of course. Lord Draker wasn't the only one who delighted in annoying her.

Before Simon could answer, dinner was announced. Regina uttered a heavy sigh. She'd forgotten all about dinner. Lord only knew what sort of mischief Lord Draker would engage in at that event.

At least she didn't have to sit near him. As the second-senior-ranking gentleman guest, the viscount was placed at his hostess's left while Regina was placed at Lord Iversley's right at the opposite end of the table.

She braced herself, expecting her host to say something about what he'd seen in his study. When several minutes passed, and he didn't mention it, she thanked heaven that he was a gentleman.

They talked of his estate in Suffolk, her father's love of horses, and Lady Iversley's interest in poetry. That last one she skirted quickly, since she could count on one hand the number of poems she knew.

Occasionally she cast furtive glances down the table to where Lord Draker sat just on the other side of their hostess from Simon, the highest-ranking male guest. Would Lord Draker be rude to her brother? Foist yet more breaches of etiquette on the company? Could he at least dine properly?

Apparently he could. He used a fork rather than eating off his knife like other country folk, he didn't hog the best dishes, and despite what she'd feared from the whisky she'd smelled on his breath, he did not drink overmuch. Only some wine, and that at a moderate rate.

The only thing that bothered her was his apparent enjoyment in talking to Lady Iversley, whom he addressed most familiarly by her Christian name. Regina didn't want that to annoy her. But it did.

Had he ever brought "Katherine" down to his famous dungeon? Probably not. Somehow Regina could not envision the poetry-loving Lady Iversley in the throes of wild passion in the viscount's dungeon. Especially when she had a handsome new husband who so clearly doted on her.

Lord Iversley had fallen silent, so she ventured an impertinent comment. "Your wife and Lord Draker are good friends, are they not?"

"Draker has been a good friend to us both in the past year." He added, with a trace of irony, "He's like part of our family."

"Is that why the two of you agreed to bring Louisa out?"

"Yes, but she's such a sweet girl, we were glad to do it."

"I confess I didn't realize his lordship had any friends at

all, since he goes into society so little, and when he does, he's so . . . so . . ."

"Rude and badly dressed?"

"I would have said 'unpolished,' but you've hit it exactly. He is very lucky to have found a friend like you who will overlook his behavior."

He toyed with his fork. "As I did earlier, you mean? Did my friend . . . er . . . do anything in my study for which I should take him to task?"

Her smile froze. "No, of course not. I am perfectly capable of handling men who . . . do not know how to behave."

His lordship chuckled. "I could tell. Although I fear it will take more than one slap to teach Draker how to behave. He has a tendency to be thickheaded."

"Really?" she said dryly. "I hadn't noticed."

"But he's had a rough go of it through the years, so I hope you'll be patient with him. Or do I presume too much from your coming here with him?"

She blushed. "Yes . . . no . . . It's hard to explain."

He eyed her closely. "My wife and I have been hoping that something—or someone—would drag him out of the hole he's dug for himself at Castlemaine. Now that someone has, I would hate to see him disappear back into his hole before he's had a chance to acclimate himself to the world."

"So would I." Lord Draker might be annoying and arrogant and determined to hate everyone and everything, but he did not belong hidden at Castlemaine, no matter what he said.

Earlier, she'd glimpsed the softer side of his lordship—Marcus, who could be tender and even vulnerable. Who experienced life only through his books because no one would dare his foul temper long enough to drag him into the light.

Did *she* dare? Could she even do it?

She set her shoulders. Of course she could. She had a wager riding on it, after all, and she meant to win, if only to see his lordship better his life. She would live up to her nickname and show him no mercy. She would haul the cantankerous Dragon Viscount into decent society kicking and screaming, no matter how rude he got or how many insults he lobbed at her.

Fortunately, he did nothing at dinner to test her new resolve. The rest of the evening passed quickly, and to her vast relief, the party broke up shortly after dessert, leaving Marcus no chance to create more trouble. Not that it would have made much difference to the guests. Everyone there already treated him as if he had the plague—he could hardly make that worse.

Nonetheless, he stayed to the bitter end, probably because he wanted to spend every possible minute with his sister. A lump settled in Regina's throat as she watched him and Louisa say their good-byes. His abiding love for his sister was one redeeming characteristic of the dreaded dragon.

But as soon as they'd entered the carriage, Marcus's belligerent manner returned. He kept his brooding gaze on her while Cicely fidgeted and Simon talked about the evening.

When Simon took a breath, Marcus finally spoke. "I was considering the opera for our next engagement, Lady Regina." He added tellingly, "Since you're so fond of music."

She tensed, not only because of his veiled reference to their aborted duet, but because he threw out the statement as if it were a challenge. Only she wasn't sure exactly what the challenge was.

"Did you have a particular opera and theater in mind?" she asked.

His eyes narrowed on her. "I thought we might attend the Italian Opera House in Haymarket tomorrow night. It's Mr. Naldi's benefit performance in *Le Nozze di Figaro*. I hear he's spectacular." He inclined his head toward Simon. "Your brother and Miss Tremaine are welcome to join us, of course. Louisa has already said she'd like to go."

"You have a box at the opera?" Cicely's shocked tone was vaguely insulting.

Marcus's eyes glittered. "No, but Iversley has kindly offered me his." He glanced over at Simon. "Unless Foxmoor has one he would rather we use—"

"Feel free to use mine if you like," Simon said, "but I'll have to bow out. I promised . . . er . . . a friend that I would attend his dinner tomorrow evening."

Regina caught her breath. She'd forgotten that Prinny had invited them both to Carlton House. And since the dinner had been discussed earlier at tonight's soiree, Marcus couldn't help but know where Simon meant to go.

A bitter half smile touched the viscount's lips. "Ah, of course. And Lady Regina will be going with you."

So *that* was the source of his belligerence. He thought she planned to renege on their bargain now.

"I would rather go to the opera," she put in, peeved that he could think her so easily discouraged.

Skepticism showed in his features. "Tomorrow night. With me."

"Why not? Cicely and I both love the opera."

"But my lady, the prince—" Cicely began.

"Will understand," she finished. Or at least she prayed he would.

Marcus's gaze locked with hers, and a change came over his face that sent a delicious shiver along her nerves. His eyes smoldered with wanton promises, reminding her of their time in Lord Iversley's study. When his hot gaze dropped to her mouth, she quickly averted her own gaze.

Lord, what had she agreed to? An opera box could be very intimate even with other people there, especially when the lights went down. She swallowed, nearly changing her mind, but she was no coward.

"Speaking of music," Simon put in, "what did you think of Miss Tremaine's harp-playing, Regina?"

"Oh, I didn't hear it." Too late she remembered why she'd missed that performance. "I . . . er . . . was . . . well . . ."

"I was showing her Iversley's study," Marcus put in.

Her gaze shot to him, but his expression was dark and unreadable in the dimness of the carriage lamps. Panic assailed her. Did he mean to ruin her, the fool? If he even hinted what the two of them had been doing—

"Iversley has quite an extensive collection of books that Regina wanted to see," Marcus went on, flashing her a faint smile, "so I gave her the grand tour."

Regina released her breath. Thank heaven the man had *some* sense.

Cicely had stiffened next to her, but Simon merely snorted. "Regina wanted to see books? I can't imagine that. I've never even seen her crack a book open."

"Haven't you?" Marcus kept his gaze fixed on Regina's face. "She seems far too clever to have avoided books all her life."

Her heart fluttered. He actually thought she was "clever"?

No, of course not. By "clever," he meant "calculating." Marcus would never pay her a compliment.

"Oh, she'll endure hearing a story read from time to time," Simon said, "but Regina has little interest in things that can't play for her, whirl her about the floor, drive her in the park, or take her shopping."

Humiliation flooded her face with heat. Cicely laid a hand on her arm, but she shrugged it off, preparing to give her brother a sharp retort.

Marcus spoke first. "Your sister may not be the contemplative sort, but tonight has shown that she does have deeper interests. Like music, for example."

She tensed and eyed him defiantly, daring him even to mention that horrible scene in the drawing room.

"She sings beautifully," he went on, "and could clearly appreciate Louisa's performance. And I've heard she plays the harp very well. I only regret I wasn't able to hear her play tonight."

She gaped at him. That was definitely a compliment. Apparently he could be a perfect gentleman when he wished. Astonishing.

Now that she considered it, why choose the opera, of all things, for them to attend? He didn't seem the sort to enjoy opera, but she had mentioned enjoying it earlier. Could he actually be doing something to please her?

Or was this a trap? Lord, she never knew what to think. His mercurial moods would drive any reasonable woman daft. Marcus possessed several advantages—wealth, a title, a clever mind. He might attain a respectable position in society if he would only behave. So why did he persist in his boorish behavior, even in his sister's presence?

The carriage slowed, and she glanced out the window to find that they'd arrived home. The gentlemen disembarked first, and Regina hung back so that Simon had to accompany Cicely up the stairs.

Leaving her to Marcus. With the lights from the Foxmoor town house behind him, his face was in shadow as he handed her down, but she could feel his sharp gaze on her, piercing her to her very soul. And when she took his arm, and they turned toward the stairs, her heart pounded. Even after all that had happened, he had this disturbing effect on her, as if she teetered on the edge of a cliff, and he merely waited to push her off.

Or catch her. She hadn't decided which yet.

As they climbed the stairs, he murmured, "We can attend the opera another night if you prefer."

"No, indeed," she said lightly. "Then you'd accuse me of not holding up my end of our bargain."

He shrugged. "If your brother isn't going, then by the terms we set, you don't have to go."

Hearing it stated so baldly made her flinch. "So you don't want me to go?"

"I didn't say that."

She hid her smile. "So you *want* me to go."

His arm stiffened beneath her hand. "I didn't say that, either. Stay home if you please. I don't give a damn whether you go with me or not."

"Then why did you offer to take me on a different night?" she teased. When he didn't immediately answer, she risked a glance at him.

The gas lamps at the top of the steps illuminated his annoyed expression. "You're a plague upon men, do you know that?"

"Why? Because I dare to expect reasonable answers from the Dragon Viscount instead of a lot of smoke and fire-breathing?"

His gaze met hers, and a reluctant admiration showed in his eyes. "Because you have a strong right arm." He lowered his voice. "And know how to use it."

Coloring, she jerked her gaze up to where her brother and Cicely were disappearing into the house. "I won't hesitate to use it again if you insult me."

They'd reached the top now, but he took her by surprise and tugged her behind the columns on the far end of the wide marble steps. By the time she realized what he was about, his mouth was on hers, hot . . . possessive . . . greedy. He took his time, kissing her so thoroughly and scandalously that her toes curled inside her satin slippers.

When he drew back, she could barely breathe, and his eyes gleamed at her in the darkness. "Do you consider *that* an insult?" he said in a seductive rumble.

She should. But she didn't. "Do you intend to follow it with some nasty comment about my preference for private duets?"

A muscle ticked in his jaw. "At the moment, I can't think of any."

"What a shame," she said lightly, struggling to conceal her reaction to his kisses. "I find them so entertaining."

Cicely appeared in the doorway and scowled when she spotted the two of them lurking behind the column. "Lord Draker, what are you doing? Regina, you must come inside."

With a taunt of a smile, Marcus caught Regina's gloved hand and lifted it to his lips. The lingering kiss he pressed to it made her body hum like a harp string freshly plucked.

"Good evening, madam," he said. "I'd better go before your duenna tosses me down the steps for my impertinence." Then he added in a tantalizing whisper, "Tomorrow night I'll make my impertinences more discreet."

She was still reeling from his presumptuous remark when he sauntered down the steps to where his carriage awaited him. Then she noticed his coachman and all his footmen looking up at her with knowing smiles. Sweet heaven, they'd probably guessed what she and Marcus had been doing behind the column.

Her face flamed as she hurried into the house behind Cicely. Why did the man always manage to slip under her guard? He seemed determined to make a public wanton out of her. If she weren't careful, he'd ruin her.

A pity he kissed so very well.

The minute she was inside, Cicely murmured, "Forgive me for not realizing what that beast was about. If I'd had any idea that the man was trying to . . . to . . ."

"It's all right, Cicely. He didn't do anything." Thanks to Marcus, she'd told more lies to Cicely in the past two days than she'd told in her entire life.

Cicely coughed. "I don't understand why you persist in this mad courtship."

"To help Louisa and Simon, of course." Turning away to hide her blush, Regina gave the footman her pelisse. "Surely you cannot think I have a romantic interest in Lord Draker."

"I should hope not! He isn't a suitable prospect for you."

Regina tensed and faced her cousin again. "If you refer to his behavior—"

"I refer to his fondness for books." Casting the footman a glance, she added discreetly, "A fondness you do not share."

Since you can't read.

A leaden lump settled in Regina's chest. Cicely was right, of course. "Then it's a good thing I'm going about town with him merely to help my brother, isn't it?" When Cicely frowned and opened her mouth to answer, Regina changed the subject. "And speaking of that, where *is* my brother? I thought surely Simon would be waiting in here to tease me."

"Begging your pardon, my lady," their butler put in, "but His Grace is with a special guest in his private drawing room."

Regina tensed. "Thank you, John." *Special guest* was the servant's code for His Highness. Why had the prince come here tonight, when he was going to see Simon tomorrow night at his dinner anyway? Could Marcus's suspicions about the prince and her brother be valid?

No, of course not. She couldn't believe it. On the other hand . . .

She glanced down the hall to the east wing. She *could* just go see what they were up to. After all, she needed to make her apologies to the prince for not being able to attend his dinner, and that would work much better in person.

Murmuring a good night to her cousin, she headed off into the east wing. It was silly even to think Marcus could be right about Simon. Her brother was ambitious, true, but he was not the sort to use a young woman so slyly.

Marcus only made such horrible claims because he believed the worst of everyone. Look at what he thought of *her*.

Though, to be honest, she was no longer certain *what* he thought of her. At first, she'd been sure he courted her merely to provoke her and Simon. And after he'd kissed her so passionately in Lord Iversley's library, his insulting remarks had seemed to confirm that he had no genuine interest in her.

But then he'd defended her in the carriage. He'd praised her singing. He'd even called her "clever." No one ever called her that. Beautiful, yes. Sophisticated, most assuredly. But clever? Not once.

She liked being called clever. Unfortunately, Marcus would not consider her clever at all if he knew the truth about her.

Cicely's words preyed on her. If Marcus learned that she couldn't read, he would think her stupid and even more shallow than he already thought her. Or he might think her damaged beyond repair. He certainly would not want her then.

No sensible man wanted a wife who might provide him with a damaged heir. It didn't matter how rich or pretty or accomplished a woman was—she had to fulfill certain duties. What if she couldn't?

That possibility depressed her.

Fortunately, she'd now reached Simon's drawing room, where she could forget about the pesky viscount. Before knocking, she put her ear to the door to see what she might discover. But she heard only the low murmurs of two men engaged in a conversation they wanted to keep very private.

Drat it all. With a sigh, she knocked, and the conversation stopped at once. Simon growled an invitation to enter.

As soon as she breezed into the room, both men rose. His Highness was the first to greet her. As she dropped into a deep curtsy, he said, "No need to stand on ceremony with me, my dear." He settled his large frame on the sturdy settee Simon had bought especially for such visits and patted the brocade. "Come sit beside me and tell me how you're doing."

Simon's scowl was meant to discourage her from lingering, but she ignored it. "I am so glad you're here, Your Highness," she said as she went to sit beside the prince. "It appears that I will not be able to attend your dinner tomorrow night. I do hope you can forgive me."

"It depends upon the reason." The prince chucked her under the chin. "And since you don't look ill—"

"Lord Draker asked Regina to join him at the opera tomorrow night," Simon put in baldly before she could figure out how to explain.

The flicker of interest in His Highness's face was unmistakable. "That's quite another matter, isn't it? I would not want to stand in the way of a courtship."

At his choice of words, Regina flung her brother a questioning glance.

Simon propped one hip on a writing table. "I told His Highness about your new beau. I thought he'd find it amusing to hear how Lord Draker fared on his first foray into polite society."

"Since when are *you* a gossip?" Regina snapped, too annoyed at the thought of the terrible picture her brother had probably painted to ask why they'd been discussing her and Marcus in the first place.

"Your brother knows I enjoy such chatter." His Highness took her hand and chafed it between his two large ones. "But do not worry your pretty head over it. Foxmoor had nothing but good things to say about you."

She didn't care what Simon said about her. What had he said about Marcus? And why should that even worry her? The prince might be Marcus's father, but Marcus hardly acted as if he wanted the man's good opinion. So why should she want it for him?

She didn't know why.

She just did.

"Did Simon mention what a fine singing voice Lord Draker has?" she asked.

The prince eyed her speculatively. "No, but I am not surprised."

He'd probably heard his son sing when Marcus was younger. Oh, how she wished she could ask him about Marcus as a boy. But she didn't dare.

"So what do you think of the viscount otherwise?" the prince asked. "Clearly you find him appealing, if you mean to forget my dinner to join him at the opera."

She cursed the blush that leaped to her cheeks, especially when His Highness tightened his grip on her hands. "He's appealing enough, I suppose," she said, trying to sound noncommittal.

"Regina means to transform him into a proper gentleman," Simon drawled.

His Highness narrowed his gaze on her. "If anyone can do it, Lady Regina can."

Thank heaven Simon hadn't mentioned the wager. "I do not mean to transform him, but to ease his way in society. I hate to see a man with such fine qualities spend all his days out at his estate."

"Draker has fine qualities?" Simon quipped. "I must have missed them."

"Then you are not as observant as I took you for," the prince snapped.

Judging from the look of chagrin on Simon's face, he'd momentarily forgotten Marcus's relationship to His Highness. "I'm observant enough to notice that the man has an interest in my sister that she does not reciprocate."

His attempt to divert the prince's displeasure worked, for

His Highness's baleful glance swung to her. "Is that true?"

"Simon misunderstands the nature of Lord Draker's interest in me," she hedged. "The man merely wants to prove to me that society is as corrupt as he believes it to be. We're engaged in a kind of contest, if you will."

"And he certainly isn't the sort my sister finds attractive," Simon added.

"That's not true." Regina colored when His Highness lifted an eyebrow. "But our interests are too different. He has little use for polite society. And I don't think he likes me much. Sometimes he even seems to despise me."

"Nonsense," the prince said kindly. "Who could despise a lovely creature like you, my dear?"

Marcus could. "All the same, I doubt he has any interest in marrying me."

Simon had apparently grown impatient with the conversation, for he left the writing table to approach the settee. "You can regale His Highness with tales of your courtship some other time, dear girl. I have several important matters of state to discuss with him privately right now, and the hour is getting late."

Since when did His Highness discuss matters of state with her brother in Simon's drawing room instead of at Carlton House?

Drawing her hand from the prince's, she rose. "Very well, I shall leave you."

His Highness rose, too. "Enjoy your evening at the opera, my dear."

She left, still burning to know what they were talking about. Could Marcus be right about Simon's intentions? Wasn't it an odd coincidence that His Highness would come here on the very night Simon had first been allowed to court Louisa?

On the other hand, if His Highness really did want influence over Louisa's future, then it made sense that he'd take an interest in Simon's courtship of her. That did not mean they were plotting anything underhanded.

They might even truly be discussing affairs of state. Marcus's ridiculous obsession with intrigue was simply making her imagine it herself. That was the trouble with letting the man kiss her—it made her think like him.

She certainly found Marcus attractive, and he'd made his physical attraction to her quite apparent. But that wasn't enough for a true courtship between two people so different from each other.

When his mouth was ravaging hers, however, she tended to forget that. So she simply *must* keep him at arm's length from now on. She mustn't let him kiss her again, no matter how gloriously he did so.

She would continue trying to civilize the beast and promote the match between Louisa and Simon, but she would be cordial and no more. Because nothing good could come of letting Marcus—Lord Draker—too close.

As soon as Regina was gone, the prince turned to Simon. "Are you sure she doesn't know what you mean to do? Your sister is more astute than she seems."

"I'm well aware of that." Simon only hoped that Draker, her new charitable project, would keep her too busy to examine his own activities. "Draker may have voiced his suspicions, but that doesn't mean she believes them."

"Then why did she agree to his mad bargain?"

"To prove him wrong in all his suppositions, just as she said." No point in mentioning the wager. He doubted His Highness would approve of such a wager involving his by-blow. "As long as Regina weighs in on my side, we're safe."

His Highness heaved his bulky frame from the settee. "Not so safe, I should think, if my son means to spend every moment with you and Louisa. How am I supposed to see my daughter and discuss her future?"

"Perhaps you should just let me tell her who you are to her—"

"Certainly not. Draker's secretive nature and his stubborn insistence that she's not mine have worked in our favor heretofore, because they've kept him from revealing to her some rather sordid details about my affair with his mother. If you tell her the truth, she'll run off to confirm it with him, and Draker will poison her against me before I even have the chance to tell my side."

Sordid details? Simon tamped down his curiosity. The secret to being His Highness's confidant was not to ask too many questions.

"When the time is right," the prince went on, "*I* will tell her that she's my daughter. But first I must get her alone, and you're supposed to take care of that."

"I'm trying, damn it. I don't see why you can't demand that the Iversleys bring her to Carlton House for a visit."

"Because if I press Iversley, Draker will certainly reveal things I'd rather not have known, especially in this tumultuous time."

"Why has Draker not revealed them before?"

His Highness waved his bejeweled hand. "I suppose he enjoys holding them over my head, the impudent scoundrel. And now he seeks to thwart me by gadding about town with Lady Regina and keeping me from seeing my daughter, damn it!"

"Patience, my liege, patience. They agreed to court for a

month, and Lord Draker won't last more than a week with Regina."

He hoped not, anyway. Simon would never survive a month of courting Louisa. A month of seeing her in blue satin and pearls, but imagining her in a lacy chemise that clung to her breasts and her belly and—

He swore under his breath as his pulse leaped into triple time. Christ, but she was beautiful. She would make some man a hell of a wife.

Not him, unfortunately. As prime minister, he would need a wife groomed to be a society hostess, not one allowed to grow wild in the country. A woman with sophistication and polish and a knowledge of her place. Louisa was both too naive and too headstrong to be a proper wife for him.

Yet he desired her. He found her innocence enormously appealing and her ungoverned tongue refreshing. She differed vastly from the calculating misses he generally met in society. If not for her connections and the future that Prinny intended for her, Simon would make her his mistress in a trice. All that wealth of black curls spread out on his pillow . . . those temptress's lips whispering naughty promises . . . those slender white arms opening to his embrace—

He groaned as his breeches grew tight. No point in thinking about it. He could never have her as his mistress. Draker would eat his liver for breakfast if he tried. And the prince would join him.

"This courtship might work in our favor if you'll only leave matters to Regina," Simon went on. "I give her a week at most to have Draker eating out of her hand. Then he'll do anything Regina asks, including letting me court his sister. You'll have your chance at Louisa yet."

"I'd better. Charlotte and William will marry soon, and I must have someone to watch over the princess whenever they travel to the Netherlands."

After the lax care that Princess Charlotte, Prinny's only legitimate daughter, had received under his estranged wife, His Highness was taking no chances. He wanted nothing to ruin this politically advantageous marriage between Princess Charlotte and Prince William of Orange. Charlotte's mother had already behaved with a shameless lack of regard for her position. Prinny wanted no taint of scandal attached to Charlotte, since she was next in line for the throne.

The prince paced before Simon. "You say that Louisa has a kind heart and good sense. Surely she will be eager to serve her half sister as a lady-in-waiting. And I will have someone I can trust to be my ears and eyes in Charlotte's household, someone I can mold."

Simon suspected there was more to this than a mere desire to have Louisa serve the princess. But if so, His Highness was not revealing it. That made him nervous. "You're assuming that Louisa will side with you, and not Draker, whom she adores. She may not be all that pleased to hear that you're her father."

"Nonsense. She's been without one for years—what girl doesn't want a father looking out for her interests?"

Simon broached another delicate subject. "She may also not be pleased to hear that I am . . . not planning to marry her."

His Highness eyed him closely. "You haven't done anything foolish, have you? Made her promises you don't mean to keep? Or seduced her into falling in love with you?" He leaned in close. "Or anything worse?"

"No, indeed," Simon said hastily. He preferred keeping

his ballocks attached to his body, thank you very much. Although he wasn't sure how much longer he could restrain his desire to kiss her. Just once. To taste that innocent mouth—

"We discussed this at the very beginning—that she would be better off married to a man whose interest in her is not political," His Highness warned.

"You're encouraging Charlotte to marry for political reasons."

"Yes, and I married Charlotte's mother for such reasons, too; look how badly that turned out. But Charlotte and I have duties, so we cannot marry where our hearts lead. Fortunately, Louisa is free to follow her heart. When she does fall in love, I want it to be with a man who reciprocates her feelings, a man capable of seeing her as more than a means to an end. And we both know you're not."

That wasn't entirely true. Simon could easily see her as more than a means to an end . . . in the bedchamber. But he couldn't exactly admit that to her father.

"Now we shall have to hope that Lady Regina does indeed distract my son enough to gain us the opening we need. Otherwise, I shall not be pleased."

And if His Highness were not pleased, Simon would lose any chance at advancement in the government.

"Don't worry, you can count on Regina. They don't call her La Belle Dame Sans Merci for nothing."

Chapter Eight

The proper chaperone should never put her needs above her charge's, even when attending favorite entertainments.
—Miss Cicely Tremaine, *The Ideal Chaperone*

La Belle Dame Sans Merci is certainly in fine form tonight, Marcus thought sourly as they arrived at the Italian Opera House. Like a society hostess at a party, she acted polite, interested . . . remote. As if she hadn't been melting in his arms behind that column just last night.

Damn her. He couldn't stop thinking about that, about kissing her mouth again, her soft, yielding—

He cursed under his breath. Had he lost his mind? This was how she sucked those other fools in, by making them clamor for the taste of her, then treating them with cool disdain.

Very well, let her play her tricks; he had a few tricks of his own. He'd proved well enough last night that the little hypocrite *enjoyed* his kisses and caresses. He would remind her of it. Repeatedly. Remind her what a courtship entailed, what a suitor had a right to expect. If that didn't drive her screaming from him, then nothing would.

They'd reached Iversley's box to find that it was prominently situated in the first tier. Good—Regina couldn't avoid having the whole world see her enter on his arm.

Better yet, "box" proved to be a generous term for the closet Iversley had rented. Regina seemed none too happy about it when she halted just inside the door. "Perhaps we should use Simon's box. There's more room."

"This looks fine to me." Marcus let his gaze linger on her. "Very cozy."

"It does have a marvelous view of the stage," Louisa said brightly.

"From what I understand," Marcus said, "the view of the boxes from the other boxes is all that matters to ladies at the opera."

"How would you know?" Louisa raised her voice to be heard over the din of the other patrons. "You've never been to the opera."

"That wouldn't keep your brother from voicing his opinion," Regina said archly. "Why obtain any facts before making pronouncements about society?"

"Actually, I *have* been to the opera," Marcus said. "In my salad days, I was as eager to ogle opera dancers as any other unlicked cub. So unless matters have changed since then, I doubt anyone is here to listen to the music." He certainly wasn't. He liked a good song as much as the next man, but opera was downright silly. "Are we staying in Iversley's box or not?"

"Yes, let's." Winking at her brother, Louisa took the arm of Regina's cousin. "Come, Miss Tremaine, we'll sit in the front."

Marcus bit back a smile at how deftly his sister had positioned him with Regina behind her chaperone. As Regina took her seat in the back row, he waited until she was well settled before he slid the other chair closer to hers and sat down.

He could tell from her stiff posture that she was not pleased. Good. And just so she'd have something to stew about, he laid his arm on the back of her chair.

She raised an eyebrow, but he merely smiled. She knocked her reticule onto the floor. "Oh, dear," she said in a voice loud enough to carry, "I've dropped my reticule. Lord Draker, if you would be so kind . . ."

He had no choice but to pick it up, which meant removing his arm from the back of her chair. When he straightened to hand her the pearl-encrusted bit of nothing, she'd inched her chair flush against the wall.

Sly wench. Obviously she thought a private dalliance was fine, but she seemed determined to hide their association from her friends.

He wouldn't let her. "Forgive me," he lied as he bent closer. "I forgot my promise to make my impertinences more discreet." Deliberately, he took her hand.

Just as deliberately, she snatched it back, a faint blush touching her cheeks. "I would prefer that you not be impertinent at all."

"I thought it was merely the possibility of someone's seeing my impertinences that bothered you." He laid his hand on her thigh, and when she reached to remove it, captured her hand in his. She tried to tug free, but he held firm.

Her gaze shot to him, annoyed, then calculating. "Do you have my copy of the translation, sir?"

"You know very well that I do. You entrusted it to me in the carriage."

The opera house sold libretto translations at the performance, but apparently she had connections to buy hers ahead of time. She said it was so that she could read it beforehand and not miss the music. He suspected it was just so she could turn up her nose at everyone who had to buy theirs at the opera house.

"Well then," she said, eyes gleaming, "may I see it?"

It was sandwiched between their chairs, where he'd placed it when they'd sat down. And short of becoming a contortionist, he could not reach it without releasing her hand. Which she apparently knew very well, blast her.

"Where's the copy I bought?" he countered.

"Louisa and Cicely are using it. So if I may just see mine..."

With a scowl, he dropped her hand. Dragging out the cheaply bound pamphlet, he started to hand it to her, but she snatched it from him and rose in one fluid movement, edging over to stand beneath the lamp in the corner of the box.

The orchestra tuned up. Soon the music would begin. He gazed up at her. "Do you intend to stand there the entire evening, reading it out to us?"

The lamplight flickered over her flushed cheeks. "Of course not. I merely wanted to check something in the third act."

Since she had only turned one page, she was nowhere near the third act. He smiled. "It's farther back—bring it here, and I'll find it for you."

A sudden panic flashed in her eyes. "I'm perfectly capable of looking for it myself, thank you."

Her voice had risen enough over the clamor to make her heard by their companions. Miss Tremaine turned to shoot them both a wary glance. Marcus stared hard at her, until at last she coughed and returned her gaze to the stage.

"Come sit down," he told Regina, growing irritated by

her determination to keep him from touching her. "It's about to begin."

The door behind them opened, and a male voice said, "I thought that was you over here in Iversley's box. Didn't I tell you that was Regina I saw, Henry?"

"Indeed you did, Richard. Indeed you did."

Henry and Richard turned out to be men about Regina's age. At her amiable greeting, they squeezed into the box, along with a younger fellow they called Tom.

As Marcus stood, Regina introduced the gentlemen with her usual serene grace. Henry proved to be Lord Whitmore, heir to the Earl of Paxton. The other two were his brothers. Apparently the three were also Regina's cousins. Very adoring cousins, judging from how they looked at her.

Insolent pups. Now they were crowding round her, complaining about the small quarters and urging her to join them in *their* box. As if Marcus were invisible.

When she refused, and they continued to press her, Marcus rose to his full height. "The lady said no, so if you value your necks, you'll take her at her word."

Louisa rose swiftly. "Now, Marcus," she said in a placating voice, "I'm sure the gentlemen don't mean anything by it."

"Come, Draker," the one named Richard chimed in, "we're merely concerned for the lady's comfort. How can she enjoy the opera in this tiny box?"

"She'd enjoy it better without a lot of chattering idiots swarming about her," Marcus retorted.

Whitmore stepped up to him. "Now see here, you overgrown—"

"Henry," Regina put in swiftly, laying her hand on his arm. "I'd like some refreshment before the opera begins. Would you accompany me to the lobby?"

Triumph gleamed in Henry's face. "I'd be honored, cousin," he said, with a smirk for Marcus.

The four of them vacated the box, leaving Marcus standing there seething.

As soon as the door shut behind them, he whirled on Miss Tremaine, who was sitting quietly in her chair. "Well? You're her chaperone. Do you generally let her go off alone with any Tom, Dick, and Henry?"

Miss Tremaine shrugged. "They're family. She'll be perfectly safe with them." She fixed him with a baleful glance. "They're also gentlemen."

Yes, he could tell what sort of gentlemen the asses were. "Fine, then I'll go." He hurried out the door, ignoring Louisa's and Miss Tremaine's protests.

All right, so he was behaving like an idiot, but he hated the idea of Regina alone with those three. He hated how they looked at her. He hated how they spoke to her. And he damned well hated that she'd rather go off with them than spend one more minute in his presence.

She'd made a bargain, confound her, and now she wanted to bend the rules by running off with those other fools. If she wanted to end their bargain, she'd better tell him to his face, where Louisa could hear it. If not, she had no business hiding their courtship from the world.

He wandered the theater for a few minutes with no success. Then, while pushing through a throng of people standing near some pillars, he heard a voice on the other side say, "Good God, Regina, I can't believe you tolerate that devil."

He froze, instantly recognizing the Eton clip of one of her cursed cousins.

The man went on in a snide voice. "We were shocked

to see you here with the man. What does Foxmoor say about it?"

"My brother has no say in whom I allow to accompany me to the theater," she said. "And neither do you or your brothers, Henry."

Marcus scowled. She hadn't used the word "court," had she?

"We're your cousins. We're concerned."

"Lord Whitmore is right, Lady Regina," a female voice put in. "The man is appalling. Aren't you simply terrified to be near him? You know what they say—"

"It's all nonsense. Trust me, he can be perfectly amiable when he wants."

Marcus stood there flabbergasted. She was defending him? To her friends?

"Draker must not have wanted to be amiable when we were upstairs," another of her cousins said, "because that was the rudest lout I've ever met."

"And did you see his hair?" one of the women said. "Good gracious, you'd think he'd never even heard of scissors."

"Or a razor. Or a tailor. Or a decent boot maker."

They all laughed, and he tensed. Silly buffoons. Frivolous asses. And Regina wasn't defending him now, was she? She was probably laughing right along.

He stepped out from behind the pillar, a snide remark on his lips, but it died when he realized Regina had gone. Somewhere between her defense of him and the laughter, she'd left. And one of her cousins was missing, too.

His anger burned even hotter. Ignoring the squeak one of the women made when she saw him, he scanned the lobby. He spotted Regina's lace-capped head next to Whitmore's perfectly coifed one just as they disappeared up the stairs.

Damn her to perdition. He would *not* let her keep company with some other fellow when she was supposed to be keeping company with him. He shoved through the crowd, his temper rising with every step. It was high time he reminded Lady Regina of the terms of their bargain.

Chapter Nine

*Any time you let your charge out of your sight,
you invite the devil Mischief to wreak
his willful havoc.*
—Miss Cicely Tremaine, *The Ideal Chaperone*

Out of the frying pan into the fire, Regina thought, as Henry led her up the crowded stairs. She should have insisted that her other cousins come along, but she'd been in too much of a hurry to escape her so-called friends and their evisceration of Marcus. If only Henry hadn't stepped in when she'd asked Richard to take her back to her box. Henry was the last person she wanted to be alone with.

Sure enough, at the top of the stairs, he tugged her toward the right.

She tugged him toward the left. "The box is this way."

"I want to talk to you. Alone. Your brother's box is empty at the moment, and you and I never got to finish our last discussion."

She sighed. They *had* finished it. He simply refused to accept it, which was why she'd avoided him ever since. She needed to put an end to his assumptions once and for all.

She let him lead her into Simon's spacious box, but stopped him when he started to close the door. "No need for that." With the lights going down in the house, it would be very dark in here with the door closed. Too dark.

He faced her with a sullen expression. "You said you'd consider my offer."

"No, I said I couldn't marry a man whom I regard as a brother."

"That's ridiculous. It's been years since we gamboled about in your family's deer park like little savages. God knows I don't think of you as a sister."

"Perhaps it's time that you do."

"Why? I have everything you could require in a husband, including a substantial fortune. You have no sensible reason for refusing me."

Except that she found him pretentious and boring. Henry's idea of a riveting evening was to gossip about everyone in his acquaintance. He probably gossiped about *her* when she wasn't around. "I'm sorry, Henry, I simply don't bear those sorts of feelings for you. And I never shall."

"You haven't given me a chance, that's all." Taking her by surprise, he shut the box door and dragged her into his arms. "But if you'd let me show you—"

He kissed her before she could stop him. She didn't resist, first stunned, then curious to see if his kiss would affect her as profoundly as Marcus's. But like the few other men who'd dared to kiss her, he'd honed his skills on many a pretty woman, and his calculated talent left her cold.

She wrenched her mouth from his. "That's enough, Henry. I am not interested in you that way."

"Nonsense." He gripped her so that she could not escape his embrace. "Give it a chance."

Panic shook her when she couldn't wrestle free. "Let go of me now, drat it!"

His face turned ugly. "They're right about you," he

hissed in her ear, as she struggled against his hold. "You're a cold little bitch, aren't you? You tease and flirt, but when a man shows you any genuine affection—"

"Release her, or I'll make you regret it," a voice growled.

Marcus! The door was now open and his massive form filled the doorway. Henry let her go with a speed that would have been insulting if she hadn't known what a coward he was. He faced Marcus warily. "This is none of your concern, sir, so if you will leave us—"

"Do you want me to leave, Lady Regina?" Marcus asked, without shifting his gaze from Henry.

Behold the dragon. His clenched fists, powerful bulk, and fiery face were the very picture of dragonly fury, a barely leashed force awaiting only her word to fly out and destroy everything in its path.

Other men had sworn to fight for her. This was the first man she believed might actually do it. A thrill shot down her spine. "Please stay, Lord Draker. Henry was just leaving."

Henry whirled on her. "Regina, you can't mean you prefer—"

"You heard her." Marcus stepped into the box. "I believe your friends are looking for you downstairs."

Henry hesitated. Fortunately, the idiot's brain actually functioned once in a while. With a tight little bow, he exited the box, leaving Marcus and Regina alone.

Now that Henry was gone, she didn't know whether to be delighted that Marcus had shown up or annoyed that he'd taken it upon himself to interfere. "How did you find me?"

"I followed you. I didn't trust your cousins."

"Or me, apparently. I could have handled Henry myself, you know."

With a glance at the rest of the boxes in the house, he closed the door, then stepped closer. "I could see how well you were handling him."

"You didn't give me the chance. When you came in, I was about to use my 'strong right arm' on him. That would have stopped him."

"It didn't stop me from kissing you on your doorstep last night," he murmured into the darkness. He was much closer now.

She shivered deliciously, but didn't move. She had two choices. The wise one was to rebuff him as swiftly as she'd rebuffed Henry. The foolish one was to see where this led.

Earlier this evening, she would have made the wise choice. But Henry's pathetic kiss had shown her one basic truth. She'd never been attracted to any man as powerfully as she was to this one. Despite his grousing. Despite the beard and rude manners and the way he always kept her unsettled.

Or perhaps the unsettled part was what attracted her. "I could have stopped you last night if I'd wanted to," she admitted.

"So why didn't you?"

"I didn't want to."

His eyes glittered dangerously in the semidarkness. "But tonight you wanted to stop me. Tonight you wouldn't even let me hold your hand."

"Because I-I wanted to teach you some manners," she lied.

"I'm rather thickheaded sometimes." Suddenly his hands were on her waist, drawing her behind the curtains at the back of the box, giving her a chance to resist. "Perhaps we should repeat the lesson."

The husky words sent a thrill of anticipation coursing

through her rapidly heating blood. Breathless, she slid her hands up the mighty arms that engulfed her. "Perhaps we should."

That was all it took to have him kissing her. And it was every bit as wonderful as she remembered, hot and sweet and silky. His mouth consumed hers, taking everything with that amazing boldness he showed in all that he did. But where Henry's boldness had appalled her, Marcus's only made her want more.

She clutched eagerly at his brawny shoulders. How nice to be out of control for a change. And this was so very out of control. They were alone in the dark; no one could see them behind the curtains. Certainly no one could hear them, with the noisy patrons conversing over the performers. If anyone did hear, they would probably assume some doxy and her companion were making use of an empty box.

At times like this she wished she were his doxy, especially when he plundered her mouth like a marauder, possessing it so thoroughly that she felt melded to him like wax to a wick, the two of them erupting into flames together.

His mouth left hers to burn a path of fire along her jaw. "You defended me to them downstairs. Why?"

"You heard us?" she whispered, cursing her friends for their snide tongues.

"I heard them behaving like asses. I heard you defending me."

"They don't even know you," she choked out, though it was hard to speak when he was nibbling her earlobe and laving her ear with his heated tongue.

"I don't know you, either," he whispered against her ear. "I thought I had you figured out. I thought it was only the public nature of our association that bothered you. I thought that was why you acted as if you disliked me. But then you defended me to your friends."

"I don't dislike you. I never disliked you."

He nuzzled her neck, his beard tickling her sensitive flesh. "Then why have you been so cool to me tonight?"

"Because this is unwise . . . you . . . and me."

"Of course it's unwise—what difference does that make?" His open mouth caressed her exposed shoulder, and a shiver ran through her.

"It makes a difference to me. I always try to act wisely." *Most of the time.*

"I don't. I never have."

She smiled against his hair. "I know. You'd much rather thrash about, insulting people."

He froze. "You mean I don't behave as you'd like. Is that why you think it unwise for me to kiss you? And want you?"

Her heart began to pound. "You don't really want me." *You would despise me if you knew I can't read your precious books.* "That's why it's unwise."

Drawing back, he fixed her with a gaze so intensely black it seemed to swallow her up. "I suppose this is how you get all the men to grovel at your feet—by pretending not to know what you do to them." His gaze scoured her throat and shoulders and breasts. "Because you have to know that men want you."

Her temper flared. He was just like the rest of them. "My body, you mean. Yes, I do know that men want my body. So what does it matter if I've got one more to 'grovel' at my feet?"

Shoving him away, she whirled and headed for the door, but he caught her around the waist and dragged her roughly back against the hard wall of his chest. A shiver swept her as her bottom pressed against his muscular thighs.

"Do you expect me not to want your body?" he murmured against her ear. "Because I don't think that's possible. And if that's why you're angry . . ."

The hint of amusement in his tone only fired her temper further. "I'm angry because you want *only* my body. You've made it clear time and again that you think me shallow and frivolous, so you couldn't possibly want me for my good temper or my common sense or my character."

"If I wanted only your body," he growled, "I wouldn't be here, putting up with your sharp tongue. I can purchase a complacent beauty in any high-priced brothel in London."

She stiffened. "If you think such a crude statement will do for an apology—"

"I'm not apologizing. I won't apologize for wanting any part of you. I know I'm crude and uncivilized and not fit to kiss your hand. I just don't care."

He splayed his hand over her belly, bunching the satin as he fit her more firmly in the shelter of his chest and waist and thighs, every inch of him as rigid and unyielding as his words. She ought to fight him. She ought to dig her fingernails into his arm, kick back at his shin . . . do anything to make him let go of her. She shouldn't even listen to his words.

Because they affected her. And because even though he was crude and uncivilized and all those things she thought she hated . . . she didn't mind it in him. Oh, what perversity was that?

He pressed his lips to her ear, then went on in a voice tinged with anger. "Do you think I like desiring the sister of the very man I despise? A woman who only tolerates my kisses because she needs an adventure to liven her life?"

"That's not true," she whispered.

"Isn't it? I've gone over and over it in my head, and I can think of no other reason for your letting me hold you. Or do this." He scattered kisses along her jaw. "And this." He sucked her neck, an action she found oddly sensuous. "And even this . . ." His hand slid up to cover her breast.

She was so shocked at first she couldn't speak. No man had ever dared or even attempted . . . Did he think she would allow . . .

She reached for his hand, but then it began to move beneath her fingers, slowly, carnally, fondling her through her gown as if she were some . . . some . . .

Doxy.

Her head fell back against his chest. Oh, Lord, perhaps he was right; perhaps she did want adventure. Or perhaps she'd just gone so long without letting any man near her that she was tired of holding men at arm's length.

No, not all men. Just him. He was the only one she wanted close. But why? Because he was outside of society? Or because she'd simply lost her mind?

"If it's adventure you want, dearling," he murmured, "I'm happy to oblige."

"No . . . I mean . . . I don't know why I let you . . . do this to me."

"I'm not complaining." He nipped at her earlobe, which sent an erotic thrill humming along her flesh. "I'm only praying I don't wake up too soon."

"You're not asleep." Or else she was, too.

"I might be. It wouldn't be the first time I've dreamed of you." Still holding her with her backside pressed into his groin, he drew her farther behind the curtains into the blackest depths of the box.

She went willingly, tantalized by the idea of his dreaming about her. When he continued fondling her breast, she choked out, "What sort of dreams?"

He caressed her other breast, wringing a long sigh from her lips. "Last night I dreamed I heard you singing. I went through Castlemaine following that siren's voice of yours and found you in my dungeon. All your talk of chaining women in it must have brought that on. Because despite what the gossips say, I only go in my dungeon when I'm in too foul a mood to be around people, and I need to vent my temper."

"Was I . . . chained?"

"No. But I was. After I entered."

"So what was *I* doing there?"

"You don't want to know."

The growled whisper only made her breath quicken. "I do."

"You were sitting with a harp cradled between your legs. And you were naked from head to toe, with only the harp to shield you."

She gasped at the shockingly provocative image that leaped into her mind.

"The second I entered, chains wrapped themselves around my wrists, jerking me back, keeping me from touching you," he went on in a guttural voice. "I stood there helpless, envying that damned harp for getting to lie between your thighs and brush the very places I wanted to touch . . . like your breasts . . ." He slid his hand inside her bodice to caress her bare flesh. "Your silky breasts."

When he plucked at her nipple as if it were a harp string, pleasure resonated through her. He played her deftly, soothing and provoking her by turns. She groaned as his fondling grew bolder, more outrageous, but she could not bring herself to stop him. Sweet heaven, was this what it was like to have a man touch you intimately? This was what she'd be giving up if she never married?

"I wanted to stroke your belly . . ." Slipping his free hand down, he splayed his fingers over her abdomen, then dragged them lower and lower until—"And this." He cupped her between the legs, right on the spot where she felt suddenly tight and tender. "God, how I wanted to touch this."

Oh . . . dear . . . Lord. He rubbed her hard down there, and she nearly leaped out of her skin. His caress made her thrum with unfamiliar desires. She laid her cheek against his shoulder, not even trying to stop him from touching her. Even though it was the most scandalous thing anyone had ever done to her.

And the most exquisite.

When his stroking made her moan, he rasped, "You like that, do you?"

"I . . . I don't know . . ."

"I can feel that you like it." His voice grew gruff. "But only because you don't have to look at me. Only because you can imagine it's someone else—"

"Never." She twisted around to face him. "I've never allowed any man these liberties, I assure you."

"No?" His eyes gleamed in the darkness as he drew her close, his other hand cupping her breast deliberately through her bodice.

"No." She caught her breath as he stroked and kneaded her, his gaze hot on her face. "Marcus, we shouldn't—"

"Shh, dearling." Taking her by surprise, he dropped to one knee and clasped her about the waist. "Let me taste you," he whispered, planting a kiss to the inner valley between her breasts. "One taste to enhance your adventure—"

"I never said I wanted . . . an adventure."

Not one this scandalous, anyway. His mouth was so hungry, so bold. This went too far—she could not let him . . . she mustn't let him . . . She clutched his head, meaning to draw him back, but his thick hair engulfed her hands in a silky mass and she couldn't resist stroking it, burying her fingers in it.

And now he was drawing down the bodice of her gown to bare one breast to his intent gaze. Excitement vibrated along her every nerve, making her tighten her fingers in his hair.

"Marcus, what are you . . ." She trailed off as his mouth seized her breast as boldly as it had seized her lips earlier. Oh, heaven . . . how delicious.

And what he did to her nipple with his tongue, good Lord!

"God help me," he tore his lips from her breast to murmur. "Even here you smell like sun and honey. So warm . . . so sweet."

He returned to sucking her breast while his hand fondled her other breast beneath her gown. He strummed one nipple and tongued the other until her blood beat wildly.

Then she was pressing his head into her chest, wanting more of the erotic thrills surging down her, undulating along her belly to throb madly in the secret place below that he'd stroked before.

He removed his hand from her breast, only to drag her onto his bent knee. She gasped as his rigid thigh pressed right on that spot between her legs, setting every nerve thrumming.

His mouth seized her other breast this time, sucking it with blatant hunger. Her heart's mad drumming drowned out the tiny voice of conscience.

But not the music. Beyond the curtain a soaring, lilting aria sounded, a fitting counterpoint to the hot licks of his tongue over her nipple and the pulsing between her legs that she only seemed able to ease by rocking against his thigh.

"Yes, dearling, like that," he whispered against her breast. "That will make your adventure all the better."

"I wish you'd . . . stop calling it that . . ." Rubbing against him did feel exquisitely adventurous. Deliciously pleasurable. The more she rocked, the more her need seemed to tighten in that one aching spot, like a harp string wound in the tuning until its note arched higher and sweeter and purer—

A sudden burst of thunderous applause erupted around them, the sound shattering all her pleasure. Blinking, she drew back from him. Sweet heaven. She tugged hard on his hair. "Marcus, we must stop."

"Yes," he growled as he laved her nipple with his tongue, ignoring the way she pulled at his head. "Soon, dearling, soon . . ."

"Now," she said firmly. "The first act must be ending."

He lifted his head. "It hasn't been long enough, trust me."

She had no idea how long it had been. When he was kissing and touching her, she lost all track of time. "I'm sure the lights will come up any moment, and we cannot be seen coming out of the box together unchaperoned."

When he just stared at her, his eyes blazing hot and hungry and his hands locked on her waist, she added in a whisper, "Please do not let me be ruined."

His hands slackened. "Damn." He didn't try to stop her

as she scrambled from his knee. "Confound it all to hell."

If they did not leave soon, they would be caught together. But no respectable woman wandered the theater alone, either. "Come on!" she cried, jerking at his arm to make him rise. "We have to go!"

He rose stiffly, but then the applause petered out, and the music continued. "It was just the end of the aria. We still have time, thank God."

She peeped around the curtain at the stage, wishing she could remember what Cicely had read to her from the translation yesterday. "But the first act will surely end soon." Straightening her gown, she cursed herself for letting matters go so far. "We have to leave the box while no one's in the hall to see us."

"I can't. Trust me, if I go with you into the light right now, you'll be ruined the second anyone sees me."

She stared at him uncomprehendingly.

He flashed her a rueful smile. "A woman can hide her arousal, dearling. A man cannot."

A blush stained her cheeks as she remembered the outrageous information she'd wrangled out of her married friends about men and lovemaking. She resisted the scandalous impulse to drop her gaze.

"Can't you . . ." She waved her hand vaguely in the area of his groin. "Can't you do something?"

Fire flamed in his face. "I could make love to you on the floor, but somehow I don't think that's what you mean."

"Certainly not!"

"Then we'll have to wait it out." His tone grew ironic. "Tell me about your cousin Whitmore. That will dampen my . . . er . . . ardor in a hurry."

The request took her by surprise. "What do you want to know?"

"Why was he bothering you?"

Oh, Lord. With a shrug, she glanced away. "He wants to marry me. I said no. Again."

"Again?"

"He asked before, and I refused. He chose not to accept my refusal."

"So how many marriage proposals have you refused, anyway? Four? Five?"

"It hardly matters."

"How many, Regina? And tell me the truth, or I'll ask Miss Tremaine, who will surely tell me just to spite me."

Drat him and all his questions. It was exceedingly difficult to discuss such things with a man who'd only moments before been tempting her to sin. "Eleven," she snapped. "If you count Henry."

"By all means, let's count 'Henry.' And what's so wrong with Whitmore that you refused him twice?"

The applause sounding in the house gave her an excuse not to answer. "Come on, we can't wait any longer, no matter how your ardor is doing."

"Believe me," he retorted, as she opened the door, "my ardor is about as dampened now as a man's can get."

When Regina peeped out to find the passageway deserted, she nearly collapsed with relief. "Quickly now," she murmured as she drew him out. "We'll just tell Cicely and your sister that we were visiting old Lady Montgomery's box. The countess is so forgetful that even if anyone asks, she'll say we were there." She cast him a small smile. "She likes me."

"Everyone likes you, Regina," he muttered.

"Even you?"

He had no chance to answer, for as they rounded a bend, they came face-to-face with Henry. And his brothers were with him, blocking the path and forcing her and Marcus to halt.

"Step aside, Whitmore," Marcus ordered.

Henry glanced past them at the empty passageway, his face turning a mottled red. "The two of you have been in Foxmoor's box all this time?"

"Don't be ridiculous," Regina said coolly. "We were visiting Lady Montgomery in her box."

"Liar," Henry said in a vile tone. "You've been with this blackguard. You won't give me one minute alone with you, but you'll let the Dragon Viscount—"

"I'd hold my tongue, if I were you," Marcus broke in. "You're speaking about a lady of impeccable reputation."

"It won't be so impeccable when people hear about this," Henry retorted.

"Don't be a fool, Henry," Richard put in.

Before anyone could say another word, Marcus grabbed Henry by the throat and thrust the young lord up against a wall, his feet dangling off the ground.

"You will not say anything to anyone," Marcus hissed into Henry's face, which was already turning red as he struggled for air.

Drat men and their tempers. Praying that the passageway would stay empty another moment, Regina grabbed Marcus's arm. "Lord Draker, put him down!"

She might as well pull on a lamppost, for Marcus didn't even seem to notice. He shook Henry as easily as he might wring a chicken's neck. "You won't say a word, Whitmore. Because if I hear that you have, I will cut off your tongue and shove it down your goddamned throat. Do you understand me?"

The other two men gasped, as much at his speaking profanity in the presence of a woman as his threat of violence.

"Marcus!" Regina's cheeks flamed. "For heaven's sake, put him down!"

"Do you understand, you little ass?" Marcus slammed Henry against the wall. "Do you?"

Henry managed something like a nod, and Marcus released him abruptly. Henry crumpled to the floor like a hot-air balloon collapsing. As his brothers hurried to his side, her cousin pushed himself to his feet, and croaked, "You don't fight like a gentleman, Draker."

"No, I don't," Marcus growled. "See that you remember that the next time you think to drag a lady's reputation through the mud."

The man had lost his mind—did he really think such tactics would solve anything? He was lucky Henry was too big a coward to call him out. And though Henry might keep silent about her and Marcus, he would never keep silent about Marcus's rough manner and coarse speech.

Marcus held out his arm to her. "Shall we go?"

The box doors burst open, spilling people into the corridor around them. She had no choice but to let him lead her away from her still-gaping cousins. As they navigated the halls her temper soared. Marcus had just made everything infinitely worse. Did he have no sense of how to behave in public? No understanding of the rules?

Either he had none, or he chose to ignore them. But why? She could not believe his mother hadn't instilled some knowledge of appropriate behavior in him. So why did he ignore his upbringing at every turn?

He practically invited people to insult him. But their insults clearly bothered him, or why would he have been so snide last night when he'd thought she was cutting him? He was a proud man, yet he behaved in a manner sure to invite contempt and condemnation.

Then there was his behavior toward her. One moment he was sneering at her; the next he was kissing and caressing her with a tender passion that made her blood heat just to think of it. None of his actions made any sense.

They entered the Iversley box to find Cicely pacing and Louisa looking positively frantic.

"Where on earth have you been?" Louisa hurried up to Regina. "One of your cousins came looking for you and said that you'd disappeared with Lord Whitmore. Then he mumbled something about Marcus, and we thought something might have happened—"

"Your brother has been busy terrifying the patrons," Regina bit out.

Marcus cast her an incredulous look. "I was defending *you.*"

"By half strangling my cousin?"

"He deserved it. He was going to—"

"Nonsense," she broke in. "If you'd given me the chance, I would have reminded Henry that gossip is a sword I can wield as well as he. He wouldn't dare malign me, knowing that I would retaliate by telling people I refused his suit. That would mortify him."

"You refused Lord Whitmore?" Louisa's gaze flitted from Regina to Marcus with clear interest.

"No doubt he failed to meet her ladyship's high standards," Marcus growled.

"Or Regina simply didn't think they would suit," Louisa said helpfully.

Marcus snorted. "I can't imagine why. He has everything Lady Regina is looking for in a husband—title, wealth . . . a condescending manner."

"That's not what she's looking for." Louisa cast Regina an uncertain glance. "Tell him that's not what you want."

"Oh, pay your brother no mind." Regina's temper flared. "He only says these things to annoy me."

And disturb his sister. In the past two days, Louisa had doubted her more often than she had in the whole time of their friendship, and all because of the insults her bitter brother continued to—

The light dawned. *That* was why he was behaving like this, doing his best to make Regina despise him. Oh, Lord, now it began to make sense—his contradictory behavior, his insults, his snide manner.

He thought she was shallow, heartless, and fickle, and he wanted Louisa to think so, too. Because if Louisa could be made to doubt Regina's character, she might also begin to question Simon's.

Of all the sneaky, conniving tricks! This wasn't about courting her—that's why he didn't try to impress her with compliments or dress to please her. And here she'd thought he actually wanted her.

Tears filled her eyes; she blinked them furiously back. What a fool she'd been. He'd probably thought to prove her a wanton, too, perhaps even ruin her. She'd been too blinded by her stupid physical attraction to him to realize it. She ought to consider herself fortunate he hadn't come right out and told Henry what they'd been doing.

But she didn't feel terribly fortunate just now. She felt used, manipulated by a man more expert at it than any of those society members he loathed.

Well, not anymore. If the dragon intended to devour a virgin before he'd stop terrorizing the countryside, he was about to discover how unpalatable this virgin could be.

Chapter Ten

*A discourteous gentleman should
never be tolerated.*
—Miss Cicely Tremaine, *The Ideal Chaperone*

Marcus knew he was in trouble. He should never have touched Regina, never have tasted her, never have let her entwine him in her spell. Why else had the thought of Whitmore's ruining her reputation turned him into a slavering beast? Even a boor like him could tell when he'd lost control, and a man should never lose control around his enemies.

Marcus glanced across the carriage to where Regina sat stiffly gazing out the window while her duenna eyed him from beside her with a distinctly malevolent satisfaction. No doubt Miss Tremaine was glad he'd argued with her cousin.

A pox on her. A pox on them both.

Regina had ignored him for the remainder of the opera, conversing only with Louisa or Miss Tremaine, turning no glances his way, and in general treating him like the only discordant note in her social symphony.

He wouldn't let her get away with it. Yes, he'd gone too far with Whitmore, but she ought to be glad he hadn't beaten the man to a bloody pulp. That's what he'd wanted to do the minute that weasel had threatened to slur her in society.

Stifling an oath, he glanced out the window. If he'd been thinking with something other than his cock, he could have used Whitmore's accusations to his advantage. Regina would have ended her bargain with Marcus if he'd confirmed even a small part of her idiot cousin's claims.

Instead, he'd browbeaten the man into silence. And why? Because of some chivalric impulse as out of place as the courtly gesture of tossing one's cape down across a mud puddle. Because after tasting her sweet flesh, he couldn't stand to watch her reputation reduced to rags for it.

And she was rewarding him with coolness. He'd foolishly let Regina know how badly he desired her, and now she thought to make him pay dearly for it.

The hell she would. "Tomorrow night, we'll go to the theater with Foxmoor and Louisa," he told her firmly. "That new fellow Edmund Kean is at Drury Lane."

His sister, who sat beside him in the carriage, perked up. "That would be lovely. Don't you think so, Regina?"

"I'm sorry." Regina kept her gaze fixed out the window. "I'm attending the Hungate ball tomorrow night. But Simon and I will look for you and Louisa there."

A burning anger settled in the pit of his stomach. "I wasn't invited." And she damned well had to know it. "That means Louisa won't be going, either."

"But Marcus—" Louisa began.

"We can go riding the next day, however," he went on. "If Foxmoor is free."

"He might be free, but I am not," she said in such an excruciatingly correct tone it infuriated him. "I have already agreed to attend a friend's party that day. But I'm sure Louisa and Simon would be delighted to join you."

"Oh yes—" Louisa began.

"What about the day after that?" he growled, his temper rising.

"That's Sunday." Regina leveled a hard glance on him. "I go to church."

"How very pious of you," he snapped.

"I pray for the souls of those who delight in their wickedness," she said sweetly.

"Like your cousins, perhaps?"

Her lips tightened. "Like certain gentlemen I know, yes."

Louisa laid a hand on his arm. Marcus shrugged it off, his temper soaring. "What about Monday night, then? Kean will still be at Drury Lane." Damn it, he had not meant to make it a request. He refused to beg her. She'd had him on his knees once tonight—she would not get him there again.

"Monday night I am otherwise engaged. And also on Tuesday." When he opened his mouth, she added in her most sugary tone, "Wednesday night I'm attending the assembly at Almack's. I don't suppose you have a voucher?"

He snorted. "I would sooner cut off my right hand than solicit a voucher from that lot of vultures."

"What a pity, then, that you need your right hand for strangling gentlemen."

"Damn it, Regina—" he began, coming to the end of his patience.

"Indeed, my social schedule is so crowded this time of year, I don't know when the four of us shall be able to meet again. You three must go on without me. But I shall check my schedule when I get home to see if I can fit you in sometime the week after next." Her brittle smile made him want to shake her.

She meant to punish him for not behaving like a gentleman. But was she also trying to get out of their bargain? The instant punch to his gut made his temper flame higher. She'd better not be. Regina had agreed to a courtship, and she was damned well going to hold up her end of it or reject him in front of his sister, where it might do him some good.

The coach shuddered to a halt. As the footman scurried to open the door, Marcus said, "Stay here, Louisa, while I see the ladies inside. I won't be long." Then he leaped from the carriage before Regina could protest.

After handing down the two females, he escorted them up the long stairs. Regina's overlight hold on his arm irritated him. She could hardly stand to touch him now, but only an hour ago she'd been melting beneath his kisses and caresses. Damn the woman.

As soon as they were inside, he turned to Regina's cousin. "I'd like a word with Lady Regina alone, Miss Tremaine."

That sent Miss Tremaine into a dither. "Oh, I don't know, I—"

"It's all right, Cicely," Regina put in. "I'd like a word with his lordship myself. It will only take a moment."

After that clipped statement, she marched off down the hall with all the regal grace of a true aristocrat. He stalked after her, painfully aware of his ungainly size and heavy gait.

Why the devil had he inherited Prinny's bulky frame instead of the man's princely manners? It was damned inconvenient.

He thought of how perfectly Regina had fit in the slender Whitmore's arms, two elegant people elegantly entwined in an elegant kiss. Until she'd started fighting the bastard.

Marcus's kisses had been more like the attack of a ravening wolfhound. And then his annoying size had forced him to kneel just so he could suck her breasts . . .

Not that she'd protested it. Her eager response to his kiss had merely whetted his hunger. Especially when she'd looked so appealing with her blond hair temptingly swirled and coifed and her female flesh plumped up so sweetly it would make any man weep to taste it. Great God, how could he have helped himself?

He could still hear her soft moans of arousal, remember her nipples growing hard as pebbles beneath his tongue. How dared she renege on their bargain after welcoming his advances—

"Well?" She turned to face him. "What did you want to speak to me about?"

With a start, he glanced around. He hadn't even noticed they'd reached a sitting room, probably hers. He'd followed her blindly, like a slobbering lapdog.

Careful, man. She'd probably led him deliberately into this enclave of frothy fripperies and spindly chairs that would snap the minute he dropped his massive body into them. She wanted to remind him that she wasn't meant for ungainly louts like him, but for refined gentlemen.

"You think to punish me with this coldness, don't you?" he ground out.

"I don't know what you mean."

"The devil you don't. Ever since that moment in the corridor when I—"

"Throttled my cousin? Used unconscionably coarse language? Tried to ruin my reputation forever?"

He bristled. "Whitmore was the one trying to ruin you, and you know it. Damn it, you ought to be grateful that I took care of it."

"Grateful! Your barbaric behavior made an enemy not only of him, but of his brothers, too. If you had used some restraint—" She broke off, then took a steadying breath. "Which leads me to what I wished to discuss with you."

This was it. She would break with him. It was exactly what he'd been waiting for—so why was he suddenly finding it so hard to breathe?

"It seems I misunderstood your reasons for courting me."

That put him on his guard. "What do you mean?"

"You said you wanted someone to ease your entree into society. I thought that you wanted to support Louisa. Yet whenever you are in society, you are rude to whomever we meet."

"Why be polite to that lot? They'll despise me no matter what I do."

"That's ridiculous—if they despise you, it's only because of how you act. And I can hardly blame them. You insult me and them at every turn, you make no attempt to adhere to gentlemanly manners, and you dress as if you're going to a wheat-threshing instead of out into good society."

"I'm only being myself. You knew what I was when you met me."

"I assumed you were being rude to me then because of my brother. I never dreamed that you lacked any knowledge of proper social behavior whatsoever."

He scowled. "I don't. I'll admit I overreacted when Whitmore made his threats, but that doesn't give you the right to renege on our bargain."

"Who said anything about reneging on our bargain?"

"That's what I call it when you refuse to let me accompany you anywhere."

She cast him one of her cool, condescending smiles. "You misunderstand. I am merely putting you off until we can resolve this situation."

He eyed her warily. "Oh?"

"If we begin lessons at once, you should be ready in no time."

He blinked. "Ready for what?"

"To go back into society. If you and I are to keep courting, you cannot continue to fumble about, insulting people willy-nilly. I do have a reputation to maintain." He gaped at her as she paced the room, ticking things off on her fingers. "Since you're so fond of books, I'll send you the most recent ones on deportment for gentlemen. We'll consult with Lord Iversley about a tailor, and I'm sure Simon would be willing to explain to you all the rules of appropriate gentlemanly—"

"I am not going to be tutored by your damned brother!" he exploded. "There's nothing wrong with my clothes, and I behave as I please. It has nothing to do with not knowing the rules."

She turned slowly to face him, her eyebrows arching high. "Do you mean to say you *choose* not to follow the rules of gentlemanly behavior?"

"Damned right," he growled.

"But I don't understand. You insisted that we have a proper courtship, that it not be private, that I be seen in public with you. I assumed that in return you meant to treat me the way a man who is courting a woman generally does—with courtesy and respect. But apparently it's only a proper courtship for me. For you, it's . . . what? I am trying to understand."

Uh-oh. This was not how he wanted the conversation to go. "It's . . . er . . ."

"Surely you know that behaving badly shames both me and your sister. So why do it?" Her eyes narrowed. "Perhaps because this is not a proper courtship after all? Because it is only your scurrilous way of trying to make me give up on Louisa and Simon?"

His blood chilled. Had she guessed what he was up to? "That's absurd."

"And all your talk of wanting a beautiful woman on your arm? Was that a lie, too? And your kisses and your claim to desire me?" Her hands were shaking now, and her lower lip trembled.

He stifled an oath. "You know damned well I desired you . . . I *desire* you . . . I—" God, she was talking circles around him.

"You desire me. Yet you do not want to please me."

"I didn't say that," he growled.

"You certainly said and did nothing to make me think otherwise. So how can you blame me for thinking you were toying with my affections for your own vile purposes? The way you claim Simon is toying with Louisa's?"

The comparison hit him like a blow to the chest. Something had gone badly awry during this conversation, but he'd be damned if he could figure out where.

La Belle Dame Sans Merci is used to turning men inside out, remember?

"I hardly think I could toy with a woman who's rejected eleven proposals of marriage," he shot back, desperate to regain his footing in the deepening morass that suddenly surrounded him.

Anger glittered in her eyes. "So you decided that my having past suitors made it acceptable for you to toy with me."

"Damn it, I wasn't toying— I meant—" He swore a foul

oath. "You're twisting this all around. You know how I feel about society. Why should I follow their ridiculous rules?"

"Because you're courting me?" When he scowled, she added dismissively, "Never mind. I think I understand now."

He stiffened. "Understand what?"

"If you did not set out purposely to toy with me—" She paused to cast him a brittle glance. "That is what you claim, isn't it?"

"Of course," he bit out, more uncomfortable with this conversation by the moment.

"Then it must be as I said at first—you don't know how to behave publicly." She gave a heavy sigh. "I should have seen it before. You are simply too proud to admit it. All your grousing and protests—they're precisely how a man behaves when he's out of his element and doesn't want anyone to know."

"Out of his element?" he said uneasily.

"I suppose I shouldn't have made it worse by pointing out your need for lessons in gentlemanly deportment."

"I do not need lessons in deportment!" he roared.

"There's no need to shout," she said primly. "It's all right. You needn't be ashamed of it with me." Her face showed nothing but pity.

Pity, damn her!

A million shades of red exploded in his brain. Nobody pitied him, not her, not his sister, nobody. Perhaps he floundered a bit when he was in society, but that was only because of how those asses treated him. Did she expect him to be *nice* to them? When they were rude to him? To smile and bow and—

The devil he would. He thrust his face right down to hers. "I do not need lessons in a damned thing. I simply choose not to cater to your insane whims and society's silly rules."

"Forgive me, but that's what incompetent fellows always protest when they don't know how to dance or behave properly or say the right things. But I am perfectly happy to help you learn—"

"I do not need your help! I do not need anyone's help." Realizing he'd sunk so far into the morass he might never get out, he decided that retreat was best. "I've had enough of this nonsense. Good evening, madam."

As he stalked toward the door, she called out, "Lord Draker?"

"What?" he snapped without breaking stride.

"Since you cannot behave as a gentleman and do not seem willing to learn how, I am afraid I shall have to forgo the pleasure of your company."

He halted. "You're refusing to hold to your end of the bargain after all."

"I agreed to a proper courtship. And you clearly do not know what that is."

"Confound it all, I do know—" He broke off, realizing he had sunk in way over his head. "Fine. Then tell your damned brother to go to perdition. Because if I don't have your company, he doesn't get Louisa's."

He stormed out, nearly colliding with Miss Tremaine, who was eavesdropping outside the door. He paused just long enough to cast her a dark glance. "Congratulations. You're rid of me at last."

Then he fled.

Chapter Eleven

*Young charges can be sly in their ways. A good
chaperone must anticipate every eventuality.*
—Miss Cicely Tremaine, *The Ideal Chaperone*

Marcus threw himself into his carriage and roared at the
coachman to go on. A pox on her, a pox on them all. He
must have been insane to enter into such a nightmare bargain in the first place. Lessons! The chit wanted to get him
lessons in deportment, for God's sake!

"Marcus, are you all right?" Louisa asked from the seat
opposite his.

"I'm fine." Wonderful, now that he'd banished Lady
Lofty from his life.

No more nights spent at his brother's town house to
avoid the long drive back to Castlemaine. No more livery
costs for his horses and carriage. No more dressing for the
evening just to have a haughty female criticize the cut of
his coat.

No more sparring with that razor-tongued witch. No
more stimulating exchanges. No more hot, ravening kisses
in the dark. No more forbidden tastes of her honey-sweet
flesh . . .

Damn the wench, why did she do this to him?

It didn't matter; it was over now. So what if she thought he was incapable of behaving himself? That's what he wanted, wasn't it?

No, damn it. He wanted to prove that her friends were a pack of wolves who would tear the average gentleman to shreds. That his sister would never be welcomed among them because of their idiotic expectations.

Not because he couldn't follow the rules. He could be as much a gentleman as the next fellow if he chose.

That's what incompetent fellows always protest when they don't know how to dance or behave properly or say the right things.

Great God, she was driving him mad!

"Marcus?" Louisa said, into the rumbling noise of the carriage. "Did you mean what you said? That Simon and you and I could go riding together?"

Damn. Now he had to deal with Louisa's expectations. "The situation has changed."

Even in the grey half-light of street and carriage lamps, he could see his sister's frown. "How so?"

"Foxmoor will no longer be accompanying you places."

An alarming paleness spread over her cheeks. "Why not?"

"Because he won't, that's all."

Louisa glared at him. "I take it that you said something horrible to Lady Regina. That's why she was so cool to you. Oh, Marcus, what did you do?"

He hadn't told Louisa of his bargain with Regina, but his sister was no fool. She had to know that his association with Regina would necessarily affect hers with Foxmoor. "What makes you think *I* did anything? She's the one with the lofty standards and the condescension and—"

"She's perfectly lovely, and you know it." Louisa settled

back against the squabs with an exasperated sigh. "But you just had to go and ruin things with her."

"I refuse to court a woman who's always trying to make me into something I'm not."

"You mean a gentleman?"

Not Louisa, too. Was he ever to escape this female snobbery? "I'm already a gentleman, damn it."

"You don't act like one. It's just as I told Simon—"

"Simon?" Had things already progressed so far that they were on a first-name basis?

She colored. "Yes. He and I have known each other for over a month now."

He rolled his eyes. "Haven't you ever wondered why a wealthy duke of such great connections would court the daughter of our rumor-laden mother?"

"As a matter of fact, I have. So I asked him about it. And he told me he'd met our mother as a boy and thought she was a good person."

"Compared to whom? Jezebel?"

She frowned. "I know Mama treated you harshly sometimes, but she could be kind—"

"How would you know? She was never around. She didn't care enough about either of us to stay home."

Louisa flinched, then turned her gaze out the window. Damn. He hadn't meant to dredge that up and wound her feelings.

But when she returned her gaze to him, her eyes were sharp as a pair of hat pins. "This is not about Mama. I'm in love with Simon—that's all that matters."

This night got worse by the moment. "But is he in love with you?"

She set her shoulders. "I believe so, yes."

"Has he said so?"

"Not yet. But we've only begun to court. And now you mean to end it before I can even find out how he feels."

"He's not good enough for you, and as your guardian, I must act according to my conscience."

"You thought he was good enough for me when you were courting Regina."

He opted for honesty. "Actually, I didn't even then. But I believed that you would see the truth if I gave him the chance to court you."

"Which gave *you* the chance to court Regina." She sniffed. "So now you expect Simon and me to part, simply because you stupidly hurt her feelings."

"Are you mad? Hurt her feelings, indeed. You saw how coldly she treated me this evening."

"Because you behaved like an ill-mannered lout. I don't blame her. If you ever treated me like that, I'd never speak to you again." She leaned forward to clasp his hand with that earnest expression that always boded trouble. "When you want to, you can be perfectly charming, like when you talk to Lady Iversley. So I don't understand why now that you have a woman who is interested in you—"

"Lady Regina isn't interested in me." He jerked his hand from her grasp. Louisa was supposed to condemn that confounded female, not take her side. "She considers me beneath her touch. If you can't see that, you're blind."

"You're the one who's blind. Haven't you seen her watching you?"

He stared at her. "What do you mean?"

"Regina watches you with those furtive glances a lady uses only for a gentleman she wants."

Ruthlessly, he ignored the sudden leap in his pulse. *If Regina wanted him, it was only to satisfy her virginal cu-*

riosity with a dangerous male. "She watches me to mark my many lapses in gentlemanly behavior."

"Oh? Then why does she ask me so many personal questions about you?"

He caught his breath. "Like what?"

"Where you went to school. Why you won't spend money on clothes." She arched an eyebrow. "If you've always been such a grump."

That a respectable woman, *any* woman, would ask about him stunned him. Yes, Regina had responded to his kisses, but he'd never guessed she might be interested in him otherwise. The possibility intrigued him. Which made it dangerous. "What did you tell her?"

"You'll have to ask *her.* I would never relate a private conversation."

"You just related—" He bit back a curse, fighting the urge to take his sister over his knee for the first time in his life. "Never mind. I don't care what you gossiping females said behind my back."

She sighed. "Oh, Marcus, I know you like her. Why not apologize? Do what you must to get her back?"

"I am not apologizing to that harpy!" Not if he could help it. He couldn't do much about Regina, but he could damned well control his sister. "Regardless of the situation between Regina and me, you are not to see Foxmoor."

She thrust her chin out mutinously. "No?"

"No," he said firmly. "And that is my final word on the subject."

"I see."

His eyes narrowed. "You will obey me in this."

"Of course. Whatever you say."

"No protests?" he said uneasily. "No objections?"

"None." She cast him a distinctly Regina-like smile, and his blood ran cold.

She'll resent you even more for your stubbornness, Regina had told him at Castlemaine, *which will give her justification for deceiving you at every turn.*

God help him. Louisa would do it, too. Being out in society had emboldened her. If he stopped going about with her in London, he'd have only the Iversleys to rely on—who were absorbed with their new marriage and their new baby and who weren't entirely convinced that his concerns about Foxmoor were valid.

Damn, damn, damn.

He could join them in chaperoning Louisa, but that meant going into society and seeing Regina at every party, with sycophants like that confounded Whitmore slobbering at her feet. He'd rather have his fingernails removed with pincers.

Not that he could get himself invited to the parties Louisa would want to attend, anyway. Although his association with Regina had garnered him an invitation or two, those would dry up as soon as she asked her friends to stop inviting him.

Which brought him back to relying on the Iversleys to watch Louisa.

He gritted his teeth. Too bad he couldn't lock his sister in the dungeon. But Regina was liable to find out and engineer her escape, then give the girl refuge in her own home. *Foxmoor's* home. Better to have his enemies right under his nose where he could keep an eye on them.

Perhaps it was time to change his tactics. His first plan hadn't worked the way he'd wanted; Louisa was still on Regina's side. And if Regina told his sister that she'd thrown him over because he was some drooling idiot who didn't know "gentlemanly deportment," Louisa would make his life hell. Or they'd both join forces against him, God forbid.

A "proper" courtship might be more effective. He could keep an eye on Simon and Louisa more easily if he wasn't always trying to infuriate Regina, and the result would be the same in the end. Because if he behaved like a gentleman and Lady Lofty saw that society condemned him anyway, she would still break with him.

But Louisa wouldn't be able to blame *him* for it. Once she saw Regina heartlessly spurning him despite his efforts to please, Louisa would surely side with him. Then she'd break with Simon, too, for how could she let him court her after his sister had mistreated Marcus?

"All right, you win," he said. "I'll get Lady Regina back."

"And Simon can still court me?"

Her hopeful expression made him groan. "For the moment."

With any luck, his new plan would put her squarely on his side. If it didn't, he just might have to resort to his dungeon after all.

Perhaps he should put Regina in it, instead of his sister. A variation on his dream last night flitted through his mind—Regina locked up in his dungeon, offering to do anything that might please him. Regina kneeling at his feet, her hair tumbled about her shoulders, her siren's mouth begging him to take her to his bed. Regina naked, without a harp to shield her from his gaze—

"So how do you mean to get her back?" his sister asked.

His fantasy evaporated, leaving him uncomfortably aroused. Setting his hat on his lap, he forced himself to concentrate on her question. "I don't know."

"Might I make a suggestion?"

He sighed. "Why not?

"If you want to impress Regina . . ."

Hours later, Marcus found himself on the threshold of the Blue Swan in the pouring rain, demanding to see his half brother. After leaving Louisa at the Iversleys, he'd gone to Byrne's house, only to learn from the butler that Byrne never came home before 4:00 A.M. Such was the life of a gaming club owner.

And since this was the first time Marcus had entered the club through the front, the porter gave him trouble.

"But you aren't a member, sir," the man said, his upper lip curling in distaste at the sight of Marcus's unfashionable overcoat and dripping beard. "No one can enter who is not a member or a guest of a member."

"If you don't fetch the owner at once, I swear I will—"

"Draker!" his brother exclaimed, coming out into the hall. "What the hell are you doing here?"

"Trying to see you," he snapped.

"By coming through the front door of my club?" Byrne waved the porter aside. "What a novel idea."

"Very funny." Marcus stepped inside and stamped his feet to dislodge the mud that had accumulated in his travels about town. "I'm not in the mood for your humor tonight."

As the porter took Marcus's soaked coat and hat with a look of disdain, Byrne chuckled, not the least bit perturbed. He led Marcus to his offices. "What's wrong that would bring you out in this weather?"

"Nothing that eradicating the entire female race wouldn't cure."

"Ah. Woman trouble."

They entered the office, and Byrne closed the door.

"Women are a plague upon the earth." Marcus headed for the fire to warm his chilled hands.

"You're just now discovering that?"

Marcus cast him a foul look. "You don't seem to have trouble with them."

"Because I keep them in their place. The minute one of them starts trying to make my life a misery, I move on to the next."

"I don't have that choice. One of the troublemakers is Louisa."

"Can't help you with that, I'm afraid. I have no sisters, thank God. So if you're here for advice—"

"I'm here because I need a favor."

Byrne's eyes burned with curiosity. Though Marcus, Iversley, and Byrne had all sworn to lend each other aid whenever asked, Marcus had never required Byrne's help before. "What sort of favor?" he asked.

Marcus stared into the fire. "I need a voucher for Almack's."

"I already told Iversley that the Lady Patronesses don't meet until Monday. While I'm sure that Louisa's application will be approved, I can't guarantee—"

"It's not for Louisa." He gritted his teeth. "I need one for me."

There was a long moment of shocked silence. Then Byrne began to chuckle. Then laugh. Then howl like a pack of children run amok.

Marcus whirled to face him. "It's not that funny."

"Oh yes . . . it is . . ." Byrne choked out between guffaws. "The idea of you . . . in that place . . . with all those humorless bitches . . ."

"Can you get it or not?"

Byrne's laughter died. "My God, you're serious."

"Of course I'm serious. You think I'd come here in the wee hours of the morning just to tweak your nose about something like that? I've got better things to do with my time."

"Like go to Almack's." Byrne erupted into laughter again.

Marcus wanted to choke him. "If you *can't* get me the voucher—"

"Then nobody else can either," Byrne put in quickly, as Marcus's dire glance stifled the rest of his fit of humor. "As it is, I'll have to call in every marker to manage it."

"Isn't one of your former mistresses a Lady Patroness?"

"Yes, but even she can only go so far to sway the rest of them."

"I thought they tend to approve men of title because they're good catches."

Byrne snorted. "Somehow I doubt that the term 'good catch' includes men who bear nicknames with the word 'dragon' in them. Or who wear thick beards. Or dress in clothes more outdated than the lowest servant's. Or—"

"Enough. I take your meaning." Confound it all, the man was as bad as Regina. "I can't do anything about what I'm called, but I thought you might suggest . . . that is, if you have a tailor you use regularly—"

"Certainly," Byrne said, thankfully staving off the rest of his humiliating speech. "My fellow will get you fixed up in no time or kill himself trying."

"I'll need the voucher—and the clothes—for the assembly Wednesday."

"You don't ask for much, do you?" Byrne sighed. "I can't get you a voucher by then, but I can get you a Stranger's Ticket. Assuming Louisa receives her voucher, you can attend as her guest . . . *if* you pass muster when you present yourself to the patronesses."

Present himself? Like some schoolboy? Marcus nearly told Byrne to forget the whole thing. But to get Regina back, he had to do this right. "Fine."

"You'll have to promise to behave with decorum."

"Of course."

"Are you sure you know how?"

Not entirely. Now that his initial anger at Regina's comments had waned, he realized there was some truth to her words. It had been years since he'd even attempted to be correct in society. What if he'd forgotten how? What if he made a fool of himself?

He snorted. As if they cared how he behaved—no matter what he did, they would shun him. But he had to make the attempt, for Louisa's sake.

"Marcus?" his brother prodded.

"Yes, with decorum. You'll have to remind me what that is."

His brother grinned. "Certainly. To the extent that *I* know what it is." His grin faded. "There's more, however. You'll have to cut your hair."

"I know."

"And get rid of your beard."

Damn. He'd started growing it on the day a maidservant fainted at the sight of his scar. The whiskers had covered his face for nigh on nine years now. "My scar will show," he said tightly as he picked up the poker to stoke the fire.

"The Lady Patronesses care less about scars than fashion. And with the war over and our brave soldiers coming home, scars are all the crack."

He doubted that his would be, but he had no choice.

"Fine," he said, staring down at the hot poker. "I'll shave off the beard."

A long silence passed before Byrne said, "She really got to you, didn't she?"

Lost in the past, he said, "Who?"

"La Belle Dame Sans Merci."

Marcus thrust the poker onto the rack. "Don't be absurd."

"She's quite a beauty. And I suppose she knows it, too."

You want only my body . . .

He stiffened. "Yes, she knows it. But she's not vain about it, if that's what you mean."

"Ah. And is she as heartless as they say?"

"She's refused eleven proposals of marriage," he said evasively. "What do you think?"

His brother stood and lowered his voice. "I think you should be careful, man. The woman was bred for better fellows than you."

Marcus rounded on him with a glower. "First you, then Iversley. What sort of sniveling coxcomb do you two take me for? I told you this is just a bargain. I'm only courting her to keep an eye on Foxmoor."

"So you say. But she's brought many a man to his knees in the past."

"I know how to guard myself against her kind of woman, for God's sake. I was twenty-two when I left society. Before then, I suffered often enough through jokes about my size and my lack of interest in the fine arts of cravat-folding, card-playing, and empty flattery." He gave a harsh laugh. "Then there were the many girls too high in the instep to countenance the attentions of a young man with a Jezebel for a mother. Even though the law considers me legitimate, I've had gossip about my parentage whispered by plenty of those 'refined' girls—"

"So have I," Byrne broke in. "But I spent years learning how to turn my unfortunate birth to my advantage. I've figured out what makes those 'refined' women want a man, and I use it to have them groveling at my feet."

"Behind their husband's backs."

"And in front of them, if I can get away with it." Byrne's eyes sparked blue as sapphires. "No one calls me bastard to my face anymore, you can be sure of that. Most of them can't afford to get on my bad side." For a moment, he looked more menacing than any demon spawned by hell.

Then he forced a smile. "But you, dear brother, have spent the last third of your life in a cave. And now a stunning female has deigned to let you court her, which you can't help but find flattering—"

"I am not the smitten fool you and Iversley take me for," Marcus snapped. "I have matters well in hand. So do I get my Stranger's Ticket for Almack's or not?"

"I'll do my best." A grin creased his face. "But God help Almack's if I succeed."

Chapter Twelve

One is always safe with one's charge
at Almack's.
—Miss Cicely Tremaine, *The Ideal Chaperone*

Regina's fingers flew over the strings of her harp as she searched for the configuration of notes that would express her discontent. But the harp just wasn't made for that sort of music. What she needed was a soulful violin. Or cymbals. That she could bash upon a certain man's head.

"Are you sure you don't want some tea?" came a plaintive voice from the table across the room.

Cicely was scribbling in that little book she always carried, the one that she called a diary. Regina wondered, rather unkindly, what Cicely could possibly have to write about in a diary. Her life lacked any real excitement.

Rather like Regina's. She scowled and attacked her favorite piece of music with a vengeance, wishing it sounded less . . . pretty. "I'm not in the mood for tea."

"Perhaps you would like me to read to you—"

"No!" When Cicely winced, she softened her tone. "I am definitely not in the mood to hear a book read." Or to remember that Marcus preferred them to her.

Her fingers fell slack on the strings.

"You're better off without him, you know," Cicely said.

Regina's head shot up, and she colored to see her cousin eyeing her as if she could read every thought in her head.

"That's why you've been snapping at everyone lately, isn't it? Because the two of you argued and Lord Draker ended your courtship?"

"Don't be absurd. He didn't end it; *I* did."

"Because he wouldn't do what you wanted."

And because he was lying to her for his own horrible purposes. She'd tried to wound his pride, make him admit that he'd been using her to drive Louisa and Simon apart. But instead of wounding *his* pride, she'd shattered her own.

It had been four days since he'd stormed out of here. Since then, not a word. How could Marcus abandon their agreement so casually?

"I don't know why it disturbs you so," Cicely went on. "He's not good enough for you. You've ignored many a finer gentleman. Why, you generally don't even spare a second thought for a man after he leaves your presence."

True. But those gentlemen generally pined for *her*. And that's what Marcus should be doing, crawling back to her on his knees, begging her to forgive him.

She snorted. Dragons didn't beg. They consumed and devoured and lumbered about, setting fire to things for the sheer fun of it.

The way Marcus had set fire to her passions.

I stood in chains, envying that damned harp for getting to lie between your thighs and brush the very places I wanted to touch . . .

As heat flamed in all those places, she jerked back from the harp, nearly oversetting it. Dratted oaf. Wasn't it enough that he invaded her sleep, provoking dreams of wildly improbable situations that all ended with his doing naughty things to her? Must he now intrude upon even her favorite pastime?

Every time she settled the harp between her legs, she remembered his hand rubbing her down there, firm and warm and erotic. Every time her breasts brushed the gilded sound box, she imagined his mouth sucking her nipples . . .

She groaned. This was ridiculous. "I wouldn't care in the least what Lord Draker did if not for how it affected Simon and Louisa," she told her cousin.

Cicely eyed her closely. "It doesn't seem to have affected them at all. Granted, Miss North has claimed to be indisposed for the past three days whenever your brother called on her. But apparently he was allowed to see her today."

This was the first she'd heard of any of that. She'd put off telling Simon about her argument with Draker, expecting him to mention it any moment. Yet he hadn't. "How do you know?"

Cicely shrugged. "Simon told me he was going there when he asked my advice regarding a gift he was bringing her."

"Why didn't he ask me?"

Cicely busied herself with straightening the sheet music. "He said he did not want to tempt your foul mood."

"Well, he might have gone to see her, but that doesn't mean he was allowed in."

"He must have been. He told me later that his gift was a success."

"Oh." Falling back against her chair, Regina stared blankly into space. When Marcus had stomped out of here, he'd said he would put an end to any courtship between Simon and Louisa. Yet he hadn't. What did that mean?

"What are you two doing in here at this late hour?" said a voice from the doorway to the music room. "It's nearly five o'clock."

Regina jerked her head up to see her brother leaning in. Ignoring him, she returned to practicing her harp.

"Hello, Simon," Cicely said.

He glanced over to her. "Aren't you going to Almack's this evening?"

Cicely looked expectantly at Regina.

"No," Regina said. "I'm not in the mood."

"She's not in the mood," Cicely repeated primly.

"Deuce take it, Ciss, I heard her." He stalked in and headed for the harp. "Regina, you always go to Almack's when there's an assembly."

Regina's fingers fairly flew over the strings. "I'm skipping a night. What do you care?"

"Don't take that tone with me. What the devil did *I* do?"

Thanks to you, I entered the dragon's lair and came out singed.

She couldn't entirely blame him for that. "I'm sorry. I don't feel like going out tonight, that's all."

The thought of making small talk for the millionth time with people who cared only about their fashions and the latest *on-dit* held less appeal than it used to.

Simon jerked her harp forward, leaving her fingers plucking thin air.

"Simon!" she protested as she reached for the instrument.

He hefted it out of her reach. "You *have* to go. I'm taking Louisa tonight."

How could that be? "You hate Almack's."

"Yes, but she just received her voucher, and she's dying to attend, so you and Cicely must come along to chaperone. Lady Iversley is indisposed, probably with the same cold that plagued Louisa this week. But Draker said it would be all right as long as the two of you come, too."

Her heart pounded. "Lord Draker was at the Iversleys? You talked to him?"

"Of course. He was being his usual rude self, insisting that Louisa could only go if you went, but that shouldn't surprise you. That *is* part of your bargain with him, isn't it?"

Not anymore. Why hadn't Marcus told him? Could the man have changed his mind about Louisa and Simon? And if he had, what did it mean? That he had relinquished the battle entirely to her?

Impossible. The man was too thickheaded to do such a thing. But if he had some other purpose for this new tactic, she could not figure out what it might be.

"Does Lord Draker mean to go to Almack's, too?" she asked, trying for a nonchalant tone. "He told me he doesn't have a voucher."

"I suppose that's true. And he didn't mention going, so he probably isn't."

Now she was thoroughly confused. If he didn't go, then he was entrusting Louisa to her and Cicely and Simon. When he didn't trust *any* of them with his sister. What was she to make of that?

"But he did ask after you," Simon went on. "Said he'd been too busy at Castlemaine to come to town the past few days."

"I see," she said dully. Oh, yes, she understood perfectly.

He'd simply decided to ignore her for a while. The wretch refused to do as she asked, but he probably thought to weaken her resolve with this gesture. Perhaps he assumed that a few days apart from him would soften her temper.

Arrogant beast.

"So there's no reason for you not to come with us tonight," Simon went on. "You can enjoy yourself without Draker around to muck things up."

"While that is an appealing prospect, I am not in the mood to field people's sly questions and comments about him. Besides, you really don't need me along. Cicely is sufficient as a chaperone. And since Lord Draker won't be there, he won't care that I'm not."

"He said you had to come."

"Then he knows what he has to do to gain my compliance." Realizing how much she'd revealed, she rose to retrieve her harp.

Simon eyed her closely. "I take it that something serious happened between you and Draker at the opera."

She clasped her harp by the neck. "I don't know what you mean."

He glanced over to where Cicely was drinking in every word. "Ciss, go dress for Almack's. Regina will be there in a moment."

"I will not," Regina protested, but their cousin was already headed out the door. She never disobeyed a direct command.

As soon as she was gone, Simon faced Regina. "I saw Whitmore today."

Alarm seized her. She forced her voice to sound calm. "Did you?"

"He took me to task for letting a man like Draker spend time with you. I explained to him about our wager—"

"You *what*?" She shot him a glare. "What right did you have to do that?"

"I was doing you a favor. He wants to marry you, and I didn't want to ruin your chances by letting him think you're seriously considering marriage to Draker."

"For your information, Henry has already asked me twice to marry him, and both times I turned him down."

"I see." Simon surprised her by smiling. "I can't say I'm disappointed. The man's a silly ass, but since you prefer silly asses in general—"

"I do not." A blush suffused her face. How could her brother understand her so little?

But then, they hadn't exactly spent much time together. By the time she'd grown old enough to know him, he'd already gone off to Eton. After his return, he'd spent all his time with the prince and his friends. Even after Father died a few years ago, and Simon became head of the family, he'd taken for granted that she could handle her own affairs and left her to do pretty much as she pleased.

Until recently.

"All the same," Simon went on, "Whitmore made some vague statements about Draker's not being a gentleman worthy of you. And when I pressed him, he wouldn't give any details."

Thank heavens. "He's only jealous."

Simon arched an eyebrow. "I asked Cicely about it, and she claimed not to know what happened. Either she's lying, or she really doesn't know, and since Cicely never lies to me, it must be the latter. So I expect *you* to tell me."

Dropping her gaze from his, Regina ran her finger over the harp's intricately carved and gilded neck. "Henry insulted Lord Draker, and the viscount was his usual rude self. That's all there was to it."

"I doubt that." Stepping up to the harp, Simon set his

hand on the gilded wood next to hers. "Since Whitmore will be at Almack's tonight, perhaps I should speak to him again. He might be more forthcoming about what happened if I offer him some incentive, like a promise that I will fully support his suit."

Her gaze shot to his, and the sudden steely blue of his eyes made her shiver. "You wouldn't tell him such a thing—why, you just called him a 'silly ass.' "

"True, but who knows what I'll say if I'm bored. Without you and Cicely and Louisa at Almack's to distract me, I'll have nothing to do but talk to Henry."

She glared at him. This was blackmail. Very effective blackmail. She wasn't entirely certain Marcus's dire threats would keep her jealous cousin from voicing his nasty suspicions if he thought it might profit him. "All right, I'll go to Almack's. But I can't promise to be good company."

He shrugged. "I don't need you to be good company. I just need you to be there."

When he turned and sauntered out of the room with his usual smug assurance that he'd gotten his way, she succumbed to the childish urge to stick out her tongue at him.

Drat her brother. And drat Marcus, too, for putting her in this position. She couldn't let Simon find out the truth about the encounter between Marcus and Henry. He would almost certainly make a fuss about it.

But hours later, as she and the rest of their party approached the grand staircase through the crowded foyer, she regretted letting Simon bully her into coming here. What was wrong with her? She liked assemblies. She enjoyed the dancing and the conversation; she delighted in seeing who was wearing what.

If it had all grown a little wearisome in recent years, it was only because she worried about whom Simon might marry and bring into their household. It had nothing to do with boredom on her part. No, indeed.

So why were her spirits flagging just at the sight of the long, spare ballroom with its six towering windows that loomed like dreary sentinels above the throng? Why did even the orchestra sound tinny tonight?

This was absurd—she refused to let Simon or Marcus or Henry or any of the men bedeviling her life destroy her enjoyment of an evening of dancing and music. She would dance her feet off tonight if it killed her.

She danced with Mr. Markham, widely considered to be a wit, then picked apart his every bon mot. She danced with Lord Brackley, and then couldn't follow his intricate footwork, although she generally matched him step for step.

An interminable hour had passed by the time the smooth-tongued Lord Peter Wilkins took her to the floor for a reel. Thank heavens the reel allowed for little conversation. If she heard one more high-flown compliment voiced by one more gushing gentleman eager to impress her with his superior wit, she'd surely scream.

Whatever had happened to actual conversation? Or for that matter, blunt honesty? And why did she suddenly crave such a preposterous thing?

"You'll never believe who just came in," Lord Peter murmured, as they took their places and waited for the music to begin.

"Who?" she asked, though she doubted it was anyone she cared about.

"Your latest beau. Draker."

She froze. How could *he* be here? Louisa had said nothing, and the Lady Patronesses would never have given him a voucher, even if he'd been willing to ask for one.

On the other hand, was even Marcus insane enough to force his way into Almack's? Half-afraid to look, she turned toward the door, her heart pounding. Then her breath caught in her throat. Because the man who skirted the ballroom was not the Lord Draker she knew.

This man was a prince's son, regal in manner and walk and appearance, especially appearance. He wore the latest fashions, and his unkempt, overly long hair had been cut and styled in waves that framed the stark contours of his now-shaved face.

Her pulse stammered into an erratic rhythm. He'd shaved off his beard, bought new clothes, and somehow, miraculously, attained entrance to Almack's.

Was it for her? Because of what she'd told him? Or for some other reason she could not fathom? She was almost afraid to believe he'd done it for her—he'd disappointed her too bitterly before.

And yet . . . he'd shaved off his beard, just as she'd once asked him to do. That had to mean something.

Especially considering that the thick scar bisecting his right cheek was every bit as severe as he'd claimed. Oddly enough, it was perfectly straight, not the jagged scar she would have expected from a fall from a horse. It was long, too, stretching from the upper curve of his cheek right down to the edge of his chin. That he would have willingly exposed the scar he'd said was too unsightly for a lady made her heart race.

That wasn't the only thing making her heart race. If not for the scar, he'd be blindingly handsome, especially when dressed in such fine clothes. His snow-white cravat had clearly been tied by an expert, and his coat of ebony silk fit him so exquisitely that only Beau Brummell's tailor could have matched it.

And Lord, those knee breeches! She dragged in a breath. She'd guessed that he had fine legs, but it had been hard to be sure from his ill-fitting trousers. Now she knew she'd been right, for the well-wrought muscles in his thighs and calves were displayed to good effect in the requisite white breeches and stockings.

All of a sudden, she remembered how glorious it had felt to rub her secret place against those firm, amazing thighs . . .

Chastising herself for such outrageous thoughts, she jerked her gaze up, only to find Marcus staring right at her. While she gawked at him as shamelessly as the rest of the idiots around her.

Heat flooded her face. But before she could do more than smile at him, the music began, and she had to dance.

If you could call it that. It was difficult to pay attention to the steps when she burned with a hundred unanswered questions. How had he managed to get in? Why had he come? *Was it for her?*

Her gaze wandered to him more often than she liked. Now he was speaking to his sister and Simon. When her dance with Lord Peter was done, she saw him take Louisa to the floor while Regina herself was led there by some dull fellow with whom she'd forgotten she'd agreed to dance.

Two more tedious dances with tedious fellows followed while he partnered Cicely, of all people, then a widow notorious for her many lovers. Earlier, Regina had thought the woman interesting. Now she thought her far too pretty.

When the widow flirted and smiled and seemed to be enjoying his company, Regina chafed at the sight of it. The entrance of the Iversleys moments later completed her misery. So much for Marcus trusting her to chaperone.

He'd only used that as a ruse to get her here, so she could witness his grand appearance.

So that was the way of it, was it? Marcus thought to come here and prove her wrong by looking devilishly handsome and lordly while he danced attendance on every doe-eyed female who batted her eyelashes in his direction?

Fine. Let him have his fun. She would not give him the satisfaction of showing that she cared. Because she didn't. No, indeed. Not one jot.

She was so busy not caring that by the time the waltz came, she had no chance to compose herself before he appeared before her, over six feet of finely groomed, exquisitely dressed male. To her chagrin, she began to quiver with anticipation. Drat the man.

Her agitation increased when he gave her a courtly bow, and said, "If you are not otherwise engaged, may I have the honor of this dance?"

A courteously worded request—would wonders never cease? She could only manage a nod.

As they found a spot on the floor, her pulse beat a thunderous rhythm. She'd never danced with him, despite having allowed him the most outrageous liberties.

A delicious shiver swept down her spine as he faced her and took her gloved hand in his. With his other hand, he clasped her waist, keeping the several inches between them that propriety demanded. It was only when she dared to look into his face that she saw him gazing at her with anything but propriety.

Whatever starch was left in her spine drained away, and all her questions burst out of her mouth at once. "What . . . how did you . . . When did you . . ."

"Don't tell me I've rendered La Belle Dame speechless at last." A faint smile touched the lips that looked far more sensuous without a mustache shading them. "I hadn't thought that possible."

As heat leaped into her cheeks, she tipped up her chin. "I thought you'd turned yourself into a gentleman, but if you're already resorting to insults—"

"Teasing, not insults." His smile broadened. "You said you wanted me to behave like a gentleman; you didn't say I had to be boring."

As if he could ever be boring.

The music began, and he swept her into the waltz with the grace that comes of plenty of practice. Yet another astonishment. She could understand his being able to manage the country dances, but the waltz was recently come to England. Not even everyone at Almack's had mastered it.

"How on earth did you learn to dance the waltz out at Castlemaine?" she asked, as he turned her expertly around the floor.

"Who do you think partnered Louisa in all her dancing lessons?" He frowned at the crowd around them. "Though I confess I've never had so little space to dance it in."

Only then did she notice how the crowd had closed in, every couple straining to get closer, to hear what was going on between La Belle Dame and the Dragon Viscount now that he'd shown up looking like a lord.

"Everyone's curious about you, it seems," she said, "and they're not alone. I'm dying to know what you're doing here."

A dark smile touched his lips. "You didn't think an incompetent fellow like me could get in, did you?"

She winced to have her words thrown back in her face. "I thought you wouldn't make the attempt. Don't tell me you actually stooped to solicit a voucher from 'that lot of vultures,' as you termed them."

"No. Another man solicited it on my behalf, a man who himself would never be allowed to darken these hallowed halls. Fortunately, my title and name were enough to gain me a 'Stranger's Ticket.' They let me in as Louisa's guest."

Which meant he'd had to present himself to the Lady Patronesses for approval. Her blood quickened. That could not have been easy for him. So what was she to make of that? "That explains how you came to be here. But not why."

"You know perfectly well why. You issued a challenge I could not ignore."

"What challenge?" she said, pretending ignorance.

"To prove that I'm not an idiot who can't carry himself in society." He jerked his head to indicate a nearby couple sneaking none-too-subtle peeks at them. "Not that it matters. It's just as I told you—I could be clothed in pure gold from head to toe, and they would still regard me with contempt."

"Look again," she said softly. "That is not contempt on their faces."

He swept his gaze beyond her. She followed it, wondering if he could see what she did. Yes, there was an ample amount of curiosity on most of their faces, but that was all. Only the people who'd already met him—and been insulted by him—eyed him askance, and even with them it was more wariness than contempt.

His gaze swung back to her, and his mouth tightened into a grim line. "They're all staring at my face. At my scar."

She hesitated. If she simply dismissed his scar as unimportant, he would not believe her. Better to be honest. "Of course they are. It's splendidly awful."

He arched one brow. "Not quite how I would have described it."

"That's because you're used to it. But the rest of us . . ." She let her gaze linger on his scar. "We can't help looking at it. It's like a brand distinguishing a Thoroughbred from a lot of nags. It sets you apart."

His grip on her hand tightened. "A brand? Interesting choice of words."

She examined it, noting how it puckered. "Not really. It resembles a severe burn I once saw. I heard that you got your scar in a riding accident, but it doesn't look right for that."

Judging from his suddenly rigid posture, she'd hit upon the truth. "How would you know what a scar from a riding accident looks like?"

"I volunteer at the Chelsea Hospital from time to time. I've seen enough healed wounds to know the difference between a burn and the sort of gash one would get from a fall."

"*You?* Volunteer at a hospital?" he said, his tone skeptical.

"Careful now," she warned. "You're veering dangerously close to ungentlemanly territory. And after you've done so well, too."

He bristled at her deliberate attempt to provoke him, and she waited for the inevitably rude response.

It never came. He gathered in his breath as if setting himself to an onerous task. "Then perhaps we should change the subject."

A surprised smile broke over her face. "Yes, perhaps we should."

Not that she wanted to. He hadn't confirmed how he'd received his scar. She was convinced it was a burn, but how did one get burned so badly there and nowhere else?

"So does this mean that you plan to let Louisa and Simon court, after all?" she asked.

"As long as you let me court *you*. I think I've proved I can be gentleman enough to suit your finicky tastes."

She arched one eyebrow. "Not yet, you haven't. Dressing well and dancing one waltz without insulting me scarcely proves anything."

"Then I'll have to do better, won't I?" His hand caressed her waist, causing her silly heart to flutter. "And perhaps later, you can reward me for my efforts."

"Virtue is its own reward," she said primly.

He laughed, the low rumble curling a knot of longing in her belly. "We aren't talking about virtue, dearling. We're talking about nonsensical requirements that you ladies impose on us men to make us fit for your company. And if I follow them, I expect something in return." He bent close. "If you know what I mean."

Her pulse burst into a gallop. "I know you're being impertinent."

He grinned. "As I recall, you enjoy some impertinence from time to time." His eyes smoldered down at her. "In its proper place, of course."

Swallowing hard, she dropped her eyes to his immaculate cravat. She should not encourage his presumption. But five nights of reliving every caress of his presumptuous hands and mouth and tongue had whetted her appetite for more. More kisses. More fondling.

More outrageous advances.

Now he was holding her much too close. She could smell the bay rum and soap on him. The sheer size of the man enthralled her, made her feel protected, safe . . . desired. Dangerously desired. "You shouldn't hold me so close."

"Probably not," he murmured.

"People will talk."

"Let them."

Thank heavens the waltz ended before he had reduced her to a spineless ninny in his arms. But his words lingered as he led her from the floor, his gloved hand lying warm and possessive over hers. *Perhaps later, you can reward me for my efforts.* Sweet heaven, the very idea sent her senses reeling.

Which was probably why she didn't notice Lady Hungate's approach until the pesky woman was upon them.

The marchioness eyed Marcus through her lorgnette. "I don't know what the Lady Patronesses were thinking to allow you into Almack's, sir."

Regina tensed.

"I could say the same for you, madam," Marcus drawled. But just as Lady Hungate's brow lowered in a scowl, he added, "We are both too clever for the likes of Almack's. Thank God they were too blinded by our other charms to realize it."

Regina held her breath, watching the odd display of emotions over Lady Hungate's face—first disbelief, then wariness. But since Lady Hungate prided herself on her cleverness, her face settled at last into a cool smile. "So you no longer wish to see me horsewhipped, Lord Draker?"

Regina held her breath.

He lowered his voice to a husky whisper. "Haven't you heard the rumors about me, Lady Hungate? I always like to see pretty ladies whipped. But only in my dungeon, and only for our mutual enjoyment."

Oh, Lord. Mutual enjoyment from such a thing—was the man daft? To Regina's astonishment, the marchioness snapped open her fan, fluttering it furiously as she turned to Regina with an arch look. "Take care, my dear. I'm not sure you're ready for the sophisticated tastes of his lordship."

Casting Marcus a smile that could only be called coy, she sashayed off like some fifteen-year-old chit fresh from the schoolroom.

Regina let out her breath in a whoosh. "I can't believe you just said that to her. And that she didn't cut you dead right there."

"I can't believe it either," he admitted ruefully. "But you did once tell me to use the rumors to my advantage. And I couldn't deny I'd ever mentioned horsewhipping."

"You were lucky she reacted so well to your . . . ridiculous insinuations."

Marcus gave a short laugh. "Luck had nothing to do with it. Lady Hungate and my mother were good friends once upon a time; both had a taste for the bawdy and the outrageous. In her younger days, Lady Hungate was rumored to have a lover with . . . shall we say . . . 'ridiculous' tastes."

"But surely a woman would not . . . could not . . ."

"Enjoy such a thing? Some women do, though I can't imagine why."

"But Lady Hungate?"

"Why do you think she brought horsewhipping to my mind the first time?" He winked at her. Marcus actually winked! "I did have a life before my exile at Castlemaine, you know. And my mother was an inveterate gossip."

"So was mine, but . . . but—"

"You think she would have told her innocent daughter about such things? Hardly. But that doesn't mean they don't exist."

She gazed at him with new awareness. He was not as cut

off from society as she had assumed. He could handle himself when he chose. "I was right, wasn't I?"

"About what?"

"You *were* behaving badly to break Simon and Louisa apart. Courting me was only a tactic to provoke one of them into breaking off their courtship."

He searched her face. "Let's just say I didn't see the need to exert myself."

Though he was finally being truthful about his aims, his honesty rankled. "And you do now?"

Covering her hand with his, he smiled. "You should know the answer to that. What man has ever stayed immune to your charms for long?"

His words too closely echoed his flattery of Lady Hungate. She wasn't sure she liked this insincere version of Marcus. "Do not insult my intelligence. I know you never intended this to be a real courtship."

"Did *you* intend it to be?" His gaze narrowed, burning into hers. "If you want truths, madam, perhaps you should offer some yourself. Your only reason for agreeing to the courtship was to help your brother. For all I know, you are part of his scheme to bring Louisa under Prinny's influence."

"Louisa is my friend—I would never betray her friendship." She lifted her chin. "And if that was my aim, I would certainly never have let you kiss me."

"You did that to satisfy your dangerous taste for adventure."

"That wasn't the only reason I let you kiss me," she whispered.

His fingers tightened painfully on her hand. "Wasn't it?"

Although her cheeks flamed, she forced herself to meet his gaze. "No."

He looked as if he meant to say something else, but then Cicely appeared and launched herself fully into her role as chaperone.

Leaving Regina to wonder at her own boldness. How could she have been so foolish as to admit his effect on her? She shouldn't give him reason to believe she might welcome his attentions. It was one thing when she'd been sure he intended the courtship to annoy her and Simon. But if his miraculous change genuinely stemmed from his desire to please her, if he truly meant to court her . . .

She imagined herself as his wife. In town, they would attend the theater and the opera, sharing kisses in the boxes, sneaking caresses in the carriage. At his estate, she would be his lady of the manor, dining with him, managing his staff, consulting with his steward on household accounts—

As if she could even read them. Her heart sank. What a futile fantasy. She could never have such a marriage. And what about her children? Even if they were spared her affliction, how could she endure the humiliation of not being able to read to them, or having them think her stupid? Having *him* think her stupid?

She could never marry Marcus or anyone else. But for the first time in her life, she wished she could.

Chapter Thirteen

*Nothing keeps a young lady on her best behavior
around young gentlemen better than the threat of
a loose-tongued brother.*
—Miss Cicely Tremaine, *The Ideal Chaperone*

That wasn't the only reason I let you kiss me.

The statement clamored in Marcus's head for the next hour. He'd come here to prove once and for all that Regina's friends were too heartless for Louisa; now that had all gone to hell. Initially, he'd received the same condescending glances, sly asides, and cruel treatment he'd come to expect whenever he went into public, but that had faded before long. Now he found only deferential curiosity, a grudging acknowledgment of his right to belong.

At the center of it stood Regina, in white lace and blue silk. For once, her golden hair was adorned with flowers instead of a hat. She glowed like spring at its warmest, and her public manner toward him matched her look. She glanced at him long and often, on the dance floor and at the lemonade table. From far across the room. And now from right beside him, where she'd stayed ever since they'd returned from their waltz.

She stood surrounded by the usual crowd of fawning

admirers, both male and female, yet *he* was the one she graced with her smile, *he* was the one with whom she conversed the most.

He didn't know what to make of it. Had he been wrong, not only about her, but about the rest of the lot? Might he even have been wrong about Foxmoor and Louisa?

No, he could not believe that. While Regina might not have anything to do with Foxmoor's scheme, he knew Foxmoor had one.

"What do *you* think about the war, Lord Draker?" Regina asked. "Is Boney beaten at last?"

He dragged his attention back to the conversation between her and an assortment of her friends who seemed astonishingly content to stand in the same circle with him.

His first impulse was to admit that he didn't give a damn about the war one way or the other. But he was already growing used to squelching such "ungentlemanly" responses. "Boney can hardly escape Elba with a phalanx of English soldiers guarding him."

"Especially if the English soldiers are as big as you, my lord," said a young woman with a heavy Spanish accent, the cousin of one of the other ladies. When he glanced at her, she lowered her eyes shyly. "And as strong."

He blinked. Great God, was she flirting with him? He couldn't remember the last time *that* had happened, if ever. "I should think a Purdey rifle would be more useful for keeping Boney in check than any Englishman's brawny arm," he said gruffly, uncomfortable with such flattery.

"Do you shoot, Draker?" asked another voice, this one male.

He eyed the fellow warily. "Occasionally. I have to keep the quail population in check at Castlemaine, or they'll eat the fleece right off my sheep."

To his astonishment, they laughed at his puny joke. Genuinely laughed. And he wasn't even trying to be witty.

"So what sort of firearm do you use?" asked another lordling, one closer to his age. "James Purdey does make a good flintlock, I'll grant you, but I prefer Manton. His rifles fire truer."

"Have you seen Purdey's newest design?" Marcus retorted, at ease with his subject. "I hear it's superior to the one the army is using now."

They continued talking about firearms until one of the ladies asked, "Is that how you got your scar, Lord Draker? From a flintlock?"

He tensed, but before he could say a word, Regina answered from beside him. "It was a riding accident, nothing unusual for an active man like his lordship."

And as easily as that, she turned the thing he'd spent a lifetime cringing over into a badge of honor. Regina swiftly changed the subject to a discussion of the opera they'd attended, and to his amazement, no one seemed to mind.

He shot her a bemused look. She hadn't voiced her own opinion about how he'd received his scar, one that was surprisingly close to the truth. Why hadn't she? To protect him from more rude questions?

The conversation floated on, and her eyes met his, her tender look making his breath catch. This is what it would be like if he married her. She would defend him, even when he didn't need defending. She would attend every function on his arm, dance with him whenever he pleased, dine with him nightly . . .

Share his bed. And everything else, too.

A strange flood of yearning rose to choke him. What if he could actually be part of the world, *this* world? What if he could have a real future, a wife and children and friends? What if he took his rightful place in society—

Damn her for putting such thoughts in his head. It was bound to lead to trouble; it always did. Yet he couldn't stop thinking about it. To have a life beyond Castlemaine, a life like anyone else . . . all his plans to use Regina to separate Louisa and Simon paled in comparison to that danger-ously tempting idea.

Steady now, he warned himself. Such thoughts were highly premature. La Belle Dame had refused eleven men; why should she accept the twelfth?

Why *shouldn't* she? He was eligible enough—his title, wealth, and birth would have made him sought after in so-ciety if not for his outcast status. Now that his status was improving, things might be different.

Perhaps he could make it possible. Regina did enjoy his kisses; that much he knew. And he could provide her with every physical comfort, if she could be content to live away from town for part of the year. Surely he could make it so she didn't *want* to leave his side. Give her a child or two, and she would be tied irrevocably to him and Castlemaine.

That never worked for your mother.

No, but his mother had been tempted into sin by the devil himself. If Regina became his, he would keep her well away from such devils.

He forced his attention back to the conversation swirling around him, about one gentlemen's refurbish-ments to his estate. Regina's comments were surprisingly astute. He'd never guessed that she knew what an oriel was or had any opinion whatsoever about projecting eaves. Perhaps her interests were broader than he'd thought.

"I hear that your father did extensive renovation to

Castlemaine some years ago," one gentleman said to Marcus, forcibly dragging him into the discussion. "Was he able to keep the work to a reasonable length of time?"

"It took a few years, actually," Marcus answered. "As a boy, I thought scaffolding in the dining room was normal."

The Spanish girl, who'd edged over to stand next to Regina, gazed at him with rampant curiosity. "Castlemaine is your home, Lord Draker?"

He nodded.

"It is a castle, no?"

"No, Silvia," her female cousin, Lady Amanda, said in a superior tone. "I'm sure it is not really a castle. You haven't been in England long enough to understand how things are, but plenty of things have 'castle' in their name that have nothing to do with castles."

When the girl blushed crimson, a snide retort sprang to Marcus's lips. But before he could put Lady Amanda in her place, Regina smiled down at the mortified foreigner. "Actually, it *is* a castle, dating back to . . . what?" She turned to Marcus. "The early fifteenth century?"

"Or thereabouts." He relaxed, touched not only by her handling of the girl but her interest in his home. That was a good sign, a very good sign indeed.

Eyes twinkling, Regina told Silvia, "It even has a dungeon."

"Truly?" the girl said, her gaze swinging to Marcus's. "A real dungeon?"

The women's enthusiasm was infectious. Marcus smiled. "I've been told it was used as such during the reign of Henry VIII, but since then it's served mostly as storage for meat or wine or whatever the present owner chooses."

"And what do *you* keep in the dungeon, sir?" Lady Amanda asked, with a coy flutter of her eyelashes.

Another flirting female. Amazing.

Regina snorted. "Nothing of interest to you, Amanda, I'm sure."

Marcus's gaze shot to her. She couldn't actually be jealous, could she?

"Oh?" Lady Amanda retorted slyly. "How would you know unless you've seen it? You must have seen his estate, to know so much about his 'castle.'"

Regina colored. "Well . . . I . . . that is—"

"Her brother is quite enamored of my sister," Marcus said swiftly. "Of course they've visited Castlemaine." As Lady Amanda and her companions exchanged knowing glances, he decided it was time to put an end to this dangerous conversation. "Now, if you will excuse us, I promised the next dance to Lady Regina." He held his arm out. "Shall we?"

She took it with a grateful smile, and they walked off toward the ballroom. As soon as they were out of earshot, she murmured, "Thank you."

"I take it that Lady Amanda would delight in seeing you ruined."

"Amanda is only happy when everyone else is miserable."

He shook his head. "And that is the sort of woman you consider a friend?"

"That is the sort of woman I consider a necessary evil," she countered. "Tell me, did you enjoy your conversation with the gentlemen about rifles?"

"I suppose," he hedged.

"One of those men is Amanda's brother. He is a perfectly amiable fellow and someone I enjoy talking to; but to have his company, I must endure hers from time to time, and so I do."

"I don't know why. I wouldn't give you a farthing for any of them."

"But surely there are people you would give a farthing for, people whose friends you endure because you enjoy their company. The Iversleys, perhaps."

"I don't have to endure their friends to have their company. And the few friends they do have are fine with me."

"Then perhaps there is someone else you would care enough about to endure their companions? Your brother, for example?"

His gaze shot to her. "Brother?"

"Oh, please, don't play the innocent with me. It is clear that you and Mr. Byrne are friends, and everyone knows you are half brothers."

"Prinny says otherwise."

"True. But he doesn't have to acknowledge Mr. Byrne as his son for people to know that he is. Just as they know that *you* are. And I'll wager that if either of you would unbend enough to approach His Highness, he would treat you with the same generosity as he's treated his other natural children."

"Even if that were true, and I'm not sure that it is," Marcus retorted, "any help he provided would come with conditions. And I am not interested in bowing to his dam— . . . to his cursed conditions."

She stopped to pull him to the lemonade table, which presently stood deserted. As he poured her a glass, she gazed up at him earnestly. "Is that why you cast the prince out of your home all those years ago?"

"I cast him out of my home because he turned my mother into a whore."

"Did he?"

He could almost see what she was thinking. *It takes two*

to make a whore. That painful truth was one he'd spent half his life trying to ignore.

And he was no more disposed to think about it now. He poured a glass of lemonade for himself. "We weren't discussing my mother," he grumbled. "We were discussing Byrne. And I don't see what he has to do with anything. Or why you think he and I are such great friends."

She shrugged. "He had to be the one who got you your Stranger's Ticket. Everyone knows he and a certain Lady Patroness were once . . . intimate companions."

"You know an awful lot about things a young lady shouldn't."

She smiled. "Thank you. I do try to keep abreast of the gossip."

"For what reason?"

"To help me distinguish my friends from my enemies."

"What a fine world you live in, that you have to do such a thing," he said, lifting his glass in a mock toast.

"And your world is different? You ignore the local gossip about your tenants? You don't know who is trustworthy or who has mistreated his family or who is too proud to take a tuppence of charity? You don't act on such knowledge?"

He drank some lemonade. "It's not the same."

"Why? Because they're not of your station? Admit it, Marcus—your world isn't that different from mine. It's made up of the good and the bad, the dangerous and the benign. And if a sensible person is to survive in either world, he—or she—must be able to tell which is which."

He had never thought of it in quite that way. "I suppose," he conceded.

"Because you've made that world yours, you under-stand it, and that's why you feel comfortable in it. But you could understand this one, too, if you chose. This is where you belong, you know. I don't understand why you fight it so."

"Because I have never belonged here before."

"You never *tried* to belong."

"I saw no advantage to it. I still see none."

"Wouldn't marrying Louisa off be simpler if you were around to watch?"

A reluctant chuckle erupted from him. "You are too clever for your own good, did you know that?"

She graced him with a brilliant smile. "No. Not until you said so."

Her smile pierced the scales that had long encased his heart, spreading a sweet warmth throughout him. He wanted this woman. It made no sense, and God knew it was foolish, but he wanted her. And not just in his bed, either.

He wanted her beside him at Castlemaine and—if need be—in a town house in London. He wanted to possess her so badly his body ached with it. She reminded him of the "woman clothed in sun" in his very own Blake dragon painting. He wanted her sun to shine only for him, only for the dragon.

But could the dragon possess the woman without con-suming her? Or being consumed by her sun? That he did not know.

"Well, if it isn't the cozy pair," said a bitter male voice behind them.

Regina's smile stiffened into a polite mask as she turned to greet the newcomer. "Good evening, Henry. How good to see you."

Marcus faced her idiot cousin, forcing himself to acknowledge the man with a nod. "Whitmore. We were just headed off to dance."

"With full lemonade glasses? I think not." Whitmore insinuated himself between them and helped himself to the depleted source of lemonade. "Besides, you need not pretend around me. The rest of these fools may fall for this ridiculous act, but I at least know what's really going on between you two."

Alarm sparked in Regina's eyes. "I can't imagine what you mean." She set down her lemonade glass to take Marcus's arm. "And we were indeed going to dance. So if you'll excuse us, Henry . . ."

She tugged at Marcus, and he started to go along, not wanting her to endure a repetition of Whitmore's accusations of a few nights ago.

"So what did *you* get out of the wager, Draker?" Whitmore called out.

That arrested Marcus. Especially when he caught sight of the panic in Regina's eyes. Extricating himself from her now-fierce grip, he faced Whitmore. "What wager?"

"Between her and her brother. You know, the one where Foxmoor wagered that Regina could not clean you up and make you presentable for society."

When Regina didn't deny it outright, Marcus went numb. "Oh, *that* wager."

Judging from the satisfied smile on Whitmore's face, the man had guessed that Marcus was unaware of any "wager." He saluted Regina with his glass. "So tell me, what incentive did Foxmoor offer to get you to take Draker on as your charitable project?"

"Don't be ridiculous, Henry," Regina said hastily. "Lord Draker is not my 'charitable project.' "

"Wager, charitable project—it's all the same. You transformed Draker into a gentleman. And judging from how everyone's talking about him this evening, you've won the wager by a mile."

The words *wager* and *charitable project* thundered in Marcus's ears as he stared at Whitmore's gloating expression.

Whitmore sipped his lemonade. "So what did you win, Regina?"

"Nothing . . . I mean, it wasn't about money," Regina whispered.

Marcus's stomach roiled. Until she'd said that, he'd hoped Whitmore was mistaken. But no, she really had made some damned wager with her brother over him. It made perfect sense. Why else would she tolerate their insane bargain? And here he'd been inventing fictions with the two of them cozily ensconced at Castlemaine—

What an idiot he was. He should have listened to his instincts instead of letting her wind her spell about him, tempting him to dive right into the treacherous ocean. He should have known she would never truly be interested in the likes of him. Why had he thought she would? Because she'd given in to a kiss or two? Let him caress her? That was probably just one tactic she'd used to win her wager.

And she'd definitely won it, oh yes. Now everyone knew he was the pathetic creature who'd allowed her sly remarks and other temptations to turn him into a slobbering lapdog like all her others. Foxmoor must be laughing his ass off.

This is where you belong, you know. I don't understand why you fight it so.

God, how could he have been such a fool?

Well, no more. But he'd be damned if he'd let her or

Whitmore know how far he'd sunk. "I'll tell you what she won." Setting down his glass, he offered Regina his arm, although what he really wanted was to wring her sophisticated little neck. "Apparently, Foxmoor didn't explain the whole of it. He refused to approve a courtship between us, citing my rough ways as the reason. So their wager was that if she could 'clean me up,' as you put it, he would give us his blessing. And how could I resist going along for such a prize?"

Whitmore paled as Regina took Marcus's arm. "Courtship?" Whitmore said, his gaze shifting from Marcus to Regina and back.

"Yes." Marcus forced a smile, although it felt as if his face might crack. "You see, Regina doesn't refuse *my* proposals of marriage." As Whitmore's face turned to ash and Regina groaned, he added smoothly, "Now if you'll excuse us, we really were headed off to dance."

Then he turned and stalked off toward the dance floor. Thankfully, she went with him willingly, for if she hadn't, he might have dragged her off forcibly.

And he didn't want to give her the satisfaction of knowing how Whitmore's revelations had affected him. Already she was undoubtedly congratulating herself for her success at winning her wager. That was all the satisfaction he meant to give her.

"You handled that very well," she said in a low voice.

Her praise burned in his gut like hot acid. Somehow he managed to sound nonchalant. "Glad to know you approve," he said tightly.

Her fingers tightened on his arm. "Marcus, it was not what you think—"

She broke off at the approach of a young gentleman with whom Marcus had seen her earlier.

"Lady Regina!" the fellow exclaimed. "You promised me this next dance."

For once, Marcus was glad she was so popular. He didn't think he could manage a dance with her right now, knowing she was assessing his performance and congratulating herself on the effectiveness of her labors.

She glanced from the young man to Marcus. "I'm sorry, Mr. Jerrold, but I forgot about it, and accepted a dance with his lordship."

"No problem," Marcus said. "You have a previous engagement. I'll wait until the next dance."

"But—"

Before she could say more, he released her arm, bowed to the other gentleman, and walked off.

He headed for the door, forcing himself to nod here and there, to behave as if nothing were amiss. He hated the pretense, but he wasn't about to throw away what he'd gained tonight. He had Louisa to consider. And since he fully intended never to set foot within ten feet of Lady Regina again, he must hold his own. So he squelched his urge to roar his anger at every man, woman, and child within hearing, even if it taxed his control to the limit.

Still, he'd be damned if he'd stay here to watch her gloat over her brilliant success. Thankfully he could leave if he wanted—he'd come here alone, so no one would think it strange if he departed alone.

He was halfway down the grand staircase when a voice hailed him from behind. He did not need to turn to recognize it as hers. Gritting his teeth, he pretended not to have heard and quickened his march toward the foyer.

The swish of her ball slippers behind him on the stairs quickened as well. Unfortunately, once he reached the foyer, he had to wait while the footman summoned his carriage, making it easy for her to catch up to him.

As she came up beside him, she said, "What do you think you're doing?"

He snatched his hat and greatcoat from the footman without even bothering to put them on. "Not that it concerns you, but I'm going home. I've had all of Almack's I can stomach for one night."

"You can't leave until we have a chance to talk," she protested.

"Did you wager with Simon that you could turn me into a gentleman?"

"Yes, but—"

"Then there's nothing to talk about. You won the wager." He spotted his carriage arriving and walked down the outer steps to meet it.

She followed him. "Marcus, please listen to me."

Without bothering to answer, he leaped into his coach and tossed his coat and hat onto the other seat. But before the footman could close the door after him, she clambered in and sat down, right on top of his coat.

He glared at her. "I would advise you to get out of my coach, madam. I'm leaving now, so unless you plan to go for a ride—"

"You wouldn't drive off with me in your coach," she said stoutly. "You know it would ruin me. Come back to Almack's so—"

"John!" he called up. "Drive on!" As the carriage rumbled off, he scowled at her. "Now's your chance. I'll tell him to halt, but only so you can get out."

She swallowed and nervously glanced out at the rapidly receding lights of Almack's. Then a stubborn look came over her face, and her gaze shot back to him. Thrusting out her chin, she crossed her arms over her chest. "You'll have to throw me out then. Because I'm not leaving this coach until we talk."

Damn her. The fact that she had cared enough to come after him was already assuaging his anger, but if she started spouting excuses . . .

No, it didn't matter what she said. She wanted to bring him to his knees—that's what she always did with men. Whatever she'd won in her wager would be the last winnings she'd get at his expense. He would make sure of it.

Chapter Fourteen

Be warned that men are waiting to ruin your charge the moment your back is turned.
—Miss Cicely Tremaine, *The Ideal Chaperone*

"Suit yourself," Marcus retorted. "Stay in the coach if you please. I don't give a damn."

Regina winced at the vitriol in his voice. Her impulsive act would surely come back to haunt her, but if she let him go now, she would almost certainly never see him again. She simply couldn't bear that prospect.

After witnessing his expression of betrayal when Henry mentioned the wager, she refused to let Marcus continue thinking that she had used him so abominably. She couldn't blame him for his reaction, but that didn't mean she would let him shut her out of his life for it.

"*Now* can we talk about this?" she asked.

"Nothing to talk about," he grunted, shifting his gaze to the window.

Drat him. The dragon was back, protecting himself with scaly armor and fiery breath while he retreated to his cave.

She didn't have time for that. Even a duke's daughter could not ride off unchaperoned with a gentleman. She would be compromised if anyone discovered it, which they were sure to do if she didn't resolve the situation swiftly.

"I think there's plenty to talk about." Somehow she must provoke him into discussing this. "For one thing, you as good as told my cousin that I'd accepted an offer of marriage from you. And we both know that was a blatant lie."

Though he stiffened, her words didn't get the rise out of him that she'd hoped for. "Feel free to set your cousin straight. I don't care what you tell him."

The man was so stubborn! "And if I tell him that he misunderstood about the wager? That you were never my 'charitable project'?"

"Tell him whatever you please."

"Drat it, Marcus, you know I don't see you that way."

A muscle worked in his jaw. "I know how you see me, madam. I just don't care."

Oh yes, he did, the sullen devil. No amount of his new-found formal correctness could hide that. "How can you think I would agree to a courtship just so I could take on some sort of 'charitable project'? Surely you realize I have better things to do with my time than try to mold a man as stubborn and surly as you into my image of a gentleman."

"Ah, but you had the wager to make it worth your while, didn't you?"

That cursed wager. "Just so you'll know, Simon was the one who suggested the wager *after* he found out I'd agreed to let you court me. He assumed I was doing it so I could 'improve' you, so he thought to put conditions on it. I nearly refused. Until he said what the terms were, and I saw an opportunity to determine if he truly intended to marry Louisa."

"There's no need for this explanation," he ground out. "I don't care about your wager."

"Stuff and nonsense. You think all this has been about some silly wager that I barely thought of. Don't you even want to know what our terms were?"

He turned even more stiffly formal. "Not really, Lady Regina. Whether you won a new harp or gown or piece of jewelry is of no consequence to me. You've said your piece. Shall I turn the coach around?"

"No, you shall not!" The arrogant fool clearly didn't believe a word she'd said. "If Simon won, I was to stop interfering in his courtship with Louisa. And if *I* won, he was to ask you formally for her hand and *abide* by your decision. It was not about a new harp, drat you! It was about making sure Simon was not using Louisa! I figured if he agreed to the wager, then he was sincere. That's the *only* reason I agreed to it."

For a moment, she thought she'd reached him. His jaw seemed to soften. But then he sucked in a shuddering breath and turned a cold gaze on her. "There's no need for you to invent something you think might soothe my pride. I don't really care why you made the wager. We both used each other, and we both got what we wanted. So we're done now."

"The devil we are! And what do you mean, 'we both used each other'?"

His expression grew shuttered. "Whitmore was right—I needed a way to enter society again, and you provided that, even if you only meant to win your wager. But now that I know I can enter society on my own, I don't need you anymore. So I thank you, but I have no more use for you."

The cruel words took the breath from her. Had he truly

shown an interest in her only because she could help him reenter society?

No, she couldn't believe it. His pride was wounded, and he was striking back. She wouldn't let him. "So our kisses and caresses meant nothing to you except as a means to an end?"

He shrugged. "You were bored and wanted an adventure; I obliged you. It was the only way to make sure you kept helping me."

"I see." Oh yes, she saw, all right. Saw that she had him cold. If he'd claimed to have lost interest in her, she might—*might,* mind you—have believed him. But she didn't believe for one minute that he'd never desired her. Even the Dragon Viscount was not *that* good at hiding his feelings.

She unbuttoned her gloves, first one, then the other. When she stripped the first one off, she thought she saw him tense. "And I guess now that you have what you really wanted from me, you can stop pretending to desire me. Is that what you're saying?"

He hesitated a fraction of a second, his eyes riveted to her hand removing her other glove. "Right."

Setting her gloves aside, she leaned down as if to readjust her slipper, but really so she could display her bosom to fine advantage. She tried not to roll her eyes at the way his gaze swung unerringly to her low décolletage. Men could be so predictable. "You mean that you are not attracted to me in the least."

"Not in the least," he echoed hoarsely.

Taking him by surprise, she changed seats to sit beside him. Then while he was still caught off guard, she laid her bare hand on his thigh. "So you are not affected when I do this."

He swallowed. "No, indeed."

Reaching up with her other hand, she caressed his smoothly shaven cheek. "And this does not move you."

"It . . . no . . . I am not moved."

She pressed her mouth to his ear. "I don't believe you." Then she kissed his ear. And his close-cropped hair. And his cheek that still smelled of shaving oil.

His breath came now in harsh gasps. "Only because you're . . . not used to . . . having a man resist you."

"I don't believe you, because it's not true. And we both know it."

Continuing to stroke his opposite cheek with her fingers, she kissed a path to his mouth. He swore under his breath. When she nibbled his lower lip, he jerked back from her. "Stop that," he said in a low rasp.

"Why? I thought you didn't desire me?"

"I didn't . . . I don't. You're making a fool of yourself for nothing."

"I certainly hope not." Cupping his cheek in her hand, she turned his head toward her until he couldn't avoid looking at her. "Since I will probably be ruined after riding off with you like this, I would hate to think it was all for naught."

She kissed him squarely on the mouth. Though a shudder rocked him, he kept still, every inch of him hard and resistant. Until she ran the tip of her tongue along the firmly closed seam of his lips, eliciting a growl from somewhere low in his throat.

He jerked back to stare at her, his features carved into a mask of sheer raw hunger, his eyes hot. "Damn you," he swore as he dragged her onto his lap. "Damn you," he bit out as he caught her head in his hands. "Damn you to hell," he groaned, seconds before his mouth took hers.

It was the most glorious kiss of her life, so powerful she would have swooned if she'd been the swooning sort. She threw her arms about his neck and gave herself up to the intoxicating pleasure.

She'd won at last. She wasn't sure *what* she'd won— after this, she could no more return to holding him at arm's length than she could stop breathing. But she didn't care about that. Marcus was kissing her with all the passion and fervor that made her feel alive, and nothing else mattered.

After endless moments of his mouth consuming hers and his hands roaming freely over her waist and hips, he tore his lips from hers. "Are you happy now?" he growled as he scattered feverish kisses over her cheeks and chin and throat.

"Because I proved that you still want me?" She arched her neck to give him better access. "Yes, deliriously happy."

He sucked hard on her neck. "Haughty witch. Impudent siren." Lifting his mouth to her ear, he nipped the lobe. "You couldn't rest until you reduced me to the same slobbering lapdog state as all your other suitors."

"If this is you being a lapdog, I shudder to think how you would be as a mastiff. I assure you, I have never allowed any slobbering lapdog suitors to carry me off in their carriages alone."

He drew back to stare at her solemnly. "If you stay here with me much longer, you'll be ruined."

"I know."

"Don't you care?"

The strange thing was, she didn't. Not right now. "No."

"You've won your wager, you know. You don't have to keep at your charitable project now."

She jerked back. "You are *not* a project," she cried, wounded to the heart. "And if you could still think I see you that way, I want nothing to do with you!"

She tried to scramble free of him, but he wouldn't let her. "Too late for that," he murmured in her ear, a hint of amusement in his tone. "Now that I've carried you off, dearling, I fully intend to take advantage of the situation."

His use of the endearment mollified her. So did the idea of his taking advantage of her. Still, color rose in her cheeks when he very deliberately began to unfasten the ties of her bodice. "You . . . you mean to ruin me in truth?"

"No." He tugged her bodice down so he could untie her filmy chemise. "But if you'll remember, I told you earlier I would expect a reward for my gentlemanly efforts." Opening the neck of her chemise, he bared one of her breasts to his ravening gaze. "And I intend to take it now."

Before she could even protest, he was easing her back over his arm so he could seize her breast with his mouth. Heaven help her, it was just like the last time . . . utterly . . . sweetly . . . delicious.

As her eyes slid shut and her hands clutched at his arms, his mouth seduced her breast, teasing her nipple until it hardened into an aching knot that only the swaths of his hot tongue could soothe.

Then he turned his sinful attentions to her other breast, caressing it with his mouth so expertly that he soon had her arching up against his mouth, wanting more, needing more.

That was probably why she didn't notice his free hand sliding her gown up her legs until he had it midthigh, and his fingers brushed her drawers.

"Marcus?" she whispered. "Do you really think you should—"

"Yes," he dragged his mouth from her breast to rasp. "If you don't let me touch you, dearling, I'll go mad."

"And *I'll* go mad if you touch me there," she said tartly, struggling to sit up.

"I certainly hope so." He smiled down at her, shifting her so that she was half-sitting, half-lying across his lap. His hand—his devilishly clever hand—continued its scandalous exploration until it found the slit in her drawers. "I want to drive you as insane as you've driven me for the past week."

She should protest. Instead, she waited impatiently to see how he intended to do that. Parting the linen with his fingers, he combed through her curls until he found a sensitive bit of hidden flesh. When he pressed his thumb to it in a most outrageous caress, she nearly hit the roof of his carriage.

So that was how he meant to do it . . . oh, Lord. He stroked it again, and she jumped. "Sweet heaven!"

"Not yet," he said, eyes gleaming with humor. "But I promise it will be."

He was as good as his word. While still mercilessly rubbing and teasing that one tender spot until she writhed against his thumb in search of more, he slid a finger lower to part her delicate folds, then slip inside her.

Her eyes widened at the shock of such a sinful intimacy. But even as she dug her fingernails into his coat and prepared to protest, his finger withdrew. Only to thrust inside her again. And again. And again, in firm, silken strokes that drove all the breath right out of her.

She'd heard enough about lovemaking to know how it worked, but she'd never heard about *this*. Having his finger inside her was perfectly appalling. She wanted it never to end.

Her eyes slid shut so she could focus on that treacherously wicked hand of his, doing amazing things to her, making her twist and turn and yearn for more . . .

"How's that for an impertinence?" he growled.

"Marvelous," she whispered, then groaned to hear her own blatant wantonness. "I didn't mean to say that."

"Why not, if it's the truth?" His low voice was a smoky seduction in itself. "Never be ashamed of enjoying this. God knows I love watching you enjoy it."

His labored breathing confirmed that. So did the bulge swelling beneath her bottom. That ought to have worried her, but she was beyond being worried about anything right now. Not when that same excitement she'd felt in the opera box was rising in her, higher, higher—

"Tell me the truth, Regina," he commanded as his strokes grew faster and bolder. He slid another finger inside her and she groaned, arching up into his hand like a virgin rising toward the glory of the dragon's flames. "When Foxmoor asked why you'd agreed to my bargain, did you tell him I was your charitable project?"

"No." She groaned as she struggled toward the fiery breath. "I told you . . . no . . ."

"But you didn't deny it when *he* claimed I was," he prodded.

"No," she whispered, her focus divided between his dratted questions and the heat building and building down low . . .

His strokes grew fiercer, rougher. "Why not?"

"I didn't want . . . him to guess . . . the real reason I agreed."

"What was that?"

"Because . . . in spite of the beard . . . and your churlish manner and your obstinacy . . ." She trailed off, hardly able to speak for the thrilling sensations coursing through her, fogging her brain, consuming her senses.

His motions abruptly turned teasing . . . too soft . . . too gentle.

"Marcus, please . . ." she begged him shamelessly, knowing instinctively that some release had lain just beyond her reach before he'd turned gentle.

"Answer the question," he commanded. He stroked her hard, and a groan of pleasure erupted from her that turned to a moan of disappointment when he didn't repeat the motion. "Despite my beard and all that, *what*? What was your real reason for agreeing?"

"Because I found you fascinating!" She pushed her hips up against his hand to urge him to continue. Her frustration grew acute when his hand continued to lie still, and she snapped, "I desired you, all right? Now *please*, Marcus, please . . ."

"All right, dearling," he murmured, as her words at last sank in. He not only renewed his motions, but lowered his mouth to hers. "All right."

Then there were no more questions and no more words, just his marvelous mouth plundering hers while his marvelous fingers caressed and fondled and thrust, stoking the flames, feeding the need until an explosion of light and color and white heat consumed her, body and soul. He swallowed her cry with a bold, hot kiss.

As she convulsed against him, clinging to his powerful arms, arching into his firm hand, he tore his mouth free of hers to rain kisses over her flaming cheeks and chin and neck.

"Ohh . . . Marcus . . ." she whispered when she could find her voice again. "That was . . . that was . . ."

"Sweet heaven?"

"Yes." She fought to catch her breath as the flames died to a warm glow of contentment. "Is that . . . is it always . . ."

He nuzzled her neck. "Sometimes. Not always. Though it helps if the man knows what he's doing, and the woman—"

"Behaves like a wanton?" Shame set in as she came back to earth, to the steady rumble of carriage wheels, the rush of air past the windows . . . the whisper of silk against silk as Marcus inched her skirts down past her stockings.

"Desires the man," he corrected.

She opened her eyes hesitantly, half-afraid of what she might see in his face. If he'd wanted revenge for the dratted wager, he'd found the perfect way to take it . . . making her beg for her pleasure.

But no gloating showed on his face, just that ever-present hunger that never seemed to be assuaged.

She sat up on his lap, guilt assailing her when his bulge thickened beneath her squirming bottom. "Is there anything I can do to . . . well . . ." How did one ask such a thing? "To make you more comfortable? You know . . . down there?"

He uttered a strained laugh, then pressed a kiss to her temple. "Not unless you want to be ruined in truth."

She drew back to stare at him. "Can't a man find satisfaction from having a woman touch him the way you touched me?"

Rampant desire leaped in his face. "He can. But that would not be wise now. If you touch me like that, I doubt that anything on this earth could make me return you to Almack's. And we both know I have to return you." He lifted her off his lap, setting her on the seat opposite him as a resigned note entered his voice. "I only pray that we've not been gone too long already."

"And if we have?" she asked.

His gaze met hers, ardent and intense. "Then we'll marry, of course."

She caught her breath. "You would marry me? The sister of your enemy?"

"I don't believe in making women pay for the sins of their male relations. And you know there's no other solution. *If* we are caught, that is."

"*If* we are caught," she echoed.

When she said nothing more, he frowned, then commanded his driver to return to Almack's. As the coachman brought the carriage round, Regina busied herself with restoring her clothing to its proper condition, trying not to think about the ramifications of what Marcus had just said.

Marriage to Marcus. For one heady moment, the thought of being Marcus's wife tantalized her. Then reality sank in. Her problems would not go away just because he made her his wife. If anything, they would increase.

He watched her a moment in brooding silence. Then he cleared his throat. "If our tête-à-tête results in your ruin, we *must* be married. Surely you see that."

"Of course. It's just that . . . well . . . I had never intended to marry."

He eyed her skeptically. "Never? Are you serious?"

"Perfectly serious."

He was silent for a moment. "That's why you refuse all your suitors."

"Yes."

"Why would a woman in your position, who could have any man she wanted, make such an absurd choice?"

Because I'm damaged. Because my children might also be damaged. Because I could not bear to see the disgust in your eyes if you discovered it.

She forced a lightness into her tone. "I'm simply as spoiled as you claim; I'm used to having my own way. But married women have no such freedom. Only the most indulgent of husbands will allow his wife to go where she pleases when she pleases, to stay in town as long as she likes with whatever friends she chooses."

He stiffened. "I doubt *I* could be that indulgent a husband."

She gave a hollow laugh. "You aren't even an indulgent suitor—as a husband you're likely to be a tyrant." When he bristled, she added softly, "I'm only teasing, Marcus. But be honest—you would try to keep me shackled by your side in the country all the time, wouldn't you?"

When he glanced away, she knew she'd hit on the truth.

"You would try to choose my friends, too," she went on. "I know you would. For one thing, you would probably forbid me from seeing His Highness at all or going to parties where he might appear—"

"Damned right I would." His gaze shot to her, intensely protective. "I'd never let that devil within ten feet of anybody I cared about."

Her heart began that silly pitter-patter again. "And you . . . care about me?"

"You really need to ask?"

"I suppose not." She busied herself with drawing on her gloves. "If I can sneak back into Almack's without being missed . . . what happens then?"

"I'll tell you what does *not* happen. If you won't marry me, then we do not meet alone like this ever again. We do not court, and we do not kiss." When her surprised gaze shot to him, he said, "I won't endure it. I want you too badly to dance attendance on you like all your other conquests, when all you want from me is a bit of fun."

"That's not true!"

"Isn't it? You don't want to marry, yet you behave like a woman who does. What should I make of that?" His voice grew bitter. "Unless this is how you refuse all of your unacceptable suitors—by claiming you don't want marriage when you really just don't want marriage to *them*."

"I would never be so dishonest."

"Then you'd better hope you're not compromised. Because if you are, we *will* be married, your objections notwithstanding."

They rode the rest of the way in silence, that promise hanging in the air between them. She considered telling him the truth, but it was too shameful to admit, especially if they were parting ways. And if they weren't . . . she would cross that bridge when she came to it.

As they approached Almack's, she grew heartened by the lack of a crowd outside. Only a single carriage was there, taking on passengers. But her relief lasted just until she recognized the carriage's ducal crest.

Marcus's coach had barely halted when the door was flung open by none other than her brother. His face was alight with anger.

"Come out here, you blackguard!" he roared at Marcus.

"Gladly." As Marcus disembarked, he shot her a glance that said he would be true to his word.

Despite everything, her heart leaped at the thought. Ignoring her brother, who fumed beside him, Marcus helped her out as if nothing were wrong. That seemed enough to convince her brother that she'd gone willingly.

"Damn you, Regina," Simon growled. "How could you behave so foolishly?"

"It seemed the only thing to do at the time," she retorted, oddly giddy now that the worst had happened.

A small smile touched Marcus's lips, but Simon turned livid. "This is not a joking matter—"

"Leave her be," Marcus put in firmly. "She's not at fault for this."

"Damned right she's not," Simon snapped. "*You* are at fault, and you will be the one to make this right, or I swear I'll see you at dawn in Leicester Fields."

"Don't be silly, Simon—" Regina began.

"Marcus!" cried a voice beyond them. Louisa clambered out of the other carriage and ran toward them.

It was Marcus's turn to be livid. "Damn it, Louisa, what are you doing going off alone with this devil?"

"Not alone," Simon retorted. "Cicely?"

Cicely stuck her head out of the carriage. "Yes?"

Simon smiled grimly at Marcus. "*I* had the good sense to take a chaperone."

"We were just going to look for you and Regina," Louisa said in a breathless rush. "Miss Tremaine was worried and—"

"Where are the Iversleys?" Marcus interrupted. "They're supposed to be your chaperones."

"We couldn't find them," Louisa said. "And anyway, Miss Tremaine was perfectly suitable—"

"For Foxmoor's needs, yes." Marcus glowered at Simon even more fiercely. "You knew Miss Tremaine would turn a blind eye if you made a stop at . . . say . . . Carlton House."

"Carlton House?" Louisa put in. "What are you talking about?"

"Nothing," Simon said hastily. Too hastily.

Regina eyed her brother with suspicion.

He ignored her. "Stop trying to deflect attention from your own misbehavior, Draker. I want to know what you plan to do about this insult to my sister."

Marcus took Regina's hand. "Regina and I will marry. We've already discussed it."

"How wonderful!" Louisa cried.

Although Cicely looked panicked, a calculated smile touched Simon's lips. "Good. I'll make the arrangements."

"*I'll* make the arrangements," Marcus countered. "If you'll tell me your solicitor's name, I'll—"

"Wait!" Regina cried. This was all going so fast. And her conversation with Marcus in the carriage had unsettled her more than she'd expected.

Both men frowned at her.

"What is it?" Simon asked.

She tugged her hand from Marcus's, knowing that what she was about to say was outrageous. Of course she had to marry him; a crowd was already forming beyond them, and it would take no time for them to figure out what was going on. A few questions to a footman, and they would all know—

No, she could not survive a scandal like that. Society was her whole life, and if it cut her off, she would go mad. But neither could she endure being locked up in the country for months at a time with Marcus. Especially when he found out the truth about her, which inevitably he must.

She ought to tell him now. But what if he backed out of his agreement to marry her? Then she'd be ruined, an outcast. She wouldn't let that happen. She would rather be a sacrificial virgin than a woman of no honor. Besides, marriage to Marcus didn't have to be a sacrifice if she took precautions.

"You're marrying his lordship," Simon said firmly. "You have no choice."

"I understand, but—" Regina took a deep breath. "He

must agree to certain conditions before I'll consent."

"Under the circumstances," Simon snapped, "you can't ask for conditions."

"Let her speak." Marcus glanced warily at her. "Tell me what you want."

She gazed beyond him to where Cicely stood frozen in shock. "First, you must allow Cicely to attend me at Castlemaine. She can no longer live with Simon in what will now be a bachelor household."

As relief spread over Cicely's face, Simon rolled his eyes. "Don't worry about Ciss. I'll make sure she has a comfortable position at one of my estates."

"No, I want her with me." A plan had begun to form in her mind. If Cicely could be there to help her read and manage the household, she might never have to tell Marcus of her problem. "His lordship must take her in."

"Fine," Marcus said. "Castlemaine is a big place. There's plenty of room for your cousin. Anything else?"

She swallowed. He would have trouble with her next condition. "I want a house in town. And the freedom to reside there when I wish, especially during the season." When his brow lowered, she added hastily, "You may stay with me, too, of course. But if you won't let me have my jaunts to town, I can't marry you."

"The hell you can't," Simon cut in. "Father might have tolerated your willfulness, my girl, but—"

"It's all right," Marcus interrupted. "I'll agree to that condition, too." She turned a grateful smile on him. Then he added, "But I have two of my own."

She tensed.

Simon lifted his eyes heavenward. "What the bloody hell are *yours?*"

"The first is that your sister agrees to be faithful to me."

Regina glared at Marcus, thoroughly insulted. "Of course I will be faithful."

Marcus's gaze locked with hers. "I mean faithful for life. Not faithful until you bear an heir and a spare. I won't tolerate any infidelity, discreet or otherwise. I know how your fast friends view marriage, but I view it differently. No matter what the scandal, I won't hesitate to divorce you if I learn you've been unfaithful even once. Do you understand?"

She notched up her chin. "Perfectly. And I repeat, *of course I will be faithful.*"

He searched her face and seemed satisfied by what he saw there, because he then turned to Simon. "My other condition is for you, Foxmoor."

"I will settle upon Regina whatever you require—"

"It's not about money. I will agree to marry your sister. But only if *you* agree never to see mine again."

Chapter Fifteen

Beware hotheaded young gentlemen.
—Miss Cicely Tremaine, *The Ideal Chaperone*

Marcus stood steadfast against Foxmoor's black scowl and the instant protests of the females. This was an enormous gamble. By some amazing good fortune, he'd caught Regina, and he wanted to keep her. God, how he wanted to keep her, in spite of her damned conditions.

But the sight of Foxmoor preparing to head off with Louisa had ignited his temper. Clearly the duke had been using the excuse of Regina's disappearance to whisk Louisa off for a rendezvous with Prinny.

Well, never again. He would make sure Louisa was free of Foxmoor forever.

"That's my condition, Foxmoor," Marcus repeated. "You leave Louisa alone, or there is no marriage between me and your sister."

"Go to hell," Foxmoor hissed.

"It's not negotiable."

"Then I'll see you at Leicester Fields at dawn."

"Fine," Marcus answered. "I don't care how I get rid of you, as long as you're out of my sister's life."

"Enough," Regina put in, her face pale as milk. "This is absurd. No one is fighting anyone."

"Marcus, you're being utterly unreasonable," Louisa added as she came up beside him to lay her hand on his arm. "I won't let you fight Simon."

"Then say good-bye to him, angel."

"You cannot think I would agree—"

"I'm your guardian," he snapped, "so you will agree to whatever I say. And I say that you may no longer see this scurrilous scoundrel."

"This will accomplish nothing," Regina whispered.

He glowered at her. "I agreed to *your* conditions. Now your brother will agree to mine, or I swear I will not marry you."

Her chin trembled, but she faced her brother all the same. "Tell Lord Draker that you agree to his condition."

"I will not! I'll fight the bloody wretch first—"

"You won't." She cast her brother a pleading glance. "I am not going to be the subject of endless scandal for years because you insist on fighting a duel. His lordship is being an idiot, but that doesn't mean I want to see him die. Or you die. Or both of you die."

"There can be no duel," Louisa agreed, as Marcus had known she would if brought to that choice. She stepped up to Foxmoor. "It's all right, Simon—agree to what he asks. In two years, I can marry where I please. I love you enough to wait for you until I come of age. Then there will be naught he can do to stop me."

Marcus started to retort, then noticed the blood draining from Foxmoor's face. Two years would not suit the duke's purposes. For whatever reason, Prinny seemed intent on bringing Louisa into his circle *now*, not in two years.

A slow smile spread over Marcus's face. "Do you hear

that, Foxmoor? She *loves* you enough to wait." His tone grew snide. "And I'm sure you love her enough to do the same. I tell you what. I can be generous. I'll amend my condition. If the two of you stay apart until Louisa turns twenty-one, I will give you my blessing. By then, I'll be sure that you truly love her."

Foxmoor cast Marcus a foul glance.

"That sounds reasonable to me, Simon," Regina said.

At the steely note in Regina's voice, Marcus swung his gaze to her. She was staring at her brother with a strangely disillusioned expression.

A rush of relief hit him. *She knows. She may not have known of her brother's intentions before, but she knows now.*

"And if you will recall," Regina went on with that same weary voice, "I won our wager, which means that *you* must formally ask for Louisa's hand and abide by her brother's answer. I believe he has just given it."

"I haven't said you've won. I don't call one successful night at Almack's meeting our terms."

Until now, Marcus hadn't quite believed she'd been telling the truth about the terms of the wager. But apparently she had. Oddly enough, that cheered him. If she'd been looking out for Louisa's interests from the beginning, then there was certainly hope for them.

"You said he had to turn into a gentleman suitable for society," Regina retorted. "And he did." When Foxmoor groaned, she added, "Besides, Louisa has just now entered society herself. It won't hurt her to see more of it before she becomes a wife. So why not wait until she comes of age?"

Foxmoor glanced uneasily from his sister to Marcus, but the man clearly knew he was trapped. If he pressed the issue, he would have to explain to Louisa why he was in such a hurry to secure her. Yet by amending his condition, Marcus had ensured that Louisa would abide by it, too.

"Do you agree?" Marcus prodded.

Foxmoor hesitated, then bit out, "I agree."

"You must swear it on your honor," Marcus demanded.

Foxmoor's eyes gleamed with anger. "I swear it on my honor. There, is that good enough for you?"

"I'm satisfied," Marcus retorted.

"Thank you, Simon," Regina said.

And that's when it hit Marcus. He was getting everything he wanted—marriage to Regina *and* Foxmoor out of Louisa's life.

A smile broke over his face. "This calls for a celebration," he said, feeling suddenly magnanimous. He held out one arm to Regina and one to Louisa. "Come, ladies, we might as well return to the assembly room and dispel any nasty rumors that might have begun. We have a wedding to announce."

Hours later on the ride home with Simon and Cicely, Regina stared out the window, her mind in turmoil.

Part of her was ridiculously delighted to be marrying Marcus. The other part couldn't stop thinking about the unsavory discussion that had led to it. When Marcus had made ending his sister's courtship a condition for their own marriage, Regina had wanted to strangle him. How could he humiliate her like that?

Then she'd seen Simon's face, and an awful suspicion had begun to plague her. It would not go away. She didn't dare voice it until they were alone, however, because she could be wrong. She prayed she was wrong.

As soon as they arrived at the town house Cicely went off to bed, and Regina and Simon went to her sitting room. She chose her words carefully to avoid putting him on his guard. She needed honesty from him, if such a thing existed.

"I want to thank you for your sacrifice, Simon. I'm sorry you have to postpone your marriage plans because I acted foolishly. I feel so guilty for putting you in that position—"

"Nonsense, dear girl, you've done me a favor."

"I don't see how." Unable to look at him, she walked to her writing desk—her useless, ornamental writing desk—and pretended to search for notepaper. "Now you have to wait two years to court Louisa."

"Do you really think I shall stop courting the girl because your idiot betrothed makes me swear not to?"

No, she didn't. Unfortunately. "So you plan to see her behind his back?"

"It's perfect. After your marriage, you'll go off on your honeymoon—"

"Honeymoon?" she squeaked, temporarily distracted from her questions.

"Of course you'll have a honeymoon trip. Why shouldn't you?"

Oh, Lord, a trip alone with Marcus. Without Cicely to help her.

She shook off her panic. She would talk Marcus out of it somehow. And even if she couldn't, how much reading could she possibly be expected to do on her honeymoon? Honeymoons were for—

She blushed. Perhaps she could manage it without Cicely, after all.

"As I was saying," he went on, "while you're on your

honeymoon, I can easily arrange to see Louisa and convince her to go against her brother's wishes."

His words brought her forcibly back to her suspicions. Her awful suspicions.

"If I have her compliance," Simon continued, "it won't even matter when you return, since you'll keep Draker happily distracted at Castlemaine while I—"

"Arrange secret meetings between His Highness and Louisa."

A shocked silence was her answer.

She turned to face him. "That *is* your plan, isn't it?"

"I have no idea what you're talking about."

Her temper exploded. "Don't lie to me! Because of you, I involved myself with Lord Draker, so I think I deserve the truth."

He shot her a defensive glance. "His Highness merely wants one damned meeting with his own daughter—"

"His daughter?" Regina said. "Louisa is the prince's daughter?"

"Of course. Why do you think he wants to offer her a place at court?"

"Marcus said nothing about her being his daughter. And I thought his mother and the prince were estranged that year."

"Yes, but you know Prinny. There was a chance encounter, and as usual he . . . er . . . indulged himself. And Louisa was born nine months later."

"That doesn't necessarily mean she's Prinny's."

"Her mother said that she was, and he believes her. But her bloody ass of a brother doesn't want to believe it, so he won't permit any meeting between them. And His Highness insists that he tell her about it himself in person."

I'd never let that devil within ten feet of anybody I cared about. "So you and the prince hatched this faux courtship to deceive the poor girl into—"

"Your Draker left us no choice, damn it!"

"No," she said, her stomach roiling. "He was too clever for you. He told me all along that this was your plan, but I never believed him. I couldn't imagine that you would be so underhanded."

Her brother's eyes narrowed. "Then you don't know me very well."

Betrayal sliced through her. All the things she had done, everything she'd set into motion, and all so he could . . . could . . . what? "Why, Simon? Why does His Highness want her at court so badly that he would perpetrate such a deception?"

"Stop saying that! It's not a deception. I've made no offer for her."

"You might as well have. Your every compliment was a promise. Tell me, Simon, have you kissed her?"

His face looked thunderous. "That is none of your concern."

"So you kissed her. And led her to believe—"

"I did what I had to for my regent, yes." He explained about Princess Charlotte and her impending marriage.

With every word, Regina's stomach sank a little more. "I suppose you get some reward out of this."

He stiffened. "I plan to be prime minister, Regina. That has always been my aim, as you know."

Her hands began to sweat. "So did you ever intend to marry Louisa? Did you love her even a little?"

He raked his fingers through his hair. "It's not that simple."

"Yes, it is." She thought of her friend, professing her love to Simon so innocently tonight. "You love her, or you don't love her. Which is it?"

His features grew stony. "I did not ask her to love me. It was not part of my plan. I can't help it if she—"

"Believed your flatteries to be sincere? Thought that your attempts to see her were motivated by truly tender feelings? How *could* you?"

"You have no right to point the finger. Did you have any feelings for Lord Draker when you agreed to his courtship? Or were you just using the poor man to get what you wanted?"

"The only thing I wanted was *your* marriage. Besides, Marcus and I both knew our courtship was only a bargain." At least it had started out that way. "Louisa knew nothing of your true intentions. And what are they, anyway? At least tell me that marriage to her is part of your 'plan.'"

He tensed. "You know perfectly well Louisa would not make a good prime minister's wife."

"Oh, Lord!" She felt complicit in something dirty and wicked even though she wasn't complicit in the least. "You *lied* to me when you accepted that wager. You never even intended to marry her."

"You said I had to ask formally for her hand and abide by his decision. Since I knew he'd never accept me, I was in no danger."

"No, only Louisa's heart was in danger."

"If she deluded herself that I meant to marry her, that is not my concern."

"Not your— You danced attendance on her, flattered her, gave her gifts, and Lord knows what else while always intending to tell her in the end that it meant nothing. What kind of wicked creature *are* you?"

He glared at her. "One who serves his future king with complete loyalty. As every subject should. As *you* must."

She shook her head. "You're daft if you think I shall look the other way with this. I shall not let you continue to deceive—"

"You will do whatever I say." He stalked toward her, his handsome features alight with determination. "You will keep silent about my plans, you will keep your bloody husband entertained, and you will let me finish this without any interference. Do you understand?"

"I will not!"

"You will. Or I'll tell your precious 'Marcus' you were part of my plans all along."

The blood drained from her face. "You couldn't be that cruel."

"I could, trust me. If you tell him—or Louisa—what's going on, I'll tell him you knew from the beginning. That I sent you to his house to distract him and maneuver it so I could get close to her."

"He won't believe you," she whispered.

Simon laughed harshly. "The man trusts you so little that he made your fidelity a condition of marriage. He *belabored* the point. Do you really think he would trust you in this?"

"He would." But even she didn't believe it. As recently as this evening, he'd accused her of being part of Simon's plans. If Simon confirmed those suspicions, Marcus would surely take his word for it.

"If you're so certain of him, go ahead and tell him all," Simon said coldly. "See what happens. Just remember that after I reveal how you've betrayed him, *you'll* have to live with the consequences. If you tell him before the wedding and he chooses to believe me, then there may be no wedding. That should really enhance your standing in society. And if you tell him afterward—" He cast her a grim smile. "I do hope all those rumors about his dungeon are false."

"I hope they aren't," she spat. "Because when he finds out what you're doing, he will surely throw you into it. And starve you for a month."

For a moment, he looked shaken by her bitter words. Then he steadied his shoulders with a condescending smile. "Now, now, you really shouldn't talk that way. Blood is thicker than water, dear girl."

"Don't you call me 'dear girl' ever again. I am not your 'dear' anything. And you are no brother of mine if you force me into this."

"I'm not forcing you," he said wearily. "Just explaining what I'll be compelled to do if you do not go along." Stepping up to her, he placed his hand on her shoulder. "But if you do comply, I swear never to let him know that you were privy to my plans. You can act surprised when he finds out that Louisa has chosen to live at court with her father."

"Her *father!*" She shoved his hand away. "The prince has never been a father to Louisa. He's only being one now so he can get something from her." Her breath came hot and heavy. "Marcus is twice the man you'll ever be. It breaks my heart to think of deceiving him."

"Then you should not have interfered in my affairs. I never asked you to make that silly bargain with him. I sure as hell did not ask you to go off in a carriage alone with him tonight."

"Because you knew I would never do it for *your* deceitful reasons." But she'd done it for her own, so she was as guilty as he.

"But you did do it, and now you must live with the consequences. Are you with me? Or shall I have a friendly chat with my future brother-in-law?"

Her blood ran cold at the very thought of how Marcus would regard her if he believed Simon's accusations. "You swore on your honor to stay away from Louisa," she said in a last-ditch effort to sway him. "Would you break your word?"

"I swore an oath to my regent that is higher. If Draker demands satisfaction for my broken promise, I will give it to him." He eyed her coldly. "But if you care for him, you'll make sure he doesn't demand satisfaction. Because I'm a very good shot."

Yes, he was. And for all she knew, Marcus couldn't hit a building at twenty paces. "All right. I'll keep silent. But I will never forgive you for this. Never."

He said nothing as she strode out into the hall. Perhaps he sensed he was on the verge of having his eyes scratched out. Or perhaps he was proud of himself for triumphing over her. Whatever the case, he would soon discover that she was not the sort to lie down and play dead simply because he commanded it.

She headed straight for Cicely's room, praying that her cousin was still awake and would agree to help her. Normally she'd have to twist Cicely's arm to get her to act against Simon, but now that he'd spoken casually of banishing her to the country, she might not be so kindly disposed.

And Regina intended to use that to her advantage. Between her and Cicely, they could make sure Louisa was never vulnerable to Simon's machinations. One way or the other, Louisa would always have someone on her side.

Chapter Sixteen

*Your charge's wedding need not ruin your future.
A clever woman will have already made herself
indispensable to the family by the time her charge
is married off.*
—Miss Cicely Tremaine, *The Ideal Chaperone*

For the past nine years, Marcus had assumed that weddings were for other people. The farmer's daughter marrying the brash young tenant. The aging schoolmistress marrying the local apothecary. The lady in the society column marrying her society gentleman, whose cheek *wasn't* scored by a hideous scar.

Yet now he stood before a bishop, scar and all. He clasped the delicate hand of the most beautiful woman in England, nay, the world. And he was making her his wife.

Astonishing.

Yes, the wedding was a hurried affair, done by special license. Yes, it was small and private, without all the fuss Regina was probably used to. But it was still a wedding, and she was willing. Or mostly willing. The few times he'd seen her in the past week of wedding preparations she'd been rather formal with him. Still, she spoke her vows without hesitation.

But without eagerness either. Who could blame her? Stunning dukes' daughters did not marry ungainly and reclusive louts like him, then settle happily into boring lives in the country away from fine society.

I must have the freedom to come and go to town as I please.

He scowled. Confound it all, he would *make* her be happy with him. He would keep her so satisfied at Castlemaine, in bed and out, that she would forget about town. He'd already leased the town house she'd demanded, but he'd be damned if he'd let her spend any time in it alone. He refused to follow his parents' path, even if that meant keeping her by his side every waking hour.

The bishop pronounced them man and wife, but when Marcus went to kiss her, she dropped her lashes demurely. His gut tightened. Regina was never demure. Cool, yes. Reserved, sometimes. But not demure. Did she already regret their marriage?

Not if he could help it.

Instead of giving her the polite peck on the lips that their guests probably expected, he tugged her into his arms and kissed her soundly, determined to lay his claim to her as publicly as possible.

When he drew back, amid polite titters among the guests, her breath came in quick gasps, and the spark was back in her eyes. Even if it *was* a spark of anger, it was better than her sudden modesty. He wouldn't let her be modest, not with him and not today.

After a week craving the sweet taste of her mouth, he was ravenous for her. And he meant to make her ravenous for him, too. Tonight he would make her his, totally and irrevocably. *His* wife. And God help her if she denied him.

They faced the guests, then made their quick way down the aisle of St. James's Church.

"I suppose you're quite pleased with yourself," she

grumbled under her breath. "I swear, sometimes you make me—"

"—wish that you hadn't come after me that night at Almack's?"

She cast him a startled glance. "No." Then she added, "But did you have to remind *everyone* why we're marrying so hastily?"

A grim smile touched his lips. "I'll do whatever it takes to show your sniveling suitors that you're no longer available."

"Surely the wedding did that," she shot back.

But the sharpness had left her voice, and she wore a ghost of a smile.

Outside, a lavishly decorated open landau waited to take them to the wedding breakfast at Foxmoor's mansion. As they waved at guests and bystanders, he said under his breath, "Can't we skip the breakfast and head straight to the honeymoon?"

She avoided his gaze. "Do men of your size ever skip meals?"

He lifted her hand to press a quick kiss into her palm. "Depends on what they're hungry for. The sort of meal I want right now is best eaten in private."

Her blush brought his every muscle to attention. "Behave," she said, in a throaty whisper.

"I'll try. For now, anyway."

Unfortunately, the wedding breakfast was designed to ensure good behavior. They had no privacy from the moment they arrived at Foxmoor's. There were an ungodly number of guests for a small wedding. Besides Miss Tremaine, the Iversleys, and Byrne, several lords and ladies from Regina's usual set had attended, half of whom he'd never even met.

Whitmore and his brothers were in attendance, too, although that didn't bother Marcus. During the endless congratulations in the receiving line, he found it immensely entertaining to gloat over the sullen Whitmore. He made sure the man was watching every time he bent to whisper in Regina's ear or took her arm or touched her hand. By the time Whitmore finally left—earlier than his brothers—Marcus was actually beginning to enjoy himself.

Except for one other annoyance. Even if Foxmoor was on his best behavior, even if having him at the wedding couldn't have been avoided, Marcus didn't like having him anywhere near Louisa.

As he and Regina left the receiving line, Marcus looked for Louisa and frowned when he saw her in close conversation with Miss Tremaine. "When did my sister and your cousin become such fast friends?"

Regina's smile looked forced. "Why shouldn't they be friends? Cicely is now a guest at the Iversleys', so they'll be in each other's pockets a great deal."

"I still don't understand why Miss Tremaine couldn't stay at Castlemaine or our new town house."

"She's sickly—I did not want her staying alone anywhere."

"My servants would have taken good care of her."

"All the same, Lady Iversley does not mind having her as a guest, and I feel better knowing that someone is looking out for her."

He supposed he should count his blessings that the damned woman wasn't coming on their honeymoon. He'd had a devil of a time convincing Regina not to bring a lady's maid.

Still . . . "Your cousin had better not be planning to help your brother break his promise."

"She's loyal to me, and she knows I would never countenance such a thing. Even if he would attempt it."

She wouldn't look at him, and that made him uneasy. "He'd attempt it, you can be sure. I don't trust your brother."

Her gaze swung him. "Do you trust *me?*"

Not when it comes to him, I don't. But he wasn't fool enough to say that aloud. "Of course I trust you."

"Then believe me when I say that Cicely can be trusted, too." Regina's gaze drifted back to Louisa. "If you're still concerned about Simon, why don't you tell Louisa your suspicions? Put her on her guard."

"She wouldn't believe me. She already knows how suspicious I am of the prince and his friends—she would accuse me of having an unjust bias. And to convince her, I'd have to tell her—" He broke off, cursing his quick tongue.

"Tell her what?"

He sighed. As his wife, she might as well know the truth. "That there's some question about her parentage, at least in Prinny's mind. He claims she's his."

She seemed oddly unsurprised to hear it. "I take it that you disagree?"

"She's not the prince's daughter, no matter what he says."

"Are you sure?"

"Circumstances make it impossible. And Prinny knows it, too. If he thought she was his, he would have challenged me for guardianship long ago, like he and Mrs. Fitzherbert did with Lady Horatia Seymour's girl."

"But Minney had no immediate family to claim her after her mother died, just uncles and cousins."

"None of whom believed that Prinny was her father,

even though her mother had been his mistress. Yet the prince fought for guardianship of the girl."

"Perhaps he doesn't fight you because he knows Louisa is in good hands."

Marcus eyed her askance. "He knows how much I despise him. That insult to his pride alone should make him fight me."

She was silent a moment. "Would it be so awful if Louisa *was* His Highness's daughter?"

Anger knotted in his belly. "I've lived most of my life knowing I was a fraud—not a true heir to a prince and not a true heir to a viscount, either. I knew I was the illicit product of a union despised by the Church and abhorred by respectable people. I was the very symbol of all that is wrong with our society. I would not lay that burden on anyone, but especially not on Louisa."

"She is a grown woman now. She can handle the knowledge."

"Can she? I don't see *you* telling her that your brother is an ass who wants her only for political gain."

Paling, she glanced away. "Because it's not true." She added in a whisper, "And if it were, it would break her heart."

"Exactly. That's why I don't want her to know about any of this. I'd rather separate them. I can endure playing the awful, overprotective brother if that's what it takes to give Foxmoor time to grow tired of this maneuver and give up."

"And if he doesn't give up?" When he raised an eyebrow at her, she added, "I mean courting her, of course."

"If he persists in any of it, I will have his head." He shot her a stern look. "And if you help your brother, I swear I will have yours, too."

"I have no intention of helping him if it means harming

your sister." She added in a quiet voice tinged in sadness, "Whether you believe it or not, I have never wanted anything but the best for Louisa."

"Good."

But the whole conversation left a bad taste in his mouth that was not wiped away by the costly dishes provided at the breakfast. Regina was keeping something from him. He sensed it. He just couldn't figure out what it was.

His unease lingered even after the breakfast ended and they climbed into his carriage. Both of them were somewhat tipsy from champagne, and she had changed her gossamer wedding gown for a rather formidable traveling costume. The peach-colored thing was fastened right up to her chin by an untold number of tassels and was finished off at the top with a many-pointed collar. It practically shouted, "Don't touch!"

It might not bother him so much if she didn't also take the seat opposite him, instead of next to him. That did not bode well for the evening.

Trying to settle her, he reached in his pocket and pulled out what Louisa had given him earlier. "Here," he said, tossing the envelope into Regina's lap as the coach rumbled off. "Louisa asked me to give this to you when we set out. I imagine it's some female nonsense welcoming you to the family."

But his gesture seemed to worry more than soothe her. With shaky hands, she tucked it inside her reticule. "Thank you."

"Aren't you going to read it?"

"I'll read it later."

"I don't mind if you read it now."

"I prefer privacy when I read my letters. Just so you'll know."

"I see." But he did not see. Was this how she meant their marriage to be, stiff and formal and "private"? That didn't sit well with him. But how could he change it?

They rode for some time in awkward silence before she asked, "Where are we going?"

"It's a surprise."

She swallowed. "One I will like?"

"I certainly hope so. It will give us the chance to be alone."

"For how long?"

"However long we wish."

She sucked in a breath, then stared down at her hands. "We're not going anywhere . . . too remote, are we?"

That put him further on his guard. "What do you mean?"

"There will be servants who can send a message for me?"

"If you want. To whom will you be sending messages?"

"I'll want Cicely to know my direction in case she needs to reach me."

"Fine." Her questions and strange reliance on her cousin exasperated him. "As long as you're not planning to have her show up, send her all the messages you wish." He eyed her closely. "Are you afraid of being alone with me?"

She shot him a guarded glance. "No, of course not."

"Then what's wrong? You were less prickly with me when we weren't even betrothed than you are now as my wife."

She forced a smile. "Every woman is nervous on her wedding day."

"Then I have the perfect cure." He reached across the carriage and hauled her over and onto his lap.

"Marcus!" She trying to wriggle free. "It's broad daylight!"

"It's nearly dusk. Besides, we're married." Before she could protest further, he kissed her deeply. At first she seemed oddly timid about returning the kiss, but it didn't take long for her natural sensuality to assert itself.

When her arms crept about his neck, he growled his approval and kissed her with a week's worth of longing. He wouldn't deflower her in his carriage like some uncivilized beast, but he could damned well prepare her for the deflowering later. They would reach their destination in only a couple of hours, which left him plenty of time to rouse her hunger and ease her virginal misgivings.

If he could last that long. Each kiss led to a hotter one until he thought he might perish if he didn't soon taste her sweet flesh.

He bent to kiss her neck, then nearly blinded one eye. "What the devil!" he swore as he jerked back. He poked at her deceptively lacy collar. "What are these pointy things?"

"It's a ruff," she said indignantly. "With wire in it to make it stand up."

"It's lethal," he grumbled. "Did you *want* me not to touch you?"

A musical laugh cascaded from her. "I didn't even think about that when I had it made. *La Belle Assemblee* calls it 'the most elegant and novel' carriage costume to appear in a long time. Don't you agree?"

"It's novel, I'll give you that."

"I thought it looked fetching."

"Fetchingly draconian, perhaps."

Her eyes twinkled. "Then it's perfect for the Dragon Viscount's wife."

He cast her a grudging smile. "The Dragon Viscountess. It suits you. Only *you* would choose clothing designed to torture a man."

She arched one eyebrow. "It never occurred to me that you might attack me as soon as we entered the carriage."

"Then you don't know your husband very well." He nipped her earlobe. "I can see I shall have to help you pick your gowns from now on. Because I don't intend to suffer this torture every time I try to kiss my wife."

"Oh, the poor dragon," she teased. "Thwarted by a traveling costume. How shall you ever hold your head up among the other dragons?"

"There better not be any other dragons," he whispered in her ear. "I mean to be the only one."

He knew he'd said the wrong thing when she flinched and drew back. "I swore to be faithful to you. And you said at the breakfast that you trusted me."

"It's not you I don't trust. It's the other dragons."

"I did not marry any of those other dragons. I married you."

"Because you were forced," he said, voicing one of his misgivings.

"I had other choices. I did not take them."

"None of them were good choices," he bit out.

"True. But I am happy with the one I made."

"Are you?"

"I'm sitting here on your lap, aren't I?"

"Dressed in the most diabolical gown ever to grace the female form."

She chuckled. "I shall never wear it again."

"You most certainly will—whenever you're around one of those other dragons, and I'm not nearby. I'll put it on you myself."

Eyes gleaming, she cupped his jaw. "You are perfectly adorable when you're jealous."

He glared at her. "I'm not joking. I won't share you with anyone."

"Neither shall I. Share *you* with anyone, I mean."

He gaped at her. "You can't seriously think that would be a problem."

"Did you not see how the women at Almack's were flirting with you?"

"Perhaps a few," he muttered, mollified that she'd noticed. And cared. "But only because I was a curiosity. Given the choice between their handsome suitors and a man with my hideous disfigurement—"

"It is *not* a hideous disfigurement," she said fiercely. She ran her fingers along the length of it. "I think it's rather dashing."

She was only trying to jolly him out of his bad mood. Oddly enough, it was working. "Dashing. Right."

Her hand caressed his cheek. "Now that we are married, will you tell me how you came by it?"

"Great God, why would you want to know that?"

"Because I am your wife. I want to know *everything* about you." She straightened on his lap. "If you do not tell me, I shall poke at you with my ruff."

A reluctant smile touched his lips. "All right. I don't need any more scars, thank you."

"You did not get it in a riding accident, did you?" she prodded.

With a sigh, he settled her more comfortably on his lap. "No. You were right at Almack's—it's a burn. From a hot poker."

A frown marred her pretty brow. "There? On your face?"

"The person wielding it didn't mean to strike me on the face. If it had struck my broad back as intended, it probably would only have singed my coat and stunned me, but I turned as it came down, and it hit me full across the cheek."

"Oh, my poor darling." Her face filled with pity. She ran her fingers over his scar as if to erase it with her tender touch. "How you must have suffered."

Darling. She'd called him "darling." He should have told her about his damned scar ages ago. "It hurt for a while, yes," he said gruffly. "But it would have been much worse if not for my precocious sister. The poor mite insisted on dressing it every day with some newfangled remedy she'd read about in the *Lady's Magazine*. Whatever it was, it helped heal it quickly."

"Louisa was there?"

"She didn't see it happen, no, and I never told her the full circumstances. But she was home with me at the time, yes."

Her eyes narrowed. "This happened at Castlemaine? What horrible person dared to do such a thing to you in your own home?"

"You don't want to know this." Shame engulfed him. He shuddered to think what she would make of it.

"I do want to know. I'm your wife. You can tell me anything, darling."

Darling. There was that wonderful word again. He'd never expected to hear it from any woman's lips, much less hers. It dissolved all his reluctance to answer. "My mother did it."

For a moment she just gaped at him. Now she would realize how appalling the family she'd married into was, and regret her hasty act.

But the only expression on her face was outrage. "Your mother? Your *mother* did this to you? How dare she! I swear, if she were here right now, I'd . . . I'd . . . well, I'd do something truly awful to her. Strike her own son with a poker indeed—what was wrong with the woman? Was she deranged?"

Her outrage on his behalf took him aback. "Not exactly. She did it in a fit of temper. She wasn't thinking rationally."

"I don't care. *Nothing* justifies a woman's striking her son with a hot poker."

He found himself in the unprecedented position of having to defend his mother. "She was stoking up the fire when I told her and Prinny I wanted them gone from Castlemaine, now that I was lord. That so infuriated her that when Prinny protested, and I gave him a piece of my mind, about—" He wasn't about to go into that, not on his wedding night. "Anyway, she went mad. She came at me with the poker, Prinny called out a warning, I turned, and *voilà.* I got this scar."

"She should have been shot for marring your handsome face," she said fervently.

Handsome face? His wife thought him handsome? Astonishing. "She got her just reward. Prinny was none too happy about it—or about being thrown off the estate publicly. That was the beginning of the end of their liaison. Why do you think she spread those vile rumors about all the wicked things I'd supposedly done to her, cutting her out of the will and beating her and all that nonsense? She never forgave me for ruining her relationship with Prinny."

"*She* was the one who ruined it! Why didn't you tell people that?"

He shuddered. "Tell them that my own mother despised me so much she struck me with a hot poker? I didn't want anyone hearing that. Besides, she would simply have told them I'd been beating her and she was forced to defend herself, or some other nonsense."

"But the prince—"

"—would have supported her claims. He wasn't about to have it known that his mistress was so awful a woman." He gritted his teeth. "When it came to her treatment of me, he always condoned her behavior."

"What do you mean?" she asked.

"Nothing. My point is that if I had told the truth about her, she would have engineered greater lies about me." His shame returned full force. "And it was easy enough for her to make me out to be a monster. I'd just thrown a royal prince from my home. Besides, at twenty-two, I was as inept, surly, and disinclined to suffer fools as I am now. I was already well on my way to making myself the bane of good society. I'd been getting into fights for years over the names the schoolboys called me." The bile in his gut rose to choke him. "And Father."

"The prince?"

"The viscount," he bit out.

"But the prince *is* your natural father, isn't he? I heard that the viscount returned from a six-month trip to Italy to find your mother newly enceinte."

He scowled. "Yes, the eternal mortification of my life is that everyone knows I am really a bastard. My mother could not wait until she bore the requisite heir and a spare, oh no. Her husband merely turns his back, and all it takes to have her in the young prince's bed is a few compliments and a gift or two."

"Turns his back? For six months? How long had they been married?"

"Two years."

"And he abandoned her for so long?"

"He did not abandon her," Marcus snapped. "He wanted to please her by redoing Castlemaine so that it was fitting for a woman of her rank and beauty." His mother had been from a very old family, one that had spent its later years digging itself into a deep financial hole. A hole the viscount had filled with his own wealth. "So he went to Italy to select marble and see the villas, that sort of thing."

"For six months? Without his wife?"

When she eyed him askance, he realized for the first time how odd that sounded. "She could have gone with him." He scrambled for a defense of Father that made sense. "But she preferred to be in England. In London."

"I don't know any woman who'd enjoy having her husband gone for six months, no matter what he meant to do to their castle."

"So you think she was justified in her affair," he said in a cold voice.

"Of course not." Her eyes burned into his. "But if *my* husband found my company so onerous that he preferred traveling about Italy to being with me, I would hound him until I learned why. I'd let no man get away with ignoring *me*."

Oddly enough, that soothed him. "I don't imagine you would." He brushed a kiss to her forehead. "And I don't mean to test that assertion, either."

A grudging smile touched her lips. "You'd better not."

He kissed her, the kiss rapidly turning searing. After several scorching kisses that led only to frustrating caresses through the thick fabric of her formidable gown, he was just on the verge of tearing the damned thing off her when the carriage shuddered abruptly to a halt, making them break apart.

He looked out, astonished to find that they'd already reached their destination. A slow grin curved up his lips. "We're here, dearling."

Chapter Seventeen

Instruct your charge always to be honest with her
husband. It will ease her married life considerably.
—Miss Cicely Tremaine, *The Ideal Chaperone*

*R*egina scrambled off Marcus's lap and peered out the window, but all she could see on her side of the coach was a copse of oak and beech. "Where is here?" she asked, growing more curious by the moment.

He threaded his fingers through hers. "My estate. Just not the main house."

She shot him a bemused look as she straightened her gown, then touched her hand to her mussed hair. "We're spending our honeymoon in a hunting cabin on your estate?"

"Not exactly. Come see."

A groom had already scurried to open the carriage door. As they disembarked she looked around, unable to believe her eyes. If she hadn't known better, she would have thought Marcus had spirited them right out of England only to drop them in the midst of India or Turkey. An onion dome rose into the sky, flanked by two eastern-looking minarets. The whole was embellished with golden fretwork and curvy windows and columns carved in the shape of palm trees.

"Lord, this is quite a hunting cabin," she exclaimed.

He chuckled. "My father had eclectic tastes in architecture. After a trip to India, he decided to build a miniature Oriental palace to go with his castle. We call it Illyria."

"Peculiar name."

"It's from Shakespeare." He slanted a glance at her. "I don't suppose you read many plays."

"None at all, I'm afraid," she said ironically. The servants scurried about, unloading luggage to carry inside while she gazed up at the imposing building. "How far are we from the main house?"

"A couple of miles."

What a vast estate he must have. At least they were close enough to the house that Cicely could summon her back to London if need be. Then again, giving Cicely her direction might not be easy. Regina had planned to bribe an innkeeper's servant to write and read letters for her wherever they ended up. But bribing one of Marcus's servants was unacceptable. Oh dear, she'd have to think of something else. But what?

"Father built Illyria as his retreat," Marcus explained, "so he and Louisa and I would have somewhere to go when . . . certain guests were in residence."

"Ah." She stood marveling at Marcus's Oriental palace. "It's amazing. Has the prince ever seen it?"

"No," he bit out. "Neither he nor my mother was ever allowed here."

"Are you sure? It looks very much like a renovation design he's been considering for his house in Brighton." She shot him a side glance. "And if I remember correctly, that design contains a number of dragons."

He stiffened. "Father would not have let them within a mile of this place, I promise you."

Them. The resentment in his voice saddened her. Not that she blamed him, after what he'd told her on their ride.

"In any case," he went on, "I thought spending our honeymoon here would ease you into life at Castlemaine. When we want to visit the main house and other parts of the estate we can, but if we want to stay here alone, we can do that, too." He slid his arm around her waist, his voice growing husky. "For myself, I would rather be alone with you for a while."

He kissed her right in front of the servants, and her heart leaped into her throat. *How long is a while?* she wanted to ask, but he would misunderstand her reason for the question. She could hardly tell him she was worried about Louisa.

She could only pray that Cicely would succeed in befriending Louisa and holding Simon at bay. Or that Simon didn't find a way to twist Cicely's arm, too.

Given Marcus's dreadful mother, he had good reason for being suspicious of Regina's own motives for marrying him. But she didn't know how to reassure him. Telling him about Simon would only make everything worse.

And telling him about the other . . . No, she couldn't, not yet. Until they shared a bed, he could conceivably get their marriage annulled. Her damaged mind would give him ample cause, and what a humiliation that would be.

She would wait until after their wedding night. Then if he demanded retribution for her not telling him of her defect until it was too late, she would give him whatever he demanded, no matter what it was.

She would leave the decision about children to him, too. Perhaps he wouldn't care. He might not mind having an heir who could not read. Who was feebleminded or worse.

But *he* was fine, so perhaps their children would be fine. His sturdy breeding might make up for the weakness in hers.

Yes, that's what she would pray for. Surely after all that Marcus had suffered in his life, God would not make him suffer with his children, too.

She drew back from Marcus, forcing a bright smile for his benefit. "Why don't you show me the house? I'm dying to see the inside."

"Certainly." With a knowing smile, he slid his arm about her waist. "Shall I show you the bedchamber first?"

"Now?" she asked. "I mean—"

"It's all right," he murmured, amusement in his voice. "I won't rush you. We have the whole night."

The thought stayed with her as he showed her into a neat foyer sparkling with Oriental greens and golds, and then an adorable sitting room furnished entirely with items of black lacquer and mother-of-pearl. She oohed and aahed on cue, but her mind raced with everything her married friends had told her this week about *their* wedding nights.

They'd used words like "awkward" and "mortifying." They'd said that "the first bit is nice, but the end is awful" and had reassured her that it was "over quickly, thank heavens." And every tale had ended with "But at least he gives you jewels after it's done, so it's all right."

As if that would make up for what sounded like an awful experience. Besides, she couldn't even imagine Marcus giving her flowers, much less jewels. He wasn't the flowers and jewels sort.

But he did seem very good at the kissing and fondling

part. So perhaps the act itself would not be *too* awful with him. It wasn't as if he didn't have any experience at it, after all. There were all those "beauties" he could buy at any brothel. Perhaps her friends' husbands just hadn't been very experienced.

Then again . . . she stole a glance at Marcus's broad shoulders and great height. Compared to her friends' husbands, Marcus was downright brutish in size. And he was lustier, too. She couldn't imagine a single one of her friends' husbands dragging his wife onto his lap. Or trying to seduce her in a carriage.

But Marcus would be demanding and forceful and . . . big. Dear Lord.

"Here's the kitchen," he was saying as he ushered her into a tidy little room about the size of the kitchen in most London town houses. "Are you hungry?"

Somehow she managed a smile. "After all that food I ate at our wedding breakfast? You must be joking."

"Good." His eyes gleamed as he took her in his arms. "I told the servants to leave a cold repast just in case, but I want something else for dinner."

He kissed her, and since there were no servants nearby, his kiss was searingly blatant. Yet she could not relax in his arms. Sitting on his lap in the carriage had been one thing—she had known he could do nothing to her there. Perhaps she *had* even chosen her gown with that in the back of her mind.

But there was nothing to delay their union now.

When she felt his fingers untying her carriage gown, she jerked back, blushing. "What about the servants? What if they see us here in the kitchen—"

"I dismissed them for the night. They'll return in the morning to take care of us, but I figured we could see to our own comfort on our wedding night." He searched her face. "Still nervous?"

"Only a bit," she said gamely, swallowing her anxiety.

With a decidedly dragonly smile, he took her arm. "Let's go upstairs. I have just the thing to relax you."

When he led her toward the stairs, her heart began to pound. The bedroom. They were going to the bedroom now. "Is it too late to eat that cold repast?"

His gaze burned down at her. "I tell you what. After I show you the surprise I have for you upstairs, if you still want to eat, we'll come back down. All right?"

She lifted one eyebrow. "The surprise doesn't have anything to do with . . . er . . . you know . . ."

He laughed. "No. Not directly, anyway."

That roused her curiosity enough that she made no further protests as he led her upstairs and into a large bedchamber with a roaring fire. She gazed around, momentarily dazzled by the wall coverings of patterned red silk and the brilliant gold-and-scarlet-hued Oriental carpet.

And then she saw it. The most amazing harp she'd ever encountered. Keeping its nose in the air like a queen offended by its slightly vulgar surroundings, the heavy walnut instrument sat beside the Chinese Chippendale bed. "Ohh, Marcus," she whispered, then added inanely, "it's for me?"

"Of course it's for you. Can you imagine me, with my oafish hands, playing it?"

Her delight spilled out of her in a long laugh, and she ran to examine it, feeling like a five-year-old at Christmas. The neck was ornately carved in the shape of a dragon with its long tail. Clearly the instrument had been built to order, although how he'd managed it in so short a time she could not imagine. She fingered the strings, smiling at the exquisite sound. He'd even had it tuned.

He came up behind her. "Do you like it? I confess to not knowing much about harps, but Louisa helped me instruct the fellow who made it—"

"It's wonderful." She turned to plant a kiss squarely on his mouth. "Absolutely wonderful! I love it!"

He tugged her back for another kiss so bold and hot it seared her clear to her toes. When he drew back, his eyes were gleaming. "Did you read the inscription?"

All her pleasure faltered. "T-The inscription?"

"On the harp. I had it inscribed especially for you."

"I didn't see it. But I'll look at it later." She flung her arms about his neck and lifted her mouth for another kiss. Given the choice between the marriage bed and revealing her defect to him right off, she would take the marriage bed any day.

But he pulled away. "No, I want you to read it. Come on."

Her heart sank as he tugged her over to the harp and pointed to some words engraved on a little gold plate set into the sound box. "You see?"

She nodded and pretended to examine it. "Yes. It's very nice."

His smile faded. "Nice? You think it's *nice*?"

She kept nodding, frantically trying to guess what he might have written.

"Nice," he repeated, a sudden bitterness in his tone. "Right. In other words, the less said about such a scandalous inscription the better."

"I don't know what you're talking about," she whispered.

"Don't play dumb, Regina, it doesn't suit you." He

whirled away from her with a curse. "That's what this is really about, isn't it? The gown, your anxiousness, your desire to have your cousin live with us . . . Clearly, the thought of being alone with me, being intimate with me, appalls you."

"I didn't say that!" she cried, alarmed by the bitterness pouring out of him.

"You didn't have to."

Lord, she'd really stumbled into it now. "Please, what does the inscription say?" she ventured, hoping he'd just tell her. "I couldn't make out the words."

He snorted.

"Just tell me what it says," she whispered.

A muscle worked in his jaw. "You'd like hearing me say the words, wouldn't you? You could gloat over me, then." He scrubbed at his chin with his hand, then groaned as if missing his beard. "How do you always manage to make me forget? You lull me into letting my guard down with your sweetness, then your true nature rears its ugly head—"

"*What* true nature?" Sweet heaven, what did he mean?

"That you're La Belle Dame Sans Merci, that you live to humiliate men for desiring you. Well, don't worry, madam, I won't inflict myself on you tonight."

He turned toward the door, but she grabbed his arm to stay him.

"Tell me what it says, drat you!" Tears welled in her eyes. "Please tell me."

Her panic seemed to reach him, because he pinned her with an exasperated look. "Stop this pretense. I know you read it. I made sure they didn't use one of those silly furbe-low fonts that—"

"I didn't read it," she interrupted. "I didn't."

"Then read it now."

"I can't." The words were out of her mouth before she could stop them.

"Of course you can." He took her by the arm as if to lead her back to the harp. "Here, just look at it again."

"I can't read it!" She wrenched her arm free. "Drat it, Marcus, I can't read anything!" She collapsed on the bed in a fit of sobs. "I can't *read* . . . I can't read."

Marcus just stood there, unable to assimilate her words. What did she mean, she couldn't read? Of course she could read. She was a duke's daughter, for God's sake, not some poor scullery maid. He'd seen her read things.

Hadn't he?

Come to think of it, she'd refused to read that note from Louisa. And she'd always seemed to hate his obsession with books. What had Foxmoor said? *I've never even seen her crack a book open.*

But she'd signed her name to the marriage license this very day.

His throat tightened. Yes, she'd signed it with an illegible scrawl. Not at all the ladylike penmanship he would have expected. And when he'd teased her about it, she had swiftly changed the subject.

"I meant . . . to tell you before . . ." she choked out between heart-wrenching sobs. "I should have . . . I'm *so* sorry—"

"Nothing to be sorry about," he said, belatedly hurrying to reassure her, though his mind still reeled. Taking a seat next to her, he gathered her in his arms. "Hush, dearling," he murmured, clasping her head to his chest. "Don't go on so."

Her tears tore at him. He'd never seen her cry, and to think he'd brought her to this with his stupid fit of temper—

"You're such a great reader," she whispered, lifting her tear-stained face. "I've been living in mortal terror of when you found out. Cicely usually reads for me, but with her in London—"

"Oh, God," he groaned, clutching her tightly as so many things fell into place. Why she wanted Cicely to live with them. Why she liked parties better than books. Why she'd refused to sing with him at the soiree. Because she really *hadn't* known the song. And she couldn't read it.

Guilt cut through him at the thought of how he'd humiliated her publicly for not singing with him.

"I wanted to tell you before," she whispered into his waistcoat, "but I was too mortified. Then after I was compromised, I was afraid you would refuse to marry me. And now—" Her sobs subsided, but the gaze she lifted to his face was still achingly teary. "Please don't annul the marriage. I couldn't bear the shame. I'll do whatever you wish . . . I'll stay in the country always . . . I'll . . . I'll—"

"Shh, dearling." He brushed a kiss to her lips to stay her begging. It drove a stake through his heart. Every nasty comment and unthinking accusation he'd ever made about her came back to torment him. "I'm not annulling our marriage, for this or anything else."

"You don't understand," she murmured, her face an ashen mask. "I can't read because . . . because . . . there's something wrong with my brain."

"There's nothing wrong with your brain," he protested, holding her close.

"But there is!" She pushed him away. "Ask Cicely; she'll tell you." The words spilled out of her, heartbreaking in their conviction. "I don't see letters properly, and when I try to read anyway I get these awful headaches. And if I bear you children and they have the same defect or worse—" Tears filled her eyes again. "Oh, I'd just die!"

"Don't even think it." He kissed her tears away, feeling as if *he* were dying. "Nothing will be wrong with our children, I promise."

This was why she'd never married, why she refused every suitor, why she could be the sweetest angel one moment and a cruel siren the next. Because she'd survived by keeping everyone away. Until he'd come along.

And what if she were right? What if her brain really *was* damaged? Feeblemindedness and lunacy did run in families. What if their children—

No, whatever else might be wrong with her, she was not feebleminded. "We'll face this together, dearling. You're my wife, till death do us part. I'm not letting you out of it, so don't even suggest an annulment."

"But Marcus, I wouldn't blame you—"

"If you persist in speaking of an annulment," he warned, "I'll assume *you* are the one who wants out of the marriage."

Her gaze shot to his, fierce and sure. "Never. I meant every word of *my* wedding vows."

His heart flipped over in his chest. "So did I." Later, he'd probe into this "damaged brain" nonsense and make her explain how a duke's daughter came to be illiterate. For now it was enough to see the old Regina reviving.

Determined to salvage what was left of their evening, he smiled and began to unfasten the tassels on her silly gown. "I can think of only one way to make sure there is no annulment."

She sucked in a breath, her eyes shining through her tears like two silver guineas in the candlelight. "What does the inscription say, Marcus?"

His blood ran high as he opened her gown to find a

silky chemise so sheer that her nipples showed through the fabric, two pink buds he already ached to taste. "It said, 'To my dear wife, the only woman I would ever want to chain in my dungeon.' "

A hesitant smile touched her lips. "That is not very . . . er . . . nice. One might even call it naughty."

"Damned right it's naughty." The blood surged through him as he lowered his mouth to hers. "And we're going to be far more naughty before the night is over."

Chapter Eighteen

Your charge's mother is responsible for informing her of what she can expect on her wedding night. But if the mother cannot or does not fulfill her duty, then you must do so.
—Miss Cicely Tremaine, *The Ideal Chaperone*

Regina reveled in Draker's kiss, so warm, so tender. Perhaps he truly didn't care. If he desired her badly enough to overlook her defect, who was she to argue?

Especially now that he had his hands inside her gown, working their incredible magic on her breasts. Sweet heaven, what a delicious feeling.

He bent his head to kiss her neck, then cursed. "*This* has got to go." He hastily untied the other tassels, then dragged off her gown. "That damned ruff has poked me for the last time."

She laughed, practically giddy in her relief that he hadn't cast her aside. "Perhaps you should chain *it* in the dungeon," she teased as he tossed it across the room.

His eyes glittered, playing hotly over her thinly clad body. "I'd much rather chain *you*."

"You'd better not," she warned. But her breath came in quick gasps, and the images rising in her head were luridly vivid.

"You might like it." He pressed her back upon the bed

until her head lay on the pillow, then took her hands and closed them around two pieces of the fretwork that formed the headboard of the Chinese Chippendale bed. Bending his mouth to her breast, he tongued her nipple through the chemise, rousing it into an aching bud. "You might find it very adventurous to be chained up in my dungeon, waiting for—"

"The dragon to come devour me?" she whispered, caught up in his fantasy.

"Oh, yes," he growled against her breast.

Where just a little while ago she'd been apprehensive about her wedding night, his outrageous words—and actions—were perversely having the opposite effect on her. Her body softened beneath the rasps of his hot tongue, grew warm beneath his sucking mouth.

He loosened her chemise ties with his teeth. But when he went to pull it down, he couldn't lower it far enough to bare her breasts, because of her arms being over her head.

So he dropped his hand to the hem of her chemise and pulled it up. He tugged her hands free of the fretwork only long enough to drag her chemise over her head, closing them back around it seconds later. "Don't let go," he ordered. "You're chained."

"Am I?"

His gaze shot to hers, heated, intent. "For the moment."

A wanton thrill coursed through her. "All right."

Next he removed her stockings and drawers, leaving her lying fully naked before him. She squirmed as his eyes raked her from head to toe. How exquisitely sinful this seemed.

Then he left the bed and went to sit in an armchair facing her. All he did was stare at her.

A delicious shiver swept her from his distinctly ravenous gaze. With the firelight playing over the stark planes of his scarred face, he actually looked like a dragon brooding over his captive female, preparing to feast himself on her flesh.

She swallowed. Hard. But still she clung to the fretwork.

He removed one boot. "I believe I like you chained." His voice was guttural, needy.

It spiked her own need even higher. "That only proves you're very wicked."

His other boot thudded to the floor. "Then how good of you to indulge my wickedness. Few women would." He rose to approach the bed, his gaze fierce and hard as it scoured her. "Even fewer would take pleasure in it."

Embarrassed that she'd shown herself to be as wicked as he, she jerked her gaze from his to scan the room. But that only made it worse, because the painting taking up half of the wall opposite the bed—a painting not at all in the Chinese style of the rest of the room—featured a whole array of half-clad nymphs. No, they were sirens, beckoning a shipful of hapless sailors to dash themselves on the rocks.

With a groan, she glanced back at Marcus. "Whose room is this?"

"Mine."

"And your father let you have *that* painting on the wall?"

He chuckled. "Hardly. I added that later." His eyes played warmly over her. "I have a particular interest in beautiful sirens."

"Like those beauties you can purchase in any brothel?" she said tartly.

"Like you," he countered. "I could never afford any beauty as priceless as you, dearling."

The blatant approval in his look burned away any lingering embarrassment, leaving her feeling restless. Hot. And strangely hungry.

Then he began to undress. He took his time about it, too, his eyes never leaving her body as he sloughed off his coat. Next he unbuttoned his waistcoat with slow, deliberate movements that made her breath quicken in anticipation. She could see the bulge in his trousers, yet he continued his maddeningly slow process.

Low in her belly, her flesh began to quiver . . . then tighten . . . then ache. She thought she might die if he didn't touch her soon.

He removed his cravat, then approached the bed to skim the scrap of silk over her highly sensitized breasts and belly and even *down there.* The cursed fabric roused her need to a fever pitch without satisfying it.

She squirmed as he dragged it one last time over her breasts before dropping it on the floor. "Now I know why they call you a dragon," she grumbled. "Because you can be perfectly beastly sometimes."

With a grin, he unbuttoned his shirt. "Ah, but you like me beastly, don't you? It feeds your thirst for adventure."

"I do not have a—" She broke off as he dragged his shirt off over his head. "Dear Lord in heaven." His chest would rival that of any wrestler's, a thickly hewn wall of flesh that narrowed down to a surprisingly lean waist.

His grin widened. "Do I meet with my lady's approval?"

"You look perfectly . . . um . . . beastly."

After shucking his trousers he lay down on the bed beside her, still wearing his drawers, though they didn't leave much to the imagination.

"Then I shall get right to my beastly duties." When he bent his head to suck her breast, she let out a long, drawn-out sigh. "Does that please you?" he rasped, then tugged at her nipple with his teeth.

"Ohh, yes," she breathed, her fingers tightening on the fretwork bars. Just the thought of being utterly exposed to his mouth and teeth and hands was firing her excitement to incredible heights.

"Do you want more?" He kissed a path down her breastbone to her belly as one of his hands fondled her breast.

"Yes, Marcus, yes," she whispered restlessly. "More. Please."

She turned her head to find the dratted sirens in the painting laughing at her. *They* would never beg for more, but she was positively shameless when it came to Marcus.

She shut her eyes against them. But when she felt his hand leave her breast, she arched up toward him. "Please . . . Marcus—"

Then his mouth touched her in a wholly unexpected place. *Down there.* Between her legs. Oh, heavens.

Her eyes flew open. Somehow he had ended up with his head between her thighs. His hands were parting the folds of her flesh as he bent his head to kiss—

"Marcus!" she protested, utterly shocked. She tried to pull her legs together, but he wouldn't let her.

"Be still, dearling." His eyes glittered up at her. "The dragon is dining."

Keeping his gaze locked with hers, he put his hot mouth right on her. Down there. Like a lover kissing her, except in the most intimate place. His tongue darted out to flick at her, and she nearly leaped from her skin.

Heaven save her. What . . . incredible . . . madness was this? She could hardly breathe. Or think. Or do anything but give herself up to the wild pleasure coursing through her.

He was even using his teeth! And it was wonderful. Amazing. Shocking. Surely the places his mouth caressed were not meant to be touched so sinfully. Or sucked so wickedly, or teased so . . . so . . .

"Marcus . . ." she breathed. "That is . . . oh . . . dear . . . oh . . ."

His mouth fondled her even more shamelessly. She writhed beneath it, seeking more. Every rasp of his tongue made her arch higher, every tug of his teeth wrung a surprised gasp from her throat until it ached with her cries. Soon she was headed toward the same sweet exultation she'd found that night in the carriage outside Almack's.

She could feel it dangling before her. If she could just . . . reach . . . that . . . amazing . . . mad . . .

He lifted his head to growl, "Oh, no, you don't, my siren wife. Not without me, not this time. Not until I can be inside you, sharing your pleasure."

"Marcus!" she cried, half in alarm, half in outrage as he left the bed. She reached for him. "Where are you going?"

"To take these off."

He removed his drawers, and she gasped. His great staff jutted out from its bed of dark hair, commanding her attention. That . . . that *thing* was going inside her? "Oh, sweet heaven."

His eyes gleamed. "I'll take that as an invitation." His gaze flicked to her hands and he added, "What happened to your chains?"

She wasn't sure when she'd let go of the fretwork. "I broke them."

A strangled laugh burst from him as he returned to the bed. "That's my wife—stronger than steel."

Before he could climb on the mattress, she grabbed his hip. "Wait!"

"No more waiting," he muttered, brushing away her hand.

"I want to touch you," she protested. "And look at you."

A dark flush stained his cheeks. "No."

"You gazed your fill of me," she persisted. "So it's my turn."

"*Now?*" he ground out.

She propped her head up on her hands. "Now."

He groaned. Nonetheless, he stood still and let her lay her hand tentatively on the mighty rod of flesh between his legs. "Someone *did* prepare you for this night, didn't they?" he rasped. "Told you how this works?"

"My married friends told me a little. But I still didn't expect . . . you . . . to be quite so . . . large."

"It'll fit, don't worry," he said tersely.

She ran one finger over the smooth flesh, marveling at how it jerked beneath her touch. He actually shook as she stroked him. Perversely, that reassured her.

"And what did Miss Tremaine tell you?" he choked out.

Regina snorted. "She said you would do naughty, embarrassing things to me, and that I must lie still and let you do them, even if I didn't like them. Because you're my husband."

"The spinster instructs the siren. Ignore everything she said."

"I intend to." She closed her fingers around his shaft, amazed by how firm it had become, and an oath boiled out of him.

"God save me from curious virgins." He thrust her hand aside. "That's enough."

"But I—"

He cut her off with a hard kiss as he settled himself between her legs. His hand found her still-aching flesh down below and rubbed it roughly, sweetly, just long enough to rouse her need again. And then it wasn't his hand there anymore, but his massive flesh, parting her, easing inside of her.

She tore her mouth from his. "You'll rip me apart."

"No, I won't," he murmured against her temple.

"You will. It's so . . . and I'm so . . ."

"Tight, yes." He paused in his motions to brush his lips over her forehead, though she could see the straining of his jaw. "That's how it's supposed to be. But trust me, men have been doing this for generations—"

"Not to me," she protested.

He gave a choked laugh. "Great God, I should hope not."

He slipped farther inside her before she could prepare herself. But oddly enough, his talking had taken her mind off what was happening below, and she was finding it easier to accommodate him.

"That's it," he whispered in her ear. "Open yourself, dearling. Let me in."

So she did. And she found it tolerable, if not exactly enjoyable. Then he came up against her virgin barrier. She could feel him inside her there, and a sudden apprehension made her tense.

He drew back to stare at her, his eyes alight. "Listen to me, Regina—"

"I know, it's going to hurt." She sighed. "I don't suppose there's any way around that part?"

A guttural laugh escaped him. "Not that I know of."

So far her friends hadn't been far wrong. The first part

was lovely. But this was just odd. And mortifying. And decidedly uncomfortable.

She braced herself. "Get it over with, then. But try not to kill me."

He frowned. "It won't . . . never mind, you won't believe me until the bad part is past."

He drove into her in one sharp thrust.

A sudden burst of pain vibrated through her insides. But it subsided swiftly, leaving behind a dull ache where he was planted deep inside her.

He hovered over her, his muscles taut. After a moment, he demanded, "Well? Are you still alive?"

She'd been holding her breath, but now she released it. "I think so."

"Good. Killing one's wife on one's wedding night is frowned upon. I'd be banished from society for certain."

His attempt at humor made her smile, despite her disappointment that this was all there was to being deflowered. Deep down, she'd really hoped it would be better than her friends had said.

"Are you sure you're all right?" he asked again, an edge to his voice now.

She wiggled her lower parts experimentally, surprised that having him inside her did not feel nearly as bad as she'd expected. "I believe I've survived."

"Not for long if you keep doing that," he choked out.

"You mean this?" She wiggled her lower body again, eliciting a heartfelt groan from him.

"If you don't stop that, I won't be able to take this easy and slow, the way I should."

"Take *what* easy and slow? I thought we were done."

"Hardly."

Hmm. If they weren't done . . . "So when I do this—"

She wriggled her bottom beneath him again. "It affects you?"

"Drives me insane," he clipped out.

Perhaps her friends were wrong after all. She deliberately undulated her hips. "I like making you insane."

"Impudent wench." He drew himself out of her. Only to go slowly back in. Then out. Then in.

How very interesting. Her lower parts grew warm and sort of tingly. She lifted her hips to meet his next thrust and nearly went out of her mind when the tingling erupted at once into a searing need.

"Ohh . . . Marcus, that's . . . ohhhh . . ."

"My words . . . exactly." He increased his rhythm. "I was right about you, wasn't I?"

"What?" She struggled to pay attention, but his driving thrusts were doing amazing things to her insides. Her belly felt all trembly and hot, and every time he came deeply into her, a new thrill shot through her.

"You really *are* . . . La Belle Dame . . . Sans Merci." His labored breath warmed her cheek. "A born temptress."

"Yes," she retorted, delighted by the thought. She might not be able to read or give him perfect children, but perhaps in this one respect she could keep him happy. "Yes, my darling."

His thrusting grew to a fierce pounding that drove the sweet tension to build in her like before. With a glad cry, she clasped him tight and arched up against him, seeking more of that magnificent feeling . . .

A hoarse groan sounded low in his throat. "Seductress," he accused. "Siren."

She turned her gaze to the painting where the sirens were cheering her on. "Yes," she said, digging her fingers into his massive arms. "Yes."

"*My* siren," he growled.

"Yes . . . oh yes . . ."

He thundered into her, around her, consuming her. He lifted his head to pierce her with a glance. "There will be no other dragons."

"No . . ." she whispered, writhing beneath him.

He slid his hand down between them, unerringly finding that tender little spot that seemed to respond so well to his fondling. "None but me."

"None." When he fingered it, she gasped. "No . . . never."

After that promise, there were no more words, just his body devouring hers, his finger building her own hunger to equal his until she was writhing against him, as eager to consume him as he was to consume her.

"Oh . . . my darling . . . oh . . . yes . . . yes . . . *yes!*" she cried out as the world exploded around her. "Marcus!"

Groaning her name, he gave one great final thrust. And as he spilled himself inside her, joining in her grand release, she clung tightly to his strong shoulders, a surge of relief mingling with her pleasure.

He was her husband now. There was no going back. Thank heaven.

Chapter Nineteen

*Teach your charge well, or when she is grown, she
will abandon your teachings.*
—Miss Cicely Tremaine, *The Ideal Chaperone*

*L*ong after Regina had drifted off to sleep, Marcus lay
awake. At last he possessed the woman he'd craved for
weeks. He'd assumed that taking her to bed would dull the
keen edge of his desire for her, but it hadn't. Even now, he
wanted to bury himself inside her again, to wake her with
kisses so he could taste her and fondle her and—

No, she needed rest and a few hours to recuperate from
his frenzied lovemaking. He could only hope that the
force of his need hadn't alarmed her. What if it sent her
running back to London to more urbane companions?

As that dour thought threatened to poison his contentment, he deliberately buried his nose in her tousled hair to
breathe her heady scent.

Somehow it soothed him. He believed that she had enjoyed their lovemaking, frenzied or no. Once they'd made
it past the difficult part, she'd thrown herself into it with
all the enthusiasm a man could hope for.

She burrowed closer to him, and he wrapped her in his
embrace. Only then was he able to sleep.

Dawn was streaking the sky when the sound of music woke him. Harp music.

Great God, he'd died and gone to heaven. And after only one rapturous night with Regina, too.

Cracking an eye open, he saw he was still at Illyria. Yet he heard harp music. Until a distinctly feminine curse sounded, and the music broke off.

That brought him fully awake. He sat up and spotted his wife not far from the bed. Seated on a stool, she was adjusting something on the harp while she mumbled to herself.

And she was completely naked. Exactly as she'd been in his dream.

His cock came fully awake, too. "I hope you plan to wake me like this every day." He tossed the covers aside and left the bed, delighted and relieved to discover that his nighttime fears had been for naught.

She glanced up, startled, then frowned at him. "I regret to inform you that your dream about my playing the harp naked shall have to stay a dream. Playing a harp naked is decidedly too impractical."

She looked so put out by that discovery that he smothered his laugh. "Oh?" he said as he stalked toward her.

"I've scraped my knees twice on the dratted thing," she complained. "And this carved wood is rubbing my shoulder raw—"

"We wouldn't want that." As he passed it, he pulled the harp forward to rest upright instead of in the usual playing position. Then he came up behind her. "Though I must admit, it makes for a fetching picture." He bent to kiss her neck.

"So did my gown. And you saw how well *that* worked."

Chuckling, he dropped his hand to caress her breast.

She sucked in a sharp breath, then leaned into his hand.

That was all the encouragement he needed. Scooping her off the stool, he carried her back to the bed. "Then we'll have to manage without the harp and the gown. All right?"

Her answer was to lift her mouth for his kiss.

Sometime later, after they were sated and lying in naked contentment, he drew her into his embrace. She went willingly, resting her head upon his chest.

"I hope I didn't hurt you, dearling," he murmured. "I should have given you more time to recover from last night."

"If I'd wanted that," she replied, pulling the counterpane up to cover them both, "I would not have awakened you by playing the harp naked. Besides, you did not hurt me. In fact . . ." A giggle escaped her.

"What are you laughing at?"

"My friends. They're such ninnies. You should have heard what they told me about their wedding nights. They had me half-convinced mine would be awful."

He arched an eyebrow. "I hope that means it wasn't."

A distinctly sirenish smile touched her lips. "You know very well that it was amazing, you self-satisfied oaf."

"You were rather amazing yourself."

She eyed him askance. "You mean I'm a shameless wanton."

"Thoroughly shameless, thank God."

"You don't mind?"

"Having a wife who takes pleasure in sharing my bed? Great God, no. Why would I mind?"

Her eyes narrowed. "You're not just saying that to save yourself a fortune in jewels, are you?"

He blinked. "Pardon?"

"My friends said the only advantage to marital relations is that their husbands buy them jewels afterward."

"Did you want jewels?"

"Not if it means giving up what we just did."

A smile tugged at his lips. "It doesn't. But I'm afraid it didn't occur to me to buy you any."

She laughed. "I knew you wouldn't. You're not the jewel-buying sort."

"I bought you a harp," he pointed out.

"Yes, and it's lovely."

"Even if you can't read the inscription."

She went still, all her exuberance fading, and he cursed himself for mentioning it. But now that their second love-making had finally taken the edge off his lust, he wanted to know how she'd come to such a pass. "You really can't read at all?"

With a shake of her head, she turned away from him onto her side.

He shifted to lie at her back, draping his arm over her waist. "It doesn't matter to me, dearling. But I do want to know how a duke's daughter could be—"

"Stupid?" she said bitterly. "An idiot?"

"Illiterate," he corrected her. Drawing her back against his chest, he nuzzled her neck. "You're not stupid at all. That's my point. How have you managed not to learn to read?"

She turned her head to stare up at him. "You don't think I tried? Hundreds of times, thousands of times? I did. I tried hard. But it never worked." Her lower lip trembled. "I told you, my brain doesn't function as it should."

"How do you know?"

She sighed. "When Cicely began my lessons—"

"Cicely? I thought she was your lady's companion."

"She is. But she's more than that. She was my governess from early on."

He arched an eyebrow. "The duke couldn't afford a governess for you?"

"Of course he could. Thankfully, Cicely talked him out of hiring one." She shifted to face him. "You see, Cicely, my father's first cousin, came to live with us shortly after I was born. Her father had just died. She was a plain woman with a poor family, so she was rapidly on her way to becoming a spinster even then. That's probably why she was so fond of me. She was the one who first noticed my problems with reading. Knowing my mother's stringent expectations for her children, she maneuvered it so that she became my governess before anyone could find out about my problems."

"Your parents didn't know?"

She shook her head. "Mother would have died of mortification. And Father rarely dealt with any of us. He spent most of his time in the usual gentlemanly pursuits and very little around his children. Even Simon doesn't know."

He frowned. "So Cicely was the only one to claim that you couldn't read—"

"I know what you're thinking. But Cicely did not 'claim' anything. She tried honestly to teach me. She would show me one letter, and I would see another. And yes, when I got older, I tested it on others. I would ask Simon to read a simple word for me, one of the few I'd managed to learn by sight. I remember distinctly asking him to read 'was,' and he told me it was 'saw.' " Tears brimmed in her eyes. "I couldn't even learn one word correctly."

"So you gave up?" he said.

She glared at him. "Of course not, but it did discourage me. Still, I might have persisted if not for the headaches."

"Yes, you mentioned headaches."

"I get them whenever I attempt to read. Cicely consulted a doctor secretly, and he said that I should not try. That my brain was clearly damaged, possibly from a fever I'd had as a child, and that continuing to tax it might further damage it. So we . . . stopped the lessons."

"And you've never tried again."

"I try from time to time, but then the headaches come—"

"Yes, I understand."

He understood, all right. Miss Tremaine had consulted some quack—or had pretended to consult some quack—and Regina, being a trusting child, had taken the damned idiot's word for it that her brain was "damaged."

He probed further. "So you don't read at all? How do you manage? It's not an easy thing to hide in society."

"Oh, I have my methods." Her smile looked forced. "If someone asks me to read, I just say my eyes are tired or I didn't bring my spectacles or I'd rather read it later in private."

As she'd done yesterday with Louisa's letter.

"If someone is very persistent, like you were last night, I either lie about what I read or change the subject." She shot him an arch glance. "Most people aren't that persistent. And they're not usually asking me to read anything scandalous, either."

"How would you know since you can't read?"

She shrugged. "Cicely is always close by to tell me what it really says when no one is paying attention. In fact, Cicely reads everything for me. She buys me the translations for the opera well in advance so she can read them to me. She writes and reads all my notes. She reads me the newspaper and my ladies' magazines—"

"Which is how you've managed to hide it all these years," he said dryly. "Otherwise, you might have been forced to learn, and then you wouldn't have needed Miss Tremaine."

She shot him a sharp glance. "Marcus, you must not blame Cicely for any of this. She has been very loyal to me. It cannot have been easy for her—never being able to leave my side, always having to read and write for me while hiding that fact from the world. The minute I need her to read something, she takes out her spectacles and does it without complaint."

"Better that than to be cast into the street."

Regina's expression grew mutinous. "She knows I would never cast her in the street."

"Does she? Your brother was more than ready to banish her to the country. If not for your need, she would have been forced to go, too. So of course she reads without complaint. For a poor relation, it's better than the alternative."

She sat up in bed to glare at him. "If you are trying to suggest that Cicely deliberately set out to deceive me about my defect—"

"No, not completely," he murmured soothingly, though that was precisely what he thought. "But perhaps she has exaggerated the problem to make you dependent upon her."

"The headaches are real! She did not invent them. *I* did not invent them!"

"Of course not." He sat up, too, cupping her flushed cheek in his hand. "But, dearling, plenty of people get the headache from doing all sorts of things. Still, they go on doing them, and they survive headaches without wreaking permanent damage on their brains."

Tears spilled down her cheeks as she glanced away. "You don't understand."

"I do." He gathered her into his arms. "Truly, I do. Headaches are awful things. I don't get them myself, but Louisa does, and I know she suffers greatly from them." He tightened his hold on her stiff body, searching for a way to convince her. "Tell me this, Regina, do you ride?"

"Yes," she bit out.

"And when you first learned, weren't your muscles very sore for days afterward? Didn't your ass . . . er . . . bottom hurt every time you sat down? Didn't your legs feel like rubber for a while?"

She went still. "Yes," she said in a more subdued voice.

"Did you then decide that there was something wrong with your legs and your bottom? That you should never ride again?"

"No." She drew back from him. "But that happens to everyone—their legs hurt and their bottoms hurt and they all know to keep going until they learn. I'm the only one who has headaches when she reads."

"How do you know? Have you asked every lady you've ever met? Every girl in a grammar school? For all you know, there could be twenty, fifty, a hundred of you ladies who get headaches when they read. There might even be men who do."

Her breath was coming quickly now, and her eyes were riveted on his face.

"If you are so reluctant to talk about it," he went on, "what makes you think *they* would? Why would they risk being called stupid or lazy? How do you know there aren't hundreds of 'brain-damaged' people wandering London as we speak?"

"What are you saying?" she whispered.

"That I truly don't believe you can hurt your brain by taxing it, dearling. But I'm certain that you'll never know unless you try."

The sudden yearning in her face tugged at his heart. Now he understood why she craved London society, why she feared being "trapped" in the country. For a lady like Regina, who couldn't read but was too clever to be content with only needlepoint and wifely duties, being in the country would be a curse.

In London she could feed her mind at the opera, the theater, the salons. Her companions might be idiots, but they were probably entertaining idiots, and they distracted her from dwelling on her "damaged brain," as she called it.

Out here at Castlemaine, she would be bored to tears. So if he wanted to keep her here with him . . .

"Later today," he went on, "I'll ride over to the house and fetch some of Louisa's old primers. If we take it slow—"

Hope filled her face. "Do you really think I could learn?"

"I know you could."

"Oh, Marcus, if you could teach me, you don't know what it would mean!"

"I can guess. Without my books to keep me company these past nine years, I would have gone mad."

A sudden cloud dimmed her face. "But what if the doctor was right? What if I turn myself into a blithering idiot—"

"You won't." He pressed a finger to her lips. "I won't allow it. And you know us dragons—we always get our way." When that didn't seem to reassure her, he tried another tack. "Besides, surely if I could brave Almack's for you, you can brave a few headaches for me."

Perhaps if she wouldn't do it for herself, she would do it for him, out of some sense of duty. Somehow, he was going to get her reading. He had to. It was the only way to keep her here with him.

"All right." She settled against his chest with a sigh. "I promise to try."

Chapter Twenty

*Your charge will follow your rules more eagerly if
she has first seen the consequences of breaking
them.*
—Miss Cicely Tremaine, *The Ideal Chaperone*

Regina had tried. And tried. And tried some more. Yet
after four days of torture, she was no closer to learning to
read than she'd been before. Worse yet, she wanted to
strangle the person who'd devised that horrible invention,
the primer. She even wanted to strangle Marcus. Because
he simply would not give up.

It was midmorning of the fifth day of their honeymoon as she sat with him in Illyria's pretty drawing room,
laboring over the primer he had brought back from the
main house. She was tired of feeling stupid, tired of the
worry on his face when she said the wrong thing, tired of
his frustration, which mirrored her own.

Most of all, she was tired of the headaches. And Marcus, curse his soul, would not forget his mission for one
minute and let her go to bed with a cold compress. Not
unless she seduced him first, which she couldn't manage
when her head hurt.

Some honeymoon this was turning out to be.

"Again, Regina." He turned a page of the red-covered

book she'd come to loathe. "Look at the shape of the letter. A 'b' has the belly to the right, not to the left. The letter that *you* are writing is a 'd.' "

"For 'dolt,' " she muttered. "Or do I have that wrong, too?"

"You are not a dolt."

"I wasn't speaking of myself." Thrusting the book aside, she sat back to glare at him. "When will you just admit that I cannot do it? After all these hours of work, I can still barely read my name, much less a book. And as for writing . . ."

"I know, I know." He rubbed his stubbled chin. "I truly thought it would be easier. I confess I have a greater respect for Miss Tremaine now than before. But if you'd just try—"

"Try!" Slamming the book shut, she leaped out of her chair. "How dare you! I've stared at these dratted books until my eyes cross and my bottom is numb from sitting, and you have the audacity—"

"You didn't let me finish, dearling." He hauled her onto his lap. "I know you've tried. What I started to say was that if you'd try not to think of it as impossible, we might get somewhere. Instead of being defeated before we even start."

A little mollified, she touched her head to his. "I only think of it as impossible because it is. Why do you insist that I can do something I've tried for years with no success?"

"Because I have faith in you," he murmured, nuzzling her cheek. "You weren't given a proper chance to attempt it before."

"I have *now*," she said. "Perhaps it is time to admit defeat."

"No!" He drew back to scowl at her. "I won't let you."

Her throat grew raw and tight. "Why is it so important to you? Can you not bear the thought of your wife being unable to read?"

"That's not it. If I thought you were content with such a state of affairs, I could be content, too. But you're not. Admit it."

"I should dearly love to learn to read, but it's not absolutely essential, you know. Once our honeymoon is over, and Cicely is living with us—"

"We don't *need* Cicely. If I have to, I'll read to you myself."

She stroked his cheek. "Don't be silly. You can't always be around to do such things."

A stubborn look crossed his face. "I certainly can. And I will."

"Louisa told me that you are far more involved in the affairs of your estate than the average lord. You won't be able to drop everything to read the housekeeper's menu or a set of instructions for me."

"I'm lord of the manor—I'll do whatever I please. I don't want you always having to rely on your cousin. Either you learn, or I'll read to you, and that's that."

She frowned. "Then what happens to Cicely?"

He shrugged. "She can live at the town house indefinitely. She'd probably prefer that—more things to do in town."

"She couldn't live alone. And anyway, I don't want you reading everything to me. There are certain things a woman likes to keep private from her husband."

His black scowl would have burned ice. "Like what?"

"Like correspondence with female friends." A flush stole over her cheeks. "And information for ladies that is of a certain . . . delicate nature." She could not endure having him read to her the latest description of a corset's fine qualities, for heaven's sake. "And when we return to town in a few days, I'll—"

"What do you mean, when we return to town? We're not going back to town anytime soon."

Her heart began to pound. "But the season isn't even over. And I thought you'd want to be in town for Louisa."

"Why? She's got the Iversleys." He searched her face. "Unless you know of some other reason I should hurry back to town for Louisa."

She forced a smile, though panic had broken loose in her chest. "No, of course not. But surely you want to be around to assess the other gentlemen who court her or offer for her. There's only a month or two left."

"I mean for us to spend that time here, so you can get comfortable with your duties as lady of Castlemaine."

She hid her shaking hands in her lap. "We can do that once the season is over." When Louisa would either marry someone or return to Castlemaine to await the next season. "But during this time of year, I prefer to be in town."

"I prefer that you be here." A muscle twitched in his jaw.

She tipped up her chin. "I could always go there alone, you know."

"Not unless I allow it."

A cold chill shook her. Until now, she had not seen any evidence of the tyrannical husband she had feared he might be. "You promised me I could come and go to town as I pleased."

"I didn't realize you meant to shirk your duties as my wife to do it."

His words got her dander up. "If you try to keep me here against my will, I shall summon Cicely to fetch me."

"How? You can't exactly send her a letter."

She colored. "I'll ask one of the servants to write a letter for me."

"Will you?" He smiled grimly. "I dare say not a single servant in your own household ever knew you couldn't read, so you're not likely to reveal it to a servant in mine."

The fact that he was right only increased her anger. "Then I shall hire someone in your little village—"

"Now *that,* my dear, I will definitely not allow."

"What? Do you mean to forbid me to do it?"

"Absolutely." When the word sent her scrambling to get off his lap, he held her firmly, his own temper flaring in his face. "I've spent half my life as the object of the most cruel gossip. The local populace has finally come to see me as a fair and just landlord who cares what happens to his land and his tenants, and you want me to give them a reason to gossip about my *wife?* To talk about how she's itching to leave me a mere week after we married?"

"I am not itching—"

"You have no idea what it's like. I can trust my servants to be loyal and discreet, but the townspeople . . ." He shook his head. "I will not allow it."

All her anger dissolved. If anyone understood that sort of pride, it was her. But the fact remained that he was trying to keep her in a prison of his own making.

"Then I shall have to walk to London," she said tightly. "Unless you mean to lock me in your dungeon?"

"Of course not." A heavy sigh wracked him. "Very well, we'll return to London for the season, if you wish."

"I do."

"But only *after* you give the reading lessons a few more days. All right?"

"All right." She should be relieved that he had relented. But she had the uneasy feeling that disaster had only been postponed, not averted.

"Besides, our honeymoon has barely begun. Surely you will not begrudge me a few more days of keeping you to myself."

"No," she said, the yearning in his tone erasing some of her unease. Of course he would be demanding right now; they hadn't even been married a week. "But I do not mean to spend the whole of it suffering through your books and my headaches. For today, at least, could we do something else?"

A smoldering heat leaped in his face. "Whatever you say," he murmured as he lowered his mouth to hers.

With a laugh, she pressed her fingers to his lips. "Not *that,* you randy devil. We do plenty enough of that already."

He released a frustrated oath. "Then what else did you have in mind?"

"For one thing, I could use a vigorous ride—" She caught herself even before his eyes started gleaming. "On a *horse.* Perhaps we could see the rest of your estate and tour the main house." A mischievous smile touched her lips. "You could even show me your famous dungeon."

His face instantly grew shuttered. "Let's skip the dungeon. The damned place is cold and dreary, with nothing in it but old wine bottles and rusty chains. It's no place for a lady."

"But all your talk about it and the rumors have made me curious."

"Only because you have a false image of it in your head. It's not what you've imagined, I promise you." He cast her a forced smile. "If you really want to see it, I'll show it to you, but I'd prefer not to stir up the rats by going down there."

Rats. Ugh. "Never mind. I'll take your word for it."

"A ride, however, sounds pleasant. And the weather's perfect for it." His mouth brushed her ear as he slid his hand inside her bodice to fondle her breast. "But first, dearling, I want a private ride. I deserve a reward after making so many concessions."

"Oh, you do, do you?" She pretended to be affronted, though her blood had already begun to heat and her pulse to race. "And if I say otherwise?"

"Then I'll just have to convince you." He thumbed her nipple until she groaned and pressed her breast into his hand. "I gather it won't be too difficult."

"You are . . ."

He kissed her neck.

". . . a very wicked . . .

He tongued her throat.

". . . dragon."

"Always," he murmured, as he kissed his way up her chin to her mouth. "But only with you, my dear, only with you."

The afternoon sun was dipping low on the horizon as they rode up to the main house. Marcus watched his wife, searching for any sign that she disapproved of his father's fanciful renovations. But her face showed that she was as pleased with it as she'd been with the rest of his estate.

It gave him hope. Perhaps now she wouldn't be so eager to return to town. She seemed to like what she had seen this afternoon. She'd exclaimed over the trout ponds, admired the vast barley fields, and questioned him on the efficiency of his dairy. Though her comments and queries had demonstrated how little she knew about running an estate, he could certainly not fault her enthusiasm.

But how long could mere enthusiasm last? Without help, she could not supervise the menus for meals, deal with correspondence regarding the hiring of servants, oversee the housekeeper's ordering of supplies, and other such things.

She knew it, too. Already she wanted to escape duties that her inability to read would make more painful. It reminded him of his mother's own cravings for the delights of town.

He shook off that thought. Regina differed markedly from his mother, despite their surface similarities. Look at her—even now her pretty cheeks were bright from their ride, her eyes sparkling with energy. Nothing like Mother, who'd found the estate boring and dreary.

Regina had a natural intelligence that delighted in any challenge—like learning to be lady of the manor. Besides, if she'd been so very happy in town, why had she sought the adventure of a courtship with him in the first place?

Yet he could not rest easy. It wasn't that he minded taking her to town. Now that he wasn't such an outcast, he might enjoy an evening at the theater or dinner at Iversley's. But he could never be entirely easy with the cream of society, where he might encounter the prince.

Besides, he liked being a country gentleman most of the time. His only complaint had been the loneliness, and now that she was here . . .

But for how long? She had him trapped. He had no wish to stay in town all the time. If he kept her here by force, she would hate him. And if he let her go to town alone, how long before she found some companion—

Damn, this jealousy was a plague upon his soul. He

wished he did not care what she did. But he cared too much. He was rapidly falling under her spell. He craved her more every day. He hated watching her suffer through her headaches, and he found himself willing to spend any sum just to bring a smile to her lips. If he didn't watch it, she'd soon have him dancing to her tune just as Mother had done to Father, and then . . .

"Are you going to show me your gardens?" she asked, drawing her mount up beside him with a winsome smile that clutched at his heart.

Great God, she looked like a sunlit garden herself, with her hair shining golden beneath a blue bonnet that turned her grey eyes the color of sky, and her spenser embroidered with a bunch of little flowers. No wonder half the men in London had wanted her. Probably still wanted her.

His heart lurched in his chest.

"Marcus? The gardens? You do have some, don't you?"

"Yes, of course. But they've been sadly neglected since Louisa left. They were hers to oversee, and our aging gardener has not carried on very well without her supervision." He eyed her closely. "Do you like gardening?"

"I like other people's gardening," she admitted with a rueful smile. "But I'm not fond of dirt and bugs. If you had to depend on me to take your gardens in hand, they would soon look quite sad." She sighed. "You chose a very ornamental wife, Marcus. I do hope you don't come to regret it."

"Nonsense," he said through a tight throat, "I could never regret it. I can always hire a new gardener, if need be. But I could never hire a wife."

A groom came running from the nearby stables, and Marcus dismounted. "Come, dearling, let's stroll through my gardens, such as they are." He handed his reins to the groom, then went to her side. "Perhaps you'll find you don't mind the dirt and bugs so much after all."

With a skeptical look, she let him help her dismount, but she remained silent as they wandered through the neat little walks beside which grew a profusion of flowers that could benefit from an expert hand.

Not hers, however. She'd made that perfectly clear.

They had just rounded the knot garden and were descending a steep hill toward the roses when a bloodcurdling scream rent the air behind them. Both of them jumped and turned, just in time to see a child of about seven come sliding down the hill on his bottom, clutching his leg.

His profusely bleeding leg.

Marcus froze as he recognized the cook's inquisitive son. But Regina didn't waste even a moment. She flew to the sobbing boy and knelt at his side to examine the leg. As Marcus hurried over, she was already unwinding the scarf about her neck and tying it above the gash to provide a makeshift tourniquet.

"I-I'm sorry, m'lord," the boy exclaimed, his eyes awash with fearful tears. "I only wanted to see . . . your lady, but I fell off the fence onto the tiller and it cut me." He lifted a panicky face to Regina. "I'm gonna die, ain't I, m'lady?"

"Certainly not," Regina said firmly. She was surprisingly unperturbed by the sight of all that blood as she examined his wound. "I've seen far worse cuts than this, on far more sickly boys, and they didn't die. A strapping lad like yourself will come through it with flying colors."

Ah, yes. She had mentioned something before about volunteering at a hospital. Marcus relaxed a little. "What can I do?"

"Let's carry him up to the house. He'll need to have this treated at once."

As they approached the back of the house where the kitchens were, they were greeted with a shriek from Cook, who'd spotted her son in Marcus's arms out the window. She rushed from the house to meet them, a couple of scullery maids following close behind. "Timmy! Lord have mercy, Timmy!"

"He's all right," Regina told Cook as Marcus carried the boy into the kitchen.

When Cook's cursory examination of her son's wound seemed to confirm Regina's opinion that it wasn't too serious, she uttered a relieved sigh.

Regina gestured to a table in the center of the kitchen. "Lay him there." She turned to Cook. "I shall need a sturdy needle, strong thread, a damp clean cloth, and some clean dry linen. And Taylor's Ointment, if you have it in your stillroom."

"Aye, we do." Cook opened a cupboard. "I've got a needle and strong thread I use for sewing up the stuffed chickens. Will that do?" Cook glanced at one of the maids. "What're you standing gawking for—go fetch that ointment."

As the girl raced from the kitchen, Cook returned her gaze to her son. "I tell you, m'lady, the boy shall be the death of me yet." She handed over what Regina had asked for. "It's the third time this month he's got himself hurt."

"Boys are like that," Regina said with a ghost of a smile. "Always ready for trouble."

But when she threaded the needle, Timmy showed himself not quite so ready for trouble, for he began to bawl like a lost sheep.

Marcus offered the boy his hand. "Here now, lad, making all that racket won't do any good. Let her sew you up, and it'll be over soon enough. Just squeeze my hand hard as you can when it hurts, all right?"

Timmy stopped wailing to fix Marcus with a fearful stare. The children on the estate were nearly all half-terrified of him, which had always bothered him. So when Regina eased the needle into the boy's skin, and he grabbed for Marcus's hand, the surge of satisfaction that filled Marcus was sweet indeed.

"That's it, lad," he murmured. "Squeeze it hard."

The boy swallowed, but kept his eyes on Marcus's face. "Is this how you got that big scar on your cheek, m'lord? Did you fall on a tiller like me?"

"Hush now, Timmy," Cook said, shooting Marcus an apologetic look.

"He got it fighting an old witch," Regina put in. "She tried to put an evil spell on him with a firebrand, so she could take Castlemaine. But even though she wounded him sorely, he held firm. Like you're holding firm now, my brave boy."

As Timmy thrust out his chest and loosened his hold on Marcus's hand, Marcus bit back a smile. His mother would have scratched Regina's eyes out for calling her an old witch.

"There, done," Regina announced as she bit off the end of the thread. "You see? That was not so bad, was it? And we can get rid of this now, too." She untied her improvised tourniquet, then smiled to see how well her stitches held.

With a scowl, Cook examined the tourniquet. "Your pretty scarf got soiled something awful. I'm so sorry, m'lady."

"It's all right." Regina shot Marcus a glance. "His lordship will buy me a new one, won't he?"

"I'll buy you ten new ones," he growled. "Whatever you want."

When Cook and the other maid exchanged surprised glances, Marcus stiffened. He might as well have knelt on one knee and proclaimed himself a besotted idiot. "Since you females seem to have this well in hand," he added with a scowl, "I'll go see to that tiller. It shouldn't be sitting out like that."

As he left the kitchen, the maid who'd been sent for the ointment entered with a box full of bottles. He was halfway out the door when he heard her exclaim, "Beggin' your pardon, m'lady, but I can't read, so I didn't know which was the ointment. I brought all the bottles in the still-room."

In alarm, he turned to go back. Cook was already handing the box over to Regina. "Here, miss, you look for it. I have to find my glasses."

He hurried inside as Regina paled and peered into the box. But before he could reach them, she picked up a bottle. As if stalling for time, she ran her fingers over the front of it.

Then an odd expression crossed her face. "No, this is laudanum. We don't want that."

He took the bottle from her. Damn, if she wasn't right. He glanced at her to find her watching him anxiously. "It *is* laudanum."

Excitement suffused her features. "I *felt* it, Marcus. I felt the letters. The first one didn't look like an 'l', but it *felt* like one. And then once I could feel it, I could see it, too."

The servants were eyeing them both oddly, but he didn't care. "Try another."

She picked up another bottle. "W . . . C . . . Taylor? Is that it?"

He grabbed the bottle. "Yes. That's the maker's name on the seal."

"Will it burn when you put it on?" Timmy asked, jerking them both back to their surroundings.

"Only a little," Regina murmured as she thrust the box of bottles at Marcus.

She swabbed the boy's sewn wound with Taylor's Ointment, then wrapped linen around it. "Timmy shall have a rather fearsome scar of his own, but it should heal all right."

"I don't know how to thank you, m'lady," Cook began.

"Nonsense." She tied off the makeshift bandage. "I'm only glad I could be useful."

It took a few more minutes to extricate themselves from Timmy and his mother, then they headed down the hall to the drawing room.

"I see you didn't lie about volunteering at the hospital," he murmured.

She shot him an arch glance. "Did you think I had?"

"I was hoping you had. Because if I'd known you were such a paragon, I'd never have dared offer for your hand."

Her blush of pleasure warmed him. "But I can't garden, remember?"

"I'll take doctoring skills over gardening any day." He covered her hand with his and squeezed. "Not so ornamental a wife, after all, eh?"

She laughed. "You haven't seen me embroider."

"What I've seen of your wifely skills is good enough for me," he said truthfully.

She toyed with the edge of his cuff as they neared the foyer, where a cluster of servants were buzzing about. "All the same, do you think we might . . . return to those reading lessons?" She met his questioning gaze and smiled.

"After all this excitement, I believe I'm ready for a tamer pastime."

His bark of laughter made the servants turn in their direction. Then a spindly figure separated from the rest and approached them.

Marcus recognized him as one of Iversley's footmen just as the man thrust a sealed letter at him. "For you, my lord."

A frisson of alarm slid down his spine as he broke open the seal. His alarm flared into anger when he read the letter.

"What is it?" Regina asked, her skin pale as chalk.

"We have to go to London."

"Now?"

"Yes, now. Your damned ass of a brother just tried to abduct Louisa."

Chapter Twenty-one

Beware the snares of a devious suitor.
—Miss Cicely Tremaine, *The Ideal Chaperone*

By the time they set off from Castlemaine in the carriage a good half hour later, Regina could hardly contain her panic. "Marcus, won't you read me the message now? You know I can't read it for myself."

He hadn't said a word to her since he'd made his chilling pronouncement. Ignoring her pleas that he read her the entire letter, he'd called for the carriage and ordered servants to pack him a bag, in case he was forced to stay in London for the night. When she'd told them to pack her a bag, too, he'd shot her a dark glance. But at least he hadn't tried to stop her from going.

So now they were alone together, hurtling toward London, with him staring rigidly out the window and her nearly frantic to know the full story.

"Marcus, please—"

"I'm sure you know what it says."

"What do you mean?"

His gaze shot to her, blazing with anger. "You knew all along that Foxmoor was planning this, didn't you?"

"No!"

"All your fussing about being in London for Louisa—you obviously knew he would try something."

She swallowed. "I'll admit I feared he might try to see her. But I never guessed he would attempt to abduct her. Simon is not generally so—"

"Calculating? Power-mad?"

"Reckless," she countered. "I can't think what he meant to accomplish."

"Her ruin," he growled. "He arranged to meet her in the street in broad daylight so he could carry her off in his carriage, damn him."

"Oh no," she moaned. "Did anyone see them?"

"No, thank God, but if not for Miss Tremaine's following Louisa when she slipped out of the house in early morning, he would have succeeded."

"This is all my fault. If anyone had seen—"

"Why is it your fault?" He crossed his arms over his chest.

Regina shot him a despairing glance. She had to tell him. It would be better to tell him the truth before a furious Simon spouted all his lies. "You must understand, Marcus. If I had thought for one minute that Simon would—"

"Why is it all your fault?" he demanded again, more coldly.

Her heart sank. "Because Simon told me the night of the assembly at Almack's that he meant to break his promise not to pursue her. He said he intended to set up a meeting between her and the prince no matter what. But I never dreamed he would go so far."

His face was the color of stone. "Is that why you didn't warn me?"

"I thought Cicely could prevent it. And she did, didn't she?"

He leaned forward, eyes alight. "Louisa could have been ruined, damn you. And you didn't see fit to tell me?"

Her hands grew clammy. "I couldn't. He said if I revealed his intentions to either you or Louisa, he would claim I'd supported his scheme from the beginning. He threatened to tell you I went to Castlemaine the first time solely at his request."

"Didn't you?" he said snidely.

"You can't possibly think I'd have been part of a scheme to harm Louisa!"

A muscle ticked in his jaw. "I don't know what to think anymore."

"If I'd been part of his scheme, why would I have charged Cicely with protecting her? When I needed Cicely so desperately myself?"

His grim features softened imperceptibly. "You should have told me what he threatened. You should have alerted me."

"Would you have believed me over him?" She drew herself up stiffly. "As he so cruelly pointed out, you didn't even trust me to be faithful to you; I could hardly expect you to trust me not to have lied to you from the beginning."

A coarse oath escaped his lips. "Your brother is an ass."

"Yes, but I knew he was right." When Marcus glared at her, she added, "And even if I'd told you, what would you have done? Take Louisa with us on our honeymoon? Lock her up at Castlemaine?"

"If I had," he shot back, "she wouldn't be in this position now."

"Yes, but that would hardly have helped her find a husband." She thrust out her chin. "I did what I thought was best—I told Cicely to prevent Simon from getting to her. And Cicely did as I asked."

"But if she had not succeeded, Louisa might have ended up—"

"I know, I know." She sighed heavily. "I shall never forgive myself for that. Still, since it sounds as if he made sure she was not seen, I don't think he meant to ruin her. All he wants is to take her to the prince for one meeting."

He glowered at her. "I suppose you approve of that."

"I don't approve of his underhanded tactics, no. But if you weren't being so stubborn, he would not have resorted to such ridiculous maneuverings. You could have taken Louisa to meet His Highness yourself, you know. Then after he stated his piece, she could have made her own decision."

"The chit is risking ruin for your idiot brother, and you think she can be trusted to make her own decisions when confronted by our manipulative regent?"

"His Highness isn't the monster you seem to think he is," she said stoutly.

"You don't know anything about him, damn it. You see the charming smile he bestows on the ladies, the seemingly amiable wit and the excellent taste in art and music. You don't see the side *I* have seen."

She sensed that she was on the brink of discovering something very important about her husband. "What side is that?"

"The one so bloated with his own importance that he thinks nothing of seducing married women like my mother and Iversley's mother—"

"Iversley's?" she interrupted. "Lord Iversley is Prinny's son?"

He blinked, then scowled. "Damn. I had no right to reveal that."

She stared at him, her mind racing. That was why he and the earl were such good friends. And why the man's wife was sponsoring Louisa in society. Sweet heaven. "Are you sure that Lord Iversley is Prinny's son?

"Iversley's father was impotent, and his mother had one liaison. With the prince. Iversley is sure, so yes, I'm sure."

"But she could have had other lovers—"

"Not from what Iversley says. She was apparently nothing like my own mother." His voice hardened. "Although that hardly mattered to Prinny—he'd bed anything in skirts."

"True, and I can understand why that would make you resent him." She chose her words carefully. "But many men in society are like that—Mr. Byrne, for example. You let *him* around Louisa. So why refuse to let His Highness near her?"

"Because once the prince has her under his control, he will do anything to get what he wants, damn it!" he spat out. "Even if he has to browbeat her or order her locked away in a dungeon—"

"Locked away in a dungeon! Don't be absurd. He would never—" Marcus's fierce expression made her blood run cold. "You didn't . . . oh, please tell me you were never locked in the dungeon at Castlemaine."

For a long moment, the only sound was the beat of the horse's hooves on the road. He glanced out the window, his jaw tight. "I was. Once."

She gaped at him in horror. "Because of Prinny?"

His gaze swung back to her, hot, angry. "Because he ordered it. His Confounded Highness did not take well to hearing what his insolent thirteen-year-old son thought of his character."

"You lectured the Prince of Wales?" she said, incredulous.

"I told him he was a vile whoreson who didn't deserve ever to be king."

"Sweet heaven," she murmured, marveling at the foolhardy bravery of Marcus at thirteen.

"I was angry, all right? What do you expect of a boy who'd heard his mother called the 'Whore of Wales' and other filthy names at school? Bad enough that I had to learn from schoolboys that I was considered a bastard, but then to have to return home and pretend he was just a family friend—" He swore under his breath.

"I'm sure that was very difficult." She tried to imagine how a boy as fond of his "father" as Marcus had clearly been would handle hearing of his true heritage from a lot of nasty children. "Any other boy might have been rather intrigued to hear that his father was royalty."

"Not if he'd ever endured having the man pinch his cheeks or demand reports on his studies. As a boy, I hated Prinny's visits. Father would closet himself in his library, Mother would turn all flirtatious, and I was left to my tutors and told to stay out of my mother's bedchamber."

His fingers tightened into fists on his thighs. "By the time I found out what all that meant, Prinny had married Caroline. For a while, he was absent from Castlemaine. I got a new little sister, and Father and Mother seemed to be getting along. I really thought we were rid of the old goat. Then I came home on holiday at thirteen to see him back in his usual spot at Mother's side, and I—" He swore under his breath. "I lost my temper and told him he was a vile whoreson."

"I suppose that's understandable."

"Not to the prince." His tone would have chilled fire. "He demanded that I apologize, and I refused. So he banished me to our dungeon for three days."

"Three days!" Her heart dropped into her stomach.

"With the rats, the dank cold, and the nights darker than coal." A shudder wracked him. "At thirteen I was stubborn as the very devil, but even I could only endure so much. When Mother came for the third evening in a row to order me to apologize to Prinny, I couldn't bear the thought of another night down there."

He spoke through gritted teeth. "I swallowed my pride, and I apologized very prettily." His angry gaze swung to her. "But I never forgave him for it. Never. And I finally got to tell him so, too, nine years later. I told him to his face how much I hated him. Then I ordered him to leave Castlemaine, take her with him, and never come back. And I got a poker across the face for my efforts."

The pain in his voice cut her to the heart. "Oh, my darling—"

"I'm not telling you this to gain your pity." The waning sun shone on his flushed cheeks. "I merely want you to understand that he's not the man you think. I'll do anything to keep Louisa out of his clutches. Anything, do you hear me?"

She nodded, but she still couldn't conceive of Prinny—jovial, easygoing Prinny—ordering his son held in a dungeon for three days.

But neither would Marcus lie. And she remembered how reluctant he'd been to show her the dungeon this morning, as well as his anger the first time she'd told him what people were saying about his keeping women there. Clearly he was telling the truth. But . . .

"Are you sure the prince ordered it? Perhaps your mother—"

"My mother was completely in thrall to the man. She did nothing unless he commanded it, I assure you."

"And where was the viscount?"

"In town. That's why Prinny felt free to visit and act the petty tyrant."

She ventured a question she knew he would not like. "Did you hear Prinny order you put into the dungeon?"

He scowled. "I'm sure I did. And he could hardly not have noticed that I disappeared for three days. And that I looked like the very devil when I came to apologize."

Her throat constricted to think of a young Marcus locked up beneath the earth, no matter who had chosen to do it. "Did they starve you?"

He snorted. "They didn't need to. Being in that miserable place was punishment enough. I had a bed and food and a chamber pot. I just wasn't allowed to come out, that's all." He hitched up his shoulders as if to shrug it off, but it looked more a shudder than a shrug. "Anyway, it was a long time ago." He leveled a hard gaze on her. "And my point is, the prince cannot be trusted. Nor your brother."

"Simon most certainly cannot." She sighed. "So what will you do now?"

"I want to hear what Louisa has to say before I make a decision."

"Promise me you won't fight Simon."

He arched one eyebrow. "Worried about your brother, are you?"

"I'm worried about *you*," she cried, hurt that he could think she would care more about Simon than him.

His rigid jaw softened. "I can take care of myself with your brother."

"If the two of you fought a duel, I would lose you both. One of you would die and the other would be forced to flee the country. I couldn't bear it, and I know it would kill Louisa. Promise me you won't call him out, Marcus."

He swore under his breath.

"Promise me, Marcus!"

"Oh, all right. But only because I can't very well keep Louisa safe if I have to flee England."

She noticed he didn't say anything about not wanting to leave his wife. Was that because he didn't care? Or because he assumed that if he ever did have to flee, Regina would go with him?

A silence fell between them, thick with tension as she mulled over his revelations. She wanted him to care. She wanted it desperately. Every time she gazed at that dear, stubborn face, her heart flipped over in her chest. After sharing his bed these past few nights while he made love to her with a fierce tenderness that melted her, she couldn't bear to have him *not* care.

Because she loved him.

Unshed tears pooled in her throat. Uncertain of his feelings, she'd kept her own under control, but he had crept around her heart anyway, as insidious as the dragon's tail carved on her new harp.

How could she not fall in love with a man who'd given up his honeymoon to try to teach her to read? Who had endured a mountain of humiliation to squire her about in public? Who cared so much for his sister that he would do anything to protect her from harm?

Tears stung Regina's eyes. She loved him all right. What else could possibly make her this weepy?

Blinking back her tears, she stared out at the dying sun and prayed that he could love her, too. That he would eventually forgive her for her part in Louisa's near ruin. Because if he couldn't, she didn't know how she'd bear it.

Chapter Twenty-two

*Remain loyal to your charge and when she is
married, she will reward you.*
—Miss Cicely Tremaine, *The Ideal Chaperone*

$\mathcal{R}$egina shivered as they were ushered into the Iversleys' drawing room. The mood was somber as a tomb. Louisa sat on a couch, flanked by Cicely and Lady Iversley, and Lord Iversley stood stiffly by the fire, his hand resting upon the marble mantel. But while Louisa's guardians bore expressions of dismay and concern, Louisa was the very image of defiance.

Ignoring his sister, Marcus headed for Lord Iversley. His half brother. Now Regina could see a resemblance, in their dark hair, their height, their chins. Marcus might be stockier, but they had exactly the same chin. The prince's chin.

Lady Iversley caught her staring, and the woman's gaze grew speculative. Did she know of her husband's true parentage? She had to. Otherwise, why had she agreed to sponsor Louisa in society? And what was it the earl had said at dinner the night of the soiree? *He's like part of our family.*

Regina snorted. Part of the family, indeed. She should have seen it before.

As Marcus reached Alec, guilt spread over the younger man's cheeks. "Draker, I'm so sorry. I swear I never thought—"

"It's not your fault. You've done better by Louisa than I could have dreamed. But when the girl acts like a fool, you can't do much to stop her."

"How dare you?" Louisa jumped to her feet. "You don't understand—"

"Hush, Louisa," Regina said hastily. "Your brother is very angry at the moment, and I would not try his temper if I were you."

Still ignoring his sister, Marcus turned to Cicely, who was coaxing Louisa to sit back down. "Miss Tremaine, I should like a word with you."

Cicely rose uneasily, her hands balling a handkerchief into a knot. "Yes, my lord?"

"First of all, thank you for your good service to me and my wife. I promise that you'll be amply rewarded for it. Now tell me exactly what happened between Foxmoor and my sister."

Cicely shot Regina a glance, and Regina nodded. Cicely's face cleared. "Forgive me, sir, but I do not know how the duke managed to communicate his plans to Louisa, or I would never have allowed it to go even as far as it did. I did try to intercept any notes or letters sent to her."

"Traitor," Louisa muttered.

For the first time since he'd entered, Marcus looked at his sister. "Excuse me, young lady, but did I just hear you insult one of your betters, a woman of advanced age and superior education, and the relation of my very own wife?"

Louisa had the good sense to duck her head, and mumble, "No."

"Good. I had better never hear it." He turned back to Cicely. "Go on."

With a nervous glance in Louisa's direction, Cicely said, "Fortunately, I am a light sleeper. My cough often wakes me early. So I heard Louisa slip out of her room. Concerned for her safety, I followed her outside. The duke awaited her in his carriage at the foot of the garden, and Louisa was nearly there when I called to her to stop. I told her if she did not return to the house, I would scream until everyone came running. Simon tried to convince her to come along anyway, but—" She glanced toward Louisa. "She knew that would be futile."

"We could never have made it to Gretna Green unless we had a head start," Louisa protested.

"Gretna Green!" Marcus snapped. "You little fool—did you really think he meant to marry you?"

Louisa paled. "He said he did."

"Drat the man," Regina muttered. She couldn't believe he'd actually lied to Louisa in order to get what he wanted. "My brother can be such an idiot."

"He's a dead idiot now," Marcus snapped.

"No!" Louisa leaped from the couch. "You must not hurt him. We did nothing wrong. We wanted to marry, and you wouldn't allow it."

"You promised not to see him."

Guilt flooded Louisa's face. "I know, but . . . well . . . I knew you would never consent, even if I waited the two years. And I thought that if it were done, and there was nothing you could do to stop it—"

"I can stop it now. Go pack your things, Louisa. You're coming back to Castlemaine with me."

"But Marcus, the season isn't over!" Louisa protested.

"The season is over for you, young lady. And I'll have

to think long and hard before I let you have another."

Regina and Lady Iversley exchanged frustrated glances. They both knew Marcus well enough to understand his reaction. And they both knew Louisa—and young women—well enough to know it was the wrong way to handle her.

"You can't take me away for good!" Louisa cried.

He set his shoulders stubbornly. "I'm your guardian—I can do whatever the hell I please. I should have done it the minute that ass started sniffing around you, but I thought you had the good sense not to be taken in by his lies."

"He loves me!" she protested. "I don't care what you say, he loves me! He told me so!"

Sweet heaven, this got worse and worse. "Marcus, you have to tell her the truth," Regina said. "If he won't, then you *have* to. You're not being fair to her."

"I don't have to tell her a damned thing," he bit out. "And stay out of this, Regina. This is not your concern."

She flinched, but did not back down. "She's my sister now, so that makes it my concern."

"You should have thought of that when you deliberately hid your brother's plans from me."

An embarrassed flush spread over her cheeks as the Iversleys both stared at her. "Marcus, please, can't we discuss this first? Alone?"

"Nothing to discuss," he said, maddening her with his usual retreat into the cave. "Louisa, go pack your things. Miss Tremaine, you will wish to do the same if you intend to go with us."

Louisa looked as if she might balk.

"*Now*, Louisa!" he barked.

She jumped, then allowed Cicely to lead her from the room.

Marcus turned to his brother. "I'm sorry she's caused

you and Katherine such grief, but I assure you I do not blame you for what has happened."

Lord Iversley steadied his shoulders. "Your wife is right, you know. You should tell Louisa what's going on. Prinny will just keep trying."

"So will Simon," Regina put in.

"I'll take care of Foxmoor, never you fear." Marcus glared at her. "And I will not tolerate any interference from you, do you understand?"

Regina bristled. How *dared* he use the same tone that he'd used with Louisa! "What I understand is that you are not thinking rationally at the moment—or surely you would not be ordering me about as if I were a child."

"As your husband, I have the right to order you about, madam. And I expect you to obey, or I swear I'll take you over my knee."

Lady Iversley rose, eyes flashing. "Marcus, really! You go too far."

"Iversley, do control your wife," Marcus growled.

Lord Iversley snorted. "The way you're controlling yours? Thank you, but I don't particularly like sleeping with one eye open." He offered his arm to his wife. "Come, sweetheart, you and I had best get out of the line of fire."

When Lady Iversley sniffed and shot Marcus an angry glance before marching off with her husband, despair gripped Regina. The old Marcus had returned, the rude lout who cared nothing for anyone's feelings, the dragon who reacted to being cornered by breathing fire. She was not going to stand here and watch him cut himself off from everyone who cared for him. "Marcus—"

He whirled toward her, his stance and expression belligerent. "If you think to soften my temper with your wheedling, think again."

"I know better than that. When you are like this, nothing will soften you. But if you'll calm yourself, you'll see that hauling Louisa off to Castlemaine without explaining the circumstances to her would be a huge mistake. She deserves a good husband and a place in society. If you deny her that by locking her up in the country, she will repay you for it in the worst way."

"Let her just try."

"Oh, she'll try, I assure you. Besides, it's unwise to jerk her out of society in the middle of the season. We should be able to squelch any rumors about her and my brother, but it will become infinitely more difficult if people see her guardian overreacting."

He scowled. "And your solution is to let her stay here?"

She breathed easier. At least he was no longer dismissing everything out of hand. "With us. If you tell her the situation, I'm sure she will behave herself perfectly for the rest of the season. Especially after I speak to Simon—"

"Not a chance. You are not to speak to that man, do you hear?"

So much for his not dismissing things out of hand. "Someone must tell him that he can no longer—"

"I will deal with Foxmoor myself. You and Louisa can clearly not be trusted around the man—he gets round you both every time. So you will leave him to me. I forbid either of you to see him."

Her pulse began to pound. "Let me see if I understand you correctly. You are forbidding me to speak to my own brother?"

The icy tone in her voice seemed to give him pause, but he stuck doggedly to his position. "Yes."

"Ever?"

His face grew shuttered. "You won't have a chance to

speak to him anyway. We're returning to Castlemaine tonight with Louisa."

She gritted her teeth. "Even if it sets the gossips to wagging? Even if she never gets to enter society again?"

"That is my decision. We are not staying in London, no matter how much you prefer society to being with your husband in the country."

"That's not true!"

"Isn't it? You've been chafing to return practically since we left. Complain all you want, but I won't indulge your whims—or Louisa's—as my father indulged my mother's. I refuse to watch my wife and my sister follow the same path—"

"As your mother? You couldn't stop your mother from choosing Prinny over her responsibilities as a wife and a parent, so now you mean to lock up me and Louisa before we can become just as reckless. Is that it?" Her own temper rising, she stepped nearer. "Louisa is nothing like your mother. And neither am I."

"Damned right you're not. You're ten times the woman she was, ten times more beautiful, ten times more alluring, ten times more good—"

"Then why don't you trust me, drat it?"

"It's not you I don't trust, but all your damned sycophants. You're also ten times more irresistible than my mother was. Those scoundrels are out there waiting to get you alone, now that you're married and don't need a chaperone."

In light of what he'd told her about his mother, she understood his fears. But that didn't mean she had to put up with them. "It takes two people to commit adultery. As long as I don't agree to it, it doesn't matter if a thousand men try to get me alone."

"With some men, it matters. You have no idea what lengths some men—"

"Spending the past few days teaching me to read a children's primer has clearly made you forget that I am not a child. I know how to handle men. I have spent the past several years successfully fending off their advances."

"You didn't fend off mine." His eyes glittered. "You indulged your taste for adventure, which is precisely why we ended up married."

"And now you mean to punish me for it?" Tears welled in her eyes as she lifted her hand to caress his cold, hard cheek. "We ended up married because I fell in love with you, you dolt. I would not have married you otherwise, no matter what 'adventures' you offered me."

For a moment, he only stared at her, stunned. Then he covered her hand with his. "If you love me, you'll return to Castlemaine and forget about London."

He might as well have slapped her. He wouldn't offer her words of love, but he would try to use her own love to control her?

"How dare you!" She jerked her hand back, fighting to suppress her tears. "I will not be your prisoner, Marcus. Your wife, yes. Your lover, certainly. But never your prisoner."

A thunderous scowl crossed his features. "You're my wife. You belong with me. And I say we return to Castlemaine. So you might as well resign yourself—"

She backed away from him, shaking her head. "I shall not let you lock me away, no matter how pretty your prison. If you couldn't endure three days locked away, how do you expect *me* to endure a lifetime?"

He stalked her like some mythical beast. "You will do as I say."

"You promised me I could come to London when I wished. You swore it!"

"And your brother promised not to pursue my sister. He broke his promise, so I can damned well break mine."

"Your promise was to me, not him. I cannot control my idiot brother. But I expect you to hold to your vows."

"As I expect you to hold to yours. You vowed to love, honor, and *obey*. So you will return with me and Louisa to Castlemaine now, or I swear that when you do return, I will bar the doors to you."

Her gasp was echoed by one behind her, but she ignored it. "You will *what?*"

"You will no longer be welcome at Castlemaine," he said, but stiffly, as if he knew he'd gone too far, yet could not bring himself to take back the words.

She shouldn't be surprised. This was how he'd punished his mother, too, by thrusting her out of his life. Why should she expect him to behave any differently with his wife?

Because his wife had never imprisoned him in a dungeon or branded him with a poker. Because his wife had only dared to question his authority. Because his wife loved him.

Still reeling from his threat, Regina turned to find Louisa and Cicely standing in the doorway while a footman strode past carrying their bags.

Louisa stared at her brother with an ashen face. "Marcus, don't be a fool."

"Go to the carriage, Louisa," Marcus ordered. "We'll be along shortly."

"But Marcus—"

"*Now*, damn you!"

Louisa turned and hurried off. Cicely watched her go, clearly uneasy.

"Miss Tremaine," Marcus said, "please remind your cousin where her duty lies."

Cicely positively shook beneath his frigid gaze. "Regina, dear, perhaps you should just go with your husband for now."

"Thank you for your advice," Regina said tightly, "but while you might enjoy living in a prison, it is not something I fancy."

"It appears, Miss Tremaine," Marcus bit out, "that you are faced with a choice. You may stay in town with my wife, in which case you will never be welcome at Castlemaine, either. Or you may return with me to act as my sister's companion. I do hope you'll make your choice wisely."

Regina glared at him. "How dare you drag my ailing cousin, after all she's done for us, into *our* argument? What could you possibly hope to accomplish?"

He fixed her with a feverish gaze. "I hope to bring you to your senses. You can hardly function well in society without her around. How will you read calling cards, respond to invitations, write thank-you notes, and all the rest?"

She felt sick. He would use her own defect against her? He was *that* far gone?

"H-He knows you can't read?" Cicely squeaked from behind her.

"He knows," Regina choked out. "He *said* it didn't matter to him. Clearly that was a lie."

His eyes blazed. "It wasn't a lie, confound it all! And I'll wager it matters a damned sight more to your society friends. Yet you choose them over me."

"No, Marcus. I choose life over a prison." She stared at his stubborn features, so full of anger. So full of fear. If she went with him now, he would never stop this madness. But if she didn't, would he ever forgive her?

She had to take that chance. She was in a fight for his soul, and she meant to win, no matter what it took. "You've spent your life hiding away in your cave to avoid the world at its ugliest. Instead, you've missed all its beauties. Well, I shan't do the same. When you decide to rejoin the world, I will be here waiting. But I love you too much to let you drag me back to die in a cave with you."

Turning on her heel, she left the room and headed for the stairs, not sure where she was going but sure that she could not stay another minute to have her heart torn out of her chest.

She heard Marcus stalk into the hall behind her. "I order you to come home with me, Regina!"

She kept ascending the stairs.

"Damn you, you're my wife!"

Yes, and he'd certainly rewarded her well for that, hadn't he? Tears filled her eyes and she brushed them away ruthlessly.

Silence filled the hall below her. As she reached the top of the stairs and headed for someplace she could release all her tears, she heard him growl, "Fine. If that's how you want it, you can rot in London, for all I care. But you will damned well rot here alone."

She froze, her tears spilling over. She heard the thunder of his boots receding down the hall and out the front door. Then she heard the unmistakable clopping of horse hooves on cobblestone, growing fainter and fainter until they merged into the other street noises.

Only then did she fall apart. Collapsing onto the floor, she began to weep uncontrollably. What if she'd lost him for good? Could she ever get him back?

Footsteps sounded on the stairs, voices murmured near her, and still she sobbed, unable to stop, unable even to drag herself from the floor onto a chair.

Suddenly an arm came around her shoulders, and a gentle, familiar voice whispered, "Here now, my dear, you will hurt yourself with such weeping."

"C-Cicely?" she said, glancing up at her cousin through her tears. "You . . . you should have gone with him."

"Nonsense. My place is always with you, dearest."

"He will make good on his threats, you know. He will cut you off entirely. And I cannot promise—"

"Shh, shh, dearest," Cicely murmured, holding Regina's head to her breast. "There is always your brother."

"No," she said doggedly. "This is all Simon's fault. I don't even want to see him." Tears choked her throat. "Besides, Marcus is probably going to k-kill him."

"Not if I have anything to say about it," another voice cut in.

She looked up to see Lord Iversley standing nearby with his wife, their faces filled with concern.

"I'll send a note to your brother at once," the earl went on, "warning him that if he knows what's good for him, he'll retire to the country until Draker's temper cools."

"Marcus will not appreciate your interference. And I do not mean to come between you and your br—" She caught herself just in time. "Your friend."

Lord Iversley's face softened further. With a glance at Cicely, he said, "Our friendship has withstood a great deal. If the choice is enduring his temper or seeing him killed in a duel with Foxmoor, I'd rather endure his temper, I assure you."

"He'll come round," Lady Iversley put in. She slid her hand in her husband's with a soft smile. "They always do."

"I wish I could be sure of that."

"You can be sure he loves you," Lord Iversley said. "But some men don't handle falling in love very well. Katherine's right—you just need to give him a few days. If you want, I'll talk to him."

"No. He must decide for himself if he wants a wife or a prisoner. He knows I won't accept the latter." Which was why she doubted it would be only a few days.

"In the meantime," Lady Iversley said, "you'll stay here with us, won't you?"

"I hate to inconvenience you. And there's always the town house—"

"Nonsense," Lord Iversley put in. "You and Cicely shall stay here, and that's an end to it." When she started to protest again, he added gently, "You don't have keys to the town house, my dear. And I'm afraid Draker might forbid the servants from allowing you to stay there anyway."

That very real possibility roused her temper enough to banish her tears. "Yes," she said bitterly, "that sounds exactly like something he'd do."

Any man who would try to take away his wife's companion in order to make her dependent upon him would certainly not hesitate to deny her any servants.

But Cicely had stayed with her, and that gave her hope.

It also gave her an idea. Swallowing hard, she stared at her cousin, then Lady Iversley. Katherine, her sister-in-law. Surely she could trust *this* woman. "As long as I'm going to be here for a few days, do you think you and Cicely could teach me to read?"

Chapter Twenty-three

*Do not forever curb your young charge's
independence. A little willfulness might stand her
in good stead later in life.*
—Miss Cicely Tremaine, *The Ideal Chaperone*

Marcus hadn't thought that living without Regina would
be this difficult. In truth, he hadn't thought at all when
he'd left Iversley's in a blind rage.

He'd had plenty of time to think about it since, however. With a sigh, he glanced at the clock presiding over
the empty dining room where he sat with his toast, tea,
and morning paper. Nine o'clock. In a short while his
steward would arrive for their daily meeting, and he
might gain a blessed two-hour respite from his tor-
mented thoughts.

But then the afternoon would yawn before him, hours
of doing nothing because he could not concentrate on estate business or investments or even the treasures in his library. Finally, he would dine alone, since Louisa would
not eat with him. Had not eaten with him since their return three days ago.

Had it only been three days since he'd left Iversley's? It
felt like three weeks . . . months . . . years. A torturous eter-
nity. His bed was empty, and his heart was hollow. And

the place at the end of the table, which should be filled by his wife—

Damn, damn, *damn!*

He thrust his untouched toast aside. He'd lived like this contentedly before, closeted at Castlemaine and tending to his estate, with only Louisa for company. He'd even gone through stretches when Louisa was so angry at him that she wouldn't speak to him for days on end. So why did he suddenly want to hurl his cup through the clock that gnawed away his life with each slow, methodical tick?

Because of Regina. Because until his wife had exploded into his life, he'd never tasted heaven, never truly known what he was missing. She had changed all that, confound the woman.

And God, how he'd lapped it up. How quickly he'd grown used to waking up with a warm, willing wife in his bed. To having her settled sweetly upon his lap while he read the morning paper and tried to help her read it, too.

To being buried inside her so deep—

He groaned. That was how a woman like her kept a man enthralled, by being so soft, seductive, and ready to please that a man couldn't help but root his cock deep inside her. Then once she had him by the cock, she led him around by it, and he was helpless to escape. If he even wanted to.

He hid his face in his hands. That was the trouble. He wasn't sure he wanted to escape anymore. Any life, even among her society friends, was better than this.

Was that how Father had finally come to accept Mother's infidelity? Because she'd worn him down? Because eventually he'd decided that any piece of her was better than none at all? Damn it, he would not let that happen to him!

"Marcus?"

He jerked his head up at the sound of that familiar resentful voice. "Yes, angel?"

"I wish to speak to you." Louisa marched into the room as regally as any queen. Great God, she already walked like Regina. Give her a few years, and society would be calling *her* La Belle Dame Sans Merci.

He stiffened. "I take it from your expression that you're still angry at me."

"I have just received a note from Lady Iversley."

His eyes narrowed. "Oh?"

"She is requesting that I send apparel for your wife. It seems Regina and Cicely are residing with the Iversleys. Because they have nowhere else to go."

"Nonsense, I leased her a damned town house."

"She has no keys, and you never instructed the servants to admit her."

He squirmed in his chair. He hadn't even thought of that. "What about her brother? She could stay with him, for God's sake." Though he didn't like the idea.

"Apparently she's too angry at her brother to stay in his house. Not that it would matter. It seems he's missing."

"What?"

Approaching the table, she tossed a newspaper clipping at him. "Read *that*."

The minute he caught sight of Regina's name, or rather, her married name, the breath dried up in his throat. Snatching it from her, he read:

Lady Draker was welcomed eagerly by her friends at the Merrington dinner party, who were anxious to hear about her honeymoon with the newly fashionable Lord Draker. His lordship had been called away

*on estate business, but accompanied by his good
friends, the Earl and Countess of Iversley, Lady
Draker shimmered in a delicate gown of French crepe
in primrose and white, with . . .*

Called away on estate business? He snorted. The
woman was ever quick to hide the truth. She would never
say, *I abandoned my husband.*

He skipped past all the fashion nonsense, then was arrested by the words, "Lord Whitmore." His heart pounding, he read:

*One wonders what Lord Whitmore did to warrant
the viscountess giving him the cut direct, but Lady
Draker made her displeasure at her cousin's presence
markedly obvious.*

Marcus stared blindly at the paper. He'd threatened to
bar Regina from his home, and she'd repaid him by cutting
the very man who'd insulted him at Almack's. Her own
cousin. A man who would leap to take Marcus's place if
she would only give him the chance.

Clearly she wouldn't. But how long would it be before
she did? If Marcus continued to brood out here without
her, how long would she stand firm? A cold fear closed its
fist around his heart. Great God, what had he done?

He kept reading, hoping for more mention of her, but
instead . . .

*Another lady's absence was also markedly obvious.
Miss North, sister-in-law to Lady Draker, and often
seen in the company of that lady's brother, the Duke
of Foxmoor, was not in attendance. Neither was the*

duke, despite his friendship with the Merringtons. According to the viscountess, Miss North's bad cold has kept her from attending parties of late. Lady Draker had no idea why the duke had not come, but we can only speculate from his previous marked attentions to Miss North that he did not want to attend any party where she was not. We will be watching this couple closely. Could a wedding be in the offing?

"Damn." He threw the clipping aside. If he'd done as Regina asked and let Louisa stay in London, nobody would be speculating on anything. It might have been possible to separate the couple gracefully with little comment, but now—

"What did you do to Simon?" Louisa shook the clipping in his face. It was clear what part of the column *she* deemed important. "If you've hurt him in any way, I swear I will never forgive you!"

"How am I supposed to have hurt him when I haven't left Castlemaine in three days?" Not that he hadn't wanted to trot off to London to strangle his brother-in-law. But he hadn't dared leave Louisa alone while he did it.

Besides, he'd promised Regina not to kill the man. And although he'd broken at least one promise to her, he sensed that she would never forgive his breaking that one. Murdering her brother was the quickest way to make his wife hate him. It suddenly seemed very important to have his wife not hate him.

"So what *are* you going to do to Simon?" Louisa asked plaintively.

"I haven't decided." But he didn't intend to let the man escape unscathed. The first chance Marcus got, he intended to speak to Byrne about a suitable revenge. His diabolical half brother would know exactly how to hit Fox-moor where it would hurt the scoundrel most.

Louisa sat down at the table. "And me? What do you plan to do to me?"

"You're just now asking that?" he said, raising one eye-brow.

"I expected you to say something that night in the car-riage, but you didn't. Since then, you've been so grumpy, I didn't want to broach the subject."

"You thought you'd give my anger plenty of time to cool, did you?"

She thrust out her chin exactly as his wife might have. "Perhaps."

He shook his head. "That was pointless. It's not a matter of anger anymore—I still hold to what I said in London. You'll stay here for now. And sometime in the fall, we will consider whether to let you have another season."

"Who's *we*—you and Regina? You drove your wife away, remember? She doesn't even feel free to live in the town house you supposedly leased for her."

The words were like a slap in the face. *He'd driven his wife away.* She was in London, apparently convinced that she must rely on Iversley's charity, and probably growing to hate her husband more with every day.

Oh, God, what if she never came back?

"What happened between me and Regina is not your concern," he said tightly.

She leaped to her feet. "Isn't it? You got angry at her be-cause she was standing up for me. She still is." Her lower lip trembled. "But it's not going to do her much good, is it? How long do you think she can keep telling people in soci-ety that I have a cold? And if . . . if no one hears that Simon has offered for me and he stays absent from society . . . how long do you think it will be before they're spreading nasty rumors about *me?*"

"They won't," he choked out. "I won't let them."

"And how will you stop them? By shouting down all the rumormongers? Going to Almack's and threatening to cut out their tongues, like you did to Lord Whitmore at the opera?"

He gaped at her. "How did you know about that?"

She paled. "Oh, dear. I wasn't supposed to say. She said you might be annoyed."

"She who?" he bit out.

"Regina. She told me and some other ladies at the wedding breakfast what happened at the opera. I think she was afraid Lord Whitmore might resent you enough to reveal it himself, so she told her side to stave off the gossip. She said she didn't want anyone to think badly of you. Not that anyone would. It was very romantic, the way you leaped to defend her honor when Lord Whitmore caught the two of you holding hands." Louisa swallowed. "But I suppose I shouldn't have said anything."

"I'm glad you did." Even if every word pounded his conscience. Regina, his clever wife, had known that her sanctified version would instantly be believed over the tale of a spurned suitor . . . as long as she told hers first.

He tried to imagine his own mother drumming up some tale to protect Father's reputation, but he couldn't conceive of it. And she certainly had made no attempt to preserve her son's. Yet Regina, the wife he'd barred from their home, had risked her own reputation to save his pathetic one.

"Marcus?"

"Hmm?" Great God, where had he gone so wrong?

"Why do you hate Simon?"

He chose his words carefully. "Because he doesn't love you as he should."

She took that in, then frowned. "I suppose you think he can't possibly love me because I'm a bastard."

His heart stopped. "Who told you such a lie? Did *he* tell you that? Did that damned ass—"

"Nobody told me. I-I figured it out on my own." Tears welled in her eyes. "It's the truth, isn't it?"

"Of course not. You're the legitimate daughter of the fifth Viscount Draker."

She brushed the tears away. "I'm not an idiot, you know. Uncle George . . . I-I mean, the prince . . . was always here, and it seemed natural that he would be. But of course it wasn't natural at all. That's why I figured I must be as much a bastard as you."

"No, you—" He stopped short. "You know about me?"

She managed a smile. It dug at his heart. "Only because of that awful argument you had with the prince before he and Mama went away."

He scowled. "I didn't think you'd heard that."

"Only some of it. Then I asked my governess about it, and she said I wasn't to talk about you being the prince's son to anyone, especially you, for it would hurt your feelings. She said it was a secret. And . . . and when I asked if I was Uncle George's daughter, she said 'Certainly not,' and I believed her."

"She was right."

"Marcus," she said, the tone far too old for a young girl, "since I've been in society, I've heard nothing but tales of the prince and his many mistresses. And I can't ever remember a time when he wasn't here—"

"He wasn't here the year you were born, and that's good enough for me. It was good enough for Father, too."

She bit her lower lip. "But I *could* be the prince's child, couldn't I? Mother took lots of trips to London. He didn't have to be at Castlemaine to conceive me."

" 'Conceive' indeed—how do you know about that sort of thing, damn it?"

At least she had the good grace to blush. "I asked Lady Iversley. I couldn't believe that my governess was right—she said babies were made when a man and a woman slept in the same bed. And since I used to climb into bed with you when I got scared as a little girl, and I didn't have any babies, I knew she was lying."

"Oh, God," he groaned. "I never dreamed your governess was telling you anything about it at all, or I would have dismissed her."

Louisa looked sad. "Do you really think I'd have been better prepared for life if I'd been completely ignorant?"

"No, of course not, but—"

"That's the trouble with you, Marcus. You think you're protecting me. But really you're just killing me. A little bit at a time. Cursing me to stay in this house forever—" A sob caught in her throat. "I swear I'll die if I have to stay here for the next year without even Regina for female company."

I swear I'll die, accompanied by tears, had been a common ploy of Louisa's in the past, but this time it wounded him. Deeply. Because it too closely echoed what Regina had said.

And for the first time, he really understood what they meant. He might just die himself if he had to stay here one more minute without Regina.

He choked back the bile rising in his throat. "All right, angel. I'll take you back to London. We'll work something out."

He thought that would end the conversation, that she would leap up, kiss him, and run off to pack while he sat here trying to figure out a way to get his wife back that didn't involve making too many concessions he couldn't abide.

Instead, Louisa just sat staring at him. "You're only saying that to distract me, because you don't want to answer my question."

He blinked. "What question?"

"Could I be the prince's by-blow?"

He started to say "no," then caught himself. *Do you really think I'd have been better prepared for life if I'd been completely ignorant?*

With a sigh, he took her hand. "Honestly, I don't know. I don't think so." He hesitated, but the voices of Regina and the Iversleys clamored in his ear, demanding that she know everything. "But I think the prince believes it."

Her hand tightened on his. "Is that why you asked if Simon had told me? Because he's the prince's friend?"

He winced. "Yes."

"And is that why you mentioned Simon carrying me off to Carlton House, the night you and Regina were caught together?"

He'd forgotten about that. "Yes."

Her hand began to tremble. "You think Simon and the prince are up to something having to do with me. That's why you don't approve of Simon."

"I . . . um . . ."

"And Regina knows, too, doesn't she? She was so adamant that we wait two years, and I thought she was merely taking your side, but then the other night she was so angry at Simon for—" She groaned. "Saying that he loved me." Her eyes filled with tears again. "He doesn't, does he? He said he did, but he doesn't."

"I don't think so, no."

"And you knew all along?" she asked, turning an angry gaze on him. "You let me make a fool of myself over him, while all the time—"

"I didn't know for sure. Regina had me half-convinced he was sincere. She believed he was sincere herself, until the night at Almack's. And then—"

"Then what?" She crossed her arms over her chest. "I want to know every detail. I deserve to know what's been going on while I've been acting like a fool."

Tears still glistened in her eyes, but now they were angry tears. She looked exactly like their mother had looked the day Marcus had thrown her out. God help Foxmoor now. Perhaps Marcus wouldn't have to seek vengeance on the man, after all—Louisa might take care of it herself.

"I don't know all of it," he began, "only what Regina managed to wheedle out of her brother that night, but according to her . . ." He explained about the prince and his plans to bring Louisa to court.

With every word, her spine straightened, and her eyes glittered more brightly, until he was sure she would turn into one of the Furies any minute, flying out across England to tear Foxmoor's head off. Marcus hoped he got to watch.

"And no one saw fit to tell me this," she bit out. "Even Regina kept it secret."

The hint of betrayal in her voice made him say hastily, "She had good reason, angel." He explained what Foxmoor had threatened, and she paled.

"Oh, Lord, the man is truly despicable!" She glared at him. "And don't say what you're thinking. Yes, you were right about him, I admit it. But if I had known even a fraction of this—"

"I didn't have any proof until recently," he said defensively.

"Yes, but you had reasons for your opinions, which you were apparently voicing freely to everybody but me. And all because you didn't want me to know about my dubious parentage." She crossed her arms over her chest. "Well, I know now. The only thing I don't know is how much of this 'courtship' was plotted by His Highness."

Marcus stared at her blankly. "All of it, I imagine."

"Not all of it. Yes, the prince might have wanted me at court, but did he tell Simon to kiss me and say he loved me and—"

"He *kissed* you?" Marcus growled, coming up out of his chair. "I'll tear the bastard limb from limb!"

"You will not." She rose, too. "We can finally hold our heads up in society, and you are *not* going to ruin that."

"Pardon me?" he ground out. When had his sweet sister turned so fierce?

"I think Simon deserves a punishment more fitting to his crime."

"And what exactly might that be?" he asked warily.

Her eyes narrowed. "Oh, I have an idea. But first I need some information. And if His Highness would go to such great lengths to bring me to court, I think he ought to explain himself to my face, don't you?"

"Certainly not."

"Hear me out, Marcus. I have a right to know how much of this whole fiasco was due to His Highness's plotting and how much to Simon's ambition."

Her hard tone made him uneasy. "I suppose."

"I want to meet with the prince. And I want Simon

there. Regina, too, since I trust her to say honestly—before His Highness—what her brother revealed to her."

His heart thundered in his ears. "The only way I'll allow a meeting between you, Foxmoor, my wife, and His Confounded Highness is if I'm there, too."

"I wouldn't have it any other way."

He eyed her closely. "Is this some sly way of trying to effect a reconciliation between me and Regina?"

"No." Her tone softened. "But if I could do it, I would. Her brother might be despicable, but she is not. You're not letting her association with Simon keep you apart, are you?"

"No."

"You can trust her, you know. *I* trust her, even after what you told me. She's never made a promise to me that she didn't keep, and she's never lied to me. And I wager if you search your heart, you'll realize it's true for you, too."

He thought back on everything that had happened between him and Regina. Even when she was keeping the truth from him about Foxmoor, she'd never lied. And he couldn't blame her for her evasions about her inability to read. God knew he'd been evasive as hell about his own past.

He might never be able to trust La Belle Dame Sans Merci, but Regina was *not* La Belle Dame Sans Merci. She showed mercy every time she overlooked his bad temper. She showed mercy every time she argued with him on Louisa's behalf.

She showed mercy when she said she loved a surly, overprotective idiot unfit to share her air, much less her bed. The question was, did she have any mercy left in her heart for him? After what he'd done to her? After what he'd said? Did he even have the right to *ask* for her mercy?

"In fact," Louisa added softly, "I'll wager that you love her. And that's the most important thing."

He stared past her to the place at the other end of the dining table where Regina would sit as his wife. If she were here. If he hadn't driven her away. "I'm not sure I know how to love, Louisa."

She took his hand. "Don't be silly. Loving is easy. It's finding someone to love you back that's hard."

Out of the mouths of babes.

She pressed his hand to her heart. "And since you've got the hard part done, the least you can do is love her. Because she does love you." She cast him an impish smile. "Although I'm not entirely sure *why*."

He tried to laugh, but nothing came out. "Damned if *I* know why."

Did Regina still love him? She'd said she would be waiting when he came to his senses, but that had been days ago. Before she'd had time to harden her heart against him, to recognize what a beast she'd married.

It would be just like him to discover what was wrong with his life too late to do anything about it. Like a fool, he'd thrown away the best woman he'd ever known, because he'd been too busy trying not to follow in Father's footsteps.

Trying to keep her from leaving him. But when he'd let his temper get the better of him, he'd given her no choice except to do just that.

Now that she'd seen the worst of him, would she even want to return? To live with him, here or in town or anywhere else? Not if she had an ounce of sense. Too late, he understood what she'd meant when she'd called Castlemaine a prison. Because any place could be a prison if you were there alone, and not by choice.

"Marcus?" Louisa said gently. "Do you think you could set up a meeting between Uncle George, Simon, Regina, and you and me?"

He sighed. "I could. It might take a day or two, though."

She let out a heavy breath. "*Will* you, then? Will you give me the chance to have my revenge on Simon?"

How he wanted to say no, to keep Louisa locked up here safe. But now he knew what a mistake that was. For Louisa *and* his wife. He wasn't sure he could do anything about Regina. But it wasn't too late to do right by his sister.

"Yes, angel. You shall have your meeting."

Perhaps then even his wife might find some mercy in her heart for him.

Chapter Twenty-four

Feeling a certain fondness for your charge
is perfectly acceptable as long as it doesn't
cloud your judgment.
—Miss Cicely Tremaine, *The Ideal Chaperone*

$\mathcal{I}$t was late in the afternoon when Regina, Cicely, and Katherine sat around the table in the immaculate Iversley schoolroom. Regina pored over a poem by one of Katherine's favorite poets. A set of carved wooden alphabet blocks were arrayed in front of her.

Regina worked at sounding out the first line. "I . . . wa- . . . wa—"

"This is too difficult," Cicely exclaimed.

"No, it isn't." Regina rubbed her fingers over the block with the raised letter that most looked like the next letter. "Oh, 'n.' That's right—it looks like an 'u' sometimes, but it's not."

For some reason, *feeling* the letters made it easier for her to identify them. She didn't know why, but after discovering it that day at Castlemaine, she'd known it was the only way she'd ever learn. It helped that both Katherine and Cicely were infinitely patient with her.

She took a breath. "I wan- . . . wan-dered . . . l-l-lonely— Lonely?"

Katherine nodded.

Regina's head throbbed, but she soldiered on. Katherine's cook had offered a posset that helped when the headache got too bad. But it seemed less painful as the days passed. She was getting used to it, just as Marcus had predicted.

She winced. She *wouldn't* think of Marcus, not now, not when she'd come so far. Otherwise, she'd start crying, and her head would throb even more. She'd been trying to save her tears for her bed at night.

She didn't get much sleep.

" 'I wandered lonely . . . as . . . a . . . clou- . . . clou—" Oh, no, more of those pesky d's. Or b's. But "cloub" didn't make sense, so . . . " 'Cloud.' 'I wandered lonely as a cloud'?"

Katherine beamed at her. "That's it. You've got it!"

Regina blinked. "I read a sentence from a real poem? Not a primer?"

"Not a primer," Katherine echoed.

"And I read it by myself." Hardly able to contain her excitement, Regina leaped from the chair and did a pirouette. "I read a sentence by myself! From a real poem!"

Laughing, Katherine leaped up, too, and they danced around like two schoolgirls. Until Regina glanced over to see Cicely crying quietly, tears streaming down her pale cheeks.

Regina stopped dancing to rush to Cicely's side. "Dearest, what is wrong? Is it your lungs?"

"No . . . N-No . . ." Cicely stammered through her sobs. "A-All these years . . . you could . . . have learned." She dabbed futilely at the flow with the voluminous handkerchief she always had at the ready. "I should . . . I should have taught you." She grabbed Regina's hand and squeezed it painfully. "I failed you. I should never have listened to that doctor. Perhaps then—"

Her heartfelt wail started Regina's own tears flowing. "Oh, dearest, no. Don't blame yourself." She enfolded the older woman in her arms. "I listened to the doctor, too. We both listened. It's not your fault."

"It is! You were a child. I was supposed to take care of you!"

"And you *did.* You have always been the perfect teacher and companion."

"But I should have done better." Cicely wiped her nose, then started to cry again. "It's just that . . . I was so afraid of your being hurt. I never got to have children, and you were such a sweet, fragile mite . . . I couldn't have borne it . . . if anything had happened to you. And the doctor did say—"

"Shh," Regina murmured, clutching Cicely tight. "I know you always had my best interests at heart."

Cicely drew back to fix her with a rheumy-eyed gaze. "It's my fault you had to marry that ogre. If not for me—"

"It's not your fault in the least, and he's not an ogre." Regina patted her cousin's hand. "Truly, dearest, once you get to know him, you will see that he's a very good man. Just a little pigheaded sometimes."

"Aren't they all?" Katherine said, taking a seat beside them.

Regina glanced at her sister-in-law. "Do they grow less pigheaded in time?"

"Not really. You just learn to get around it." Katherine smiled. "And they do make up for it in other ways."

Regina's answering smile was forced. Although she dearly missed having Marcus in her bed, more than that, she missed his cleverness, his dogged persistence . . . his outrageousness. She never knew what to expect from him.

Every rout, every ball, every party she attended now seemed dull. These days she'd much rather sit here with Cicely and Katherine, struggling through one sentence, than spend an afternoon listening to a lot of idiots converse about the weather.

Oh, Lord, now she even sounded like Marcus. But four days had passed, and she began to worry that he might never come round. Had her defiance been too much for him to accept? Was her marriage to become one of those awful arrangements where her husband lived in the country and she lived in town and they had separate lives?

She couldn't bear the thought.

A knock came outside the open door to the schoolroom, then a footman thrust his head inside. "My lady? There's a letter here for Lady Draker. I thought she might want it right away, seeing as how it's from his lordship."

Regina blushed. Their argument had been heard by every servant in the house, a mortification she'd had to live with for days. And if Marcus had sent a letter . . . that couldn't be good.

Katherine bade the servant enter to give Regina the letter. When Regina took it, it was heavier than she would have thought. Her heart sinking, she broke the seal and opened it. Two keys fell into her lap.

Perplexed, she stared at the letter, one short sheet of Marcus's bold scrawl.

"Shall I read it for you?" Cicely asked.

She wanted desperately to say no. Much as she loved and trusted her cousin—and Katherine, too—she hated having either of them read something so personal. But it would take her half a day at least to puzzle it out herself, especially with Marcus's poor penmanship. Besides, he had to know she'd be asking Cicely to read it. So it couldn't be terribly personal.

Her heart sank further. "Yes, please read it," she told Cicely, handing it over.

Donning her spectacles, Cicely began to read. " 'Dear wife, I heard that you are staying with my friends. Forgive me for not making it clear, but I never intended for you to be without a home. I'm enclosing the keys to the town house. You may go there with Cicely if you wish.'"

Regina moaned. "He's making this banishment permanent, drat him."

"I don't think so," Cicely said hastily. "He writes, 'Please tell the servants to prepare the house for Louisa and me. We're arriving in town tomorrow.' "

Regina's heart began to race. Had he come to his senses? But then why send a letter and not come here himself?

"Tomorrow?" Katherine exclaimed. "He thinks he can just trot into town as if nothing happened, and you will welcome him with open arms?"

"There's more," Cicely said. But before she could go on, an irate voice sounded from downstairs.

"I don't care what the devil you say—I know she's here. Now call my sishter . . . sister . . . down here this minute, or I'll bloody well . . . I'll bloody well . . . I'll go looking for her."

"Oh, dear," Cicely muttered. "Simon is here."

Katherine frowned. "He sounds drunk, too."

"Regina!" Simon called up the stairs. "Damn you, Regina, come down here!"

"Drunk or insane," Regina muttered as she rose and hurried to the door. She moved to the stairs and glowered down at her brother. "Go away!"

Simon stumbled up a step. "I'm not going 'way until you tell me what's going on."

He *was* drunk, for heaven's sake. And Simon rarely drank at all. Two footmen appeared to grab his arms, and he began to struggle. "Let go of me, you asses! I'm here on state business. State business, I tell you!"

State business?

They started dragging him toward the door.

"It's all right," Regina said. "Let him go." This was too odd to ignore, especially on the heels of Marcus's announcement that he was coming to town.

The footmen released him, and Simon steadied himself clumsily, straightening his coat and grumbling under his breath.

She continued down the stairs. "What are you doing here, Simon? I thought you had gone to the country."

"Because of what Iversley said? Hell, no. I'm not running away. Let your bloody husband call me out. Just let him. I'll take his bloody head off."

"You're not capable of taking anyone's head off at the moment." Grabbing him by the arm, she steered him to the parlor.

"Fetch His Grace some cold water," she called out to a footman. Perhaps if she dunked his head in it—

"I'm fine." He snatched his arm away. "I can walk by myself, damn it. And why are you here? You're supposed to be keeping your bloody husband occupied."

"Unfortunately, that became impossible after you tried to abduct his sister," she said coldly. "That's when he got angry and banished me from his home."

"What?" He shook his head as if to clear it. "Can't be. You're supposed to come, too. And that wouldn't make sense. Not if he's angry."

"Oh, for heaven's sake," she muttered, unable to make any sense out of his ramblings. She waited until they were in the parlor and he was sprawled upon a settee before she tried to get anything more out of him. "Now, what's this about me going somewhere?"

"To Carlton House. For a meeting. With your husband and Louisa."

Katherine appeared in the doorway. "He's right. Marcus's letter says that he hopes you'll allow him to accompany you tomorrow afternoon to Carlton House for a private meeting with His Highness and Louisa."

"And me," Simon snapped. "What's going on? What does Draker have up his sleeve now, damn it?"

"I have no idea." Her mind was reeling. Marcus hadn't seen the prince in years and had been adamant about never allowing Louisa into His Highness's presence. So what could it possibly mean?

"Did the letter say anything else?" she asked Katherine.

Like *I love you?* Or even *forgive me?*

Cicely appeared behind Katherine. "No. I'm sorry."

"Draker means to ruin me with His Highness, I know it," Simon grumbled. "That's why he's taking Louisa there. And if she tells the prince about—" He closed his eyes. "God save me, I'm in trouble."

"Good. You deserve it."

All Regina could think about was Marcus. What this meant for their marriage. What he was trying to tell her with this cursory note, if anything.

She turned to her brother. "Did you come in the phaeton?"

"Certainly."

"And I suppose you drove yourself? Good." She headed for the door. "I'm taking the phaeton."

"What?" He stumbled to his feet and nearly tripped over a tea table. "You can't—"

"You're in no condition to be tooling it about town anyway, and I mean to go to Castlemaine this instant."

"Have you ever driven a phaeton?" Katherine asked.

"Simon has let me take the reins a few times, yes."

Katherine lifted one eyebrow. "Perhaps you ought to wait until Alec returns from Tattersall's and let him take you out there in the carriage."

"No, indeed." She swept past Katherine and Cicely. "If I show up alone, Marcus will not dare to bar me from the house. He wouldn't want me driving back to town in the dark by myself."

"You don't really think he's going to hold to that threat now, do you?" Katherine asked as she followed her into the hall.

"I truly have no idea. After his note and the keys . . ." She let the footman help her into her coat. "I only know I cannot sit here another minute wondering what he's thinking. I have to end this, once and for all."

But as Regina headed off in the phaeton, she couldn't settle her taut nerves. It was a long two hours to Castlemaine, and she fretted over every mile. By giving her the keys to the town house, was Marcus acknowledging her freedom? Or asking for his own? Why hadn't he come himself?

Then again, the man was so cursedly proud, he could never admit he was wrong. Perhaps this meeting with the prince was meant to be his final denouncement of the man and all his friends, Regina and Simon included.

But he was taking Louisa with him, and he'd been so adamant about not telling her the truth. Had he changed his mind? Or had she figured it out? Or might both of them now be bent on vengeance against His Highness and all his friends, Regina and Simon included? Except that he meant to stay in the town house with her, and that made no sense if it was vengeance he wanted.

By the time she reached Castlemaine, she'd worked herself up into a state of high dudgeon. So help him, if he had told his butler to bar her from the place, she would drive the phaeton right through the halls of his precious Castlemaine and have the horses dance on his head!

But no one made a murmur as she drew up in front. A startled groom hurried to take her reins and help her down. An equally startled footman opened the door, and a distinctly ruffled butler met her in the hall.

It suddenly occurred to her that she had never been formally introduced to Marcus's staff. The last time she'd spoken to the butler, upon her first visit to Castlemaine, he actually *had* tried to bar her from the place.

She didn't even know his name. "I . . . um . . . am Lady Draker."

The butler colored deeply. "Yes, I know, my lady. Young James here will take your coat." He gestured to the gawking footman, who scurried to do his duty.

She let out a breath. "I need to speak to my husband. Do you know if he's here?"

"Yes, my lady. He asked not to be disturbed, but . . . well . . . he went down to the dungeon about two hours ago, carrying a bottle of Irish whisky and a painting, and frankly, I'm a bit worried."

He wasn't the only one worried. The dungeon couldn't be good for anyone, but especially not a man who'd once spent three days in it.

Then the butler's other words sank in. "He went down there with a painting?"

"I'm afraid so, my lady. That horrible one of a dragon by Mr. Blake." He leaned close. "We all hate it. It's very ugly. But his lordship insists on keeping it in his bedchamber—except when he takes it to the dungeon. Whenever he's in a foul mood."

"Right." He'd once mentioned going to the dungeon to vent his temper. If he'd been closeted down there for two hours, it must be some temper. She swallowed. "All the same, I believe I should go down there."

The butler led her to the servants' quarters beneath the main floor, then showed her to a small door set at the end of a gloomy stone hall. "This is the entrance to the stairs. It's not too far down from there."

Apprehension skittered along her spine. Joking about a dungeon with Marcus had been one thing; joining him in one after he'd been drinking whisky for two hours and keeping company with some ghastly painting was quite another.

But she'd come this far—"Thank you," she told the butler, and opened the door.

She had only descended a few steps down the dimly lit stone staircase when a disembodied voice came up from below.

"Leave me be, Louisa. I'll be fine for your confounded meeting tomorrow, I assure you, but for tonight I want some time to myself, to think over my sins." His voice dropped. "God knows I have plenty of them to keep me occupied."

Her heart lurched in her chest. He didn't sound like a man who'd been drinking. But the despair in his voice was more frightening than any drunkenness.

She quickened her steps until suddenly she burst into a very odd room, about twenty-feet-by-twenty-feet, barely high enough to permit a man to stand erect. Close and cold, it was hewn entirely from stone. A threadbare old chaise longue sat against one wall, looking incongruous amidst the moldy stone and rusting chains.

Waning daylight trickled in from one slit window near the ceiling, but most of the light came from candles. Lots of them. They were perched on stone ledges, inserted in ancient sconces, and lined up in candelabras along the wall. In the middle of them stood Marcus, with his back to her.

This was no place for anyone, not a grown man *or* a child of thirteen. Now that she saw it, she understood much about him that she'd never understood before.

A sudden hatred for his mother—and the prince— flared in her chest. How dared they try to break a mere boy all those years ago by thrusting him down here? They had convinced him he deserved nothing better, and drat him if he didn't still believe it.

No wonder he tried to gain everything by force. He didn't think he could gain things any other way. Well, it was time he learned otherwise.

A sudden scrabbling on the floor near her reminded her of what he'd said about rats, and she squealed before she could stop herself.

"Damn it, Louisa," he snapped as he whirled around, "I told you—"

He stopped short when he caught sight of her. "Regina?" he said hoarsely. Disbelievingly. "What are you doing here?"

Her heart twisted in her chest. He looked haggard, as if he'd slept even less than she had. His beautiful eyes were shadowed by pain. And his whiskers were growing back.

"You forgot to tell your butler to bar the door."

He flinched. "I didn't forget."

It took all her strength not to fly into his arms and tell him everything was fine. But she wasn't about to act as if nothing had happened. She meant to save his dragonly soul, to make sure he never did anything like this again. To force him out of his cave once and for all.

"Why did you not come to town yourself?" She allowed all her own pain to pour out of her. "Why did you not bring the keys in person instead of sending me some scurrilous letter, drat you?"

He stood there stoically, as if enduring a series of blows. "Because I was afraid you would not forgive me. I said the most horrible things to you—"

"Yes, you did. So you should have at least come in person to apologize."

Guilt etched his gloomy features. "Quite frankly, I wasn't sure you'd even see me." With a weary sigh, he dropped his large frame heavily onto the chaise longue. "And I wouldn't have blamed you."

Drat it, Marcus, fight for me. "Is that what you've been doing all this time, when you should have been apologizing? Drinking down here in this dungeon, working yourself into a fine brooding?" She walked toward the chaise longue, then spotted the painting he'd been gazing at.

Good Lord. The candlelight cast an unholy light over the ghastly thing. It was not what she'd expected—the usual picture of a scaly dragon with a long, reptilian tail. The dragon was actually a man to whom had been added some reptilian features, reminiscent of Satan himself. Marcus had certainly picked an excellent subject for his brooding.

"And I suppose you've been staring at this the whole

time." She faced him with a scowl. "Your butler is right—it *is* horrible."

He lifted the bottle of whisky in a silent toast. " 'Splendidly awful,' to quote my wife."

Tears gathered in her throat. She fought them ruthlessly. "I suppose you think it's an apt representation of *you*."

"Isn't it?" With a hint of defiance, he swigged from the whisky bottle, then wiped his mouth with the back of his hand.

"No, it is not." Walking up to examine the painting, she noted the blond woman lying at the dragon's feet. On the picture frame below the figure was a gold plate with a title inscribed on it. Regina ran her fingers along it, which helped her read it. "And I suppose you see 'the woman clothed in sun' as me."

"It fits you." He blinked. "Wait a minute—how did you know the title?"

"I read it just now. While you were apparently spending *your* time brooding in a dungeon, I was spending mine trying to learn something. And thanks to Katherine and Cicely, I have come a long way." She shot him a hesitant smile. "I read a whole line from a poem this morning. All by myself."

"That's wonderful, dearling," he said with heartfelt sincerity. Then his troubled frown returned. He set the bottle on the floor. "But that just proves how useless a husband I am to you. I couldn't even teach you to read."

His remorseful tone tore at her heart. "Teaching is not your particular strength, true. But without you, I could not have done it. Because you convinced me I could learn. Without your faith in me, I would never have even tried."

She steadied herself before she turned into a puddle of

mush in front of him. He did not need mush right now. "But that's neither here nor there." She glared at him. "Do you know what the trouble is with you?"

He eyed her warily. "I suspect you intend to tell me."

"You're damned right I do." When he blinked at her unladylike language, she said, "The trouble with you is that your half-mad mother expected you to be the same 'slobbering sycophant' to His Highness that she was, and when you recoiled, she tried to force you into it."

She blinked back tears, determined not to let him see them. "So to survive her machinations, you turned yourself into the dragon. Better that than a sycophant, right? Better that than becoming the equivalent of your whoring mother, begging for the prince's attention."

She strode up to him. "But you *aren't* the dragon, any more than I'm the 'woman clothed in sun' or the siren or even La Belle Dame Sans Merci. Yes, the dragon is a part of you, and the siren is certainly part of me."

He'd risen to stare at her, and she pressed on ruthlessly. "But you're more than that. You're a fierce protector of the innocent. You're a clever man with a taste for books." Her breath caught in her throat. "You're even a considerate lover, for all your talk about chaining women in the dungeon. And it's time you stop letting the dragon rule your life." Reaching up, she ran her finger along the thick line of his scar. "It's time you put the dragon in his place."

A low groan escaped his lips. "What if I don't know how?"

"Of course you know how. I suspected it the day I met you, but I became convinced of it when I saw you walk into Almack's so gloriously. You're the Viscount Draker, a man of wealth and privilege, the son of a future king. You're a prince, if not in name, then in character. If I had not seen the prince hidden beneath the dragon, I would never have let you kiss me or touch me . . . or marry me." Her tears fell unheeded. "I certainly would never have fallen in love with you."

Hope briefly lit his face. Then it died, and he shook his head stubbornly. "You say you love me now, but how long can it last? My own mother didn't love me, Regina. How the hell could you?"

The aching pain in his voice ran so deep that she feared she could never take him past it. But she refused to let it win.

She caught his face between her hands. "Your mother did love you in your own way, I'm sure. How could she not? She simply didn't know what to do with you. She was a will-o'-the-wisp trying to clasp a great, magnificent beast by the tail, and she couldn't hold on."

As tears filled his eyes, she looped her hands about his neck. "But I can hold on, my love. I can and I will. You will not shake me off, no matter what you do, no matter what you say. I will *never* let you bar the doors to me. Because La Belle Dame Sans Merci is part of me, too, and when it comes to you, I shall show no mercy. I will drag you out of the cave and into the light if it's the last thing I do."

Something broke inside him then, for with a groan, he crushed her to him. Then his mouth found hers, hard and achingly hungry. He tasted faintly of whisky and smelled like candle smoke and Marcus. Her Marcus.

He kissed her, deeply, thoroughly, as if trying to imprint her on his soul. Then he tore his lips from hers. "I'm sorry for what I said, dearling. God, you have no idea how sorry I am." He brushed kisses to her cheeks, her eyelids, her nose. "I'll do anything you ask. I'll go to town whenever you please, or stay here if you wish. I'll do anything you want, as long as you don't leave me."

"I'll never leave you," she said. *As long as you love me.*

Yet he had not said he loved her, had he? Some tiny part of him was still too afraid to trust her that far. Still, she truly believed he did love her. He just feared that if he said the words, she would own him. And he'd fought so long against having anyone, especially a woman, own him, that even now it was a struggle.

Which was why she meant to have the words from him tonight. And she could think of only one way he would let go of his fears enough to say them.

"There *is* one thing I want from you right now," she told him.

"Anything," he swore.

"Make love to me, Marcus."

His eyes darkened. "Oh, yes. We'll go upstairs—"

"No. Make love to me here. In the dungeon."

Chapter Twenty-five

*Your charge may choose a husband whom you
would not choose for her. If she is happy with her
choice, however, then you must be, too.
Sometimes a man improves upon acquaintance.*
—Miss Cicely Tremaine, *The Ideal Chaperone*

An involuntary shudder wracked Marcus. The very idea
of laying his lady wife down in this hellish place revolted
him. "No. Trust me, you do not want—"

"I do. And why shouldn't I?"

"Because it's filthy and unfit for a lady."

Her eyes gleamed at him like steel through a mist. "Yet
you dreamed of me here. Naked."

A strange panic gripped his chest. "I told you, I don't
know why I dreamed that. I only come down here to be
alone and—"

"Think upon your sins. Yes, I know." Taking him by
surprise, she shoved him so hard that he lost his balance
and fell onto the chaise longue. Before he could stand
back up, she had moved between his sprawled legs.

His cock instantly went hard. With a sensuous smile,
she removed the pins from her hair and shook it out. As a
curtain of gold curls fell to drape her shoulders, his breath
caught in his throat.

Nimbly, she unfastened the front of her gown. "You

come here to vent your temper where it can do no harm. Isn't that what you said?"

Her bodice fell open to reveal the sheer linen of her chemise, and his mouth went dry. He nodded, unable to speak, unable to do anything but stare at her. Even with only candles for light, he could see the rosy buds of her nipples through the fabric. God help him.

She thrust her breasts forward, as if to tease him. "What you really meant is, you come here to let the dragon loose when he is at his fiercest and ugliest. When you don't want anyone else to see him. Well, I mean to prove that I can handle even the dragon. In all his manifestations."

She shoved off her gown, and his blood beat a hot tattoo at the sight of her in that sheer chemise, her slender arms and bare neck awash in golden candlelight.

He reached for her, but she brushed his hands aside. Grabbing the hem of his shirt, she dragged it over his head. Before he realized what she was doing, she lifted his hand to one of the eyebolts fastened into the wall directly over his head. "I mean to chain the dragon," she said as she closed his fingers around it.

His heart hammering, he held on as she did the same to his other hand.

"I mean to chain him so that you'll learn how. So that chaining the dragon will become a pleasure to you, and not a fear that you are giving up your soul." Her eyes glittered as she skimmed her hands down his raised arms. "So that you will trust me not to hurt you, the next time I ask you to chain the dragon."

She stepped back to unbutton her chemise.

"What if I don't want to be chained?" he growled.

"You said you'd do anything I want. Do you really want to break another of your promises to me?"

He groaned, his groan deepening to a moan when she shimmied out of her chemise. Great God, she really was a siren. And La Belle Dame. And the woman clothed in sun. The candlelight behind her kissed her shoulders with a molten glow and turned her gilt hair to fire, but cursedly eclipsed all the places he wanted to see and lick and touch.

Bending close, she whispered, "Close your eyes."

He didn't want to close his eyes after being without the sight of her for so long. And he'd spent his three nights in the dungeon at thirteen entirely in the dark. Why did she think he kept so many candles lit down here now? During the day, the slit window provided enough light, but at night—

Glaring at her, he hissed, "No."

She set her chin stubbornly. "Close your eyes," she demanded.

"Make me."

She sucked in a breath. Then she smiled. The wickedness gleaming in her smile should have warned him. But when she leaned in to brush his mouth with her breast, her nipple hardening instantly, he didn't think twice before thrusting his tongue out to catch it.

Only to catch nothing but air.

She was now rubbing her nipple up along his scar. "Close your eyes, Marcus." This time her voice was the silky enticement of the siren. "I promise I will make it worth your while."

She slid her hand down to cup his erection, and he nearly went off in her hand right there.

His eyes slid closed. He wasn't sure how. All he knew was he wanted to taste her, and with her teasing him, he might not get to. Nor could he bear to have her hand leave him aching, empty. Alone.

With a low murmur of approval, she brushed his lips again with her breast. This time when he opened his mouth, he was rewarded with a taste of her. More than a taste. She thrust her breast into his mouth and he took it gladly, eagerly. He sucked it as if he'd never had the chance before, tongued the nipple until he heard her groan.

Triumph surged through him. The dragon might be chained, but that didn't mean he had to lie quiet. Her hand worked open his trousers, and he thrust against her fingers, hoping to coax her to "reward" him there, too.

She chuckled. "Lift your bottom so I can get your trousers down, Marcus."

Within moments she had him naked, his ass resting on the worn damask of the couch as she settled herself across his thighs. He could imagine her honeypot open and waiting, imagine her downy curls glistening in the candlelight. But he couldn't see it, damn it. He wanted to see it.

"I want to open my eyes," he grumbled.

"Not yet, my love. Not if you want me to satisfy this." Her fingers grazed the crown of his cock, and his blood pumped his erection even higher.

"Great God, Regina—"

He broke off with a choked moan as she stroked his cock with a long, teasing caress. Then her mouth was on his chest, kissing and licking and driving him completely out of his mind.

Never knowing where she'd touch him, *how* she'd touch him, made him nervous. She ran the tip of her tongue over his nipple, and he jumped. She fondled his ballocks, and he clenched the eyebolts to keep from pushing her away.

"Shh," she murmured against his chest. "Settle down,

my dragon. You know I won't hurt you. I would never hurt you. Show me that you trust me."

With soothing murmurs, she gentled him until he grew used to having her touch him everywhere at will, to having her all around him, her honeyed scent seeping into his senses, her loose hair brushing every inch of his skin. The more he relinquished his fear of letting her control the caresses, the more her caresses aroused him. Having his eyes closed made him feel every fondling more acutely, every kiss more profoundly.

But now he was so damned hard he feared he might go off too soon.

"I want to be inside you," he bit out.

"Do you?" She shifted on his lap until suddenly he felt her dewy curls brush against him. She inched forward until his cock was cradled between her thighs—not inside her, but so close to being inside her he thought he would die.

"Please . . ." He cringed to hear the word come out of his mouth. But that didn't stop him from saying it again. "Regina, please—"

"Tell me something, Marcus." She rubbed her damp cleft up the length of him, then down, and he cursed under his breath. "Why did you send me the keys to the town house?"

That gave him pause. "Because . . . because I knew you wanted them."

She nipped his nipple. "And?"

"And what?" he growled, unable to stop from thrusting against her.

"Was that the only reason?" She rubbed herself against his erection again.

He groaned. Vaguely he remembered doing this to her

in the carriage once, caressing her while he demanded answers. But he would never last as long as she had. If he didn't get inside her soon, his mind might just snap.

"Was that the only reason you sent me the keys, Marcus?" she repeated.

"I wanted you to know that I trust you."

She rewarded him for that answer by impaling herself on his cock. His eyes flew open, but she did not protest. Her own eyes were fierce and sure. "And?" she demanded.

He pushed up, trying to get her to move, but she just sat there atop him, her sweet heat engulfing him, tempting him, arousing him to painful heights.

"And?" she asked again.

"And I want you," he said, stating the obvious.

That got no response except a frown. "*And?*" she bit out, a hint of anger in her tone.

Then he realized what she wanted. Why hadn't he said the words before?

Because he'd been afraid that if he said them, she would have the advantage. She would assume she could do as she pleased, and he would be unable to stop her.

But now he didn't want to stop her. He trusted her not to hurt him or be disloyal to him. She had come back here, even after all the nasty things he'd said to her. She'd come back for him.

Any woman who would do that, who would brave the dungeon for him, who would fight this hard for him, could be trusted with his heart.

"I love you," he whispered.

Her eyes filled with tears. "Are you sure?"

"I love you." Instead of feeling as if chains closed around him, he suddenly felt free. Completely free.

A giddy joy rose in his throat. Releasing the bolts, he

caught her head in his hands. "I love you!" He kissed her mouth and her cheeks and her chin. "God, how I love you," he said hoarsely.

How could he not love the woman who'd come through the door with her heart shining in her eyes, talking about how clever and protective and considerate he was? Who'd defended him to her friends at the opera? Who, the first time he'd seen her, had stood up to him in all her virginal fury and demanded her due?

She began to move atop him. "Oh, Marcus, I love you so much, I thought I would die when you left me."

"I'm an idiot." He buried his face in her neck, in her fragrant hair. "I'm an utter fool."

"Yes, you are." She clutched his shoulders as she moved on him, up and down, gloriously hot, gloriously sweet. "But you're my idiot. And I will never let you go, do you hear?"

"Good. Because if you do, I will loose the dragon." His breathing grew labored. "I'll send him . . . flying over the countryside . . . until he finds you . . . and drags you back . . . to me."

The rush to release built inside him thrust by thrust, until he thought he could bear it no longer. Yet he waited until he heard her breathing grow labored, too, and felt her muscles tighten around his cock. Until he felt her give herself completely into his keeping.

The storm overtook him then, and his cock filled her with his seed the way he wanted to fill her with his love. As she cried out her own pleasure and strained against him, he clutched her close against his chest.

"Hold on, my love," he rasped. "Hold on to the dragon. Because I will never let you go."

*   *   *

They did not stay long in the dungeon. Now that Regina had accomplished her purpose, she wanted a comfortable bed, where she could hold her husband close and remind him that they belonged together forever.

Louisa had the good sense not to disturb them, thank heavens, so they spent the night in the master bedchamber in a daze of sweet words and kisses, of sealing the vows of their marriage as they never really had.

When she awoke near dawn to find him inside her, thrusting hard, taking her to ecstasy yet again, she could only thank whatever god had sent her out here weeks ago. Because if not for Marcus, she might have spent her entire life letting her fears about her defect keep her from finding this wild and wonderful love.

Only after they lay in each other's arms, satisfied and replete amid the tangled sheets of the spacious bed, did she venture to ask a question that had plagued her. "Marcus, what do you mean to do about Cicely?"

He shrugged. "I thought we already decided that. She'll live here."

"I wasn't sure. You were so annoyed at the thought of my needing her—"

"Only because I knew you didn't need her. I knew you could learn to read eventually." He brushed a kiss to her hair. "And because I was selfish. I wanted you to need *me*."

She snuggled close. "I do, I assure you. But while I may not rely on Cicely much anymore, she relies on me."

"I know, dearling. We all rely on you." He stroked her back. "When we go to town today, we'll bring her home, wherever we decide that home is. Besides, Louisa can use a companion, even if we stay in town for the remainder of the season." His voice grew husky. "We'll be too busy for chaperoning."

A delicious thrill shot through her, but she had one more question. "Speaking of Louisa, why did you arrange a meeting for her with His Highness?"

With a sigh, he settled her against his chest. "I realized you were right. Louisa did need to hear the truth about her possible parentage, and not just from me. I'm no longer even sure if I know the truth about anything anymore. I spent so many years resenting Prinny that I don't know who he really is. So this meeting is as much for me as for Louisa."

"It has sent Simon into a real dither." She pressed a kiss to his chest. "He came to the town house to demand what was going on."

"What did you tell him?"

"That I had no clue, of course. The answer didn't exactly please him."

Marcus chuckled.

She lifted her head to eye him askance. "You can be a very wicked man, you know. And what *is* going on, anyway?"

He only laughed again. "I know as much as you, believe it or not."

He related his conversation with Louisa, and Regina shook her head. "What can she possibly mean to do to Simon? If His Highness is the one who orchestrated the courtship, then—"

"I know, but she seems to think she has a way to strike at him. And I certainly hope she does."

"So do I."

A bemused look crossed his face. "He *is* your brother."

"Yes, and he's behaved very badly. I hope Louisa brings him to his knees."

"The way you've brought me to my knees?" he said softly, but without a hint of bitterness.

She grinned. "Oh, yes. I like you on your knees."

Eyes gleaming, he rolled her under him, then parted her thighs until he could kneel between them. "Like this, you mean?"

"Exactly."

"Siren," he murmured as he bent to take her mouth in a kiss.

And as he entered her, she decided she liked being a siren sometimes. She liked it very much.

Chapter Twenty-six

*Be careful if your charge is clever. She will lead
you a merry dance.*
—Miss Cicely Tremaine, *The Ideal Chaperone*

They'd been waiting in the drawing room for twenty
minutes, and still there was no sign of the prince. To
Regina's surprise, it didn't seem to bother Marcus nearly
as much as it bothered Louisa.

Regina cast a worried glance to where the young
woman paced back and forth. "Louisa, dear, he'll be here,
I'm sure. Don't work yourself into a tizzy."

Marcus settled back in his chair. "It's just his way of reminding us who is the one with the power, that's all."

"You know me so well," a voice said bitterly from beyond them.

Regina jumped to her feet, and Marcus followed more
slowly as the prince entered the room with Simon at his
side.

The proper bows and curtsies followed, but immediately afterward, the prince faced Louisa. "Don't you have a
kiss for Uncle George, poppet? When you were a girl, you
used to greet me with a kiss."

Stiffly, Louisa stepped forward to press one to his cheek. "If you will permit me to ask, Your Highness, how is it that I came to call you 'uncle' when we are of no relation whatsoever?"

Simon groaned, Marcus choked down a laugh, and Regina fought hard not to smile.

The prince, however, actually chuckled. "You haven't changed a bit. You always did speak your mind." He moved slowly to a chair and dropped into it.

Regina glanced at Marcus. As her husband watched the prince grimace in pain when lifting his gouty leg onto a footstool, Marcus's expression held first shock, then concern. Concern?

George caught him staring. "*I* have changed, haven't I, Draker? In nine years, I have aged twenty. That's what being Regent will do to you."

Marcus stiffened. "That's what living a life of debauchery will do to you."

Oh Lord, they'd be thrown out before Louisa even got her chance to speak.

George did no more than frown. "Ah, my son's high moral character rears its ugly head. I had forgotten how very often it emerges to chastise me."

Silence fell on the room. Did the prince realize he had just referred to Marcus as his son in front of three other people?

Simon certainly did. He'd already looked ill at ease when he came in, but now he looked decidedly queasy. She had to wonder why.

The prince gestured to Louisa. "Come, child. Your brother's message said you had a few questions for me. Now's your chance to ask them."

Louisa swallowed, but approached the prince. "Regina

has already told me that you would like me to join the court and why, but—"

"You told Lady Draker of our intentions, Foxmoor?" the prince interrupted with a glance at Simon.

"I had no choice," Simon replied. "Regina figured some of it out herself, and she threatened to tell Draker. So I told her all of it and asked her to do her duty."

"*Asked?*" Marcus snapped. "You lying ass—you blackmailed her. You threatened to tell me lies about her that would damage our marriage."

"Is this true?" the prince asked Regina.

She nodded.

"I did what I thought was my duty," Simon ground out.

"Was kissing me your duty, too?" Louisa burst out. "And saying you loved me? And telling me we were going to Gretna Green when you really only planned to take me to meet the prince?"

Simon looked positively deathly.

"Answer her." The prince's face had paled more and more during Louisa's protest, until now it was quite bloodless. "Tell the truth, Foxmoor. Did you do those things? Did you toy with her affections?"

Simon's eyes glittered. "They tied my hands. I had no choice." He gestured to Marcus. "He made Louisa promise not to see me again, and she insisted upon holding to her promise. I had to catch her alone at a ball and persuade her—" He broke off, realizing he was digging himself even deeper. Facing the prince with a stony glare, he said fiercely, "*You* told me you wanted her at court. That I was to arrange it so you could meet with her in private. I was only doing what you—"

"I did not tell you to kiss her."

Simon clenched his hands into fists at his sides. "That is true. I did that on my own."

"I also told you not to make her any promises, and you did."

"I had no choice, damn it!"

"It seems to me you had at least one choice. You could have discussed the situation further with me."

"You wanted this, and you know it," Simon growled.

The prince stiffened, then turned his gaze from his friend. "Thank you, Foxmoor. I shall decide how to act, and inform you forthwith. And now, I should like to speak to my guests alone. That will be all."

The look of betrayal on Simon's face was unmistakable. "This is not right."

"That will be all, sir," the prince said coldly. "If you will not leave, I shall have to call—"

"I'm going," Simon snapped, but his cheeks were flushed, and his eyes overly bright.

Regina would feel sorry for him, if not for what she, too, had suffered from his machinations.

As he headed for the door, Louisa called out, "Simon?"

He halted, but did not turn around. "Yes?"

"Did you mean any of it? Or was it all part of your scheme for His Highness?"

Slowly he turned, then swept his gaze from the tip of Louisa's head to her elegant slippers in a look that was as hot and covetous as any Marcus had ever given Regina. "I meant the kiss," he rasped. "I definitely meant the kiss."

Then whirling on his heels, he left.

Louisa looked shaken as she stared after him.

"Tell me what you require of me," the prince said. "Tell

me what I must do to make amends for my overzealous friend's actions."

Settling her shoulders with a resolute smile, Louisa returned her attention to him. "First, I want to know why you want me at court."

The prince's face darkened. "You mean, you want to know if you're my natural daughter."

She flushed, but did not back down. "Yes."

Marcus tensed beside Regina.

"Your mother said you were, and we did have an . . . er . . . encounter that could have brought it about. But it is equally possible you are not. Frankly, I cannot be sure." When Louisa's face fell, he added, "In my heart, however, you are my daughter. And that is why I wanted you at court. Why I still want you at court. Because I should like to get to know the woman I only knew as a girl."

Louisa smiled, and Marcus groaned beside Regina. No doubt he was thinking how fragile his sister's emotions were right now and how easily she could be influenced. And he was right. Regina could only hope that the young woman had enough sense to realize it for herself.

"I will consider your offer, Your Highness," Louisa said. "And I do understand what a very great honor it is to be asked to serve in your court. If I agree, however, I want one thing in return."

His Highness leaned forward. "You will have it, whatever it is."

"Simon's ambition is to be prime minister, is it not?"

Regina and Marcus exchanged glances.

The prince hesitated. "Yes."

"I believe he would make a good one . . . in time. After he has known something of the world. The broader world outside of England, that is."

The prince eyed her consideringly. "Yes, you may be right about that."

"An ambassadorship or governorship somewhere would educate him most thoroughly, don't you think? Perhaps in India or the West Indies. Somewhere he can't toy with the affections of sensitive young English ladies for a while."

Marcus whispered in Regina's ear, "And you thought *I* was a dragon."

"Simon will never forgive her for this," Regina whispered back.

"Good. The sooner he learns not to toy with my family—including you—the better." He squeezed her hand.

She squeezed his back.

"Foxmoor will simply refuse the appointment," the prince said.

Louisa, the little minx, sidled closer. "Not if you tell him you will withdraw all support for him as prime minister unless he takes it."

The prince cast her a hard look. "You want me to choose you over my friend and closest advisor?"

"Not at all. I am merely pointing out that I cannot serve in His Highness's court and travel in the same circles as a man I cannot trust, a man like the duke." Her lower lip trembled rather dramatically. "It would be too painful for me."

Marcus needn't worry about her anymore, Regina thought.

"Very well," His Highness said. "A governorship it is." He settled back against his chair. "And you will serve in my court."

"She said she would consider it," Marcus put in.

Louisa ignored her brother. "If the Duke of Foxmoor

takes an appointment abroad, Your Highness, I would be honored to serve in your court."

"Damn it, Louisa—" Marcus began.

"Be quiet, Draker!" The prince rose slowly to his feet. "If she wishes to accept, it is none of your concern."

Marcus strode up to him. "I am her guardian."

"Yes, and you've certainly done a fine job of that," His Highness retorted. "You kept her so sheltered at Castlemaine that it took a smooth-tongued fellow like Foxmoor only a month to convince her to run off to Gretna Green."

"At your request!"

"That is not the point. She could stand to learn something of the real world. And she can do that at court."

"She will get corrupted at court!"

"Marcus, please—" Louisa began.

"Enough, Louisa. It was a mistake coming here." Marcus glared at the prince. "You were wrong—you haven't changed one whit. You're as selfish and manipulative as ever." Striding over to Louisa, he took her by the arm. "Come, we're going home. Come, Regina."

Regina groaned. She had feared this might happen. When it came to His Highness, Marcus could not be rational.

"Come back here!" the prince called after them. "You will not walk away from me!"

"Watch me," Marcus growled as he strode resolutely for the door with Louisa in tow and Regina right behind.

"Damn you, you stubborn fool—I did not know about the dungeon!" His Highness shouted.

Marcus halted, every inch of him turning to stone. A thick silence blanketed the room, cut only by Louisa's whisper, "Does he mean *our* dungeon?"

"Louisa, dear," the prince said hoarsely. "If you would

please go with Lady Draker into the hall for a moment."

"Regina stays." Marcus faced his father with a stony glare. "She stays, or I do not."

The prince blanched. "Very well. Louisa, if you would take that door to your left, you will find a lady-in-waiting just outside. I am sure she would be happy to show you Carlton House."

Louisa had the good sense to obey.

As soon as she was gone, the prince lumbered toward them. "I take it your wife knows about your . . . er . . . time in the dungeon."

"Three days," Marcus growled. "It was three days, as you know full well."

"I didn't know, I swear it. Not until that day when your mother came at you with the poker. Why do you think she got so angry?"

"Because I told her to get out of my house," Marcus said through gritted teeth. "And to take her whoreson lover with her."

When the prince flinched, Regina laid her hand on Marcus's arm. He took it, his fingers tightening painfully around hers.

"That, too," His Highness admitted. "But that wasn't all. She knew how I would react to hearing that she'd locked you in a dungeon for three days." A sudden pain ravaged his face. "My God, Marcus, did you really think this whole business with Simon and Louisa was only about my wanting her at court? It was not, I assure you. I could think of no other way to get you to listen to me. I tried to tell you that very day you railed at me for it, but her striking you with the poker put an end to any rational conversation."

He approached them with a heavy tread. "I waited for your temper to cool, then sent you a letter. It was returned unopened. They were all returned unopened. I sent a messenger, and you boxed his ears." His voice trembled. "I kept thinking that you would surely go back into society eventually. That one day I would hear of you at some ball or other social function, and know that I might have a chance of meeting you there."

Marcus was squeezing her hand so hard that she feared he might break it.

"But you never did," His Highness said. "And then I heard of Louisa's come-out, and I saw a way to have you both. Because I knew you would do anything to protect her, even brave Carlton House to snatch her from my clutches."

Marcus said nothing still, just stared at the prince with a hollow-eyed gaze.

"Will you never forgive me?" the prince said in a hoarse whisper. "I did not know, I tell you. I would never have countenanced such a thing."

"How could you not know?" Marcus choked out. "Did you not question it when I disappeared for three days?"

"I did. Your mother told me she had locked you in your room. *Your room.* With plenty to eat and all your books at your disposal."

Marcus snorted. "Did I *look* as if I'd spent three days in my room reading, when I came to apologize to you?"

"I was too angry at the manner of your apology to notice, I confess. You stared at me with hate in your eyes while you said, 'I'm sorry.' "

"What did you expect? I'd spent three days in a dungeon with the *rats.* At night there was no light, and I huddled on the old couch my mother had left for me and tried to keep from wondering when those rats would come to gnaw at my toes. In the daytime, there was nothing to do but listen for the sound of my mother bringing me my meals and debating whether I could yet swallow my pride enough to say what she wanted—"

"You and your damned pride," the prince hissed. "You should have told her whatever she wanted the first day she put you down there, so you could get out and come to me with your anger."

"And what would you have done? Tossed her aside? What do you think she would have done to me then?"

"I would have spoken to your father, and he would have seen that she was . . . helped." The prince came nearer, his face a mask of tortured guilt. "Until she came at you with that poker, I did not realize just how . . . unhinged she'd become. She'd always been a high-strung filly, but toward the end she saw you as her only means to keep my affections. So whenever you did not please me, she . . . took whatever measures necessary to bring you round."

"And you, of course, always approved. Three days in one's room is no great fun either, after all."

"No, but I saw it as a good way to teach you that you could not speak to your future king as if he were some rogue in the street." He drew himself up stiffly. "I could not have you going about calling me a whoreson in public."

"Then you should have kept your damned prick in your trousers."

"Then you would never have been born."

That brought Marcus up short. He stared bleakly at his father.

"Marcus, I have made many mistakes in my life. But having you was not one of them. I only wish I had explained to you the situation between your father and me before I no longer had the chance."

"What was there to explain? He was your friend before you stole his wife."

"I did not steal her." He sighed. "Your father simply did not care that much about the things that mattered to your mother."

"Like status and society and—"

"Like passion. Your mother was a passionate woman, but your father was an ascetic. Passion didn't much interest him. So when he left your mother alone for so long, she found someone else to give her what she craved."

"He *loved* her," Marcus said fiercely.

"In his own way, yes. But not enough to give her what she wanted from him." He shrugged. "Books interested him. Buildings interested him. But not people." He smiled faintly. "Except for you and Louisa. He loved the two of you. And God knows you loved him." His voice cracked. "I envied him that, having your love and your respect. No matter how hard I tried, I could not gain it."

The prince glanced away, his eyes going hard. "Your mother knew it, too. So she tried her damnedest to get it for me." A harsh laugh escaped his lips. "I could have told her it was fruitless. One thing you did inherit from me is that damned Hanoverian blood. You're as willful and stubborn and proud as my father ever was." His gaze swung back to Marcus. "When Gillian started those damned rumors about you, why didn't you just deny them, for God's sake?"

"Why didn't *you?*" Regina put in, her temper rising. "You should have stood behind your son, instead of abandoning him to the wolves."

The prince blinked, as if he'd forgotten she was there. Then he scowled.

She didn't care. Slipping her hand from Marcus's, she

approached the prince. "He has spent his life alone in exile because you were too much a coward to do the right thing by him. He deserved better from you."

The prince searched her face. "Indeed he did. But I would make amends now, if I can."

"By corrupting my sister?" Marcus snapped.

His Highness uttered a weary sigh, then slowly shook his head. "If you truly do not want her here, then I will withdraw my invitation."

Marcus released a pent-up breath.

"But consider this," he went on. "A few years at court will give Louisa the society polish she will need to make the sort of match she truly deserves. A love match with a man worthy of her." His gaze met Marcus's. "It will certainly erase any rumors that might arise as a result of my ill-thought machinations with Foxmoor."

The prince had a good point, actually. The sense of it even reached Marcus, for she could see the battle raging on his face.

At last he sighed. "I will consider it," Marcus said gruffly.

That he had not dismissed the suggestion out of hand was a step forward.

Relief spread over the prince's face. "And in time, do you think you might also consider one day joining me at dinner with your wife?"

A long silence ensued, and when Regina looked at Marcus, it was to see his eyes misting. "Perhaps," he choked out at last. "Perhaps in time."

They left then, taking Louisa with them.

Some hours later, after Louisa had retired and they were in their bedchamber at the town house, Marcus said, "Do you think he's right?"

"Who?" she asked as she took down her hair.

He came up behind her at the mirror. "Prinny. Do you think Louisa would benefit from being at court?"

That he could even ask such a question was astonishing. That he valued her opinion on the subject was positively thrilling.

She chose her words carefully. "She might. It would certainly teach her enough of the world to appreciate what a good match actually is."

"Oh?" he said in a husky voice as he bent to press a kiss into her hair. "And how would you define a good match, my love?"

"One with a man who trusts you." She rose to face him. "Respects you." She flung her arms about his neck. "And loves you."

"Is that all?" he said dryly.

"Not quite." She shot him a teasing smile. "He should also have a very sturdy dungeon."

Epilogue

*If your charge marries well, then you have achieved
your purpose, but if she marries happily, you may
congratulate yourself on a job well-done.*
—Miss Cicely Tremaine, *The Ideal Chaperone*

He still couldn't see a damned thing from here. Marcus
rose, cradling his infant son in the crook of one arm as he
crossed the terrace outside Iversley's ballroom to approach the closed glass doors.

When Jasper drooled on his coat sleeve, Marcus
chuckled. "Don't let Uncle Byrne see you do that, my boy,
or he'll never hold you again."

Marcus stared through the glass, then angled the two-
month-old forward so he could see, too. "Look at Uncle
Alec and Auntie Katherine dancing the reel. Don't they
look fine? And somewhere in there, Mama is dancing with
Uncle Byrne. Poor devil. She's on a mission to get him
married these days, and he's having none of it."

Shifting little Jasper, he peered closer at the throng, then
chuckled. "It even appears that Miss Tremaine has acquired
a beau, judging from how that colonel has been dogging
the old girl all evening. Seems that having her little book of
advice published has raised her credit in society."

Then he spotted his sister. "There's Auntie Louisa, being
led from the floor by some handsome fellow. No great sur-

prise there. She has lots of handsome fellows about her, now that she's at court." Hard to believe it had been little more than a year since he'd stood here watching her dance with Foxmoor. "Auntie Louisa left her lofty post just to attend your christening party. What do you think of that?"

Marcus glanced smugly down at his son's intelligent brown eyes, wispy dark hair, and blessedly average size. Not a hint of Prinny in *this* lad, to be sure.

"No one shall ever call *you* a dragon, my boy. If they do, your papa shall breathe fire at them till they run off." He smiled. "If your mama doesn't get to the poor unfortunate first and slice him to ribbons with her sharp tongue."

"Who are you accusing of having a sharp tongue?" demanded a female voice close by.

"Uh-oh," Marcus said to his son, "here's the lady now. Mum's the word, my boy."

"Very funny," Regina grumbled. "And what are you doing out here skulking about with him in the dark, anyway?"

Marcus smiled. "The point of having this affair at Iversley's was to keep it from being a strain on you so soon after Jasper was born. Yet you were fussing over the poor boy so much, I knew you wouldn't take even a moment to enjoy yourself unless I whisked him out of your arms." He cast her a chastening glance. "Not that it did any good. I'm sure once I was gone, you started lecturing poor Byrne over his marital state. When you were supposed to be dancing."

"I *was* dancing." Her eyes lit with mischief. "And if I happened to let slip a few words about the advantages of matrimony, I was merely making polite conversation. I'm sure he didn't even realize what I was doing."

Marcus snorted, then bent his head to his son's. "Don't worry, my boy. When the time comes for you to look for a wife, I'll keep your mother well occupied elsewhere."

Regina glided up to stand beside him and stare adoringly at their son. "Don't you trust me to choose a proper wife for our darling Jasper?"

"Not for one minute. Between you and Katherine and Louisa, the only girl to pass inspection would be some milksop maid pure as the driven snow, who would bore him to tears."

She sniffed. "I suppose *you* would have him marry a fast, unmannerly hoyden who'll break his heart."

"I'd have him marry a woman like his mother." Marcus leaned over to kiss her cheek. "It certainly seems to be working well for me."

Mollified, Regina cast him a smile. "When did you turn into such a flatterer?"

"When the woman I fell in love with told me she wouldn't let me court her unless I behaved like a gentleman."

"Clever woman."

He chuckled. "Clever woman indeed. I heard from Cicely that you were reading Shakespeare only this morning."

Regina screwed up her brow. "Bumbling through, more like. But I am doing much better. I got through the whole of one play this week. Now that you've come back to town from Castlemaine, I might just coax you into reading the next play *to* me." A coy smile touched her lips. "Unless you're planning to take us all home again."

"I wouldn't dream of whisking you from London during the season."

She walked her fingers up his coat sleeve. "Ah, but there are certain advantages to being at Castlemaine. More privacy." She lowered her voice to a whisper. "A bigger bed."

He grinned. "Very tempting, dearling. Unfortunately, I promised Louisa that you and I would dine at Carlton House this week."

She eyed him closely. "You mean, you promised the prince you would let him see our son."

"I can never get anything past you. You're right, of course."

"Just as I was right about Louisa going to court?"

"I suppose," he grumbled.

Regina punched his arm playfully. "Admit it, you big lout. Serving as Princess Charlotte's lady-in-waiting has been good for her. It's given her a certain polish and style."

He sighed. "Yes, it has. Although she still hasn't married anyone."

"She will. It's better for her to take her time about it, rather than accepting the first proposal that comes her way." Her eyes gleamed up at him. "That's what I did, after all, and it certainly seems to be working well for me."

When he answered her with a warm smile that brought a dreamy expression to her face, it was all he could do not to take his wife out behind the bushes.

"I have a suggestion, darling," she murmured, in that silky voice that still made his blood race and his heart pound. Opening the glass doors, she stepped through and then turned to offer him a come-hither glance. "Why don't we give Jasper to one of his many doting relations and have a dance of our own?"

He stood there a moment with his son in his arms and the dark night behind him, staring at the woman he loved more than life.

Everything was different now. No more lurking in the shadows. No more hiding in caves. No more banishment.

"I thought you'd never ask," he said hoarsely.

Then the Dragon Viscount followed his wife into the light.

Author's Note

Readers have probably guessed by now that Regina's difficulties with reading stemmed from her being dyslexic. Dyslexia takes a variety of forms—I chose the most common for my story. In my research, I learned that some people with dyslexia learn better if taught using tactile methods, so that's why I focused on that for Regina.

The details about Princess Charlotte are all true—her father did broker an engagement between her and the Prince of Orange, but later, in the summer of the year when my book is set, she fell for another man, Prince Leopold of Saxe-Coburg, and ended her engagement to the Prince of Orange. She married Prince Leopold in 1816, only to die tragically in childbirth a little over a year later.

Lady Draker was loosely based on two of Prinny's married mistresses among the nobility, although neither woman possessed my character's cruel nature. The first lady, the Viscountess Melbourne, was reputed to have borne the prince a son, George Lamb, during her four-year stint as Prinny's mistress.

The second lady was the Marchioness of Hertford, whose husband looked the other way for twelve years while she and Prinny carried on their affair. Prinny was chummy with the marquis, frequently visited the Hertford estate in Warwickshire, and later became quite friendly with their son—who was definitely not *his* son, however, since he was born when Prinny was only fifteen.

Although the most famous poem entitled "La Belle Dame Sans Merci" is by John Keats, it hadn't yet been written at the time my story took place. But since Keats based his poem on a Chaucer translation of an Alain Chartier poem (at the time of the Regency, it was believed to be a Chaucer original), I was still able to use the phrase.

The lines "Golden slumbers kiss your eyes/Smiles awake you when you rise" are not original to the Beatles; they came from a Thomas Dekker poem, a common lullaby in England. In fact, the liner notes to *Abbey Road* credit him.

Want even more sizzling romance from
New York Times bestselling author
Sabrina Jeffries?

Don't miss

The Danger of Desire

the next installment in her
sizzling and sexy Sinful Suitors series.

Coming in Fall 2016 from Pocket Books!

1

London
August 1830

When Warren Corry, Marquess of Knightford, arrived at a Venetian breakfast thrown by the Duke and Duchess of Lyons, he regretted having stayed out until the wee hours of the morning. Last night he'd just been so glad to be back among the distractions of town that he'd drunk enough brandy to pickle a barrel of herrings.

Bad idea, since the duke and duchess had decided to hold the blasted party in the blazing sun on the lawn of their lavish London mansion. His mouth was dry, his stomach churned, and his head felt like a stampeding herd of elephants.

His best friend, Edwin, had better be grateful that Warren kept his promises.

"Warren!" cried a female voice painfully close. "What are you doing here?"

It was Clarissa, his cousin, who also just happened to be Edwin's wife—and the reason Warren had managed to drag himself from his bed at the ungodly hour of noon.

He shaded his eyes to peer at her. As usual, she had the look of a delicate fairy creature. But he knew better than to fall for that cat-in-the-cream smile. "Must you shout like that?"

"I am not shouting." She cocked her head. "And you look

ill. So you must have had a grand time at St. George's Club last night. Either that, or in the stews early this morning."

"I always have a grand time." Or at least he kept the night at bay, which was the purpose of staying out until all hours.

"I know, which is why it's really unlike you to be here. Especially when Edwin isn't." She narrowed her eyes at him. "Wait a minute—Edwin sent you here, didn't he? Because he couldn't be in town for it."

"What? No." He bent to kiss her cheek. "Can't a fellow just come to a breakfast to see his favorite cousin?"

"He can. But he generally doesn't."

Warren snagged a glass of champagne off a passing tray. "Well, he did today. Wait, who are we talking about again?"

"Very amusing." Taking the glass from him, she frowned. "You do not need this. You're clearly cropsick."

He snatched it back and downed it. "Which is precisely why I require some hair of the dog."

"You're avoiding the subject. Did Edwin send you here to spy on me or not?"

"Don't be absurd. He merely wanted me to look in on you, make sure everything was all right. You know your husband—he hates having to be at the estate with Niall while you're in town." He glanced at her thickening waist. "Especially when you're . . . well . . . like that."

"Oh, Lord, not you, too. Bad enough to have him and my brother hovering over me all the time, worried about my getting hurt somehow, but if he's sent you to start doing that—"

"No, I swear. He only asked that I come by if I were attending this. I had to be in town anyway, so I figured why not pop in to Lyons's affair?" He waved his empty glass. "The duke always orders excellent champagne. But now that I've had some, I'll just be on my way."

She took him by the arm. "No, indeed. I so rarely get to see you anymore. Stay awhile. They're about to start the dancing."

"Just what I need—to dance with a lot of simpering misses who think a coronet the ideal prize."

"Then dance with me. I *can* still dance, you know."

No doubt. Clarissa had always been a lively sort, who wouldn't be slowed by something as inconsequential as bearing the heir to the reserved and rather eccentric Earl of Blakeborough.

Clarissa and Edwin were so different that sometimes Warren wondered what the two of them saw in each other. But whenever he witnessed their obvious affection for each other, he realized there must be something deeper cementing their marriage. It made him envious.

He scowled. That was absurd. He didn't intend to marry for a very long while. At least not until he found a lusty widow who could endure his . . . idiosyncrasies.

Clarissa stared off into the crowd. "As long as you're here, I . . . um . . . do need a favor."

Uh-oh. "What kind of favor?"

"Edwin would do it if he didn't have to be in Hertfordshire helping my brother settle the family estate, you know," she babbled. "And Niall—"

"*What's the favor?*" he persisted.

"Do you know Miss Trevor?"

Miss Trevor? This had better not be another of Clarissa's schemes to get him married off. "Fortunately, I do not. I assume she's one of those debutantes you've taken under your wing."

"Not exactly. Although she was just brought out this past season, she's actually my age . . . and a friend. Her brother, Reynold Trevor, died last year in some horrible shooting accident, and she and her sister-in-law, Mrs. Trevor, have been left without anything but a debt-ridden estate to support. So Miss Trevor's aunt, Lady Pensworth, brought the two of them to London for the season."

"To find them husbands, no doubt."

"Exactly, although I think Lady Pensworth is more concerned about Miss Trevor, since the late Mr. Trevor's wife has already borne him a child who will inherit the estate, such as it is. To make Miss Trevor more eligible, Lady Pensworth has bestowed a thousand-pound dowry on her, which ought to tempt a number of eligible gentlemen."

"Not me."

She looked startled. "I wasn't thinking of *you*, for heaven's sake. I was thinking of someone less wealthy, with fewer connections. And decidedly younger. She's only twenty-four, after all."

Decidedly younger? "Here now, I'm not that old. I'm the same age as your husband."

"True." Her eyes twinkled at him. "And given your nightly habits, you apparently possess the stamina of a much younger man. Why, no one seeing you in dim light would ever guess you're thirty-three."

He eyed her askance. "I seem to recall your asking me for a favor, dear girl. You're not going about getting it very wisely."

"The thing is, I'm worried about my friend. Miss Trevor keeps receiving these notes at parties, which she slips furtively off to read; she falls asleep in the middle of balls; and she seems rather distracted. Worst of all, she refused my invitation to our house party next week, which I had partly planned in hopes of introducing her to eligible young gentlemen."

"Perhaps she had another engagement."

Clarissa lifted an eyebrow at him.

"Right. She needs a husband, and you're nicely trying to provide her with a selection of potential ones." He smirked at her. "How ungrateful of her not to fall in with your plans."

"Do be serious. When was the last time you saw any unmarried woman with limited prospects refuse a chance to attend a house party at the home of an earl and a countess with our connections?"

He hated to admit it, but she had a point. "So what do you want *me* to do about it?"

"Ask around at St. George's. See if anyone has heard any gossip about her. Find out if anyone knows some scoundrel who's been . . . well . . . sniffing around her for her dowry."

The light dawned. During her debut years ago, Clarissa had been the object of such a scoundrel's attentions, and it had nearly destroyed the lives of her and her brother. So she tended to be overly sensitive about women who might fall prey to fortune hunters.

"You do know that if I start asking about an eligible young lady at the club," he said, "the members will assume I'm interested in courting her."

"Nonsense. Everyone knows you prefer soiled doves to society loves."

That wasn't entirely true. He did occasionally bed bored widows or ladies with inattentive husbands. There were a great many of those hanging about—one reason he wasn't keen to marry. He had a ready supply of bedmates without having to leg-shackle himself.

"Besides," she went on, "that *is* the purpose of St. George's, is it not? To provide a place where gentlemen can determine the suitability of various suitors to women?"

"To their female relations," he said tersely. "Not to the friends of their female relations."

Clarissa stared up at him. "She has no man to protect her. And I very much fear all of the signs lead to her having found someone unsuitable, which is why she's behaving oddly. I don't want to see her end up trapped in a disastrous marriage. Or worse."

They both knew what the "worse" was, since Clarissa had gone through it herself. Damn. He might not have been her guardian for years now, but she still knew how to tug at his conscience.

"It would be a very great favor to me," Clarissa went on. "I tell you what—let me just introduce you. You can spend a few moments talking to her and see if I'm right to be alarmed. If you think I'm overly concerned, you may leave here with my blessing and never bother with it again. But if you think I might be right . . ."

"Fine. But you owe me for this. And I promise I will call in my debt down the road." He grinned at her. "At the very least, you must introduce me to some buxom widow with loose morals and an eye for fun."

"Hmm," she said, rolling her eyes. "I'll have to speak to my brother-in-law about that. He has more connections among that sort than I do."

"No doubt." Her brother-in-law used to use "that sort" of women as models in his paintings. "But I don't need you to talk to Keane. So I suppose I'll settle for your promise not to be offended if I also refuse your invitation to your house party."

"There was a possibility of your accepting? Shocking. But since I've never seen you attend a house party in your life—unless it was to some bachelor's hunting box—I didn't bother to invite you."

"Good," he said, though he was mildly annoyed. Marriage had obviously changed her. A year ago, she wouldn't have stopped plaguing him until she'd convinced him to attend. Surely she had not given up on him already.

Unless this was her sly way of once again trying to get him married off. He'd best tread carefully. "So where *is* this woman you wish me to meet?"

"She was right over there by the—" Clarissa scowled. "Oh, dear, that's her by the fountain, but what the devil are those fellows doing with her?"

She stalked off across the lawn and he followed, surveying the group she headed for: a woman surrounded by three young gentlemen who appeared to be—fishing?—in the fountain.

He recognized the men. One was a drunk, one a well-known rakehell, and the third a notorious gambler by the name of Pitford. All three were fortune hunters.

No wonder Clarissa worried about her friend.

He turned his attention to the chit, who had her back to him and was dressed in a blue-and-green plaid gown with a pink-and-yellow striped shawl.

Good God. Any woman who dressed that way was bound to be a heedless young twit, and he disliked that sort of woman. Unless she was sitting on his lap in a brothel, in which case intelligence hardly mattered.

As they approached the group, Clarissa said, "What on earth is going on here?"

The jovial chap with cheeks already reddened from too much champagne said, "The clasp broke on Miss Trevor's bracelet and it dropped into the fountain, so we're trying to get it out to keep her from ruining her sleeves."

"I would prefer to ruin my entire gown than see you further damage my bracelet with your poking about," the chit said, her voice surprisingly low and throaty. "If you gentlemen would just let me pass, I'd fish it out myself."

"Nonsense, we can do it," the other two said as they fought over the stick wielded by the drunk. In the process, they managed to poke Miss Trevor in the arm.

"Ow!" she cried and attempted to snatch the stick. "For pity's sake, gentlemen . . ."

Warren had seen enough. "Stand aside, lads." He pushed through the arses. Shoving his sleeve up as far as it would go, he thrust his hand into the fountain and fished out the bracelet. Then he turned to offer it to the young lady. "I assume this is yours, miss."

When her startled gaze shot to him, he froze. She had the loveliest blue eyes he'd ever seen.

Though her gown was even more outrageous from the front than from the back, the rest of her was unremarkable. Tall and slender, with no breasts to speak of, she had decent skin, a sharp nose, and a rather impudent-looking mouth. She was pretty enough, but by no means a beauty. And not his sort. At all.

Yet those eyes . . .

Fringed with long black lashes, they glittered like stars against an early-evening sky, making desire tighten low in his belly. Utterly absurd.

Until her lips curled up into a sparkling smile that matched the incandescence of her eyes. "Thank you, sir. The bracelet was a gift from my late brother. Though I fear you may have ruined your coat retrieving it."

"Nonsense." He extended the bracelet to her. "My valet is very good at his job and will easily put it right."

As she took the bracelet from him, an odd expression crossed her face. "You're left-handed."

He arched one brow. "How clever of you to notice."

"How clever of you to be so. I'm left-handed, too. So I generally notice another left-hander because there aren't that many of us around."

"Or none that will lay claim to the affliction, anyway." And he'd never before met a lady who was.

"True." She slipped the bracelet into her reticule with a twinkle in her eye. "I've always been told it's quite gauche to be left-handed."

"Or at the very least, a sign of subservience to the devil."

"Ah yes. Though the last time I paid a visit to Lucifer, he pretended not to know me. What about you?"

"I know him only to speak to at parties. He's quite busy these days. He has trouble fitting me into his schedule."

"I can well imagine." Pointedly ignoring the three men watching them in bewilderment, she added, "He has all those innocents to tempt and gamblers to ruin and drinkers to intoxicate. However would he find time to waste on a fellow like you, who comes to the aid of a lady so readily? You're clearly not wicked enough to merit his interest."

"You'd be surprised," he said dryly. "Besides, Lucifer gains more pleasure in corrupting decent gentlemen than wicked ones." And this had to be the strangest conversation he'd ever had with a debutante.

"Excellent point. Well, then, next time you see him, give him my regards." She cast a side glance at their companions. "He seems to have been overzealous in his activities of late."

When the gentlemen looked offended, Clarissa said hastily, "Don't be silly. The devil is only as busy as people allow him to be, and we shall not allow him to loiter around here, shall we, Warren?" She slid her hand into the crook of his elbow.

"No, indeed. That would be a sin."

"And so are my poor manners," Clarissa went on. She smiled at her friend. "I've forgotten to introduce the two of you. Miss Trevor, may I present my cousin, the Marquess of Knightford and rescuer of bracelets. Warren, this is my good friend, Miss Delia Trevor, the cleverest woman I know despite her gauche left hand."

Cynically, he waited for Miss Trevor's smile to brighten as she realized what a prime catch he was. So he was surprised when her smile faded to politeness instead. "It's a pleasure to meet you, sir. Clarissa has told me much about you."

He narrowed his gaze on her. "I'm sure she has. My cousin loves gossip."

"No more than you love to provide fodder for it, from what I've heard."

"I do enjoy giving the gossips something to talk about."

"No doubt they appreciate it. Otherwise they'd be limited to poking fun at spinsters, and then I would never get any rest."

He snorted. "I'd hardly consider you a spinster, madam. My cousin tells me this is your first season."

"And hopefully my last." As the other fellows protested that, she said, "Now, now, gentlemen. You know I'm not the society sort." She fixed Warren with a cool look. "I do better with less lofty companions. You, my lord, are far too worldly and sophisticated for me."

"I somehow doubt that," he said.

"I hear the dancing starting up," Clarissa cut in as she released his arm. "Perhaps you two can puzzle it out if you stand up together for this set."

He had to stifle his laugh. Clarissa wasn't usually so clumsy in her social machinations. She must really like this chit. He was beginning to understand why. Miss Trevor was rather entertaining.

"Excellent idea." He held out his hand to the young lady. "Shall we?"

"Now see here," Pitford interrupted. "Miss Trevor has already promised this dance to me."

"It's true," she told Warren. "I'm promised for all the dances this afternoon."

Hmm. Warren turned to Pitford. "Lord Fulkham was looking for you earlier, old chap. He's in the card room, I believe. I'll just head there and tell him he can find you dancing with Miss Trevor."

Pitford blanched. "I . . . er . . . cannot . . . that is . . ." He bowed to Miss Trevor. "Forgive me, madam, but I shall have to relinquish this dance to his lordship. I forgot a prior engagement."

The fellow scurried off for the gates as fast as his tight pantaloons would carry him. Probably because the wretch owed Fulkham a substantial sum of money.

Pitford's withdrawal was all it took for the other two gentlemen to excuse themselves, leaving Warren alone with his cousin and Miss Trevor.

With a smile, he again offered his arm to Clarissa's friend. "It appears that you are now free to dance. Shall we?"

To his shock, the impudent female hesitated. But she obviously knew better than to refuse a marquess and quickly recovered, taking the arm he offered.

As they headed toward the lawn where the dancing was taking place, Miss Trevor said, "Do you always get your way in everything, Lord Knightford?"

"I certainly try. What good is being a marquess if I can't make use of the privilege from time to time?"

"Even if it means bullying some poor fellow into fleeing a perfectly good party?"

He shot her a long glance. "Pitford is deeply in debt and looking for a rich wife. I should think you would thank me."

She shrugged. "I know what Pitford is. I know what they all are. It matters naught to me. I have no interest in any of them."

Pulling her into the swirl of dancers, he said, "Because you prefer some fellow you left behind at home? Or because you have your sights set elsewhere in town?"

Her expression grew guarded. "For a man of such lofty consequence, you are surprisingly interested in my affairs. Why is that?"

"I am merely dancing with the friend of my cousin," he said smoothly. "And for a woman who has 'no interest' in the three fortune hunters you were just with, you certainly found a good way to get them vying for your attention."

She blinked. "I have no idea what you mean."

"The clasp on that bracelet wasn't broken, Miss Trevor." When she colored and glanced away, he knew he'd hit his mark. "So I can only think that you had some other purpose for dropping it into the fountain."

As they came together in the dance, he lowered his voice. "And if it wasn't to engage those men's interest in you personally, I have to wonder what other reason you might have to risk losing such a sentimental heirloom. Care to enlighten me?"